FISH *of the* SETO
INLAND SEA

This book is about a family whose traditional home is by the Seto Inland Sea in Southern Japan.

There is a saying that the best fish in Japan comes from here because, as is quoted in the book, the rapid flow of water in many places in the sea makes the fish especially firm and good.

These qualities seem to mirror the strength and resilience shown by the three generations of women of the Shirai family.

Ruri Pilgrim

FISH *of the* SETO INLAND SEA

HarperCollins*Publishers*

HarperCollins*Publishers*
77–85 Fulham Palace Road,
Hammersmith, London w6 8jb

Published by HarperCollins*Publishers* 1999

1 3 5 7 9 8 6 4 2

A catalogue record for this book
is available from the British Library

ISBN 0 00 257087 4

Set in Postscript Linotype Aldus by
Rowland Phototypesetting Ltd,
Bury St Edmunds, Suffolk

Printed and bound in Great Britain by
Clays Ltd, St Ives plc

To my Father and Mother
Itsuji and Shizuko Kumoi

ACKNOWLEDGMENTS

Thank you to:

John Pilgrim who taught me English, who is a companion I can always talk to, and who is my source of inspiration.

Sophie Pilgrim who encouraged me to write this book, edited the manuscript and has been a sincere critic throughout the time I was writing.

Anita, Tom, Nick, Roxanne and Adam, who, with John and Sophie, are my constant support and with whom I share happiness in life.

Joan Day who takes on my daily worries and who made my mother's last days blissful.

Patrick Walsh, my capable and tireless agent and my unofficial godson.

Susan Watt, my most respected editor and a wonderful new friend.

Janet Law who combed the manuscript with meticulous care.

Amanda and Frances Cornford, my much loved friend and her daughter.

Sebastian Secker Walker, one of the talented people inherited from our children,

Christine Thompson,

Louise Hartley-Davies,

and all the other people

who read the manuscript and gave me their insights and an English understanding.

Martin Travers, my long-standing ally who saved me from many crises with the computer.

Mr Toshio Kimura who sent me dictionaries and books from Japan over the years and whose kind gifts gave me a better understanding of the great Japanese writers.

Ms Yoko Nakajima of Kodansha Publishing who said to me, 'Why don't you write? You can.'

Miss Yumi Tsuchida who unfailingly sends me material from Japan.

Mrs Miyuki Ota who finds me useful source books, and her daughter and son-in-law Kaori and Satoshi Yamane, and his mother Mrs Haruko Yamane who invited me to stay by the Seto Inland Sea.

With all my love,
Ruri Kumoi Pilgrim

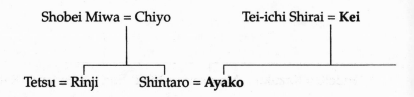

Shobei Miwa = Chiyo   Tei-ichi Shirai = **Kei**

Tetsu = Rinji   Shintaro = **Ayako**

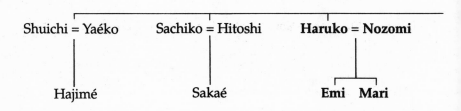

Shuichi = Yaéko   Sachiko = Hitoshi   **Haruko = Nozomi**

Hajimé   Sakaé   **Emi   Mari**

HARUKO'S FAMILY TREE

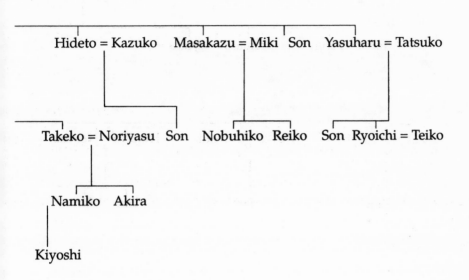

Hideto = Kazuko   Masakazu = Miki   Son   Yasuharu = Tatsuko

Takeko = Noriyasu   Son   Nobuhiko   Reiko   Son   Ryoichi = Teiko

Namiko   Akira

Kiyoshi

THE SANJOS (Haruko's in-laws)

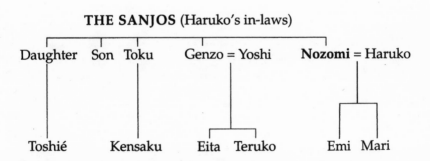

Daughter   Son   Toku   Genzo = Yoshi   **Nozomi** = Haruko

Toshié   Kensaku   Eita   Teruko   Emi   Mari

CONTENTS

PART THREE

PART ONE

1

The Landowner's Family

Shobei Miwa was a rich landowner. His land spread far beyond the village of Takao. He could walk from his house for about forty minutes to the nearest railway station without stepping on anyone else's land. In fact, it was Shobei who had sold the land for the railway and station to the government.

Shobei Miwa had two sons, Shintaro and Rinji. His elder son, Shintaro, was sent to Tokyo at the age of fourteen before the railway had been built. He was accompanied by a servant and walked on the trunk road to Tokyo, taking nearly a month. The servant carried his money, including his school fees, in a bundle firmly tied around his waist which he did not take off even when he slept at night. The rooms of the inns had sliding doors and no locks. There were many thieves. The young master and his servant kept to themselves but at the same time had to take care not to look too cautious and attract attention.

When they reached the Oigawa river, the servant would not trust the boatmen and he crossed the river carrying Shintaro on his shoulders. In the middle of the river, the water came up to his chest. Every year, until the railway was built, he made the same trip to Tokyo bringing Shintaro's expenses.

Shobei was not much worried about how Shintaro lived as a student. When a rumour reached him that Shintaro was drinking heavily, Shobei laughed and said, 'A man who cannot drink cannot succeed in life.'

He was generous about his son's expenses as well. 'Let him have a good time. One can never be young again.' He was concerned only about one thing. This was that Shintaro should come home without getting seriously involved with a woman. Shobei was anxious that his son should marry a girl from a good family known to everybody around them.

'Occasional relaxation from hard work is necessary, but you must remember to honour your obligation to your family,' Shobei wrote to Shintaro in every letter. Shobei's letters were written with brush and ink and were difficult to decipher but Shintaro knew the last few sentences without reading them.

Imperial University students were considered to have good prospects and were targeted by ambitious mothers with unmarried daughters, but Shintaro returned to his father's village, Takao, without mishap. With Shobei's influence, Shintaro's future was promising. It was as the director of a new hospital, the largest in the area, that he began his professional life. He was considered the most eligible bachelor for several counties.

Who would be the lucky girl? People speculated. There were many young ladies of suitable families. Relatives and friends were busy sounding out the possibility of a match with girls they knew or had heard about. Parents who had daughters of the right age called on people who knew the Miwas to impress their names on them. The hospital was visited by more young girls, taken by their mothers or maids with minor complaints.

Shobei rejected these proposals one after another without even telling Shintaro.

'Thank you for your concern, but he has been away so long and has just started his career. It is important for him to concentrate on his work at the moment,' was his stock reply to every one, although Shobei knew that they were well aware it was not true.

'What is he scheming for his son's marriage? Is he thinking of marrying Dr Shintaro to a nobleman's daughter?' People talked. It was generally believed that the real reason was that the girls' families were not considered good enough.

When Shobei refused a proposal from the Abes, a family richer and older than the Miwas, Shobei's wife confronted him for the first time.

'Excuse me, but Shintaro san is over thirty now. I would like to ask you what is in your mind. Shintaro san will end up as a bachelor because you are . . .' She wanted to say 'fastidious' but said, 'Well, because you are too careful.'

'We cannot have Abe's daughter.' Shobei's answer was categorical.

His wife persisted. 'But may I ask why? They say she is pretty and we have heard nothing against her. The family, of course, is beyond criticism.'

'She might be acceptable, but she has two brothers.'

'But it's good that she has brothers. What is wrong with that?'

His wife was mystified. If the family did not have sons, the girl had to stay at home and take a husband into her family to carry on the family name. She could not marry out. That was how the family line was kept. The system was called *yohshi*, adoption.

'Abe's sons are lazy and stupid. The younger one is mean as well.'

'I am sorry, but please explain what you mean. If you worry about everybody in the family, you will always find someone who is not perfect. Shintaro san is not marrying her brothers.'

'Her brothers may be no problem while the father is alive. But wait till the sons have a chance to control the family affairs. At first they will sell a bit of land away from home to pay off their gambling and womanising debts. Gradually they will get deeper and deeper into debt. The brothers will quarrel. After ten years, there will be nothing left. They will come to Shintaro to borrow and so on. Shintaro will have to be involved. Not only is he a kind fellow but he cannot stand by while his in-laws ruin themselves. The bad name of his wife's family would spoil the name of the Miwas.'

'I see. Well, I hope Shintaro san will be able to marry one day.'

'Of course he will marry.'

'But . . .'

'I have already decided on his wife.'

'You have?'

'Yes, I have. The daughter of the Shirais in the next village.'

His wife was nonplussed.

'You mean Dr Shirai's daughter?'

'Yes, Dr Shirai of Kitani village.' His tone told her that his mind was made up and that his decision was final.

'They have four sons.' She looked him straight in the eyes, which she normally did not dare to do. She was not satisfied with her husband's decision, because the Shirais were the poorest among all the candidates so far.

'And all intelligent,' Shobei replied. 'The father is a fine fellow and

5

still young. The whole family will be a great support for Shintaro and for his future son.'

'But the girl is very young. One of the sons is still a baby.'

'I know. That is why I had to wait. She has a very good reputation. Besides, she should know how a doctor's household should be run, although Shintaro's life is a bit different from her father's.' Shobei sounded smug. He had already found out a lot about Dr Shirai's daughter, Ayako.

'If you say so,' his wife conceded.

'Of course!'

When people heard that the daughter of the Shirais was chosen as Shintaro's bride, they could not understand why. The Shirais had been doctors in traditional medicine for many generations. They had been the retained doctors of feudal lords until the system was abolished towards the end of the 1880s. Since then, the present head of the family, Tei-ichi, continued to look after people in the area with his hereditary knowledge and experience. He was endowed with a progressive spirit and had already contacted Shintaro to seek advice on some of his patients. Tei-ichi was respected and popular, but the family was not well-off.

Tei-ichi's house was always full of poor patients. With backs and knees bent from hard lives, peasants brought their children who were exhausted from suffering.

Dr Tei-ichi Shirai would shout angrily, 'Why did you leave the sick child so long without bringing her to me?'

'I am very sorry . . . We have not paid you the last fees and . . .'

'Who is talking about fees? Don't you see this child is ill because of your neglect?'

They loved to be scolded by Dr Tei-ichi.

As many of his patients were poor, his fees were often not paid or were paid with small amounts of fish, fruit and vegetables. On the other hand, the merchants who dealt with the doctor's family sent their accounts twice a year, but were not too harsh in demanding payment. Shobei knew it all.

The Shirais lived in an old house surrounded by a moat and high stone walls. A wooden bridge led to a large gate and straight ahead was an open main entrance. The gate was usually closed and people used a small side door to get into the front courtyard. From the courtyard they walked round the back of the house to go in through the family entrance or the kitchen.

Tei-ichi's wife Kei was open-hearted and cheerful.

'Now, what is wrong with you this time?' she would ask a villager who appeared and stood timidly at the kitchen door. 'Come in, come in. You won't get better standing outside.'

And they would tell her their symptoms, worries and difficulties.

'It sounds exactly like what Yohei had the other day. He is fine now. Go in and see the doctor. Only, don't mention your own opinions and everything the others have said. You won't die yet.'

Kei had beautiful skin. She washed her face thoroughly every morning with rice bran in a small cotton bag and consulted a thermometer to choose what to wear for the day. The thermometer had been given to Tei-ichi as a thank-you present when he attended one of his well-off patients and it was the only thermometer in the surrounding villages. Schoolteachers occasionally brought pupils to see it. Kei did not use make-up, but her hair was always fashionably done up and she carried a parasol in summer to protect her face from the sun. The villagers called her 'okkasama', which means mother, and greeted her warmly as her neat figure hurried down the village street followed by a maid.

She would buy damaged material and sale goods at a cloth shop. She was clever at cutting and sewing kimonos and clad the whole family handsomely. All her household were well mannered and disciplined. Shobei knew this as well.

Kei also made ointment to sell. It was a simple mixture of beeswax and a few other ingredients. Although the recipe was not secret, her special skill was needed in heating and kneading. The finished product was put in sealed sea shells and was sold widely as Shirai Ointment for cuts and bruises. Kei carefully saved from the income for their sons' education. She was determined that her sons should go to the Imperial University like Dr Shintaro and succeed their father as modern doctors. But she did not have much ambition for her daughter, Ayako. She should marry one day but not into the kind of family that would involve the Shirais in spending a lot of money for a trousseau. Kei hoped that Ayako would be treated kindly by her husband's family when she married and would be sufficiently provided for. Ayako was a pretty girl so this did not seem like too much to ask for.

'Being a doctor, he must have a secret recipe for making his daughter so lovely,' the villagers remarked when they saw Ayako.

She was nicknamed 'Drop off a bridge'. This strange name came from a story about a man from another village who was crossing a narrow bridge when he saw Ayako coming towards him. Gawping at her, because she was so beautiful, he missed his step and fell into the river.

When a distant relative brought the marriage proposal from the Miwas, Tei-ichi was surprised. Until then, he had not thought of Ayako as a woman. Wasn't she running around with her brothers and catching fish in the river? The last time he saw her up a tree, he had vaguely wondered if it was time he should tell her off for behaving like a boy. Wasn't it only a few years ago? Besides, he had never considered the possibility of his daughter being asked for by the most sought-after bachelor he knew.

'Let me think about it,' he said eventually to the go-between. At first he could not believe what he had heard. Then he reconsidered.

'Why, we are not such a bad family. We have nothing to be ashamed of. And Ayako is an intelligent and beautiful girl.'

But he had not expected to part with her so soon. Ayako seemed totally unprepared for the role of a young wife in such an august family. However, if he missed the opportunity to marry her to Shintaro, he was convinced that he would never find as good a match as this most accomplished young man. Tei-ichi also wanted very much to become the father-in-law of such a well-educated doctor. He would be a fine example for his sons. Undecided, he called Ayako. She was not at all demure. She looked her father straight in the eye and said, 'Dr Miwa, otohsan? Oh, yes, I will marry him.'

'W-wait a minute. You don't have to rush. Think about it carefully,' he stuttered, confused. 'In any case, you don't know him. I . . . I am not telling you that you have to marry him.' He had expected her to be either shy and hesitant, or look totally innocent.

'I have heard a lot about him,' she said, 'and I have seen him.'

'What?'

Tei-ichi felt that his stern control of the household was crumbling in front of him.

'When did you see him?'

'I went to the station with Yasuharu san to see what Dr Miwa looks like, when he came back from Tokyo.'

Yasuharu was one of her younger brothers. The family had the custom of referring to each other with a respectful 'san' at the end of their names.

'Oh!'

'Everybody says he is very intelligent, and very kind,' Ayako said.

'You don't understand.' Tei-ichi struggled to regain his composure. 'You don't know what it means to get married. You have no idea, do you understand? You have no idea. It is not playing house. You have to leave us and your home for ever and live somewhere else with someone else.' Then he said, even more sternly, 'It is not like going to stay at your cousin's. You cannot come back. I will not allow you to come back.' But after a moment, he added wistfully, 'That is, as a member of this family. You can visit here, of course, but not to live.'

Ayako was listening respectfully but Tei-ichi did not feel that she was in any way impressed by his speech.

'Did you realise that Ayako is growing up to be a daring modern girl?' Tei-ichi complained when he was alone with Kei that night.

Kei put a cup of tea in front of her husband and sat directly on the tatami floor without a *zabuton*, a cushion.

'Has Ayako done something wrong?' she asked.

'I asked her what she thought of marrying Dr Shintaro.'

'It was kind of you to ask how she feels about it.'

'Hum!'

Tei-ichi realised that it had been thoughtful of him. A lot of girls would not be given the opportunity to express their opinion. Marriage was the union of two families regardless of the sentiments of the persons immediately concerned.

Kei had not been told about the proposal from the Miwas.

'So, are you giving her to the Miwas?'

'There is no reason why not. He is a splendid fellow. But Ayako is too young. She does not know what marriage means. She does not know anything about men and women.'

'So, what did Ayako say?' As Tei-ichi went silent, Kei prompted him.

Tei-ichi remembered his surprise.

'Amazing!' He suddenly looked animated and young, telling Kei what he had discovered. 'Kei, she is not a child any more. She said she wanted to marry Dr Shintaro. She said she knew about him already. Can you believe it? She seems to understand what marriage means.' Then he repeated, 'I thought she was only a child.'

Kei laughed. She was not disquieted. She merely said, 'Girls mature early.'

Tei-ichi felt that he was slighted by both mother and daughter. He straightened up a little. He regained his air of importance.

'She said she had gone to the station to see Dr Shintaro. Such behaviour is not allowed. From now on, teach her manners and be strict with her. You must not let her go out on her own.'

'Yes.' Kei bowed a little and stopped laughing. She admitted to herself that it had been indiscreet for a young unmarried girl of a decent family to go out with her brother, without her knowledge. But in the big house that the Shirais had to manage, there were not enough maids to accompany Ayako every time she went out. Kei had to spare Shige to accompany Ayako for sewing and koto music lessons. Kei's youngest son, Hideto, was not a year old yet. Shige's daughter, Kiyo, would have to clean the kitchen and perhaps Kei herself would carry the baby on her back while she prepared the meals . . . She could manage. It would all be worthwhile if Ayako could marry such a well-qualified man.

'We have to prepare her to become a suitable bride for the eldest son of the Miwas,' Tei-ichi was saying. 'Don't be lazy about chaperoning her. It is your responsibility.' While he was talking to Kei, he made up his mind about his daughter's marriage.

'Yes,' Kei said, looking at her folded hands on her lap.

'There will be a lot of expenses, to be equal to the Miwas. But we must do our best not to shame ourselves. We must also think of Ayako's position after she has married. We have to send her off properly. The boys' education might have to be reconsidered. I hope you understand that,' Tei-ichi told his wife solemnly.

'Yes,' Kei said again, but she was not as worried about money as Tei-ichi was. When the negotiations started, she would gently suggest that her husband have a frank talk with Shobei. Shobei must know the Shirais' financial situation. If it was money he wanted, he certainly would have accepted the Abes' daughter. He would not be as unworldly as her husband. Kei sensed that her sons' education, on the other hand, was far more important than before. They were the family assets, not a large trousseau.

She went back to the kitchen where Shige was supervising Kiyo, who was measuring rice and washing it ready for the next day. Shige had come to the Shirais as Kei's personal maid when she married Tei-ichi. They had grown up together.

'O'Shige san,' Kei called. 'Come here a minute.'

When Shige went into the *chanoma*, a small back living room next to the kitchen, Kei was sitting by the *hibachi*, an elaborate charcoal burner. An iron kettle was always placed on it during the day and from it now came the soft noise of water evaporating.

'Sit down for a minute.'

Kei pointed towards the other side of the hibachi. As soon as Shige sat down, Kei giggled and whispered, 'Ayako gave dansama such a surprise.'

She remembered how her husband was flurried and lost his usual dignified air of importance.

'He is so naive!' She kept on laughing. Shige, too, laughed.

'Oh, men are all very naive.'

'They think they are cleverer than us.'

'What happened?' Shige's husband was bringing in wood from outside and, hearing the laughter, poked his head into the *chanoma*.

'Go away. This is women's talk.' Shige waved her hand to chase him away. The two women continued to chat to each other, giving vent to feelings pent up by the strain of constant obedience.

As Kei hoped, Ayako was welcomed and treated like a real daughter by Shobei and his wife. Most of her trousseau was made up of the 'presents of welcome' from the Miwas. This did not shame the Shirais. On the contrary, people realised that Shobei esteemed the Shirais and their respect for the Shirais increased. At the same time, they appreciated Shobei's generosity. Shintaro loved his young and lovely wife. Ayako adored him. For her, there was no one as handsome, intelligent and kind as he was. She looked up to her husband with respect and worshipped him as though he was a god. Her obedience to him was sincere.

For ten years, there was nothing but happiness in the Miwa family. The villagers said, 'Even the sun shines brighter over their house.'

When Ayako produced a healthy first child, even though it was a girl, there was a celebration. She was named Takeko. Then, two years later, in the first year of a new century, 1900, Haruko was born. Slight disappointment was felt at the arrival of a second daughter, but the husband was thirty-five and the wife was only nineteen.

'We'll have more children,' Shintaro said to Shobei.

'Of course you will,' he answered.

When a third daughter was born, Shintaro, who had been telling his wife that he was not at all worried whether it would be a boy or a girl, had to walk around the garden before he went to see her to make sure he looked cheerful and pleased. The third child was called Sachiko.

It was when Ayako was pregnant for the fourth time that, one frosty morning, Shobei went to inspect his charcoal-making lodge. Wearing his padded jerkin, he bent forward and walked on hurriedly. As he came to the foot of the steep stone steps leading up to a temple, he made out a pair of women's footwear left neatly at the bottom. He was not surprised. The temple was famous for divine favours for childless women and women without sons. They would go to the temple every day and climb up and down the steps barefoot for their wishes to be fulfilled. During the day, there were always one or two women in the vicinity who had come from far away.

In the grey light, he saw Kei coming down the steps. Unaware that the passer-by was Shobei, Kei squatted once more in supplication when she reached the bottom of the steps. Kei must have been there every morning praying for Ayako to have a boy, before Tei-ichi got up. Tei-ichi's dislike of what he called superstition was well known.

And a son, Shuichi, was born. Shobei opened kegs of saké and invited the villagers. He ordered pink and white rice cakes from the largest cake shop in town and distributed them. He also donated a large sum of money to the temple. It was in honour of the quiet figure who was praying barefoot in the icy morning for the sake of her daughter and her family. It was his way of thanking her without telling her.

All day, relatives and friends arrived. They brought a large red sea bream as a symbol of felicitation, silk, cakes and other presents. In the kitchen, sushi was prepared in quantity. Only one person did not participate in the party. In the quiet inner room, Ayako was fast asleep.

That was the happiest day for the Miwas.

2

The Russians

At the outbreak of the Russo-Japanese War, the International Red Cross appointed Shintaro to be responsible for war casualties. He was one of the few doctors in the country qualified in European medicine. He was stationed on an island of Oki in the Japan Sea where the Red Cross Hospital was set up. Anticipating that the war would last more than a year, Shintaro took his wife and young family with him.

'Haruko ojosama, there is a Russian man's body washed up on the shore. Let's go and see,' a young servant said to Haruko.

He knew she would come. He was excited and itching to go, but thought that it would be prudent to take one of the children with him. It would look better than leaving work on his own. Of the four children in the Miwa family, the younger two were not old enough, while it was unthinkable to ask Haruko's older sister, Takeko. At the age of seven, Takeko was a prim young lady. Haruko was different. When she heard the servant, she neither asked questions nor hesitated.

Haruko went out through the gate ahead of the servant. Once outside the garden, the servant rolled up his *hakama* (wide trousers). Haruko hitched up the skirt of her cotton kimono. Both of them took off their *geta* (wooden footwear) and, carrying them in their hands, ran along the dusty lane leading to the sea shore.

There was a crowd of some fifty people standing on the beach looking at the body, which was lying on the sand face up. It was late spring and the breeze felt pleasant to the people who were standing around.

'Huge!' a well-tanned and bow-legged man exclaimed, looking at the body.

'If the country is big, it is natural that the people are big,' someone else said. He meant to state a fact, but the villagers broke out into fits of laughter. 'They may be big, but we defeated them.'

The Japanese navy had attacked a Russian task force and won an outright victory. Everybody was good-humoured, as though this success was a personal achievement. They forgot about the dead body for a moment. It lay as though it had never known life.

Several children tried to peep between the onlookers' legs and were scolded and chased away, but someone noticed Haruko and said, 'Ah, the doctor's daughter,' and let her get inside the circle of men.

Haruko thought that the colour of his hair was strange, like an ear of wheat. The face was unnaturally pallid. The eyes were closed. Haruko crouched down to take a closer look.

'Aren't you afraid, Haruko ojosama?' a shop-keeper asked. She shook her head. There was hardly anything that made her afraid, she thought. She was not like Takeko, who was scared of almost everything and squeamish as well.

'Look at this.' Someone standing behind Haruko pointed at the chest of the body. A gold chain with a green enamelled ball about one centimetre in diameter hung from the neck. She had noticed it but was not sure if she was allowed to touch it. Tiny diamonds encircled a small piece of glass at the top of the green ball, and threw little rainbow-coloured lights in the sun.

The man bent over the body and picked up the pendant, turning it around. Standing up, he told Haruko to look through the top. It was a small magnifying glass. When she managed to focus, she gasped. There was a foreign lady inside the small green ball. She was sitting sideways with one elbow lightly resting on a cushion. She had long reddish golden hair and blue eyes. Her shoulders were bare. She had something red and gold around her neck and on her ear.

'Haruko ojosama,' the servant whispered, and poked at her. She turned around indignantly and realised that her father was coming with several people, among whom were the head of the village and the chief of police.

Her father was busy talking to the others about identifying the body and taking it to the temple.

'Do not touch him. You must respect the dead, enemy or not,' she heard him say to the villagers. He was also saying to the police chief, 'There may be more bodies drifting this way.'

*　　*　　*

Two days before, Haruko had been to the beach with the same servant and they had seen many columns of black smoke on the horizon.

'There are fifty Russian warships.' Someone was knowledgeable. 'They came all the way from the North Sea, taking eight months.'

'Eight months!' a fisherman repeated in surprise. 'Ships like that cannot be in the sea for long without supplies. Barnacles and seaweed grow on the hull. If they are not cleaned off they will slow down the ship. Even our little boat . . .'

'Yes, yes.' The first man interrupted the chatter impatiently.

The world knew the difficulties of the task force and watched its heroic progress through the Baltic Sea and the North Sea, the Atlantic and Indian Oceans, the South China Sea, the East China Sea and, finally, the Sea of Japan. Anchorages en route were mainly hostile. The long suffering of the sailors was nearly over. The year was 1905.

The motive for this extraordinary expedition by the Russians was to secure command of the Sea of Japan by reinforcing the First Pacific Fleet based at Port Arthur. The Russians had leased this port at the southern tip of Manchuria from the Chinese. But Port Arthur had fallen and the entire First Fleet had been destroyed by the Japanese navy. The new objective of the Russian Commander Rozhdestvensky, was to carry as many of his warships as possible safely into Vladivostok, north of the Sea of Japan. The last thing he wanted was to meet the Japanese en route.

For the Japanese the confrontation with the Russian fleet was the culmination of half a century of struggle and preparation. Technology was behind. The nation was poor. Most people had only millet and dried fish to eat. And yet the Japanese had invested heavily in the navy. Those in power were conscious of the vulnerability of an island nation that lacked the natural resources to modernise. A nearby land empire in China would be a lifeline. If they lost the sea battle against the Russians, the Japanese army, which was narrowly winning in Manchuria, would be isolated. It would not take long for them to be ousted.

As the Russian ships neared their destination they had to decide whether to take the direct and shorter route to Vladivostok through the Tsushima Strait into the Sea of Japan or sail along the east of the Japanese archipelago in the Pacific Ocean. The Japanese did not have enough warships to meet them in two places. Which route would the Russians choose? This was the question in everyone's mind. The nervousness of naval headquarters permeated down to the streets. Rumour had it that a samurai in white clothes had appeared in a dream to the Empress and said, 'Don't worry. They will come to the Sea of Japan.'

Standing on the beach, Haruko saw the columns of black smoke far away above the horizon, and heard a man mutter, 'Thank God, they came this way.'

The news that Haruko and the servant had been down to the beach to see the dead body had already reached home by the time they entered the house.

'What have you been up!' Ayako sighed and smiled at the same time. 'Can't you behave like a girl?'

'How can you go and see a body!' Takeko made a show of shuddering and covered her mouth with both hands in a gesture of horror.

Haruko ignored her sister. She did not dislike Takeko, who was two years older, but she could not respect her.

In the morning, Takeko often said, 'I don't feel well,' before setting off for school. 'In that case, you had better stay at home,' her Miwa grandmother, would say and Takeko would stay at home. After all, she was a girl; she did not need an education. As a girl of a well-to-do and long-established family she would have good marriage prospects if she was pretty, and that was all that mattered. Even at school, Takeko often said she felt ill and went home, leaving her books and other belongings for Haruko to bring back later.

For Haruko, school was important. Besides, she enjoyed it. The work was easy for her. She could dominate the village rascals in the classroom. She was given prizes. And she always finished her homework before the lesson was over.

That night, the Miwa children sat on cushions placed on the tatami floor while their father had his dinner. The children usually finished their meal early around a big table with their mother. A maid sat and attended them. Shintaro had his meal later, attended by his wife. He had a small table to himself, and Ayako sat by a little rice tub with a tray on her lap. The dishes were more elaborate than for the earlier gathering. There was soup in a black lacquered bowl with gold and silver chrysanthemums painted on it, a broiled fish with garnish and more plates of vegetables in season. Saké was served as well. As Shintaro ate, he talked to his children.

'And what did you see in the pendant that you were peeping in?' he asked Haruko that night. He had seen her on the beach.

'I saw a lady. Is she Russian?' Haruko relaxed. She was not going to be scolded.

'Very likely. She must be his wife or fiancée.'

'She had jewels around her neck.'

'Did you like them?'

'The jewels? I don't know,' she said. They had seemed so unreal that she had no feelings except awe. Shintaro laughed.

'What is a pendant?' Takeko wanted to know.

'Russians are enemy,' three-year-old Sachiko said.

'Haruko.' Her father called her as she was getting ready to go to school the next day. 'I want you to come with me to the Russian hospital ship today. I will send someone to fetch you from school.'

'But I cannot miss school.' It was an awful dilemma. To miss school was bad. On the other hand, she had been told that her father's word was absolute.

'I will send a note to the teacher. It is to help me visit the wounded and make them feel better.'

'Russians?' Ayako opened her eyes wide with astonishment. She forgot her usual modesty in front of her husband and protested, 'You cannot go to the enemy place with a little girl. They will kill you.'

'No, no. They will not kill us. They are doctors like me and their patients.'

Ayako was not totally convinced but did not say any more.

'In foreign countries,' Shintaro explained gently, 'it is the wife's duty to go with her husband on such occasions.'

'Wife!'

'Yes. Wife. You see, in foreign countries, wives attend dinner parties looking like the lady that Haruko saw in the pendant, and are able to carry on conversations with other men.'

'Do foreign women eat with men from the same table?'

'Yes, they do.'

'Why?'

'Because they think it is sociable.'

Most of Shintaro's knowledge of life in Russia came from reading translations of novels by writers such as Dostoyevsky and Tolstoy.

Although she did not understand why Shintaro wanted to take

17

Haruko to see the Russians, Ayako had Haruko's special kimono, which was kept for New Year's Day, spread out on the tatami floor and dressed her daughter.

'You must stay with your otohsan. I heard that foreign men have hair all over their body like animals,' she told Haruko. A rickshaw came and Haruko climbed up after her father. He held her in front of him. She was almost hidden behind a large bunch of flowers that the servant handed to her.

'Foreign wives are like geishas,' Ayako confided to her maid, Kiyo, later.

The hospital ship was a small vessel of about three and a half thousand tons but as Haruko stood in a little boat ready to be hoisted on board, the side of the ship soared up beside her like a cliff. They were winched up in a kind of basket. Shintaro was tall among fishermen and tenant farmers but the person who approached them on the deck was of another species. He was like a bear. A reddish beard covered half of his red face around a big nose. Her mother was right. His hands were covered with golden hair even between the knuckles.

'This ojisan is the captain of this ship,' Shintaro told Haruko. Although 'ojisan' meant 'uncle' it was freely used by children for men of their parents' age. But this giant was not another ojisan. Shintaro amiably shook hands with him and talked in German. Then he handed Haruko the large bunch of flowers he was carrying for her. Pushing her gently towards the Russian, he said, 'Give the flowers to the captain.'

The giant said something. His voice was deep and sonorous. He took the flowers from her and, still talking to Shintaro, put his large hand on her head. The hand covered her head and she could see the tips of the fingers. The hand was heavy. She shuddered a little. Her whole body went rigid.

'Were you scared?' Takeko asked when father and daughter came home.

'No,' Haruko said. 'Not at all.' She had decided never to tell anyone that she had wet herself when the large hand was placed on her head.

Soon after the Tsushima naval battle, the war ended, and the Miwas went back to the family home in the southern prefecture of the main island by the Seto Inland Sea.

3

Haruko and Her Father

In the autumn after he had been married for ten years, Shintaro caught a cold and could not shake it off. His university friends, who were well-established doctors by then, were consulted. He had suffered from incipient tuberculosis as a student. It had been contained, but it seemed to have resurfaced.

Shintaro was afraid that his condition might be infectious, particularly to his family. He bought a small house not far from home along the coast of the Seto Inland Sea and stayed there. His four children were told that he would be better soon and come home, but they were never taken to see their father till his last days.

When the children were told that they were going to the seaside house, they were delighted. The oldest, Takeko, was then ten and the youngest, Shuichi, was just four.

It was balmy autumn weather and the sky was full of clouds like fish scales. The adults talked about a coming storm but all the children, except Takeko, romped about in the garden and played hide and seek. When they were hushed and scolded, Shintaro gestured that they should be allowed to play and watched them from his bed.

A maid came to Haruko to tell her that she was wanted by her father. When she went into the room, Shintaro nodded slightly to Haruko to come near him. After looking at her for a while, he said, 'Give me your hand.' When she placed her little hand on his thin veined hand, he whispered, 'Promise me to help okahsan look after Shuichi, will you? I can rely on you, can I?'

Haruko nodded gravely. She felt an enormous weight of responsibility. She did not understand how she should help her mother. She concluded that they would become very poor like a lot of her school friends. If it was so, there was no problem. She would carry water, wood, and cook meals for Shuichi. She would fight village boys if they harmed her brother. She could picture herself in a tattered kimono going to school hungry because she had given her breakfast to Shuichi. Yes, she would do that.

'Yes, otohsan, I will,' she said. Shintaro smiled a little.

It was an honour to be asked. Haruko thought she knew why she was selected. When she was five, she and Takeko were having a nap in a *kotatsu*, a little charcoal burner in a wooden frame with a cover over it. Haruko was woken up by Takeko's scream. Takeko had put her foot too near the fire. Her *tabi*, a sock, was smouldering. Haruko opened a window, scooped up snow in both hands and put it on the burning sock. By the time the grown-ups came, Takeko was still screaming but the fire was out. The burn was not severe.

'You are such an intelligent child. You are more cool-headed than most grown-ups.' Her father had patted her head then.

The night Haruko promised her father to look after Shuichi, there was a lot of rain. The sea was rough and the roar of waves was heard very close. Around midnight, a sliding door was quietly opened and Kei came into the room where the children were asleep. She woke the three girls and carried Shuichi.

When they went into the room where Shintaro lay, they were told to sit by his bedside. Shuichi was made to sit first and the girls followed. Their mother held a bowl of water and a brush for them. In turn, the children were handed the brush and told to wet their father's lips.

The doctor was at the other side of the bed holding Shintaro's wrist.

'I am sorry . . . Please look after Shuichi and the other children, and help Ayako,' Shintaro said in a low but clear voice. In Confucius' terms, Shintaro was an undutiful son, as his death preceded those of his parents and gave them grief.

'Don't worry. Shuichi will be well taken care of as the heir of the Miwas. And the other children, too, of course,' Tei-ichi said from behind Shobei. Shobei had his arms folded and did not move.

'Thank you,' Shintaro said, and closed his eyes.

The wind blew hard and bamboo bushes kept hitting the shutters. The electric bulb hanging from the ceiling swayed in a draught and moved their shadows.

The next morning, Haruko found that all the white hagi flowers had gone from the garden, blown away by the wind.

'He was blessed with too much,' people said. 'He was intelligent, handsome and rich. He had a lovely wife and children. He was so lucky that the devil was jealous of him.'

The coffin was taken back home and there was a quiet family funeral that night. The public Buddhist ceremony was held at home, three days later. Ayako wore a black kimono and the children were all in white. Shuichi was sitting nearest to the altar as chief mourner. Ayako sat next to him and then the girls in order of age.

Baron Kida, a close friend of Shobei, was the senior member of the funeral committee. Led by the head priest of the family temple, the ceremony was impressive and well attended. The house was filled with wreaths sent by the famous. They spilled out from the house through the gate into the street.

The mourners were struck by Ayako's loveliness. At twenty-eight, she seemed to be at the height of refined beauty. The black kimono enhanced her classical features. It was customary to include a black mourning kimono in a trousseau, and Kei had bought the most expensive black silk. Kei had always been frugal and Tei-ichi had been shocked at its price.

'It is not necessary to have such good quality,' he protested.

Kei was undaunted on this occasion.

'Black silk is very revealing,' she said. 'If the material is cheap, the colour is muddy and it will stand out when everybody is in black. The young wife of the Miwas cannot look unstylish.'

Pale-faced but composed, Ayako sat between Shuichi and Takeko. The expensive black silk was almost luminous. The edge of her collar against the dark kimono was so white that it almost hurt her eyes. The guests forgot for a moment the rites and incense when they saw her.

Shintaro had prepared her for the day. During his long illness, he had often talked about her life after he had gone.

'I have loved you from the moment I saw you,' he said. Ayako was unaccustomed to this kind of expression and at first she looked at him blankly. He took her hand. 'I will always love you wherever I am.'

It was Shintaro who told her to become a Christian. He thought that her simple adoration of him could find an outlet in the worship of Christ. The teachings would comfort her.

The funeral went on for a long time. Many people came from all over the area. The thick white smoke of incense and the incessant chanting of sutras continued. Shuichi stayed still all through the funeral and people talked about how good he was.

Shobei sat squarely right behind Shuichi. He kept repeating to himself, as though to convince fate, that he had to live for twenty more years. 'I have to see to Shuichi until he finishes university.'

The next day, an ox cart made a slow journey to the temple through winding village streets carrying the coffin. The villagers came out to pay their last respects to Shintaro. Most women cried, but their tears were for the four-year-old Shuichi in a white kimono, carrying his father's name tablet and walking behind the coffin. Haruko walked with him. It was either Ayako or Takeko's place to be nearest to Shuichi, but no one protested. In the family, Haruko was beginning to be regarded as trustworthy.

4

Shobei's Garden

Shobei was sitting in his study. It was a room connected to the main house by a covered corridor and faced a garden of its own. The day was fine and all the sliding doors were open. He was at a desk under the window on which were a large abacus, a lacquered box with brush and ink stone, and a wooden box containing a substantial number of documents.

The chrysanthemums in the garden were vivid yellow. He had forgotten that their season had returned. After the funeral, courtesy visits to and from relatives and friends had kept them busy for several weeks. A carp jumped out of the water of a large pond.

He remembered the day when he waded into the pond in a formal hakama and kimono with family crests to catch a carp for a member of the imperial family. That year, on the plain nearby, the Emperor had held grand military manoeuvres over three days and the Miwas were chosen to accommodate a prince. A special cook was hired from the town and the carp was duly presented to the imperial table.

Shobei and Shintaro were invited to sit at the table with the prince and allowed to share the dishes. Ayako, in her specially prepared dark blue kimono with painted and embroidered chrysanthemums, attended the table.

When the prince left, having thanked the host and his son for their hospitality, he fixed his eyes on Shintaro and said, 'You are a lucky fellow to have such a beautiful wife.'

After he had gone, Shintaro remarked, 'Thank goodness, we aren't living in the barbaric feudal period. He might have tried to take Ayako with him.'

'Don't be disrespectful to the imperial family,' Shobei scolded his son, but now he understood Shintaro's concern for Ayako's vulnerability.

Until Shintaro's illness became serious, Shobei thought he had been lucky. They lived in the south along the Seto Inland Sea. The climate was mild. The soil was fertile. The sea was productive. He invested well. And he had an excellent son and grandson to carry on the family name.

Shobei sighed and opened the polished wooden box on his desk and took out an envelope. He began to tear it up.

He could hear his own voice telling Shintaro, 'I am sure to die before you. All the instructions as regards to our property are kept here when you need them.' He also remembered that Shintaro hesitated as if to say, 'No doubt you will live for a long time yet,' but eventually he just said, 'I shall carry out your instructions, otohsan.'

Shobei's reminiscence was broken.

'Did you want me, otohsan?' Rinji, Shobei's younger son, came into the room.

'Oh, yes, sit down.' Then Shobei said, 'It's very mild for November, isn't it?'

Rinji, who was not in the habit of being received with such a sociable remark from his father, looked a little surprised. Usually if he was called, his father was ready to go straight to business. Shobei's loneliness might have made him more gentle than usual. The father and son were looking at the carefully tended garden. Rinji wondered why he had been called.

Although Shobei had never heard directly what the villagers were saying about his second son, he could have made a good guess. They were saying that at the Miwas', the older son had taken everything good with him when he was born, and left only the dregs behind.

Shintaro was tall, but Rinji was short. They had the same features, yet Shintaro was handsome, and he had a natural grace. Rinji lacked refinement. Shintaro was intelligent, but Rinji had not learnt much at school.

Shobei chose a nearby stonemason's daughter called Tetsu as Rinji's wife. It was Shobei's view that his second son needed a clever wife who could manage his affairs, and not an innocent girl who had been brought up protected in a good family.

At his marriage, Shobei gave Rinji one-third of his property and made him establish his own household independent from the main family.

'You could give Rinji half the property,' Shintaro had suggested. 'You gave me my education and I could support my family.' But Shobei had been adamant. Rinji was also given land including forests. If managed well, they produced good timber. Rinji had a new house built on the other side of the village. After eight years of marriage, he and Tetsu had no children.

When Shintaro was alive, Shobei felt no pressure to tie the loose knot in the family affairs. Now that he had gone, the bridge he had to build between himself and four-year-old Shuichi was long. Every obstacle had to be removed and the foundations had to be made solid for Shuichi's sake.

Recently Shobei had been hearing an unsavoury rumour. Tetsu's nephew, who had run away from his family trade of stonemasonry, had come home and was often at Rinji's house.

'People are saying that Tetsu is passing a lot of money to her family. She may eventually adopt her nephew as their heir,' Shobei's wife said to him one night. 'That nephew of hers does not have a good reputation. I think you must have a word with Rinji san.'

When she told Shobei this, his wife felt a sense of retaliation. She had been brought up in an old family which still prided itself on its bygone samurai status. It was beyond her comprehension that her own family should mix socially with people like stonemasons and vendors. Her own son Rinji should not have been treated like a good-for-nothing. She felt rebellious now and again against Shobei's dogmatic ruling of the family, and she had opposed Rinji's marriage as strongly as she dared.

Now Shobei turned to Rinji.

'I hear that Tetsu is passing a lot of money to her family. Is that true?' he asked without further preliminaries.

'Oh, well, you know, otohsan, how it is. She might have helped them out once or twice, a little here and there.'

'You do not have a plan for adopting your wife's nephew as your successor, do you?'

'Oh, I don't think so. Nothing definite yet, anyway.'

'Good,' Shobei said. 'You will adopt your niece Haruko. One day she can take a husband and succeed your family.'

As Rinji did not answer right away, Shobei said, 'That is the best plan for you.'

'Yes, otohsan.'

'When Haruko is a little older, I will explain to her and we will make it public. At the moment, it will suffice to decide among ourselves.'

Haruko and Shuichi. Between the two, the families would continue safely, Shobei thought.

Towards the end of the year, Shobei called on Tei-ichi.

'I came to apologise to both of you,' Shobei began to say to Tei-ichi. Kei appeared with cups of tea, bowed, and started to leave the room. Shobei stopped her.

'I asked you to give us your daughter and promised that we would make her happy. Now, I have made her a young widow.'

'Don't be absurd!' Tei-ichi was genuinely moved. 'Even if it was not long enough, Ayako had a lovely life with your family and now has wonderful children. She does not regret, neither do we.'

'Thank you.'

After a pause, Shobei said, 'I came to ask you a favour. I have been thinking about Ayako and the children a lot recently. Since Shintaro died, her days are very lonely. The children, too, need a more lively atmosphere. I wonder if you would agree to have Ayako and the children come to live with you. It is not that I am giving them back to you. If you accept, I would like to provide for them.'

Soon after that, Ayako and the four children went back to live in the Shirais' house in Kitani village. Ayako insisted on leaving most of her belongings at the Miwas until later. The children were told that they would be staying at their Shirai grandparents for a holiday. They wrapped some of their clothes in small bundles, each using a *furoshiki*, a square cloth.

'What about our school things?' Haruko asked.

'You take them with you. We will be there for a while as Yasu ojisama is coming home from Tokyo.'

'We can play with Hiden sama!' They were delighted. Hideto was the youngest of Kei's sons and only two years older than Takeko. They called him Hide niisama, older brother, instead of ojisama, uncle, but the pronunciation had degenerated to Hiden sama. He was an excellent swimmer, gymnast and runner. He was a hero among the children.

Ayako insisted on walking. She wanted to make the leaving as casual as possible. A servant carried Shuichi's *furoshiki* and the children ran and chatted.

'A nice day. Where are you going, Shu dansama as well?' Villagers stopped and asked.

'We are visiting the Shirais. My brother is coming home from Tokyo,' Ayako replied politely.

When Ayako had come to Shobei's study to say goodbye, both of them made light of the leave-taking.

'Give Shirai oji-isama and obahsama my regards, and all of you, be good. I will come and see you soon,' Shobei said to the four children.

Although his study was built away from the main house and he had seldom heard the children before, the quietness was oppressive.

'What I have done is best for Ayako and the children.' He rested his chin in the cup of his hands and looked at the garden. 'The Shirais' sons are wonderful company for Shuichi. He needs boys around him. And Ayako . . . I could not bear watching a beautiful young woman living day after day, lonely and quiet, just waiting for her children to grow up. I don't think she would want to re-marry even if she was advised to take another husband. She is thinking of Shintaro all the time. Every corner of this house reminds her of the days she has been happy with him.'

'Yes, I have done the right thing. The Shirais are a lively family, Kei san will not let Ayako dwell on memories. Ayako will eventually regain her cheerful self that Shintaro loved so much. We all did . . .'

Shobei stayed in his study all day.

5

Spring

In the spring, lots of snakes came out from between the stones of the walls surrounding the Shirais' house. Haruko and Sachiko were collecting cast-off snake skins which were like lace. It was six months since they had returned to their grandparents' house with their mother.

'Good afternoon, girls,' a tall black figure said. The two girls looked at each other and ran away from him to the back of the house.

'Where is Hiden sama?'

Shige's husband stopped cutting wood and, resting his hands on the handle of the axe, told them, 'He was with Shu dansama in the garden.' The two boys were target shooting with handmade bows and arrows. The girls ran to them.

'Hiden sama, Shu-chan.'

Hideto ignored them. Shuichi copied everything that Hideto did.

'Listen,' Haruko said, panting, and Sachiko giggled. 'The crow has come.'

'Oh, no.' Hideto stopped shooting and looked at the girls.

'I have an idea,' Haruko said. 'Let's all run away to the woods and hide. Are you coming, Hiden sama?'

If they were going to the woods, they needed Hideto to protect them from snakes, village boys and all sorts of dangers.

The crow was a nickname the children had given to Rev. Kondo because of his long black robe. He came every Wednesday afternoon from a nearby town to perform Christian services at the Shirais'. Everybody at home including the servants was expected to attend. Shobei had ordered an organ for Ayako from Tokyo and a former schoolmistress came and played it.

Not only was the service boring for the children, but Rev. Kondo had an unnaturally long face. When his jaw was pulled down to sing a hymn, the girls and young maids in the back row had to endure excruciating hardship not to burst out laughing. On one occasion, one of the maids who sat right behind Haruko suddenly slapped her on the back and said, 'Oh, no, Haruko ojosama,' and went into fits of hysterical laughter. Everybody turned around and stared at Haruko. Altogether, the service was something they did not look forward to.

Later, the children were called by Tei-ichi.

'Hideto.' Tei-ichi addressed Hideto in a severe voice. 'It was very rude of you to run away from the service when Rev. Kondo came all the way from the town to teach us lessons.'

'Yes, otohsan.'

'You should be old enough to know that. It was particularly naughty of you to have told the younger ones to run away with you.'

'I am sorry.'

Haruko's heart was beating fast, but Hideto did not make any excuses.

'Go to the storehouse.'

The storehouse was at the end of the corridor and was built to withstand fire. It had mud walls which were one metre thick and no window. Two thick oak doors separated it from the main house. At the outbreak of fire, the doors would be sealed with mud. It was dark and cold inside.

To be locked up in the storehouse was the worst punishment.

Towards night, clanging a bunch of large keys, Kei came in, a lamp in hand.

'Hideto?' She held up the lamp and called, peering inside. 'Come with me and we will apologise to otohsan.'

Kei and her son bowed to Tei-ichi. Kei said, 'Now he knows he has done wrong. He says that he will not do it again. Please forgive him.' She turned to Hideto. 'Apologise to otohsan.'

After that Kei sat Hideto down and gave him his evening meal which she had kept for him.

In the summer, Haruko, Sachiko and Shuichi followed Hideto around. When he appeared, village bullies left them alone. In order to establish this position, Hideto had been involved in a few serious fights and had again been locked up in the storehouse by Tei-ichi.

Unlike the Miwas, the Shirais had evening meals together. Now that the older boys were away at university and school, Tei-ichi, Hideto and Shuichi sat at the top of the table. One evening, Tei-ichi looked down towards the end of the table and said, 'I saw monkeys today up in a tree in the village.'

'Monkeys?' Kei asked. 'I have never seen them so far away from the mountains.'

'These monkeys I saw today were strange monkeys. They were wearing kimonos.'

'I see,' Kei said. 'You had better tell them to go back to the mountains next time you see them.'

'I will try. But I wonder if they will understand . . . After all, they are monkeys.'

Haruko and Sachiko were red in the face and hunched their shoulders, making themselves as small as possible. Ayako looked at them amused. As Shobei wished, she was treated by Tei-ichi and Kei as though she was one of the children. She was more relaxed and happier.

'When I was going on my rounds,' Tei-ichi would say at another meal, 'I saw two naked girls swimming in the river with the village children. They looked exactly like ours, but I don't suppose we have such ill-behaved children in our family, do we? What do you think, Ayako?'

Everybody, even the servants, laughed, except Haruko and Sachiko.

Tomboys ought to be restrained, Tei-ichi believed, but he wanted Shuichi to be vigorous, even boisterous. He was the important charge trusted to him by the Miwas. As a doctor, he did not think that tuberculosis was hereditary, as it was generally believed, but suspected that there might be a constitutional tendency to the disease. Shuichi was tall for his age, but his neck was thin and he looked delicate. In Tei-ichi's opinion, too many women fussed around him.

One evening, in early autumn, the sun was still high, but it was cooler and the smell of burning dry leaves was drifting in the air. The household was beginning to get busy. The bathtub had to be filled, washing had to be taken in and put away, and the evening meal had to be cooked. By the well, Shige was scaling a large fish. Shobei, who often went fishing early in the morning, had hung his catch at the Shirais' gate on his way home before the household woke up.

'Mata san,' Kei was calling.

'I sent him to town for shopping,' Shige's voice was heard.

'Haruko nesan,' Sachiko said, 'I want a notebook.' Nesan meant older sister.

'I will give you one. It is nearly new.'

Sachiko indicated her dissatisfaction by being silent.

'Let's go to town,' Sachiko insisted.

It took about an hour to walk to town and there was a tacit understanding that the children were not allowed to go on their own, especially in the evening.

'Haruko nesan, let's go to town,' Sachiko repeated. Since they had moved to the Shirais', Kei left social obligations more and more to Ayako and she was often out or away from home for a few days. Takeko had always been Kei's favourite and hung around her grandmother. Sachiko was increasingly dependent on Haruko.

As the two girls started out, Shuichi appeared from somewhere and followed them.

'Shu-chan, we will be back soon,' Haruko tried. They wanted to return home before dark. They did not want to be saddled with a four-year-old boy.

'I want to come.' He looked at Haruko.

'Where is Hiden sama?' she said, but even before she asked, she knew Hideto had been away the whole afternoon with his friends. He must be climbing up a waterfall, or hanging on vines and jumping across a stream. He would no doubt be a general assaulting 'Port Arthur'.

'All right, you can come.' Haruko stopped walking. She tidied Shuichi's kimono and tied his sash tight. She held his hand and started off on the path between the rice paddies.

They saw Matabei coming back from shopping.

He asked, 'Oh, Haruko ojosama and Sachiko ojosama, Shuichi dansama, as well? And where are you going?'

Sachiko said, 'Just over there.' She was quicker at tact than Haruko.

'Over there?' Matabei bent his head on one side and looked at the girls. 'Don't be too long, ojosama,' he said.

'Oh, no, we'll be back very soon,' Sachiko said.

They started to run. Matabei stood with a pole over his shoulder, shopping dangling from both ends. He looked after them for a minute,

31

then went home, taking steps in rhythm with the movement of the pliable pole.

When they arrived in the little town with one narrow street, the sun had gone farther down and one side of the street was almost in darkness. At the back of a small shop which sold an assortment of stationery, sweets and haberdashery, there was a large persimmon tree laden with red fruit. The persimmons were shining in the evening sun.

The shopkeeper's wife came out, wiping her hands on her apron, and opened her eyes wide in surprise.

'Oh, Shuichi dansama, and Haruko ojosama and Sachiko ojosama, that was a long way to come.'

They did not know that they had to pay for the notebook but the woman did not worry about it either. She knew she would be paid later. When they said, 'Thank you,' and went out, she called after them, 'Go home quickly. The autumn sun sinks very fast.'

'I want to go home,' Shuichi said. He must have been tired. It was getting dark rapidly and Haruko and Sachiko, too, were homesick. The worry of being scolded began to seem real as well.

'I am hungry,' Shuichi said. Haruko and Sachiko also felt hungry.

'Let's take the railway track,' Sachiko suggested. The idea had crossed Haruko's mind. If they took the railway track, it would take only about half an hour to get home, but they had been told by Tei-ichi many times that they must not walk on it. Even for Hideto, whose activities were hardly restricted at all, the railroad was an exception.

'I want to go home,' Shuichi repeated, holding Haruko's hand. Haruko made up her mind.

They jumped from one sleeper to the next, and sang songs. There were lots of lovely pebbles to collect. They came to a railway bridge. They squatted and looked through the railings. Far below, the Kitaka river was heard, but the water was dark. Their village, Kitani, was along the river, a little upstream. It was the familiar river where they swam in summer when they thought no adults were around.

Home was not far away. They could get off the railway soon after the bridge and, within ten minutes, reach the big gate.

Haruko was relieved and astounded almost at the same time. She heard the tooting of a train and, as she looked, a light was approaching rapidly.

'Sachiko san, sit here.' Her voice was harsh in her anxiety. 'And Shu-chan next to Sachiko san.'

The thought which flashed through Haruko's mind was that Shuichi should not die. She had promised her father to look after him. How her mother would cry if she lost Shuichi.

She pushed herself against the railings and told Sachiko and Shuichi to do the same. She reached behind Sachiko's back to hold Shuichi across his shoulders. The train might kill her. She hoped that Sachiko would be safe, though she might be killed as well. But Shuichi would be protected if there were two people shielding him. He had to be saved.

Now she prayed, 'Please, God, I am sorry I did not listen to Rev. Kondo. Please help Shu chan for okahsan's sake.'

It did not take long for the train to pass, thundering by.

'Shu dansama, Haruko ojosama, Sachiko ojosama.' They saw a lantern and heard Matabei's voice. A tenant farmer had told Matabei that he had seen three children walking on the railway track.

Tei-ichi had heard from Matabei how Haruko was sitting with the other two, protecting them.

'Haruko, were you not afraid yourself?' Tei-ichi asked. He was unexpectedly gentle.

'Yes, but I thought it would be all right if Shu-chan was saved. Okahsan won't cry.' As far as she could remember, Haruko had not been afraid. She had been too busy trying to save Shuichi.

Tei-ichi was silent. Haruko was surprised that she was not locked up in the storehouse. Her grandfather's eyes were a little moist. That surprised her as well. After sitting there for a while, Tei-ichi said, 'Let's go and have supper.'

By the time Haruko was ten years old, Shobei's fears about Rinji had been confirmed. It was well known that Tetsu's father was losing his business to another stonemason in the next village as he had taken to drinking. His son, Tetsu's brother, had never been promising. The family debt was accumulating. People gossiped that his daughter's marriage into a rich family had turned the stonemason's head.

'Perhaps we should divorce her,' Shobei muttered in front of his wife. 'She has no children. We could send her home. We can give her some money . . .'

It was the duty of a bride to bear children for the family she married into. The Miwas had a right to divorce Tetsu. It occurred to Shobei that the Chinese characters for 'barren woman' were 'stone' and 'woman', but his sense of decency restrained him from making a poor joke in front of his wife.

'To send Tetsu home might be a solution,' his wife said, 'but you will not be popular. Even if you gave her money, her relatives would bear a grudge against you, and they are not a small family. It will not be good for Shuichi's future.'

That was true. The little boy would need as much sympathy and help as possible as he grew up. In this part of the country, where tangerines grew in the winter sun, everything was easy-going, and a peasants' uprising was unlikely. But society was changing. The Socialist Party had been launched and the *People's Newspaper* was in circulation. There were strikes in the factories and mines. Shobei was afraid that when Shuichi grew up, the life of a landowner would not be as easy as it had been.

It was not just the material side of life that was under threat. Although Shobei himself was not directly involved in politics, he was recognised as one of the most powerful men in the area. Officials came from the local government to ask his opinion. Candidates for any government office were said to have to get his unofficial approval as the first step. For a person in such a position, a scandal about a member of his household being treated unkindly had to be avoided.

Shobei said to his wife, 'You are thoughtful. If you have a suggestion, say it.' It was the first time he had asked his wife's opinion on a weighty matter since they had married a long time ago.

'I think you should pay Tetsu's father's debt. It could not be too large for you. If the problem is drinking, the chances are that he will not be able to go back to his business. Pension him off. Then, make Haruko the rightful successor to Rinji san. No one will say you are cruel.'

Shobei folded his arms. He was not reflecting on what his wife had just said. He was simply impressed.

The duty of telling Haruko about the adoption fell on Tei-ichi.

'You know your Rinji ojisan and Tetsu obasan, don't you?' Tei-ichi began.

Haruko had never seen her uncle except at formal family gatherings. The furtiveness of his demeanour as he talked to elderly relatives was plain even to the children. Beside Shintaro he had always been an

34

undistinguished son and a mediocre brother. For the children, he had never been a respected uncle nor a friend.

The relationship between his wife and the children was even more vague. With the sensitivity of the young, they felt she was not quite one of them. Haruko once heard grandmother Miwa say to Tetsu, 'Tetsu san, wear your kimono a little longer. The mistress of the Miwa branch family has to look graceful.'

Haruko noticed that Tetsu wore her kimono as Shige and Kiyo did, showing her ankles, while Miwa obahsama and Ayako wore theirs long so that the hem almost touched the floor. Only the white toes of their *tabi* were seen peeping in and out as they walked.

Interpreting Haruko's silence as expectancy of what was coming, Tei-ichi pressed on.

'As you know very well, Rinji ojisan and Tetsu obasan do not have children, and they want someone to succeed them. Miwa ojisama thought that you would be a very good person to become their child and carry on their name.'

Haruko was bewildered and stared at Tei-ichi. She did not understand.

In spite of himself, Tei-ichi felt uneasy as his granddaughter gazed at him.

Haruko did not look as though she was going to be tall and slender like Ayako. She would be more like Kei, dainty and lively, but she had inherited her mother's eyes. They were large and liquid, and the fold of her eyelid was not common among the people around them.

He looked away. He felt that he was unable to explain to a ten-year-old why it was advantageous for the family to inherit Rinji's property. It was too pragmatic for the innocent.

'It will be to Shuichi's advantage in the future,' he said, and felt the remark struck a chord.

Haruko did not understand why becoming Rinji's child would help Shuichi, but the children were not in the habit of asking questions of grown-ups.

'Of course, your Rinji ojisan's house is not far away, and you don't have to stay there all the time. Even your surname is not going to change. It is just that when you grow up, you will succeed him.'

'Do I have to call them otohsan and okahsan?' Haruko asked anxiously.

'No, you don't have to, if you don't want to.'

She had not grasped the full implications and Tei-ichi's tone was reassuring. She could do nothing but trust her grandfather.

'For Shu-chan's sake, I will do it.'

'Thank you,' Tei-ichi said solemnly.

As Haruko came out of her grandfather's study, she saw Ayako sitting on the verandah. The sun was shining on her thick coiled hair, making it look deep purple. She was bending over a cloth spread on her lap and peeling a persimmon. More fruit lay in a shallow bamboo basket placed near her. Sachiko and Shuichi were sitting on either side of her. Sachiko moved closer to her mother and made a place for Haruko on the same *zabuton*.

Ayako had a kitchen knife in her right hand and skilfully turned round and round a persimmon held in her left hand. An orange ribbon grew longer and longer and hung from her hand. When the fruit was peeled, she cut it into four pieces, put them on a plate and stuck a toothpick into each one.

As she handed the plate around, a waft of clean gourd water scent that Kei made for the family as a lotion passed over the children.

Ayako picked up the last piece left on the plate and ate it herself.

'Very sweet,' she said smiling at the children. She picked up the peel from her lap and put it in the basket. Then she bent down again to peel another fruit.

'M-m-m,' Shuichi uttered. Ayako put down the persimmon she was holding and held out her palm to let Shuichi spit out a stone. She wiped her hand with the cloth and picked up the fruit again.

Haruko suddenly thought that it was unfair that she was to be taken away from her family while the other children could live peacefully in such a loving atmosphere. Why did she alone have to go to her uncle's house when she hardly knew him?

'I have to go and live with Rinji ojisan,' she said, and unexpectedly tears started to roll down her cheeks. They were warm and salty. Ayako looked up.

Sachiko said, 'Why?' and started to cry herself. 'Oh, no, I don't want you to go away,' she wailed.

'I don't want you to go away, either,' Shuichi cried, too.

Ayako put down the knife and said, 'Look, you don't have to go, if you don't want to. Don't cry,' and put her arms around the three children, holding them tight. 'There is nothing sad about it. It is to keep our family together. There is nothing to worry about at all. God will be with us always.'

Desperation surged through Haruko. She felt the helplessness of her mother without realising it. Still in his mother's arms, Shuichi stroked Haruko's hand. She smiled at him. She had to go to Rinji ojisan's house. She would go because that would help Shuichi.

In Rinji's house, there were no thick pillars blackened by time and polished by generations of hands like the Miwas' main house or the Shirais'. Each room was elaborately decorated but small.

'Come this way,' Rinji said, and took Haruko to a tiny room built into the garden. 'Use this as your own. See, you have your own room. Pleased?' and he left her.

She sat on the tatami floor. Takeko would not be able to stay here, she thought, as she imagined how dark and quiet it would be at night. She untied the *furoshiki* she had brought with her and, since there was no desk, spread her school books in front of her. Crouching, she opened them.

As it was getting dark and cold, Tetsu came.

'We will eat now,' she said, and led the way to the kitchen. A simple meal of rice, miso soup and cooked beans was ready for two. A bowl of pickles was in the centre of the table. Tetsu ate without speaking. She picked up a piece of pickle with her chopsticks and noisily crunched it. Kei and Ayako would certainly frown. It was good manners to take a piece from the bowl into your own plate and eat it. When Tetsu finished eating, she poured tea into her rice bowl. At the Shirais', tea was served in a tea cup.

'I will show you how to wash up,' Tetsu said. Haruko had never done any washing up and she noticed that Rinji and Tetsu did not have maids. Getting water from the well was not easy, but she felt grown up. When the washing up was done, Tetsu followed Haruko to her room and showed her where the futons were kept. Obviously Haruko was not going to be given a lamp and there was nothing to do but to go to bed.

She wondered how Sachiko was. Neither of them had ever slept alone. Sachiko had a habit of wetting her bed, and she often crawled into Haruko's bed early in the morning. When Ayako was away and the wind woke them up, all three children slept huddled under one cover. What would Sachiko do? When Shuichi woke up in the middle of the night with nightmares, would Kei be able to hear him scream and sob?

The sliding door was opened and a man's voice said, 'You have to get up.' Haruko jumped out of bed. At the Shirais', Kiyo softly called them from outside before she came into the room. Each child had a shallow box into which Ayako or Kei would put the clothes they needed for the day. Haruko found that she had gone to bed without changing. She had to go to school in a wrinkled kimono. It was grey and cold. She shivered.

'From today, you are a child of this family,' Rinji said. 'You have to learn lots of things. To get up early is the first important thing. One shouldn't be idle. Now, the first duty of the day is to clean the verandah.'

'Children have to be disciplined,' he had told Tetsu. 'The worst thing that can happen to a child is to be spoilt.' He was determined to educate Haruko to be an obedient and hard-working woman capable of managing a house.

Tetsu came out with a bucket of water and a floor cloth and left them in front of Haruko without speaking.

'I will show you how to clean the floor,' Rinji said. In front of the astonished Haruko, he knelt down on the floor with his knees apart and his heels together. Supporting himself on his spread-out left hand, he moved the cloth with his right hand from left to right and then, having turned the cloth upside down, wiped the boards this time right to left. He continued this way gradually going backwards. His bottom swayed rhythmically with the motion and Haruko thought it was most undignified. It was comical, too. It was something that she certainly had to tell Sachiko. Ayako would smile and Kei would laugh, Haruko was sure.

In what period of his life had Rinji taken up cleaning the floor, Haruko wondered. She had never seen a man doing housework. At the Shirais' even Matabei, who did almost everything else, was not expected to clean inside the house.

She received the cloth from Rinji and tried to wash and wring it as he did. The water was icy, and she thought of Tetsu's large hands. When the cloth was soaked with water, it was too voluminous for the child's hands to wring it. It was heavy and dripping.

'Watch it!' Rinji shouted. 'Water will mark the floor. Wring it tight. Tighter. Tighter. I will teach you how to sweep the rooms after breakfast.'

Haruko was alarmed. 'I must go to school,' she said. Already it was getting late.

'You don't have to go to school today,' Rinji told her. 'We have more important things for a girl to do.'

Haruko had to dust the sliding screens. She had to polish shelves and sweep the tatami floor. All morning, the house was quiet except for the noise Haruko was making.

Rinji had very few visitors. At the Shirais', there were always lots of people coming and going. First of all there were patients. Then there were relatives. Merchants called. The most popular merchant among the children was a man from the cake shop in town who came a couple of times a week. He brought a shallow box slung round his neck. The box was neatly sectioned and in each little square, there was a sample of an exquisite cake. They were mostly rice or bean-based and not only tasty but had lovely colours and shapes. Their names were artistic, too, 'Spring Rain', 'Shower of Petals', 'Autumn Mist', 'Chrysanthemum in the Evening Sun', 'Dawn', and many more. The samples of cake changed according to the season. The cake man would be given a cup of tea while Kei was deciding what to order. The children often sat around hoping that their grandmother's choice would fall on their favourites.

The tofu man called every day as Tei-ichi had a piece for dinner with ginger and spring onions. Kei made a special citron and soya sauce for that dish. The man carried a pole across his shoulders with a tub hung from either end. He had a little brass trumpet that he would let the children blow if Tei-ichi was not looking. In summer, a goldfish man would call and, from her brocade purse, Ayako would give the children money.

Once a year in the autumn, a man came from Kyoto with a large bundle on his back. Even if it was a chilly day, he wiped his bald head with a folded handkerchief when he put down his load in the living room.

'Are you all well? Dannasama and young dannasama as well?' he would inquire politely. He brought silk. It was not the sort of material which Kei bought for daily kimonos; the silk was for special occasions such as New Year's Day when they had to dress up. The kimono dealer held the end of rolled material and, with a flip of his arm, spread lengths of cloth one after another across the tatami floor. Kei and Ayako would be deep in consultation, discussing and examining each piece.

'I thought this would particularly suit young Miwa okusama,' the man would say to Ayako. To Kei, he said, 'Since you have given me such long patronage, I will make it as cheap as possible. If you just stand, please, allow me.' He draped a long and narrow cloth over Kei's shoulder.

'What do you think, young Miwa okusama?'

Then they began to discuss the linings to go with the kimono material.

Kei and Ayako usually bought several pieces of material for the whole family, and, finally, presents for the servants were put aside as well.

Only the tofu man came to Rinji's house.

On the fourth day after Haruko arrived at Rinji's, Matabei came early in the morning bringing some fish and vegetables as presents.

That evening, Haruko was washing rice by the well at the back of the house. She heard a whisper, 'Haruko nesan.' At first she thought it was her imagination. She was thinking of Sachiko and home. It was icy cold. She felt miserable and homesick.

'Haruko nesan.' It was Sachiko calling her from behind the hedge.

'Quick!' Sachiko said. 'I came to get you. Let's go home!'

Involuntarily, Haruko looked around. 'I'll get my school things.' She tiptoed into her room and got all her books and pencils. She left her clothes.

Matabei had heard from the tofu man of Haruko's plight and, having been there himself, told Kei and Ayako.

'Poor Haruko ojosama! Please being her home. She is too young and the dansama of the branch family does not know how to treat children. After all, he has no experience with them.'

Kei and Ayako were already concerned as Sachiko had been telling them of Haruko's absence from school.

While the grown-ups were discussing how to deal with the situation, Sachiko heard them and decided to rescue her sister.

The two girls hurried out of the gate. Once outside, they ran. Evening stars were beginning to appear in the pale blue sky. After a while they were out of breath and stopped. Their cheeks were red but their hands were cold.

'Haruko nesan,' Sachiko said. Haruko took Sachiko's hand and they walked home.

That night, Matabei carried a lantern and hurried back along the same path. He had two letters from Tei-ichi to deliver, one, a letter of explanation to Shobei, and the other, a letter of apology to Rinji.

6

Haruko's Uncles

The drama was soon forgotten in the excitement of the approaching New Year's celebration and Haruko's uncle Yasuharu's home-coming for a holiday from Tokyo.

Tei-ichi was just as pleased as the others to see his son but, to maintain his dignity, he made himself look specially glum on the day of Yasuharu's arrival. Even so, he could not keep himself away from the rest of the household.

'Kei.' He came out from the consulting room. 'Yasu might like a hot bath after a long journey.'

'Yes,' Kei replied. 'Mata san has it ready.'

'Hum! One does not want to make a fuss, but I thought it was essential.'

After ten minutes, he came out again.

'Kei, what are we having tonight? He is coming home just for a holiday. You don't have to make anything special. Get the front path swept, will you? One's front garden always has to be clean whether Yasu comes home or not.'

In the afternoon, Matabei brought round a cart. The children crowded around it and walked to the station with him. When Yasuharu appeared at the ticket barrier with a porter behind him, the children shrieked, 'Yasu ojisama!' The station master came out from his office to greet him. Passengers who got down from the same train bowed and wished him a good holiday before they parted.

A rickshaw was ready for Yasuharu. Shuichi sat on the cart with the luggage and the rest of the children sometimes ran in front, sometimes dragged behind, chatting and laughing.

The front gate of the Shirais' was wide open. Yasuharu was to enter the house from the formal open porch and not through the back entrance. The eldest son was the next important person to Tei-ichi in the family and Kei made sure that all the formalities were observed. The members of the household gathered at the front porch to welcome him home. Tei-ichi stayed in his study.

When Yasuharu went in to greet his father, Tei-ichi said, 'Oh, is it you?' and, as though he had just remembered that his son was coming home, turned round from his open book. 'How are you? You look well.'

'Thank you, otohsan. I am very well. I am glad you are keeping well, too.'

After formal exchanges, Tei-ichi released Yasuharu saying, 'You must be tired after your long journey. I understand there is a bath ready for you. Relax and let's hear your news later.'

Yasuharu always brought back lots of presents. For his nieces, there were little silk pouches. Takeko was given a pair of red patent leather *zori*, a pair of sandals.

'Let's see.' Kei and Ayako admired them. 'As may be expected, anything you buy in Tokyo is very well made.' Both women turned the *zori* and examined them.

'Isn't it a lovely colour, okahsan,' Ayako said to Kei, and eventually to Takeko, 'Put them away carefully. You can wear them on New Year's Day when we go and see Miwa oji-isama and obahsama,' and the sandals were given back to Takeko.

They admired Shuichi's kaleidoscope, an English dictionary for Hideto, ribbons and hair ornaments and pencil cases, water pistols and toy boats. 'How nice!' the women exclaimed. He would bring appropriate presents for Kei and Ayako and the servants.

When everybody was happy, Yasuharu said, 'Haruko, I hear you had quite an adventure. This is specially for a brave girl,' and he gave her a book. It was thin but about twenty centimetres wide and three times as long. On a glossy green cover, three bears in European clothes were dancing together. The title was written across the cover but Haruko could not read it.

Inside there were more beautiful illustrations of three bears and a girl. She had blue eyes, and golden hair like the Russian soldier whom Haruko had seen on the beach.

The next day, another family member arrived. Tei-ichi's younger brother, Haruko's great-uncle, had gone to a Buddhist temple as a novice when he was a little boy. It was the traditional way for a boy of intelligence to be educated. He had become a priest of high position. With a shaven head and wearing a simple black robe, the venerable man would visit his old home to pray for the ancestral spirits. He was always accompanied by a young novice who looked after him.

Villagers came to pay their respects to him one after another, then they went round to the back of the house and asked for his bath water. No one knew how it had started but the belief was that if one drank this noble priest's bath water, it would purify the mind and keep the body healthy.

Tei-ichi told them off whenever he found out.

'Holy Man? Don't be ridiculous. I have told you before. What a disgusting idea. Matabei, empty the bath tub immediately. Drinking bath water, indeed. You will all die of cholera one day.'

'They still come for your uncle's bath water,' Kei said to Yasuharu. 'Country folk are so superstitious.'

Yasuharu laughed indulgently. He knew that his mother was also full of odd ideas.

'Do you remember the Takanos of Miura village?' The talk of superstition gave Kei the chance she had been waiting for. 'Their son Fusataro san was at school with you.'

'Ah, Fusatan.' Yasuharu involuntarily resorted to the childhood nickname. 'A very nice guy. He went to Waseda University. I met him in Tokyo by chance some time ago, and we had a meal together.'

'He is the representative of his village now and comes often to see otohsan. Both of them are very keen on the problem of diet and sanitation.'

'Oh, that's good. I want to go and see him one day.'

As the conversation was going in the direction that she wanted, Kei was encouraged.

'You know Fusataro san has a younger sister.'

Yasuharu said he did not remember, and now realised what was coming.

'Okahsan,' he said, 'I am not against marriage. On the contrary, I know it is important for me to marry.'

He then told Kei that his world was no longer confined to Kitani village or to the prefecture. For that matter, his horizon was beyond Japan.

'The Ministry of Education has set up a scholarship for medical researchers to go to Germany and study. I haven't talked to otohsan, yet, but I am thinking of applying for it in a few years' time. I will get his consent when I know better what I am doing. You see, okahsan, there are things that I want to achieve before I am saddled with responsibilities.'

The news that Yasuharu planned to go abroad did not shock Kei unduly because, in her mind, the distance between Kitani village and Germany was not much further than that between Kitani village and Tokyo. She accepted his view on marriage calmly, and embraced his ambition. Yasuharu told her that he wanted to specialise in ophthalmology and the study of trachoma.

'Oh, Yasuharu san.' She was pleased. 'How marvellous! Go to Germany or anywhere and study as much and as long as you need. When you come home, you can cure Yone san, Katsu's okahsan, Ken san of the Matsudos and . . . oh, they will be so relieved.'

'Okahsan, it will be a long time before anyone can cure Yone san and everybody else,' Yasuharu told her in haste. He was horrified to imagine that when he came home next time, there would be a queue of villagers and their friends and relatives waiting for him to cure their trachoma.

'It does not matter. I will be a good mother for the doctor of trachoma and wait until the time comes.'

'Can I be a doctor, too?' Haruko suddenly said from the corner of the room. As she had been quietly looking at her new book, both Kei and Yasuharu had forgotten that she was there. Some of her schoolfriends had eyes caked with mucus. Although she did not know what they were suffering from, the Miwa children were warned by Kei not to hold these friends' hands.

'I want to be a doctor and cure people,' she said. Her grandfather wore a white apron to see his patients, but her uncle wore a smart white coat when he helped grandfather. She had thought that she would become a teacher, but being a doctor seemed more interesting and exciting.

Kei looked at Haruko affectionately and smiled. 'Oh, what an idea! Girls cannot be doctors. It's a man's job. But you will be a lovely bride one day like your okahsan, won't you?'

It seemed the new year opened a new page for the Shirai family. On the seventh of January, it was the custom to have rice gruel with seven kinds of herbs for breakfast. In the mountain areas, people often had to look for tiny shoots under the snow. On the fifteenth, to mark the end of the New Year's celebration, they had rice gruel with red beans. The battledore and shuttlecock that girls played, and the kites that boys flew, were all put away.

As if he had been waiting for the holiday season to end, Tei-ichi announced, 'Kei, I will stand as candidate to be a member of the Prefectural Assembly.'

Kei received the news calmly. For men, the world was changing and progressing, but her role remained the same. She accepted and gave support as always.

She had heard Tei-ichi say many times that hygiene was more important than medicine – 'The way they live, it is a miracle they don't get ill' – and he had been excited about a plan for a health-care centre.

She had never thought she would be a politician's wife, but she would do her best. Kei suspected that there was another reason for Tei-ichi's decision to direct his efforts in a different direction. Whenever Yasuharu came home, there were villagers who came in with sheepish grins and asked, 'Eh, I wonder if the young Dr Yasuharu is at home?' Tei-ichi would say with a wry smile, 'Cunning rascals. Drinking bath water and wanting a new doctor.' Although Kei's interpretation was simpler, Tei-ichi felt that the time had come for a new generation of doctors with knowledge and technology. Experience alone was no longer enough to gain people's confidence. He had suspected this for a long time, perhaps since Shintaro came home from university.

Kei calculated that with his reputation and the respect he had among people, he would succeed in being elected. As though she had planned it all along, she said, 'It is very good timing.'

Their second son had been adopted by a landowner's family in a nearby village. Their third son, Masakazu, Kei said, would not need any more education.

'Why?' Tei-ichi wondered why she was telling him about their sons and also why there would be no more expense for Masakazu's education. Their third son had always been a worry for Tei-ichi. Shobei had said that the Shirai boys were all bright but he had overlooked Masakazu. He was a kind, cheerful boy but would not be able to go to university without great expense for special tutoring, and even that might not achieve the aim.

Kei argued, 'Any more education for him would be a waste of money.'

Tei-ichi had always thought of Masakazu as a failure. Many times he had sat with the boy till late at night trying to teach him things he could not grasp. The more annoyed and angry Tei-ichi became, the more confused the boy became until he could not answer questions that even Haruko was able to get right. But Tei-ichi was nevertheless determined to go on trying harder to make him like his other sons.

'He is not good at school, but that does not mean he is not worthy,' Kei was saying. 'He is kind and honest. The post master in town promised to employ him if you agree. He can work from this spring when he finishes school. He will be able to have a contented and respectable life.'

Although Kei did not name him, Rinji was in her mind.

As for Hideto, Kei said, he was a bright boy. If it was difficult to send him to university, he could go to military college or naval college. They were free.

'It does not matter if we have to sell our land now,' she went on. 'Kitani village is too small for our children. They should go out, and get their places in the wider world. Your ancestors would be proud of you if you spend what they passed on to you for the sake of the people around here.'

'Oho!' Tei-ichi stared at his wife. If Haruko had been present, she would have understood that Yasuharu's ambition had inspired Kei. 'You have grown to be a great woman.' Tei-ichi disguised his surprise by teasing.

'Oh, no,' Kei replied modestly. 'I am just repeating something Yasuharu san told me the other day.'

Tei-ichi Shirai's campaign had hardly any opposition, particularly after Shobei offered his wholehearted support. Shobei's trust in the Shirais as a mainstay for his family, expressed before his son's marriage, had been fulfilled.

Tei-ichi was busier and within a few years had risen to the position of Chairman of the Assembly.

In the spring, Masakazu started to work at the post office. Kei bought him the first bicycle in the village. On the morning of his first day, she lit new candles in the recess where the ancestral name tablets were placed. She made Masakazu sit by her and both of them prayed.

'I thanked our ancestors that you have grown up to be a fine man,' she said. 'I am sure they are very proud of you.' She handed him his lunch box. She stood at the gate and watched him ride away until he waved at her and turned a corner.

The villagers were getting used to hearing the bell of the bicycle through the early morning mist, and a cheerful 'Good morning.' 'Kuma san, if you want to write to your son again, I'll do it for you. Come to the post office.' 'Thank you very much, Masakazu dansama. I'll come to see you tomorrow, if it's all right with you.' Watching his disappearing back, they would say, 'The young dansama of the Shirais are all hard-working and well educated.' Kei's plan was successful.

'It is better to be a chicken's head than an ox's tail.' Kei was breezy when talking to Ayako about her younger brother. 'He is respected now and appreciated. He would have been miserable among scholars.'

'What does that mean, obahsama?' Haruko asked, laughing. 'Why is he a chicken's head?'

Kei was serious. 'It means, it is much better to know one's place than to hang at the bottom of more able people and be undistinguished. Remember it. It is an important lesson in life.'

As for Hideto, Kei was confident and hardly worried about her youngest son. He was now a boarder at a school in town. Although he was mischievous, he was popular among his friends. Kei secretly believed that he had the potential to become a great man. He would be a hero among heroes, she thought. The school tolerated most of his adventures and he was given only minor punishments.

It was mere boyish misbehaviour. On winter evenings, when the boys were hungry, the vendors came around calling, 'Baked sweet potatoes! Baked sweet potatoes!', or, 'Buckwheat noodles. Hot noodles!', over the school walls. The vendors had earthen barrels with burning charcoal on a cart, and the sweet potatoes were hooked and baked inside. It was always Hideto who had to go and buy them for everyone, as he was the best able to climb up on the high wall of the boarding house.

One night, as Hideto carried a hot newspaper bag and jumped down into the school premises, a teacher was waiting for him. He was also involved in many fights, mostly defending weak boys from bullies. All the incidents were duly reported to his parents and they both ignored them.

'He has already been punished at school,' Tei-ichi would say. 'Leave him. If he is still like that when he is eighteen, then, I will disown him.' Kei secretly loved these stories which she thought gallant and fun. But when he participated in a strike against the school authorities, the matter could not be left unattended. It was an incident concerning a young history teacher. He was enthusiastic about democracy and freedom and excited the boys with an idealism bordering on anti-imperialism and anti-militarism.

This was at a time when twelve people had been sentenced to death just for being accused of planning the assassination of the Emperor. Socialism was a dangerous word. The Military Police were increasing their influence. Although Hideto was not a senior pupil or the main agitator, taking part in the strike was judged to be a grave offence. Tei-ichi was not only Chairman of the Assembly but also by then the head of the parents' association of the school. The school hesitated to publicise his son's misconduct. If it was known that Hideto was treated generously because he was Dr Shirai's son, Tei-ichi's name would be tarnished. On the other hand, if Hideto was either suspended or expelled from school, it would affect his future.

Kei visited the headmaster, the deputy headmaster, the class teacher, and all the other teachers, even the kendo instructor, and apologised to each one. She was the wife of the Chairman of the Prefectural Assembly and a doctor who was widely known and respected. Her family was also closely connected with the Miwas, but she humbly and politely asked everybody to forgive him as in future he would be strictly supervised. All the teachers sympathised with Kei. She was admired as 'a very accomplished lady'.

'What has he done?' Haruko asked Kei.

'Boys get passionate about new ideas. That is the way they learn. Only those who are stupid never get into trouble when they are young, but only stupid ones go on being trouble after they grow up,' Kei said.

'What trouble, obahsama?'

'Oh, politics. Something that we women do not have to understand.'

And it was not long before Hideto proved himself worthy of his mother's efforts.

The summer holiday came and Yasuharu returned home. He brought with him a friend who was a paediatrician. The children were told to

49

call him Dr Komoto but, in spite of the formal address, he was soon joining in with wrestling, games and other lively activities. Haruko's English alphabet progressed from 'apple' to 'pen' with Dr Komoto's help.

The days passed, happy and uneventful, until the day that Yasuharu, Dr Komoto, Hideto and Shuichi decided to go sea fishing. Early in the morning, they left, both Yasuharu and Dr Komoto in *yukata*, cotton kimono, and Hideto and Shuichi in cotton shorts, all wearing straw hats. The day promised to be fine. They carried rice balls that Shige had made. The rice balls had cooked seaweed inside instead of the usual pickled plums. Pickled plums prevented the rice from going sour but, if taken fishing, Shige insisted, there would not be any catch.

'Oh? That won't do, Shige san. Thank you,' Dr Komoto said politely. Yasuharu just opened his mouth and laughed noiselessly.

At the shore, a fisherman was waiting for them with a small boat. He said, 'It is windy further offshore. Come home early before the weather changes.' But the sky was deep blue and the temperature was rising. The sun was already strong. They got into the boat and the fisherman pushed it out into the water.

'Shu-chan, you must get as tanned and strong as Hideto,' Yasuharu said. Yasuharu, Dr Komoto and Hideto rowed the boat in turn until they were a long way from the shore. They were all happily fishing when Dr Komoto said, 'Oh?' and looked up at the sky.

The wind was getting cool and he thought he felt a raindrop on his face. But he did not pay further attention as Yasuharu and Hideto did not seem to be worried. They were brought up in the area, he thought, they should know. But although they had grown up near the sea, neither Yasuharu nor Hideto had much knowledge or experience of boats. Yasuharu looked up at the sky as large drops of rain started to come down on them.

'It will pass,' he said, and asked Shuichi if he was cold. Shuichi was catching the rain water running down his cheeks by sticking out a lower lip. He shook his head. The boat began to sway and he was a little afraid but he trusted his uncles and was quietly holding on to the side of the boat.

As the wind rose, wave after wave crashed into the small boat.

'Hideto, scoop up the water in the boat with your hat,' Yasuharu said and Dr Komoto and Hideto started to bail out water.

'Shu-chan, you help us, too,' Hideto said and Shuichi joined them. The boat was lifted up by a big wave and crashed down and reeled round. Despite all their efforts, they were soon ankle-deep in water.

'Shu-chan, come here,' Yasuharu said, and pulled him to his side.

'Which way is the wind coming from?' Dr Komoto said. In the middle of the storm, Hideto thought the question was silly and inconsequential, but then it occurred to him that Dr Komoto might be trying to compose himself.

'It seems to be blowing us along the shore,' he answered.

At home, the three girls were sitting around Kei sewing dolls' clothes. Ayako was not at home, having gone to a relative's wedding party. The pieces of cloth the girls were given were mostly dark-coloured cotton with stripes. Silk remnants were kept to make cushions for guests or sleeveless tops, but Kei gave them each a small piece of brightly coloured, patterned silk. The material was carefully smoothed with a flat-iron. Kei had taken it out from a chest of drawers with large iron handles.

As they all bent down around Kei's sewing box, Tei-ichi said from the verandah, 'Has Yasu not come home yet?'

'No, he has not come home,' Kei said.

Tei-ichi's voice was heard calling Matabei. The girls had not noticed but the raindrops were causing ripples on the surface of the pond. Plantain leaves swayed and rustled. Kei said, 'You stay here,' to the girls and hurried to join Tei-ichi.

Matabei ran out barefoot into the rain towards the sea wearing a waterproof cape.

'Yasuharu is with them. They will be all right,' Tei-ichi said, and went back to his study. The rain was getting harder.

The girls felt restless and put away their sewing. Shige came into the kitchen and started to make a fire in the range. The dark and damp kitchen became steamy and hot. Shige said, 'Don't worry. Mata will soon bring them back.'

While it was getting dark inside the house, it was not yet dark on the sea, but the rain was coming down harder and the bottom of the boat was full of water. The straw hats were no longer useful. Many times the boat nearly capsized and Yasuharu realised that it would soon start to sink.

'Hideto,' Yasuharu called. 'You are the best swimmer in the prefecture, aren't you?'

Hideto said, 'Yes,' but the sea around them was so different from the sea on the day of the swimming competition.

'Hideto,' Yasuharu called again, keeping his balance. 'Carry Shuichi on your back and swim back to the shore.'

Hideto could not believe what he was hearing. It was true he was the best swimmer in the prefecture. For two years he had come first at the all prefecture swimming competitions for the adults. He had never felt tired, even after swimming a long-distance race. He remembered the sight of many heads behind him all in a line as though they were strung together by a long string, and the roll of drums from boats with flags bobbing up and down. The sky was blue and there were spectacular summer clouds. There was also sweet crystallised sugar thrust from the boats in a long-handled spoon.

Hideto was about to say, 'I cannot do it. It is not possible,' when his brother ordered him with all the authority of an eldest brother. 'Don't think. Just do it. We have to save Shu-chan . . . Look there!' Yasuharu had seen the faint glimmer of lights.

Yasuharu untied his sash and passed it across the little boy's goose-pimpled back, under his arms and around Hideto's chest. He crossed it in front, wound it back and tied it securely.

'Go!' Hideto jumped into the water. Even though he was the best swimmer in the prefecture, for the sixteen-year-old, an eight-year-old boy was heavy. Tossed about by the waves Hideto swam. Shuichi was holding on to him tightly.

At the shore, a big fire had been built. Women and children were out, and as the children ran near the fire, mothers and grandmothers scolded them. Men were calling, 'Shuichi dansama, Yasuharu dansama, Hideto dansama, Doctor Komoto,' in turn.

Somebody shouted, 'Oh, there's Hide dansama and Shu dansama!' Hideto appeared, staggering in the light of the torches, supported by a group of men who had formed a search party down the coast. One of them carried Shuichi.

Yasuharu and Dr Komoto arrived a few minutes later. They had abandoned the sinking boat shortly after Hideto.

Hideto was sitting in front of the fire, hugging his knees. Kei stroked his back. It was the first time Haruko had seen her grandmother cry.

She was saying, 'Oh, well done. You are brave. Well done,' with a tear-stained face.

They could not find Tei-ichi. Only Matabei knew where he was. He was standing alone on a cliff overlooking the sea, but Matabei did not tell anyone.

The next day, Tei-ichi called Hideto. He said, 'I will give this to you,' and gave him an antique sword forged by a famous swordsmith. It was the most precious treasure belonging to the family.

7

The Flood

Autumn came earlier than usual that year. Haruko was now fourteen years old. The rain which started in September continued without stopping into the middle of October. At first the Kitaka river had roared and foamed, swollen by the heavy rains. The volume of water increased until, for the past few days, the river was lapping at the top of the dyke. The water looked ominously quiet. It was dark and flowing swiftly.

The dyke had contained the river for as long as the villagers could remember. People stood by the water and shook their heads. That day, the river was higher than ever before. It was already overflowing here and there in thin streams, and crabs were crawling around.

The wind got up in the afternoon. People finished work early and secured their shutters and doors. When Masakazu arrived home and put away his bicycle in the old stable, he saw his father washing his feet by the well.

'Oh, Masa, you crossed the river all right?' his father asked.

'I came home over the New Bridge, otohsan. Good job it was finished,' Masakazu replied. The concrete bridge connecting Kitani village to the town had been finished earlier in the year. Shobei had donated generously to its completion.

'Ah, the New Bridge will be all right, but it may be only a matter of hours until the dyke bursts. If that happens, several houses in the village will go under water.' Then Tei-ichi said, 'Masa, when you go in, ask someone to bring a towel out for me.'

Almost at the same time, Kei appeared with a towel and a pair of dry *geta*. 'I am sorry. I didn't realise you were home.'

'Have you seen the river?' Kei asked both of them, as she squatted and dried Tei-ichi's feet.

'I was telling Masa that houses of the Miwa tenant farmers might be flooded.'

'Use this.' Kei stood up and handed the towel to Masakazu. She asked both of them, 'Shall I send Mata san to get the women and children from those houses?'

'That might be an idea. Masa, you go and alert the youth club members. 'We'll send Yohei and Mata to the three houses nearest the river.'

'Yes, otohsan.' Masakazu went back to the stable and brought out the bicycle he had just put away.

'Yohei.' Tei-ichi called Shige's husband. 'Go to Kawabata and bring people from those three houses nearest the river. Take Mata with you.'

'O'Shige san,' Kei was heard calling. 'Cook plenty of rice and make rice balls for the people who are coming. We need lots of hot water as well.'

'Can we help make rice balls?' The girls came to the kitchen.

'Yes, yes, we need all the help we can get. Ask your okahsan to find you aprons.'

'Oji-isama, can I go with Mata san to the river to help people?' Shuichi asked.

'Oh, yes, you can go, but stay with Mata and do not go near the river, do you understand?'

Watching the boy running after Matabei, Kei remarked, 'He is getting clever. He knows I wouldn't say "yes".'

'He is ten. You shouldn't pamper him.'

Kei was quiet but she still shuddered when she remembered how close he had come to drowning.

As the darkness fell, the rain beat down harder. Masakazu came home and was going out again.

Tei-ichi called him back. 'How is it? Do the upstream villages seem to be holding all right?'

'So far we have not seen any sign of disaster, otohsan, but I don't think some of the bridges are strong enough. I just came back to leave my bicycle. The wind is so strong that it's difficult to ride.' He called out. 'Okahsan, I am going with the others to help the villagers upstream. Don't worry about me, if I am late,' but his voice was almost drowned in the torrents of rain.

'I hope Shu-chan is all right,' Kei said to Ayako, peering outside.

'He is not stupid, okahsan, and Mata san will not let him out of sight,' Ayako replied. 'Besides, although he wouldn't go up, the top of the dyke is quite wide. People can't fall into the river easily. You know very well no one ever has.'

'No, but he must be soaking wet. You get his dry clothes ready and let him have a hot bath when he comes home.'

Kei peered outside once more before she went back to the kitchen.

The wind became stronger towards midnight and brought more rain. About fifteen people including children were evacuated from their homes and came to the Shirais'. Kei did not hesitate to open up the rooms reserved for guests and special occasions and the whole household tried to settle down for an uneasy night. Outside the wind was howling.

It was about four o'clock when the rain began to subside. Once the storm had passed, the dawn brought a beautiful day such as people had not seen for a month. Shafts of golden light shone through clouds. The white feathers of pigeons on the still-wet roof were pink in the sunlight. Sparrows chattered. The hills in the distance were the colours of autumn and the leaves left on the trees were washed clean and shining. Masakazu arrived home caked with mud and without shoes. He had a bath and breakfast, and left for work. At every house, people were hanging their clothes out to dry.

A large area of the rice paddies was flooded and the water stretched far, reflecting the white clouds in the serene sky. Big trees had been washed downriver and lay sideways here and there gathering debris. Upstream the damage was considerable but in Kitani village, two houses had gone and there were no human casualties.

In the afternoon, a servant arrived from the Miwas, and Kei and Ayako realised that they had not sent a message of inquiry to Shobei and his wife. The Miwas' house was on high ground and there was no cause for worry, but it would have been a matter of courtesy to have contacted them.

'Oh, Zen san,' Ayako said. 'How are otohsama and okahsama? We are sorry we haven't been in touch with you yet. We had so many people last night, and we are still in a muddle.'

'They are all right, young okusama, although dansama seems to have caught a chill. He says he will come to see you tomorrow. He wanted to know if you need a hand.'

Ayako remembered that whenever there was anything unusual,

however insignificant, Shobei would call on the Shirais himself.

'Is otosahma all right?'

'He says you should not worry.'

The day before, when the wind had been getting stronger, Rinji had called in to see if his parents needed any help. Seeing that everything had been in order, he had had a cup of tea and left soon afterwards. Shobei had stayed home and, after supper, had gone out without anyone noticing. Later when his wife had realised that he was not in his study, she had not been too concerned. He had a group of friends with whom he played the game of Go and she had thought he might have gone out to meet them, although it had not seemed like a good night to go visiting.

'Actually, dansama walked upstream to see how his land and farmers were. I don't think he realised how quickly the dyke would burst there. He was trapped in the flood till the youth club members rescued him early in the morning.'

Ayako frowned. She excused herself and quickly changed her kimono. To Kei she said, 'I know he would come himself unless he felt really ill. I will just go and see how he is.'

'Take your overnight things with you and stay there tonight. I don't want you to come back in the dark.'

After Ayako left, Kei spent the afternoon alone worrying. She had never known Shobei to be ill. He was vigorous and had not shown much sign of ageing, but she realised that he was in his late seventies. Time had passed quickly.

Kei remembered a saying, 'An old man should not have a cold shower'. It was a warning to old men against rash behaviour. There was a particular reason that the news of his illness disturbed her. She went into the *butsuma* where the ancestors' name tablets were kept and prayed.

As she sat in supplication, she could hear in her mind Shuichi's shrill voice calling, 'Oji-isama! Oji-isama!' It had been in the spring. Tei-ichi told the boy off for running around like a puppy. He said, 'A man should never hurry, Shuichi.' The boy said, 'Yes, oji-isama,' but could not hide his agitation.

'Now, what is it?' Tei-ichi asked.

'There is a gigantic white snake in the *butsuma*, oji-isama. You should come and see. It's hanging between the lintels like a bridge. Something bad is going to happen.'

'In spring all snakes come out of hibernation. It is not at all unusual to see one in the house. A lot of them live among the stones of the wall.'

'But o'Shige san said that this one is the old spirit of the house. He comes out only when a bad thing is going to happen. Last time it appeared, otohsan died.'

'Tell Shige we have only one old spirit in this house and that is me, oji-isama.' Shuichi looked at his grandfather and saw that his eyes were dancing with fun. 'It is not just in spring that I am around. I am always here to guard the house. Nothing bad will happen in our family.'

Shuichi laughed and seemed to have dismissed the white snake from his mind, but Kei had not forgotten. She and Shige shared the same beliefs. Since then, she had felt uneasy whenever something happened to a member of her household. If Ayako had a cold, she had been more worried than before. Every time Shuichi set off on an adventure, she had prayed for his safety. In Shobei's case, it was unfortunate that Rinji had not offered to undertake the inspection himself or at least accompanied his father. One thought followed after another and Kei sat in the room for a long time. Eventually she got up and told herself that, after all, Shobei would get better. He might have stayed home realising himself that he ought to be more careful.

Ayako's stay at the Miwas' was extended from a week to two and then three. Instead of their mother coming home, the children were called to the Miwas'. When Haruko arrived with the other children, she saw by the entrance a broad-brimmed oilskin hat and a coat that had once belonged to Shintaro. Shobei had come home wearing them and soon afterwards had taken to his bed. No one had thought of putting them away.

When Haruko had seen him on her way home from school a few days before the flood, Shobei had been wearing the oilskins.

'Oji-isama,' she had called, as he had not noticed her and passed by.

'Oh, Haruko.' He had looked surprised, then he smiled. 'Is everything all right?'

'Yes, oji-isama.' She had nodded.

'Good. Good.' He had looked as though he had wanted to tell her something but large drops of rain had started to hit them.

'Hurry home. You'll get wet. I'll see you soon.'

He had stood and watched her go. He had looked as robust as ever.

While her sisters shied away from their paternal grandfather, Haruko respected him and at the same time felt close to him. Her father had trusted her and she felt the same sympathy from his father as well.

Haruko was surprised to see how Shobei had changed within a few weeks. His face was ashen and gaunt.

'I am scared,' Takeko whispered when they came out of the room. Shobei's wife, Ayako, and a nurse took turns to sit by him.

Tei-ichi had just gone and Rinji arrived.

'How is he?' he asked, moving his lips without making a sound.

'Just the same, but he had a small amount of rice gruel,' his mother replied in a low voice. 'Come and have supper with us.'

Shobei lay in his study and away from the main house, but everybody tiptoed and tried not to make a sound. During the meal, however, there was some conversation and an exchange of outside news.

'I will go and sit by oji-isama,' Haruko offered, 'so that the nurse can come and eat. I am not hungry. I will eat later.'

'Thank you, Haruko san.'

She went into the room quietly. Her grandfather looked asleep but when the nurse closed the sliding screen, he gestured to her by a slight movement of his hand to come near him. He spoke to her in a hoarse faltering whisper.

'Your speech . . . was well-written.' He stopped and Haruko waited. 'General Akashi . . . was very . . . impressed, so was I . . . and the headmaster.'

There was a smile on his face.

Shobei was referring to a general who had been invited by Haruko's school to give a talk to the pupils and, as was often the case with a distinguished visitor to the area, Shobei had invited him after the talk to his house for dinner.

General Akashi was an unusual hero of the Russo-Japanese war, Haruko was told. His achievements were reputed to have made a significant contribution to Japan's victory, but he had never met the enemy in the battlefield. As a colonel, he had spent the entire war in the capitals of Europe, meeting the leaders of anti-Tsarist underground groups, helping them with funds which had been entrusted to him by the Japanese government.

When it became known that the school was going to invite General Akashi and had selected Shuichi to make a speech of thanks, Shobei called Haruko to give her some advice. Everybody, including the teachers, counted on Haruko to write Shuichi's speech.

At the school, General Akashi's talk had been about the courage of other people who were passionate about saving the Russian people from destitution, and the surrounding countries from Russian tyranny.

Shobei impressed on his fourteen-year-old granddaughter that courage was needed to pursue a career with little public recognition.

'You . . . should have been a . . . boy,' Haruko's grandfather repeated from his bed in a voice which was barely audible. Haruko nearly replied, 'So that I could be a spy, oji-isama?', but she noticed that his breathing had become more laboured. His windpipe began to make a whistling noise.

'Are you all right? I will call someone.' As she was going to stand up, his eyes gleamed for a second. He was clearly impatient and agitated. He seemed to try to draw Haruko's attention to the shelf above his head on which she could see a wooden box.

'The box, oji-isama?'

He looked satisfied and relieved. He breathed, 'Your Shi' . . . oji-isama . . . okahsan.' His eyes were closed. His head rolled a little sideways.

'Someone, come quick.' Haruko ran out of the room, shouting. The first person who came running out was her uncle Rinji. He collided with Haruko and nearly knocked her off her feet. As she reached the main house, she looked back and saw her uncle coming out of the room. He was carrying the wooden box under one arm. As he ran, he looked like a picture of a devil with wide open eyes and flowing hair. His free arm was moving from front to back as though he was swimming in the air, staggering with the size and the weight of the box.

On a clear autumn day, a long cortege went through the village. Shuichi was again the chief mourner and walked behind the coffin, but this time he was no longer an infant, and was wearing a black kimono and hakama. Haruko in a white kimono walked behind with Ayako and her sisters.

From Shobei's village and also from the surrounding villages, a lot of people came to see the last of their landowner.

They whispered and shed tears as Shuichi walked by. 'Poor child! He was born into such an excellent family, but he has had to attend two funerals and he is only ten years old.'

After the funeral, the Miwas' big house was in turmoil with a crowd of relatives and friends milling about losing each other and finding unexpected acquaintances. Everybody had thought that Shobei would live for a long time.

Tei-ichi followed the priest to the entrance and thanked him. As he was walking back to the living room, he saw Haruko waiting for him in a corridor.

Oji-isama,' she said. 'Have you found out what happened to the box Rinji ojisan took with him?'

'What box?' Tei-ichi had totally forgotten about it, although Haruko had told him everything that had happened.

'Oji-isama, I have told you already. The wooden box that Miwa oji-isama always kept in his study. He had it by his bed after he had been taken ill. He has told me many times that it has important documents.'

'Why, isn't it in his study?' The question was just a reflex. He did not mean it. He knew very well that the box was not in the study. He reflected on his carelessness and as the implications dawned on him, he was belatedly alarmed. He had not fully realised the importance of the contents of the box. He saw impatience and concern in his granddaughter's face, even a little reproach.

'Oh, I know. I am sorry. I have been so busy. I'll talk to Rinji ojisan. He must be keeping it in a safe place. Don't worry. Leave it to me.'

Having told Haruko to leave the matter with him, he wondered what he could do. Shuichi was Shobei's heir and no one could dispute his legal position, but his material inheritance was a different matter. Tei-ichi needed documentation to act on his grandson's legal status. He would approach Rinji but if Rinji's intention was to seize the family fortune by force, recovering it in any civilised way did not seem possible.

Soon after the funeral, Rinji moved back into the main house. Rumour had it that he began vigorously collecting repayment of the loans that Shobei had made.

'There is no one more dangerous than a fool,' Tei-ichi muttered. He was worried.

Shobei's brother intervened and suggested that they should take the financial situation and the issue of the missing will to court. Tei-ichi opposed this strongly on the grounds that a family dispute right after Shobei's funeral would disgrace the honourable man and his family.

'If the worst comes, I am able to look after my daughter and her children,' he insisted in front of the relatives.

Eventually Rinji agreed that some property and the rent from it should be given over to Shuichi for his education on condition that Rinji would manage the money till Shuichi was twenty-five. That was all that Shuichi was to receive out of everything that Shobei, one of the largest landowners and the richest man in the area, had carefully guarded to pass on to his grandson and his future descendants. As for Ayako and the three granddaughters, there was a piece of land already notified under their names with Tei-ichi as their guardian.

8

Takeko is Seventeen

A year after Shobei's death, Takeko finished school, and by that time there had been a few marriage proposals for her. When a family friend came to talk about the prospect of a match for her daughter for the first time, Ayako could not help feeling a slight shock, although she had been conscious of the possibility for some time. She herself had married at an even younger age. Takeko was certainly not too young to marry.

'It is eighteen years since I married,' Ayako was thinking while she watched the visitor's mouth which moved incessantly, telling her and Kei about a family that she thought suitable for a daughter of the Miwas. Living with her own parents as though she had never left them, Ayako had pushed away the idea that one day her pleasant family life had to be broken up and that, one after another, her daughters would leave her.

In a few years, Haruko would leave home and then Sachiko, too. When Shuichi left for Tokyo to go to university, which Ayako hoped he would, then what? Yasuharu would marry. Masakazu would marry. Even Hideto would marry. Everybody was kind and considerate to her in the family, but eventually she would have to leave and live with Shuichi and his wife. Where would that be?

'I thought it would be really a very advantageous match for you,' the woman was saying. 'I'm sorry to say it, but your family is not exactly as it was a year ago, is it? They are saying a lot of things about Rinji san, and although I told them that it is all foolish nonsense, you know how they are, those village folks, if you listen to them. I told them, after all the Miwas are a distinguished family. But I must tell you that in a few years time, they will forget about Shobei san.

Rinji san seems to be wasting a lot of money on some sort of investment that the son of that stonemason is involved in. They are crooks,
those people. As I was saying, you don't have to take what they are
saying seriously. This is a great match and honestly you cannot expect
a better one . . .'

Ayako excused herself and went to the kitchen where Kiyo was
arranging a fine tea-set on the table.

'Where is o'Shige san?' Ayako asked, as it was usually Shige who
made tea for guests.

'She is out in the back somewhere. She says she doesn't like that
lady.'

'Oh.' Ayako feigned surprise and took the tea tray. As she went
back into the room, the woman turned to Ayako.

'I was just telling your okahasama. The Matsudo family are even
bigger landowners than your father-in-law used to be. But they say
they do not mind having a daughter-in-law from a poor family so
long as she is pretty and good. To tell you the truth, they don't need
any more money.'

In a flat voice, Kei cut in. 'Thank you. We know who the Matsudos
are. But we don't know anything about their son who, I assume, is
the one who might marry our Takeko. How old is he and what sort
of person is he?'

'Oh, a very nice man. Very nice, indeed. He is, I think, about
twenty-three or thereabouts. He is at home. He went to school, but
school was not interesting enough for him.' She laughed, making a
short 'ho ho ho' noise through a puckered mouth.

'I see,' Kei said. 'It was so very kind of you to think of us. As you
said yourself, more or less, a girl without a father does not exactly
have good prospects for marriage. We know our place and we would
like to find our Takeko a match which is suitable for us. Thank you
for coming.'

'Okahsan,' Ayako said, after the visitor had gone, 'is it wise to
make an enemy of her? She will spread some kind of fabricated story.'

'I will not let anyone insult us in our own house. In any case, who
wants a man who could not finish even basic schooling? You can tell
he is a good-for-nothing, lazy lad.'

The name Matsudo did not reach Tei-ichi, as mother and daughter
did not bother to repeat the conversation to him, but the following
proposal was brought to him directly. An acquaintance came to sound

out a match with a family running a large draper and haberdasher shop called Tagawa-ya. It had an extensive frontage opening on to the busiest street in a big town which was the political as well as the commercial centre of the prefecture.

Tei-ichi would have said that it was not a convincingly good match, but he found himself less particular than before.

'A merchant?' Kei raised her cleanly-arched eyebrows. Tei-ichi had felt the same mental reaction when he was told about the match.

Nearly half a century had passed since the collapse of the Tokugawa feudal regime. Tei-ichi reflected, 'What a lot of social and technical changes and progress we have experienced.' Yet, he had to admit that he was not entirely against the old rigid class system. After all, when he was born, feudal lords were still travelling up and down the main roads to and from the capital which was called Edo and not Tokyo, in palanquins surrounded by samurais each bearing two swords and wearing a topknot.

Samurais were at the top of the class system in those days. They had the right to kill anyone, anywhere. The rice-growing farming class was the next in rank. Rice was important. The economic power of each feudal domain was determined by the amount of rice it produced. The samurais' stipend was calculated in rice. Then came the artisan class. The merchant class occupied the bottom position. They were not allowed to wear silk, and their houses were inspected lest they should be too luxurious. Dealing with money was despised and the profession whose ultimate purpose was the accumulation of wealth had to be at the bottom.

When Tei-ichi was little, his father told him a story about a castle which was besieged, and how the defending samurais had to eat the mud walls to survive. Even then, those who accompanied their lord to the peace negotiations in the enemy camp did not touch the food offered to them. They were so proud, and could withstand material temptation.

If he told such stories to his sons they would listen, but Tei-ichi knew that to his sons these were only epic tales. Times had changed.

'Well, we are living in a new age,' Tei-ichi said to Kei and Ayako. 'We cannot be prejudiced against new ways of thinking in the modern world. Our feudal period ended because the samurais could not maintain themselves economically and had to rely on merchants. You see, the standard of life was going up and up, yet the amount of rice produced could not be increased beyond a certain limit. It was the economy . . .'

Tei-ichi showed his scholarship and would have gone on lecturing them with his interpretation of the arrival of the Meiji era, but the women did not seem to be impressed. They listened respectfully, but as soon as they were left alone, Ayako said, 'It's sad to think that the status of the Miwas has fallen, okahsan. In the olden times, no one considered it proper to think of such a match, however prosperous their business was.'

'Oh, it is good to have a lot of proposals. To accept or refuse is our prerogative. We would worry about our fallen status if nobody thought of match-making with us,' Kei said, trying to cheer up Ayako and herself, and added with conviction, 'It's not the Miwas' status which has sunk. It is the Tagawa-yas' status which has gone up. That is what otohsan calls the new age. In ten years' time, the likes of them will be members of the Prefectural Assembly and the National Parliament.'

In the end they decided to go ahead with the prospective match with Tagawa-ya. The draper's son was in Tokyo. After graduating from one of the universities, he was staying on to study English, they were told. He had been hoping to go to Europe to learn business, as he was convinced that soon the time would come when people would wear more European clothes than the traditional kimono. However, the situation in Europe was taking an ugly turn and war was about to break out. He would stay home and wait for an opportunity. For the same reason Yasuharu's plan of going abroad was postponed. It was 1914. Archduke Ferdinand had been assassinated and the ripples from Sarajevo were felt as far away as Kitani village.

When Tei-ichi heard of Tagawa-ya's son's ambition, his last feelings of hesitation disappeared and he positively looked forward to the successful conclusion of the negotiations.

Kei and Ayako wanted to settle Takeko's marriage within a year or two at the latest. There were two more daughters to think of and it was necessary for the eldest to marry, otherwise she would hinder the younger ones' chances. Encouraged by her family, Ayako visited the go-between friend's house.

'We are very grateful that you have taken the trouble to think of my daughter, Takeko. We think that the match with Tagawa-ya san will be very desirable and I came to ask you to proceed with the negotiations.'

The friend also expressed in formal language her pleasure at being of use and promised to do her best to arrange the match, but she was slightly confused about who Ayako was until she had time to think about it.

'Surely she could not be older than her late twenties. No, if this is Takeko san's okahsan, she has to be at least about thirty-four.' The friend was calculating in her mind and admired how young Ayako looked.

Tagawa-ya himself was a plump and happy-looking man, with humble manners. On several occasions, when Kei and Ayako had visited the draper's shop, he had been sitting among the young employees, greeting a customer, telling his assistant what to do, being consulted about what to buy. The shop was always full of customers and they could tell that the business was flourishing.

Ayako and the Shirais needed at least a year to prepare for the marriage. Once the marriage was finalised, there would be much to do. Since Takeko was marrying into a family which handled kimono materials, it might not be necessary to have a lot of kimonos made, but a chest of drawers, a dressing table, a desk, bedding, all had to be specially made. The lacquered utensils had to be ordered from Kyoto. Good lacquering would take over a year.

Since Ayako's wedding had been organised mostly by Shobei, it was Tei-ichi's first experience of handling arrangements, and when he was shown the shopping list, he said with a sigh, 'They say three daughters are the ruin of a family, and they are quite right.'

Ayako had made up her mind to spend all that Shobei had left for his granddaughters on their weddings. It was the last luxury the Miwas would be able to afford.

About a month after Ayako had asked the go-between to proceed with the marriage negotiations, she came back to Kei and Ayako to tell them that Tagawa-ya was very pleased about the prospect of having Dr Shirai's granddaughter as their son's bride. They had sent someone to Takeko's school to find out about her, and had heard that she was a very polite, gentle lady and there had never been any problems.

Tei-ichi was known among his neighbours as an honourable person, particularly since he had intervened in the family feud over the inheritance.

'They also heard about your second daughter, Haruko san,' the go-between friend said, 'and should you have already accepted another proposal for Takeko san, they would be pleased to ask for Haruko san. She seems to be a highly intelligent young lady and Tagawa-ya san thinks that she would be a very suitable wife for his son who also likes books and studying. After all, we are in a modern age. It is not shameful for a girl to like studying.'

'That is very thoughtful of Tagawa-ya san, but Haruko is still only fifteen and we hope Takeko will make a good wife for their son,' Ayako answered politely.

The Shirai side wanted to settle the negotiations and exchange the gifts of engagement as soon as possible and were disappointed when nothing happened for a few months. The next step was to set a date for the meeting of the two young people before the marriage was finalised.

'Tagawa-ya san is saying that their son is coming home from Tokyo next month, and then we will know when to get together,' was the message.

'We'd better visit Mrs Kawamatsu with some presents,' Ayako said to Kei, referring to the go-between friend. 'She has been coming and going between our houses for some time.'

'When all is formalised, we will give her proper presents. For the moment, you will go to her taking perhaps a bottle of saké and a box of cake,' Kei suggested.

Another month had passed without further news. One day, Mrs Kawamatsu finally returned but when they saw her, they knew the news was not good before anything was said.

After an exchange of seasonal greetings, the visitor said, 'I will not beat about the bush. I will be straightforward and say I come to apologise today. Tagawa-ya san is so embarrassed and angry as well.'

Tagawa-ya's son had already met someone whom he intended to marry, but knowing how his family would react, he had been waiting for a good opportunity to tell them. The young lady was the daughter of his landlady.

'After all, he is a well brought up young man and does not know what people are really like. That crafty landlady must have tricked him. The whole Tagawa family is upset. Tagawa-ya san is very angry and he is saying he will disinherit the son. Certainly Tagawa-ya san will not give him permission to marry this young lady in Tokyo. They don't know anything about her family, of course. Tokyo women are so dangerous.'

She leant forward and lowered her voice. 'Apparently women dance with men. Would you believe such disgraceful behaviour? Of course, for a young man from the countryside, there must be so much temptation.'

After the friend left with lots of apologies and stories of orgies going on in the capital, Kei and Ayako each let out a deep sigh. The rumour had already spread that Dr Shirai's granddaughter was marrying Tagawa-ya's son, and they had not bothered to deny it.

Once Tei-ichi had become enthusiastic, the whole family began to believe that it was a most desirable marriage.

'Never mind. There will be better proposals. We might be thankful in the end.' Kei tried but could not help feeling humiliated. 'It's Tagawa-ya's fault,' she said. While there was a prospect of the Tagawa family becoming her relations, she called them Tagawa san or Tagawa-ya san when referring to the shop, but now she put them down as Tagawa-ya. 'They should control their son. Yasuharu san would never be trapped by women in Tokyo. Look at Shintaro san, too.' Then she declared with dignity, 'We are glad that we do not have to marry our Takeko to such a feeble-minded merchant's family.'

In November another proposal came. It was from a rich landowner's family in Kyushu, and Tei-ichi said, 'This is a proposal from far away.'

There had been a lull since Tagawa-ya, and both Kei and Ayako were on the point of giving up the idea of getting the marriage settled within a year.

'In this day and age, when people are going abroad, Kyushu is just next door,' Kei said, and Ayako came round to agreeing, though she still regretted the abortive liaison with Tagawa-ya.

'The father of the bridegroom-to-be died several years ago, and the young man is the head of the family now,' they were told. 'That is why he has remained a bachelor until the age of thirty. He is a hard-working man and liked by everybody in the area. He is introducing improved rice varieties and organising a cooperative.'

'I think he is an ideal man.' Tei-ichi was pleased but Kei insisted that they find out more about the family.

The mutual acquaintance came back and said, 'The bridegroom's side wants everything settled as soon as possible. There could be an unexpected hindrance if the negotiations are prolonged. Why don't you say yes first and then sort things out. The bridegroom-to-be is saying that any time you are ready, he will come and meet your family. He is very enthusiastic.'

'We can't say yes without knowing whether this man has brothers and sisters, or other details about him,' Kei said, and Tei-ichi sent someone to find out about him. As it was already the beginning of December, the settlement would be in the new year, no matter how much they hurried.

'Do you think she'll marry this time?' Sachiko asked Haruko. They had not been told about the negotiations with Tagawa-ya's son but knew everything that was going on.

'Why does he want to get a wife from so far away, that's what I'd like to know,' Haruko said precociously, and added, imitating Kei's tone, 'Aren't there any women in Kyushu?'

'Oh, Haruko nesan,' Sachiko giggled. 'But it's funny that they want to hurry so much, don't you think? He has waited for so long to get married.'

Early in the new year, Tei-ichi received a letter from a friend in Kyushu, whom he had asked to find out about the family of the bridegroom-to-be.

Dear Dr Shirai,

New Year's greetings to you. May I use this opportunity to wish you and your family a very happy and prosperous year. It has been a long time since I last saw you and it has always been in my mind that I must write and thank you for all the advice and help you have given me. Thanks to you, we have been able to expand our pharmaceutical business and we are doing very well. I would like to visit you soon and tell you all about it.

As for what you asked me to find out, the family is certainly well off and respected and there is nothing negative to report about the person himself. But I regret to say that he has a sister who is confined to the house and nobody has seen her for a long time. According to the tradesmen and servants, she was born deformed and seems to have the intelligence of a three-year-old. There is another similar case in one of his aunts, I was told.

The young man himself is very popular and I do not

want to destroy his chances of happiness but on the other hand I have to inform you of the facts.

If there is anything further that you want me to do, please do not hesitate to ask me. I hope to see you soon, but meanwhile I wish your granddaughter the happiness she deserves.

'I wonder if there is something wrong with us,' Ayako asked. 'Why do all the proposals turn out to be inappropriate?'

'It is quite usual for marriages to come up against a lot of problems. Most old families have a skeleton or two in the cupboard,' Kei said. In fact, both of them were in a way relieved that Takeko did not have to live far away.

After this the marriage proposals came to a standstill and several months passed. Takeko was eighteen. Both Kei and Ayako were worried and there were new reasons for wanting to hurry Takeko's marriage.

Haruko came home one day and asked if she could take the entrance examination for the Women's Medical College in Tokyo. She had found out about fees in detail.

'Please, if I could use the money that you reserved for my marriage, I would go and live with Yasu ojisama. Then it will not cost much. I will be able to work as their maid.'

'Where did you get such an idea? Of course not! A woman doctor? It's so indecent.'

'Okahsan, it is more indecent to go and ask a man doctor to look at you.'

'Haruko san, I don't want to hear you say such a thing.'

After a few days Haruko came home from school and said that if she was not allowed to go to the Women's Medical College, she would like to go to the Women's Teaching College for Higher Education in Nara.

'Okahsan, that's free. The government pays for fees. If you let me go, I will pay you back whatever I spend when I become a teacher. I will help Shu-chan as well.'

'A working woman!' Kei and Ayako were horrified. Now more than ever Takeko's marriage had to be settled so that Haruko could be safely married off.

Tei-ichi realised how lucky he had been with Ayako's marriage, and reflected on what a fine man Shobei had been. He wondered what Shobei would have thought about his inability to find a suitable husband for his granddaughter.

'There is no one like Shintaro san, anyway,' Ayako said.

The next year Haruko would graduate from the girls' school. Then they would have two girls at home. Kei and Ayako sighed.

The summer passed uneventfully.

Ayako noticed that the air felt fresh one morning.

'The autumn is coming,' she said, making tea.

'The tea smells particularly beautiful this morning.' Kei sat and took a cup from Ayako.

Shige came in and whispered, 'That woman has come again.'

'What do you mean by "that woman", o'Shige san?' Kei frowned. Shige was obviously not in a mood to say any more and left, showing her displeasure by her rigid posture.

'I'll go and see.' Ayako got up.

There was the woman who had brought the first proposal.

After formal greetings and gossip, she came to the point.

'I said to myself, I must find a nice husband for that beautiful young lady. I have not seen her for a while but if she is like you, Ayako san, she must be beautiful. I still remember how lovely you were at your wedding.'

Then she asked if she had heard of a Count Ki-i.

'Is he the man who distinguished himself in the Meiji revolution for his service to the Emperor?'

'Indeed he is. The Count himself is dead now, but he has two sons. Well, actually one son is legitimate but the second son is a child of his mistress. This mistress's son was given some assets and established a branch family.'

Ayako was listening to the genealogy of a far-away nobleman, wondering where the story was going. Sachiko looked in from the verandah. Ayako scolded, 'This is not a child's place. Will you go and play with the others.'

'I am not a child,' Sachiko answered back.

'Sachiko san, do what you are told. So sorry, she is so undisciplined.' Ayako apologised and made a mental note that she had to talk to Sachiko. In a few years' time, she had to be presented to people as a suitable girl for someone.

'This branch family has a son and daughter,' the woman resumed. 'The daughter is already married into a well-known industrialist's family.'

The son had been to France. The woman did not know the purpose of his trip to France, but gentlemen of his position did not have to have reasons to go abroad. He had come home and was looking for a suitable bride.

'So, when I heard about him, I immediately thought of your Takeko san. Having been in foreign countries and among blue-eyed girls, he missed a nice girl from home, and he wants to marry someone who has dark hair and lovely eyes like you, ho ho ho.'

After she had gone, Ayako told Kei about the Count and his mistress and the illegitimate son and his sister, and that he wanted 'a dark-haired girl with lovely eyes like me'. They looked at each other and laughed.

'There must be a lot of "nice girls" or "girls from good families who have dark hair and eyes he likes",' Ayako said. 'Why ours?'

'That's exactly what I thought when Shobei san asked for you as his son's bride.'

'Yes, okahsan, but that's different. In Tokyo, there are so many people.'

'Not if you really want someone beautiful and good, perhaps.'

Yes, those Tokyo girls were flippant and immoral, both thought, remembering the girl who had seduced the prosperous draper's son.

9

The Maple Tree

Members of the Shirai household rarely visited the Miwas' main house now that Rinji lived there, but Haruko and Shuichi had to go and see Rinji once a month. Matabei always accompanied them. At the end of every month, on the day that the rent had been collected, Rinji would hand a part of it to Shuichi as had been arranged. Rinji would make Shuichi count the money while Haruko watched. Then Haruko would write a receipt in the name of Shuichi and both of them would bow and say, 'Thank you, Rinji ojisan.' Matabei would carry the money and the three of them would go home together.

Haruko and Shuichi also went to the main house at the end of every school term, but for these occasions they went through the garden to a small annex where Shobei's widow lived quietly. She had Shobei's Buddhist name tablets and, as when Shobei was alive, the children's school reports were placed in front of the tablets and the three of them prayed. There were always fresh flowers and offerings of fruit and cakes.

The reports were, as always, wrapped up in a silk *furoshiki* specially kept for the purpose. It was green and had a good-luck symbol of a crane painted in the middle. This was the last such visit for Haruko. She had just graduated from the girls' school at the top of the whole year.

At the end of every school term, ever since Shuichi had started school, Haruko had accompanied him to the Miwas' to show Shobei his school report. In those days, Shuichi would place his small hands, which had been scrubbed by Ayako and Kiyo, on the tatami floor. He bowed. He recited in a piping voice everything he had been instructed to say.

'Oji-isama, thanks to you and the ancestors, I have finished this term without mishap. I have done my best and here is my report.' Shobei would listen straight-backed with his hands on his lap and his eyes half closed.

'I am very glad. Thank you for coming. Let's show the report to your otohsan first,' Shobei would reply gravely. After they prayed together, Shobei would look at the report. Shuichi did well at school. Shobei would invite all the schoolteachers for dinner at the end of every term to thank them.

Haruko was proud of her own report, too. It always said 'outstand-ing', and the character 'excellent' filled all the columns. Kei and Ayako were obviously pleased but would just say, 'Oh, well done.' Haruko wondered sometimes whether they would say the same thing if she received something other than 'excellent'. Tei-ichi showed more enthusiasm, but Miwa oji-isama was the best. After he examined Shuichi's report, he looked carefully at Haruko's, and said, 'You are an exceptionally clever girl. You should have been a boy.' She thought, 'Perhaps girls are chickens. I am after all the head of the chicken', or, 'What did Kei obahsama say? "A maple tree can never be an oak." Girls are maple trees and inferior from birth. We have to accept it.'

Then they were given tea and cake. Miwa obahsama joined them and Shobei would tell her how well they had done. Shobei would be relaxed and smiling, and tell them how pleased he was with the way they were growing up.

It was on these occasions that he would say to Haruko, pointing at the wooden box kept on the shelf by his desk, 'Haruko, this box has all the things you need when I am gone. When that happens, you must remind your Shirai oji-isama and okahsan about it. Don't forget. It is very important.'

He once showed her the papers kept inside. There was a large envelope which, he said, had all the documents about his loans. 'With-out these, nobody knows where to collect the money that I have lent out. Then these are about our land and rented houses. These papers are called bonds. They are the same as a lot of money. These docu-ments explain what I am leaving to your okahsan and also to each one of you for your marriage. Here is a list of antiques that are worth a lot of money. Most of them are family heirlooms and will go to Shuichi but some will be yours when you grow up . . .'

*   *   *

Shuichi and Haruko sat with Shobei's wife in the room which used to be his study and in which he had died. The same ornaments were displayed on the elaborate shelves but no box. Haruko had kept Rinji's behaviour on the day of her grandfather's death to herself. She had not described what had happened in detail, even to Tei-ichi. She wondered if her Miwa grandmother had guessed.

Her Miwa grandmother congratulated Haruko graciously. 'Oji-isama would have been so pleased.' She was always softly spoken. 'Now, what are you going to do with yourself?'

The question was unexpected. Everyone assumed that Haruko would stay home and learn a few things like sewing, flower-arrangement and the tea ceremony while waiting for her grandparents and mother to find a suitable husband. Haruko felt warm towards her grandmother.

'I don't know, obahsama,' she said. 'I wanted to go to college but I am not allowed.'

'I am very sorry that you are a girl. Oji-isama said so, too, many times. Do you remember? I wish I could help you. Women should not remain ignorant, be dead and buried before the age of twenty. We women are not supposed to have independence in this world and who knows about the next one. They say a woman does not have a home in three worlds: she lives in her father's house as a child, her husband's house when married and her son's house in her old age.'

Nobody spoke. She sighed and added, 'I wish your father was alive instead of me.'

Haruko and Shuichi walked home side by side. Skylarks trilled, and cherry blossom covered the mountainsides in a pink haze. Shuichi no longer held her hand. She wondered when he had stopped. Now Shuichi was a little taller than Haruko.

'Are you getting married soon?' He broke the silence.

'I hope not. Takeko nesan has to go first.'

'Haruko nesan, why don't you run away? Run away and go to college?'

'I would if I could.'

'Why can't you?'

'There is nowhere I could go, Shu-chan. I have no money to live on if I left home.'

'Haruko nesan, don't get married. Wait till I grow up. I will make lots of money and send you to college.'

She walked behind him so that he would not see her tears. Even if she managed to go to Tokyo, she could only go to Yasuharu's lodgings and he was helping Hideto. She wished Hideto were older. When he came home for New Year, he told them about Dr Komoto's mother who was looking after the three of them.

'She believes in beans. Every evening she goes out to buy beans boiled down in soya sauce and we eat it with rice for supper and she puts the rest in our lunch box with rice. I'm waiting to see if I become addicted or I hate beans so much that whenever I see any I'll come out in spots.' They all laughed.

'You need more nutrition than beans.' Kei was concerned.

'Oh, beans are good for you, okahsan. We as a nation eat nothing but miso, soya sauce, cooked beans, tofu, they are all beans, and look at us. We have one of the finest navies in the world. We beat the Russians although we didn't get much for the effort.'

It was Hideto who told Haruko about the Women's Medical College.

'You will have no problem getting in there.'

'How can I afford to go, Hideto sama?'

'Haru-chan, I wish I could help you. I would if I could. All I can say now is to come to Tokyo and join in our bean feast.' Then he added seriously, 'Poor girl! Life is not fair for you, is it?'

All the people who would help her were helpless.

Haruko thought she would go to Tokyo anyway. She would ask if she could go just for a few months to learn, she would say, koto music or flower-arrangement, or anything, and then once she was there she might be able to find her way.

She had been tossing and turning at night. Some nights she decided to find some way of earning a living. Tokyo seemed big enough. She could sew. She had once seen someone painting designs on plates and cups. Perhaps this could be a way of making money. Some nights she despaired. When she was wandering the streets of Tokyo in a tattered kimono and hungry, would she be able to keep up her ambition? How would she pay for college?

Neither Kei nor Ayako was averse to the idea of her going to Tokyo when Haruko put it to them.

'She might settle down after a trip away from home,' Kei said.

'Haruko nesan, are you really going?' Sachiko was nearly in tears. 'I wish I could come with you.'

'I may be back very soon. I will write to you, I promise, and you can come to see me soon, too.' But Haruko thought: I might disappear into the big city. I will let Sachiko san know where I am. She can keep a secret.

Haruko packed only a few things.

The evening before Haruko was to go to Tokyo, Sachiko complained of a pain in her toe. She had trodden on a thorn which had sunk in deep and Haruko had taken her to a nearby doctor. He had used a scalpel and made a small incision to get it out.

'You look hot.' Haruko looked at her sister.

Ayako felt Sachiko's forehead and said, 'You have a temperature. You must have caught a cold. Go to bed. I'll ask oji-isama for medicine.'

Soon Sachiko's temperature soared. Tei-ichi untied the bandage on her toe and looked.

'Mata,' he called, 'go to town and bring the doctor.' He named another doctor he knew better.

'I'll go,' Masakazu said. 'I'll be quicker with my bicycle.'

'Toxaemia?' Tei-ichi asked the doctor who examined her.

'I am afraid I agree with your diagnosis,' the doctor nodded gravely. 'When was her toe looked at?'

'Okahsan, Haruko nesan,' Sachiko cried. 'Help me! It's so painful. Are you going to Tokyo?' She was delirious. 'Okahsan, I can wear this. She said I could borrow her kimono while she is in Tokyo.'

The doctor from town was saying in a low voice in the next room, 'We'll see, but if there's no improvement, we might have to amputate her leg. It's a matter of hours before we have to decide.'

'No!' Haruko went into the room. For a moment she forgot the social niceties that her grandparents and Ayako had strenuously impressed on her. From a standing position, one did not address older and respectable people who were sitting on a tatami floor. The two men turned and gaped at her. She sat down.

'Please, oji-isama. You cannot amputate Sachiko san's leg. What kind of life can she have? No one will marry her. No, you have to do everything, anything, but that, oji-isama.'

'Haruko, we are discussing other options and help from other doctors.'

Sachiko was breathing hard but was sleeping. The towel placed on her head became warm immediately and Ayako and Haruko had to change it frequently and constantly to fetch cold water from the well.

Sachiko's leg was swollen and purple. 'I wish I were a doctor,' Haruko kept on thinking, 'then I would know what to do.' It was hard to sit and do nothing while every second, she thought, the poison was advancing that much further into Sachiko's body.

'Okahsan, do you remember a doctor called Sakamoto sensei who came down once when otohsan was alive?' Haruko asked suddenly.

'Oh, yes, they were students together, weren't they?'

'Okahsan, send a telegram and ask him to come.'

'What?'

'Okahsan, get him.'

'Haruko san, he is such a famous doctor. He must be very busy. We cannot send a telegram and tell him to come.'

'It's a matter of life or death. Ask oji-isama to tell Dr Sakamoto what he has to bring with him. He is Shu-chan's guardian. Oji-isama has his address. Ask Masa ojisan to send a telegram. You can apologise and do anything you have to later.'

Ayako stared at Haruko.

'Okahsan, her leg might have to be amputated. She will never be able to marry. Shu-chan will have a crippled sister to look after. Nobody will marry Shu-chan.'

Tei-ichi was heard saying, 'Shuichi, you go to bed. You have school tomorrow. You are not going to worry so much that you can't sleep, are you? There was a general called Napoleon. He could win one battle after another because he could always sleep, anywhere.'

'That's not true,' Shuichi protested. 'He could do with very little sleep.'

Haruko wondered fleetingly where Tei-ichi had learnt about Napoleon. All his books seemed to be written in classical Chinese.

'All right. No doubt you are right about Napoleon, but a man should stay in control in any situation.'

Masakazu came in a few minutes later and whispered to the two women who were sitting by Sachiko, 'I have the telegram which otohsan has written. I'll wait for his answer, then order a rickshaw to pick up Dr Sakamoto from the first train in the morning. Is there anything else I should be doing in town?'

Ayako and Haruko shook their heads.

'I won't be long.' He stood up. In the next room, they heard him say as he was going out. 'Shu-chan, go to bed and leave the field to the soldiers as oji-isama said.'

'What happened at Waterloo?' Shuichi's voice piped up.

'There were too many mosquitoes buzzing around in the marsh and for once he could not sleep.'

'Okahsan, I can look after her. You should go to bed. When Dr Sakamoto arrives, you take over.'

Although Ayako always looked healthy and youthful, she did not have much stamina, and if she had a sleepless night, or there was a change in the weather, she easily caught a cold. It was probably because she had been brought up without facing any real crisis on her own, Haruko thought. To have lost her husband was a devastating event but even then she had been well protected.

Haruko knew, though, that the next morning, she would be perfectly prepared to meet Dr Sakamoto. She would be beautiful and know exactly what to say and how to treat him.

'Okahsan, we will take turns. I will sit here till morning. You can come and take over. If there is any change, I will wake you up. But she will be all right. If you can't sleep, just lie down.'

Having persuaded her mother to go, Haruko sat by Sachiko and watched the sleeping red face.

Kei came in quietly. 'Haruko, it was too bad, wasn't it? But you can go to Tokyo as soon as Sachiko is better.'

Haruko had completely forgotten about going to Tokyo.

'Obahsama,' she said, 'if Sachiko san has to have her leg amputated, please let me stay home and not be married. I will look after Sachiko san.'

Kei nodded. Her lips quivered. Eventually she said, 'I'll get tea for you. Do you want anything to eat?' Haruko shook her head. Kei left the room.

Haruko went out to the well now and again to get cold water. The sky was full of stars. Tei-ichi came in and looked at Sachiko. 'It was a good idea to call Dr Sakamoto,' he muttered and after a while went out. Shige came in with tea. Kei sat with Haruko again for a while. Everybody looked as though they were holding their breath and waiting for the arrival of Dr Sakamoto.

Haruko felt that she had never spent time in such an incoherent and vague way. She thought of the river where she and Sachiko had swum together, flowers they had picked together, but towards the early morning, she was not sure if she was dreaming. Occasionally she prayed that Sachiko would be safe. Sachiko slept on, thanks to Tei-ichi's painkillers.

Haruko went to wash. There was some light in the eastern sky. Soon cocks would start crowing. Ayako came in freshly dressed and looking in control and almost at the same time there was a commotion at the front of the house. Dr Sakamoto was ushered in.

That evening, Sachiko was visibly better but she would be left with a lot of scars on her leg and her small toe had almost gone, which she had not yet been told.

'Haruko nesan, haven't you gone to Tokyo?' was the first thing Sachiko said.

'No, Sachiko san. I think you wanted me to stay so much that you stepped on a thorn deliberately.'

They both laughed and felt happy.

Sachiko took a month to recover and return to school.

'Haruko nesan, I'll bring back the work I missed. Help me, won't you?' Sachiko said in the morning. Under a white bandage, the toe had healed but she did not want her friends to see the little stump.

'I told you I would. Go on. You will be late.' Haruko urged her as though she was impatient but she was pleased to be asked. Helping Sachiko and Shuichi with their homework was the most interesting part of her day. Either nobody remembered, or they did not bring up her plan to go to Tokyo. Anyway, summer was coming soon and then Yasuharu and Hideto would both come home. Tokyo would be empty, she thought.

'Where are you going?' Haruko asked Takeko. One of the big guest rooms was full of lively-coloured kimonos spread out and Takeko was standing in the middle to be dressed by Ayako.

'We have to get Takeko san's photograph taken,' Ayako explained, standing behind Takeko and tightening a heavy, wide sash.

Sitting on the tatami, Kei was saying, 'I think a lighter-coloured kimono would have a better effect.'

Ayako stopped what she was doing and came to look up at Takeko from the front, kneeling by Kei.

'Yes, I think so.' Kei nodded to confirm her thoughts, her eyes still on Takeko. 'The dark colour would make the photograph gloomy.

And I think patterns with straight lines would not suit her. They would make her look hard. How about that chrysanthemum kimono we had made for the New Year?'

'Oh, yes.' Ayako looked around and dragged another kimono out of its paper wrapping. With a movement of her arms, she spread it out. Ayako had worn a kimono with a chrysanthemum pattern years ago when the family had the honour of entertaining a member of the imperial family, but while Ayako's had small flowers here and there, Takeko's was a colourful design of large flowers with some petals embroidered in gold and silver on a white background.

'That is better.' Kei was satisfied.

'I'm tired of standing,' Takeko complained, and neither Kei nor Ayako paid any attention.

'Which sash shall we have?' The two older women started to open some more wrappings.

'Why do you have to have a photograph taken?' Haruko asked, having watched them for a while.

'A count in Tokyo whom Takeko might marry wants her photograph.'

'Okahsan, it's not the Count,' Ayako corrected Kei. 'It's his grandson.'

But Kei's attention was on Takeko. 'Ah, that's better. Look, her face looks much brighter. Put on that obi with the oblong pattern.'

The three black-and-white photographs, one from the front, one from the back and one from the side, were given to the woman who was acting as a go-between. They were duly sent to her cousin in Tokyo who was teaching flower-arrangement at the Ki-i household, and after a while, in return, she sent back a photograph of a young man.

'He is like a stage actor,' was Tei-ichi's remark, and everybody knew that it was not meant to be a compliment. He did not approve of a man who looked 'like a woman', which summed up a slender and fair man with delicately handsome features.

Kei was quiet in front of him but said later, 'You can't tell a man from one photograph,' which implied that she did not want to dismiss him entirely. Ayako thought he looked acceptable. Takeko looked at it and coloured a little. She held it a little longer than one might have done under the circumstances, but did not make any comment.

When Haruko said, 'Let's see,' Takeko held it against her breast.

'Oh, come on, Takeko nesan.'

Takeko did not hand the picture to Haruko but held it in front of both of them.

'Oh!' Haruko did not know what to think. The man looked straight into her eyes and she felt embarrassed. She burst out laughing.

'What is so funny?' Takeko asked.

'Strange child.' Ayako turned to Haruko but unexpectedly Tei-ichi started to laugh and everybody's attention was directed at him. Haruko explained to herself that there was something odd in the behaviour of a man who had travelled as far as France, yet tamely submitted his photograph to a family flower-arrangement teacher in order for her to find him a wife. But, of course, Haruko thought again, he might not know that in a village far from Tokyo, a family was looking at his photograph and making various comments and laughing at it. He might be horrified if he knew.

'Takeko nesan likes that man in the photograph,' Sachiko whispered in Haruko's ear, and giggled.

'He has exactly the sort of looks that she likes.' Haruko was a little cross. She had recently realised, as Ayako had some time ago, that marriage would break up the family. If all went well, Takeko would go and live in Tokyo, and they would not be able to see her often. Haruko had never had much in common with her older sister, but Takeko had a place in their family life and would leave a gap behind her.

Although they took the trouble to send the photographs of Takeko, Tei-ichi and Kei lost enthusiasm for going on with the marriage, as Yasuharu was sceptical about the young man's character.

'To me, he seems a typical playboy,' he had written, and his letter was soon followed by a newspaper cutting.

It had recently rained a great deal, causing landslides in Hakone, a popular mountain resort near Tokyo, and a famous hotel was nearly destroyed. There were a number of casualties. Among the guests were a Mr Ki-i and his companion, a certain lady, who narrowly escaped. The article claimed that she was Mr Ki-i's common-law wife and a former geisha.

10

The Medicine Store

The blue sky promised a warm day but the air was fresh in the early morning. Most of the back yard of the Shirais' house was still in shade.

For the past few days the women of the Shirai household, all three generations, had been busy unpicking winter kimonos and the covers of the bedding. Everything had been washed. Now Ayako and her two daughters spread the cotton cloth out on long boards and brushed over them with starch. Kei was handling silk using tenterhooks.

'I heard a cuckoo this morning,' Kei said, while her hands were swiftly moving from one side to the other, hooking both sides of a narrow strip of material using *shinshi*, bamboo shafts with pins attached to both ends, to prevent it curling up. The cloth was stretched between a wooden fence and a hook driven into the wall of a shack. The *shinshi*s were arched neatly one after another at short regular intervals. 'Perhaps today or tomorrow our fishmonger will bring this year's first *katsuo* fish.'

Fresh green leaves, cuckoos and *katsuo* fish traditionally symbolised the coming of summer.

'*Katsuo* is good, of course, but I am looking forward to having *chinu*. Miwa otohsama often caught it in summer, didn't he?' Ayako, who was squatting in front of a tub, stopped wringing cloth, looking up at Kei and narrowed her eyes in the sunshine.

'Oh, yes. Yesterday, our fish man already had *kisu* with him. I wonder what he will bring today.'

'Okahsan, fish in Tokyo is awful. The flesh is soft and crumbles in your mouth before you bite it. If you want to enjoy eating fish, it has to be fish from the Seto Inland Sea,' Ayako said. She had been to Tokyo a couple of times to help her brothers settle down.

'Mmm. Of course. There are a lot of places in the sea where the flow of water is rapid. They say that's why fish from the Seto Inland Sea is firm. Men are the same. Hardships will make a real man. Oh, by the way, remind me to ask Yohei san to get ginger from the storage room.' The deft movements of Kei's hands finished one strip and she returned a few tenterhooks left in her hand to a box.

Haruko thought that her grandmother must have been thinking of her youngest son, Hideto, when she talked of hardships. His allowance was small. He wore *geta*, wooden clogs, as he could not afford shoes and socks. Last time he was home, he laughed.

'Okahsan, don't worry. The more you wear socks, the thinner and holier they get, but the more you walk barefoot, the stronger your feet get. My soles are thicker than the soles of shoes. Rain or snow, they won't break.'

Kei continued silently working on another piece of cloth for a while but, noticing Haruko and Takeko watching her, chuckled.

'There was no time for your okahsan to practise all these skills before she married. She can't do it very well even now.' She examined the needle of a tenterhook she was about to use and put it aside. 'Women are more and more educated these days and know less and less about house-keeping. It's important to keep one's house well. Home is the basis for all happiness.'

She finished the strip and glanced at her work ready to be starched. She turned and checked what the others were doing. 'I used to do all the work for the whole family on my own, sometimes carrying Hideto san on my back. He was such a naughty boy and could not be left alone for a minute.' Her face was soft. 'I never had time to worry about educating myself. I lived only thinking otohsan should be happy and able to work and hoping the children would grow up safe and well.'

It was a statement of satisfaction. Haruko wondered if the remark was aimed at her recent restlessness.

'O'Shige san, why are you looking so excited?' Ayako asked Shige as she appeared from the house, panting and red in the face.

'Jinsuke of the medicine shop eloped with the daughter of the noodle shop man last night, and the whole town is gossiping about them.'

'Jinsuke?' Kei and Ayako turned to Shige together. 'So what happened to the medicine shop?'

'That's why I came back quickly. It's been shut since this morning.'

The Shirais owned the only medicine shop in town. It was one of the few properties belonging to them. Rather than rent it out, they ran it themselves. It was quite successful and was bringing in a moderate income.

'The daughter of the noodle shop?' Takeko joined in. 'I went to school with her. The fair girl with a round face.'

Why did they have to elope? Haruko wondered. Aloud, she asked, 'The noodle shop man will not object to his daughter marrying Jinsuke, will he? What is wrong with him?'

Shige licked her lips. She swallowed. Then she breathed out brusquely, 'He made her pregnant.'

'Oh.' Haruko coloured a little, although she tried to receive the news nonchalantly.

'Silly man! What's the good of running away?' Kei spoke. 'Why did he not come to me? I would have talked to the noodle shop man,' but there was a more urgent problem for her to sort out. Haruko understood.

'I'll go.'

'Go where?' Ayako looked at Haruko.

'I'll go to the shop and see what has to be done.'

With the women of her family, Haruko had learned that it was more effective to state what one was going to do rather than plead with them. 'Please obahsama,' would make Kei defensive.

Kei nevertheless considered for a minute.

'Well, yes, then. Just go and see what has to be done. Take Mata san with you. Somebody has to go and sort the shop out, anyway. Come home and tell me what is happening.'

Kei handed Haruko a large wrought-iron key and, with Matabei, Haruko hurried to town. It was an adventure. She congratulated herself on how well she had handled the situation.

The front of the shop was closed up with wooden shutters, as Jinsuke had left the night before, and several people were standing in front of it gossiping. One of them was pushing himself against a crack in a shutter trying to peep inside.

Haruko and Matabei walked along a narrow gap between the shop and a neighbour's house to the back. They had to pass by a hole made for night soil. The stone lid was covered with green lichen and there was a bad smell.

'Step carefully.' Matabei watched as Haruko gingerly followed him over the slimy soil. At the back there was a communal well and a woman was doing her washing with a child tied on her back.

'We didn't notice anything till this morning,' she ventured without being asked. 'He seemed such a hard-working and honest man. It was a real surprise. We didn't even know that he was so intimate with the noodle shop man's daughter.'

He must have been an honest but timid man, Haruko thought, and wondered where they were and what they were doing. It was good of him not to have rejected her as a lot of men would. It might be quite exciting for the girl to go away and live her own life with the man she loved. Haruko shrugged her shoulders.

'Those people from other villages can't be trusted,' the neighbour muttered, standing up ready to wring her washing. Water ran down the cloth and splashed on her bare feet and ankles.

Matabei pushed the door open and, as they went in, there was enough light coming through chinks in the shutters for them to see. It looked orderly.

'The first thing is to open the shutters,' Haruko said, but Matabei shook his head.

'Haruko ojosama, I think we'd better check what is missing before we open the shop. Nobody will come for a while because everybody knows that Jinsuke has gone.'

'Is there an inventory book?' Haruko asked, and surprised herself when these words came out so naturally.

Matabei went up a narrow steep stair. When he came down, he looked around the small downstairs back room and muttered, 'I think he has taken all the cash and perhaps some of the goods as well. The book has gone. He might have destroyed it. Now we don't know what he has taken.'

'You would expect that, wouldn't you?' Haruko replied. She thought it was a grown up and smart thing to say.

'We trusted him completely. We'd better inform the police.' Matabei was looking in the drawers.

'What do we do now? Shall we open the shop anyway? If I write down what we sell today, Mata san, we can check later on what Jinsuke has taken.'

All day Haruko was kept busy. Curiosity brought a lot of people and a group of children stood in front of the shop and stared. Matabei shooed them away several times.

'Mata san, I don't know the prices of some of the things.'

'Lots of money is going to be lost now that we don't know who was given credit, either, Haruko ojosama. What a mess.'

That evening Kei said, 'Kenji will work for us at the medicine shop from tomorrow but Mata san says someone has to sort out the books.'

'I'll do it,' Haruko said quietly, so that nobody noticed how delighted and excited she was at the prospect of getting out of the house and doing something.

Kenji was the son of a tenant farmer and had been in Takeko's year at primary school. Kei asked him to help with the shop because he had done well at school. He had been at home helping his father in his rice paddies. When Haruko arrived at the shop the next day, he was already there sweeping the shop front and sprinkling water.

'Good morning,' he bowed. Although he tried to avoid talking to Haruko, they had to consult with each other many times during the course of the day as neither knew where things were or how much they should charge for certain medicines.

'Oh, it was cheaper when Jin san was in charge,' a customer said and Kenji would come to Haruko.

'Haruko ojosama, did you hear her? Shall I let her have it for what she says until we find out exactly how much it used to be?'

'Yes, of course.'

'Haruko ojosama, if you stay here tomorrow morning, I will go to the wholesalers and find out what has been bought and how much certain things are.'

'Yes, that's a good idea, but what about the medicines which dealers bring here themselves? We can't get in touch with them, can we? They come from far away.'

'No, but no good worrying about them. They will not come back during the summer months and by then we will know more about our stock.'

'Oh, goodness, perhaps we have to pay those wholesalers.'

'Haruko ojosama, you must not tell anyone that we have lost the inventory. I will deal with them when necessary. Don't worry. Leave it to me.'

Haruko looked at the peasant boy. She looked at him for the first time. He was tall and broad-shouldered. His hair was slightly wavy, which was unusual and charming. He had beautiful white teeth and his eyes were bright, unlike those of most other village boys. In spite of his strong features, he had long eyelashes.

'Yes,' she consented meekly.

When the shop was not busy, he climbed up a ladder and counted everything kept on the high shelves, cleaning at the same time.

The shop had high glass cupboards on both sides and a low glass case in the middle.

A man came in. Haruko recognised him as one of the Miwa tenant farmers.

'My daughter . . .' he mumbled. 'Dr Shirai some time ago gave her medicine for her coughs. Can we have the same medicine?'

Haruko looked in a drawer and found a prescription in Tei-ichi's writing.

'Eh, Dr Shirai said I could get the medicine on credit. I will pay in the autumn.'

'All right.' Haruko found the medicine and wrapped it up.

'Haruko ojosama.' Kenji came down from the ladder when the farmer had gone. 'Some peasants are very poor, that is true, and we all know how much Dr Shirai has done for them. I am one of the people who was saved by him. But most peasants have learned to be very cunning. It is not because they were born sly, but it has been necessary for them to get the best out of any situation. One has to be kind and sympathetic, and as one of them, I appreciate that, but don't let them think of you as a soft touch . . .'

He was suddenly embarrassed by his speech and quickly went back up the ladder.

That night Haruko said to Kei that it would take quite a while to reorganise the shop.

'We'll get someone from town.'

'No, obahsama. Now that I have done a little, I'll carry on.'

'How is Kenji doing?'

'Oh, fine, I think.'

It was socially unacceptable for a man and a woman to spend time together alone after the age of seven. Confucius had taught so, but no one in the Shirai family thought it was socially incorrect to leave Haruko and Kenji together. They belonged to different classes and it was inconceivable that they would have romantic feelings towards each other as man and woman.

Haruko did not know whether Kenji stayed at the shop or if he went home every night. She did not know whether he cooked meals in the corner where there was a kitchen stove on the earth floor, but every morning when she arrived, he had opened and swept the shop. The fire was burning and he made tea for her. Haruko sat behind the counter and listed stocks and did the accounting. Kenji did everything else. They rarely spoke to each other. He had learned which medicines were popular and which needed restocking. He went to the wholesalers. He read the instructions and explained to customers what the medicines were for and how they should be taken.

Haruko noticed that there was an old English textbook by the kitchen range.

'Are you studying English?' she asked.

'Only at night and in the morning when I am waiting for the water to boil.'

He did not elaborate and she did not ask further.

'You have worked quite hard, haven't you?' Tei-ichi said one evening about a month later. 'When Jinsuke ran away, I thought I would close the shop. But it seems everything is sorted out. Well done! Jinsuke hadn't taken much after all apart from the money, did you say?'

'No, oji-isama and, well, Kenji . . . manages the shop very well.'

While they were working, Haruko tried to avoid calling him by his name. Her family called him Kenji but she felt it would be rude to say his name without using 'san' when he was older, capable and clearly intelligent. Yet it was awkward to call him Kenji san.

'Excuse me,' she called one day. Kenji stopped cleaning a shelf and turned round. His eyebrows went up. That was his way of asking 'What is it?', a gesture which had become familiar to Haruko by then. A warm feeling rushed through her. She said, 'I was going to tell you that you've got a cobweb on your hair.' He put his hand up to brush it off. 'No, no, on the other side. Just above Kenji san's left ear.' Since then, she had addressed him as Kenji san.

Haruko's grandfather said, 'I have known that Kenji was an intelligent boy since he was very little and always wanted to give him the opportunity to study but I couldn't myself. I have managed to find him a sponsor.'

'Oh?'

'I have been talking to Lord Toda about him and he says he will have Kenji at his Tokyo mansion as a servant and send him to night school. It's up to him from then on. It's not easy but I am sure he'll get through.'

Lord Toda was the descendant of the former feudal lord of the area and now a member of the House of Lords.

Haruko thought of Kei's comments about fish of the Seto Inland Sea. She asked, 'So what will happen to the shop?'

'We have found Jinsuke. He is very sorry, so I told him that I'll forgive him just this once. After all, he is an honest chap, and hard-working, too. He desperately wants to come back. We'll get him married and he can continue managing the shop. Running away and taking money was wrong, but when one thinks of the motive behind it, you can understand. Between a young man and a young woman . . . what happened is quite natural.'

Kei looked sharply at Tei-ichi.

The next day Kenji did not mention Lord Toda or his new life. In the evening, he brought the English dictionary and the grammar book that Haruko had found in the store at home and loaned him. They were books that Hideto had used some time ago. She had left them by Kenji's books and he had not mentioned them, but Haruko knew that he was using them.

'Haruko ojosama, it was very kind of you. Thank you very much. Jinsuke san will be back from tomorrow and I will leave, and . . .'

'If they are useful, you can keep them. Hiden sama will never want them.'

'Thank you. Then I would like to borrow them. I will bring them back one day.'

'Yes.'

'Haruko ojosama, are you going home soon? It's getting late.'

'Yes.'

'I will come with you if I may. It is getting dark and I also want to thank Dr Shirai and okkasama and say good-bye.'

He walked behind Haruko. A hazy moon was in the sky. Just right for a scene of elopement in a play, Haruko thought. The scent of flowers was in the air, which she had not noticed before. Daphne? Or had their season passed?

Haruko did not dare turn round to look at him but she knew that he was walking a few steps behind her carrying a small bundle of books and perhaps some clothes.

Inside the Shirais' gate, she met Matabei with a lantern.

'Oh, Haruko ojosama. I was just coming to meet you. You are rather late today.'

'Thank you, Mata san, I had to tidy the books.'

Kenji started to follow Matabei towards the kitchen where Sige or Kiyo would sit him down to wait and then take him to see Tei-ichi and Kei. Haruko was about to go into the house through the family entrance. There was a rhododendron bush near the door. The white flowers were small and modest but scented. She stopped and breathed in hard before she said, 'Goodbye, Kenji san. Look after yourself and good luck.'

He also stopped, turned round and bowed. He hesitated and then called Haruko who was moving towards the door, 'Haruko ojosama.'

'Yes?'

'I will come back one day, to thank you.'

'Yes.'

'I have your dictionary and the book, too.'

'Yes.'

He bowed again and the tall strong back was seen in the pool of light from the house for a moment but then was swallowed in the darkness behind the house.

11

The Chief Engineer San's Friend

A new power plant was built up the Kitaka river and the construction of a dam had changed the shape of the river since the days when Haruko and Sachiko had swum in it. It was not just the landscape which had changed; the nearby town had expanded and become more lively. The land between Kitani village and the town, all of which used to belong to the Miwas, had gradually changed hands from Rinji to developers and small houses were being built along the road.

The new chief engineer of the power plant lived in one of those houses. He was about thirty. A village woman was hired to go every day to do the cleaning and washing.

'A very nice man,' she nodded. 'No trouble. Always very polite.'

He found a stray dog or, as the people said, the stray dog found him. The dog followed him everywhere and lived under the raised floor of the chief engineer's house. In the morning he trotted after his master to work. He curled up under his desk in the office, went with him for inspections, and sat by him in the evening while he had saké and chicken shish kebab at a tavern. When his master went away for a day on a business trip by train, the dog waited for him all day at the station.

'Chief engineer san with a dog' was well known in the area but if someone had asked for him by his name, most of the villagers would have shaken their heads. They had not learned his name, nor the dog's.

Chief engineer san wore a western-style suit and the loop of a watch-chain shone in front of his jacket. In summer, his white linen suit, which the town laundry man was proud to wash and iron, was immaculate. He was dark and well built but not tall. He was friendly and fun, but he had never talked about himself.

'Why isn't he married?' they wondered.

'He might have been jilted,' someone suggested.

'Where?'

'Oh, in Tokyo, I should imagine, don't you? That's why he decided to take up a post in the country. He looks too smart for a place like this.'

That sounded plausible. He was obviously a well-educated and refined gentleman and could have lived in a big town, if not Tokyo.

One night, the tavern-keeper asked, 'How is saké here compared with Tokyo?'

'Tokyo? Oh, it's good here, too.'

A customer who sat near him and had been drinking saké said, 'Chief engineer san, how about women? They say Tokyo women are beautiful.'

'Oh, there are beautiful ladies and ugly ladies just as anywhere else.'

'Was she lovely, eh?' another light-hearted voice chipped in.

'Who?'

'You don't have to hide from us. We all know. Don't worry if one woman left you. There are lots more lovely ones about.'

His quizzical expression changed to one of mirth.

'Oh, I see, yes,' he said. 'She was like a willow in the spring breeze. She had skin like a drop of pearl. Her eyes were . . .'

'Ha, ha,' the customer said. 'That's enough, chief engineer san. Don't tease us.'

'You started it. The night is young. You must hear me out.'

Although nobody found out what happened or who she was, if there was such a lady, they all laughed a lot. Eventually he got up.

'Could you let Puck have a piece of meat?'

'Puck?'

'My best and most faithful companion who would never leave me unlike my spring willow.'

'Oh, I see.'

After he had left, they all shook their heads still repeating and laughing at things he had said.

'At least we know his dog's name now,' the tavern-keeper said.

The chief engineer was the centre of village conversation again when he invited the older children from school to see the power plant. He showed them around and explained in simple terms how electricity was produced. He also accepted a request from a boys' school in town to give a talk about electrical engineering.

Shuichi was excited when he told his family about him over dinner.

'He explained physics very well. He is better than you, Haruko nesan.'

'That's not fair. I have never been taught physics at school.'

'I know, I know. I was just teasing you.'

'It's really interesting. I might become an engineer. He said he would teach me mathematics.'

'Did you ask him?' Ayako wanted to know.

'I asked him some questions and said I'd like to learn more. He said he'd teach me if I am interested.'

Through Shuichi, the Shirais learned a little about the chief engineer, including his surname.

'He makes difficult problems very easy. I think it's because he understands everything so well himself,' and the family could tell that the chief engineer, Mr Katsura, was filling the gap that the absence of Hideto had left in Shuichi's life.

'When we cook something special, we'll send some to him,' Kei said.

When the sushi was made, Ayako called Takeko. 'Takeko san, go with Kiyo, and take this to the chief engineer san.'

'Does it have to be today?'

'Of course it has to be today. Why?'

'I don't want to go out today. It's hot, and it's such a long walk.'

'Oh, you are lazy. It's not polite to send Kiyo on her own; on the other hand, it will be too much if I go.'

Haruko knew what was coming next.

'Haruko san.' Ayako turned to her. 'Will you go?'

'Why is Takeko nesan always treated like a princess and I like a slave?'

'Because I am the eldest,' Takeko said. Haruko did not argue. Once Takeko said she did not want to do things, nothing would make her. If she was forced, she could fall ill quite easily and not only manage to look ill but develop some symptoms as well.

Haruko sighed and went to change her kimono. Unlike Takeko, she did not like flowers and butterfly patterns. She liked stripes and checks.

They also differed in choice of fabric. She did not like soft silk. She wanted to be spruce like Kei rather than an inactive princess. But stripes and checks were only for daily kimonos, and not for formal occasions. As Haruko appeared in her new arrow-patterned kimono in white and purple, both Kei and Ayako admired her.

'That was a good choice. That sort of pattern would not suit Takeko at all, but you look lovely. A kimono looks good only when the person enjoys wearing it,' Kei said, without taking her eyes of Haruko. 'Take a parasol,' she added. 'We don't want a sunburnt young lady.'

'Tell him how grateful we are, won't you? Shuichi san enjoys his company so much.' Ayako came out as far as the entrance.

The chief engineer's rented house had been hastily and cheaply built. It was very small. In a year or two, Haruko thought, the front doors would warp and become difficult to slide open.

'Excuse me,' Haruko called, standing in front of the lattice doors. They had frosted glass and she was aware of someone inside, but there was no answer.

Kiyo went round the back. When she returned, she said, 'He is coming now. He was putting on his clothes.'

The sliding front door was already sticking and, as he forced it open, the chief engineer stumbled out.

'Oh, I beg your pardon.' He blinked. He looked healthy and young. On a warm Sunday afternoon, he must have been relaxing on his own. He adjusted his *yukata* which he had put on in haste. 'Please excuse me. Won't you come in?'

Haruko took the sushi from Kiyo and put it down on the side.

'I am Shuichi's sister. I came to thank you on behalf of my family for teaching Shuichi. He is very happy to come to you.'

'Oh, it's a pleasure. He is such a pleasant boy. We get on very well.'

'My grandmother has made this for you and I hope you will like it.' She pushed the plate a little towards him.

'Oh.' He raised the cover and peeped inside like a child. He grinned. 'I haven't eaten such a dish for ages. Please thank your grandmother. Give my regards to Dr Shirai and your mother, too.'

Everybody bowed.

When the woman who looked after him returned the sushi plate, several large summer oranges were piled on it. They were covered by a piece of cloth which Kei folded and gave back to the woman. A family crest of two arrows side by side in a hexagon was dyed in the middle.

'I don't know what kind of family background he has, but he is undoubtedly a polite and sensible person,' Kei remarked. 'Is he from a family connected with Lord Mori, I wonder, as his family crest suggests?'

'He isn't like that at all, obahsama.' Shuichi laughed.

'Like what?'

'Like Lord somebody. He is young and friendly.'

'Don't be silly. A lord does not have to be old.'

Kei's curiosity was to be satisfied soon afterwards. Lord Toda asked Tei-ichi if he would consider marrying one of his granddaughters to the chief engineer.

'He is a son of an old samurai family in Kyushu.' Tei-ichi passed on his newly acquired information to Kei and Ayako when he came home. Lord Toda told Tei-ichi that the Katsuras were connected with Lord Mori and had been a distinguished family once but, for the last few generations, they had gradually gone down in the world. The chief engineer himself was the second son, and would not have any prospect of inheritance from his family. But he was a Tokyo Imperial University graduate and a brilliant man. His future was assured. His qualifications were far more valuable than a small inheritance.

'The young man has said to Lord Toda that he would be happy to leave the marriage arrangements with Lord Toda if we accept him as he stands in his shoes.'

'Then he is better off than Hideto san. Hideto san told us that he has no shoes to stand in.' Ayako giggled.

'It's not a joke. It's your daughter's marriage.' Kei scolded her daughter.

'I think this is the best proposal so far. I have asked around among the people. He is very popular. A man who is popular among men is trustworthy, as against a man popular among women.' Tei-ichi looked at his wife and daughter.

'I know he is popular, but we would like to know a little more about what he has been doing between university and the time he came here.' Kei was cautious.

Ayako took a train to Tokyo. She was not unfamiliar with the capital as she had been there several times before to help Yasuharu and Hideto settle down. She met the president of the large electricity company that employed Noriyasu Katsura. Ayako was satisfied with Noriyasu's credentials and the president was even more impressed by Ayako. 'What a beautiful and accomplished lady,' he repeated to the people around him. 'He is very lucky if his fiancée is like her mother.'

'If chief engineer san is marrying Dr Shirai's granddaughter, he must be thinking of settling down here.' The villagers were delighted.

'I wondered once if Takeko would ever marry,' Ayako mused.

'There has never been a real worry, but when the wind is right, the sailing goes so smooth.'

Tei-ichi invited Noriyasu for a formal interview at home. Takeko was to bring tea and that was the first time she would see him.

Kei and Ayako helped Takeko to put on her kimono. It had *kikyo* (balloon flowers) and *hagi* (bush clover) over the fading background of purple to pale blue. It suited Takeko well and made her look gentle and graceful.

'It is not quite the season for *kikyo* and *hagi* flowers yet, but the kimono looks so good on her,' Ayako said.

'It's fine to wear something which is a little early in the season.' Kei told her.

'What is he like?' Takeko asked Haruko who came in with a glass of water that Takeko had asked for.

'I didn't look at him properly but I think he is good-looking.'

'What you call good-looking is not my idea of a handsome man.'

'You'll soon see him yourself.'

Haruko handed the glass to her sister who sat down and sipped water gingerly, trying not to spoil her lipstick.

'He is a funny chap,' Tei-ichi chuckled later. 'He said he did not mind whatever or how much Takeko was going to take with her, but his house is very small and the foundations are not strong, so it might be better not to bring too many pieces of furniture and too many things. His work requires him to be at the power plant, which is not in the middle of town obviously, and he thinks he is going to settle here. I told him that although Takeko would not bring a big dowry and trousseau, there is a piece of land that belongs to her, and we would give its ownership over to him.'

'What did you think of him?' Haruko asked Takeko.

'I don't know what he looks like from the front because he was talking to oji-isama all the time and I put the tea cup on the table and sat there listening to them.'

'Didn't he say anything to you?'

'He asked me if I have been to Tokyo.'

'Without looking at you?'

'He did look at me, then, but I felt too shy to look at him when he talked to me.'

Tei-ichi said, 'A steady, reliable kind of man. It does not matter how he looks. The type which women like are no good at all.'

Takeko and Haruko looked at each other.

'I hear he likes drinking. Perhaps you had better talk to him one day. It's not good to drink too much when he is young,' Kei suggested.

'A man has to be able to drink to get on in life.' Tei-ichi was not concerned.

Shuichi was delighted about his sister's marriage to his hero.

'Shuichi is the happiest,' Tei-ichi laughed.

'Haruko nesan,' Shuichi whispered later when they were alone.

'Yes?'

'I am convinced that he didn't realise that I have three sisters. I think he thought he was marrying you.'

'Oh, Shu-chan, of course not. They met. No, no, he liked Takeko nesan.'

'He does like her all right, but at first it was you he liked. He asked me a lot about you and I could tell.'

'Don't be silly. I saw him for only about two minutes.'

'He said the other day, "I didn't know you had more than one sister." I told him I had three too many.'

'Cheeky boy.'

Haruko wondered. She liked him, too, but it did not matter. She could call him 'niisan', older brother, and that was rather nice.

The wedding was to be in late September. It was a pleasant time of the year.

'It's nice and easy when you don't have to do much and there are no in-laws to worry about, but I feel I have forgotten something,' Ayako complained to Kei. 'In a way it's better to run around having too much to do.'

'You have to remember there will be three more weddings and plenty of opportunities to run around.'

But, after all, enough kimonos to last for the next ten years had to be prepared. New bedding was ordered. A lacquered box of ink stone and brushes. A small lady's desk. A chest of drawers had to be bought.

Takeko sorted out her collection of ribbons and various small girlish things, putting aside what she wanted to keep.

'If you need help, call me,' Haruko said.

When Takeko went away to Kyoto with Ayako to buy more clothes, Sachiko found Haruko looking inside a box which Takeko had put aside to take with her.

'What are you doing?' Sachiko was surprised. Haruko put her finger to her lips without turning around and continued to try to search for something under handkerchiefs and embroidered neckpieces. As Sachiko watched her, Haruko took out a photograph from the bottom of the box.

'Haruko nesan, who is it? What are you doing to Takeko nesan's things?'

'Sachiko san.' Haruko turned. She looked so serious that Sachiko was a little scared. 'I am convinced that what I am doing is not only right but very important for her happiness and his. Do you remember you said Takeko nesan likes this sort of face?'

Haruko showed Sachiko the photograph of the Count's grandson.

Sachiko nodded, surprised to see the nearly forgotten image of the man.

'She likes this sort of face, but she is playing with fire. I caught sight of it the other day and decided to destroy it for her sake. She thinks that it does not mean much. She hasn't even met the man, but she is stupid. How would he take it if he finds out? I think he is a very sensitive man, although he looks strong.'

Sachiko shivered.

'Don't worry. We'll destroy it.'

Haruko and Sachiko went to the kitchen. The fire was not made and they put it under the embers. The photograph, pasted on a thick piece of gilt-edged cardboard, curled up and gradually smoke started to rise. Finally it caught fire and went up in a puff.

Sachiko took Haruko's hand.

*   *   *

After her marriage, Takeko came to the Shirais' almost every day.

'You are lucky you have no in-laws,' Kei said.

'He said I could do whatever I like while he is at work.'

'He is such a nice man.'

Takeko shrugged.

One afternoon, Noriyasu came to the Shirais unexpectedly. He and Tei-ichi were talking for some time alone, and that was how Haruko's marriage was settled.

'Noriyasu says that one of his best friends is coming to visit him. He is also an electrical engineer and is working for Siemens. It's a big German company. This friend is due to go to Europe, mainly Germany, to study. Noriyasu says he knows everything about this friend, in fact, more than the friend himself does.' Tei-ichi laughed. 'That's what he said. If the man is like Noriyasu, I have no objection.'

'Well, well. Where is he going to live?' Kei asked.

'Not far. In Kyushu.'

'Kyushu, not far?'

'Compared with Germany, it's practically in the same village.'

'It is,' Kei thought. Her oldest son Yasuharu had been studying in Germany. She thought of the white envelopes with lots of stamps which Masakazu brought back from the post office. When the family wrote letters to Yasuharu, it was either Haruko or Masakazu who wrote the address on the envelope, as they were the only ones who could write the European script.

'With new coal mines opening up and a steel manufacturing business developing, Kyushu is the centre of industrial growth. All capable men are going to Kyushu.'

'Is that what Noriyasu san told you?' Kei asked.

'I don't have to wait for Noriyasu to tell me. Anybody who is familiar with the *"zeitgeist"* would know.'

'With what?'

'Something women don't have to worry about.'

'So what kind of family is he from?'

'Noriyasu said that he is also from a once-good-but-now-ruined sort.'

'We seem to be specialising in once-upon-a-time families, don't we?'

'You are getting a little presumptuous.'

'Oh, not at all.'

'Women over fifty are all saucy.'

For Tei-ichi to be so talkative was an indication that he was in a good humour.

Compared with Takeko who had gone through so many proposals, Ayako felt it was a little too easy, but there was nothing to complain about.

'What is his name, Noriyasu san?' Kei asked.

'Nozomi Sanjo, obahsama.'

'Goodness, it sounds like a name of a court noble.'

'Him? Court noble?' Noriyasu responded with his vivacious laugh.

Noriyasu's friend was invited by Tei-ichi soon afterwards.

'He's here.' Sachiko rushed into the room where Kei and Ayako were getting Haruko ready.

'Behave yourself,' Kei scolded her.

'What is he like?' Haruko asked.

'Ummm, he is quite like niisan, but he is not dark like him. He had a white suit on like niisan.'

When Haruko took in the tea tray, Nozomi Sanjo was kneeling in front of the *tokonoma*, the recess, where a scroll was hanging. The scroll was a treasure belonging to Tei-ichi. He brought it out of the store and hung it there without really expecting it to be appreciated but to honour his guest. The calligraphy was old and difficult to decipher, but this guest not only had some understanding of its value but clearly liked it, and Tei-ichi was delighted.

The man was taking his time looking at the scroll and Haruko could see only his kneeling back and a pair of soles put together. One of his socks had a hole and she suppressed a giggle. Whether Tei-ichi had noticed it as well, Haruko could not tell, but he scowled at her.

Haruko reflected on the difference between this man's preparation and her own. Since this morning, she had been bathed and her hair was washed. A hairdresser came from town and put her hair up. Kei and Ayako endlessly discussed which kimono was better for the occasion. Ayako wanted a kimono with a bamboo pattern dyed and embroidered over a green background. Kei objected on the grounds that the colour and the pattern were too severe for the occasion. She was in favour of one with various coloured ivy leaves over off-white. Eventually Kei's choice was accepted but, in between, Haruko had to have two more kimonos draped around her to be scrutinised. By that time, Takeko and Sachiko had joined the party and everybody gave their opinions. Her appearance was most important on that day. There was no time for her to be nervous.

He must have just got up, shaved and put on a suit and any old socks, she thought. He finally turned round and went back to where he had been sitting.

'Thank you very much for letting me have the opportunity of looking at such a precious scroll,' the young man said.

'Do you like calligraphy?' Finding someone who shared his interest, Tei-ichi was animated.

'I don't know much about it, but recently someone sold me a Sanyo script.'

'Hoh!' Tei-ichi was impressed. 'You own a writing of Sanyo!'

'Only a small piece. They say there are a lot of imitations of the poet's writings, and I hope the one I bought is genuine.'

The two men were deeper and deeper into their interest in old scripts and looked as though they had forgotten the purpose of the meeting. Nozomi Sanjo was sitting with his back to the garden. The strong sunlight outside made the room under the deep eaves dark in contrast and Haruko could not see his face clearly. Also, she was not sitting facing him.

'I am afraid I am not like your son-in-law, Katsura. He is a clever man and such fun. I am quite dull compared with him and don't have any hobbies to name,' the man said eventually in answer to Tei-ichi's question and turned to Haruko.

'Do you have any hobbies?' he asked. She was sitting a little away from the table, almost behind Tei-ichi.

'I do a little painting,' she said. That was another thing she wanted to learn properly but Kei and Ayako were convinced that art students were immoral. Perhaps he will think I am immoral, she thought, although she did not know exactly what immoral meant. She vaguely associated the word with drinking and being rowdy.

'That's very good,' he said. 'Do you do oil or water-colour?'

'Water-colour.'

'What was he like?' Sachiko asked.

'I couldn't see very well. But he wears glasses.'

'He is another one.' Tei-ichi laughed. 'He said he did not want any trousseau. He hasn't got a house yet. He rents a room in someone else's house, although he will find a house as soon as possible. Besides, he says a lot of possessions are a nuisance.'

Noriyasu supplied a few more pieces of information. His friend was the third son of a poor farmer. The headmaster of his school offered to take him into his own home so that he could continue his education and eventually the headmaster and the post master sent him to university.

'He says he was interested in archaeology but decided to do engineering, thinking of better salary prospects, so that he could return the money those two men had entrusted to him.'

Tei-ichi had heard talk of a new generation of elite students who went into the Ministry of Foreign Affairs or banking and were marrying girls with good fortunes. Noriyasu and Nozomi were equally elite but of a different breed. They were trying to steer their own destiny.

Sparrows were chirping noisily outside. It was not often that Haruko was woken up by them. On the futon alongside her, Sachiko was fast asleep. They had stayed up chatting till the early hours as both knew that it was the end of their life together.

Haruko did not think that married life would be difficult, seeing Noriyasu and Takeko. Takeko seemed to have more freedom than when she was at home. Sometimes Noriyasu took his wife and her sisters to the theatre at the nearby town. He was fun. He was interested in kimonos and enjoyed seeing them dressed up. He often offered his opinions about fashion, colours, hairstyles. Haruko hoped Nozomi would be as easy-going when they knew each other.

Haruko could not go back to sleep. She got up and changed into an old kimono. This was going to be left behind. Kei would unpick it, wash it and give it to the maid, Kiyo. Haruko could imagine Kiyo sitting in front of Kei being taught how to sew in the house when she would no longer be there. It was strange to think that life at the Shirais' would go on without her exactly as it always had.

In the kitchen, Shige was squatting in front of the fire. Steam started to force itself out from under the heavy wooden lid of the rice pot. Shige looked at Haruko as though she was going to say something, but turned away. She pulled out pieces of smoking wood from the mouth of the clay oven and put them in a lidded pot. Leaning against a pillar, Haruko watched the familiar scene.

'Are you up, Haruko? You know it rained last night.' As always, when Kei came out from her bedroom, her hair had been tidied and her kimono showed its crisp folds. She was ready for a new day.

'Yes, I heard it, too.'

'But it's going to be fine today. It's a good omen to have rain before a wedding.' Kei took out a clean apron from a drawer and tied the string over her obi. 'The rain makes the ground firm and fertile.'

Soon Tei-ichi and Ayako were up and the house began to bustle with preparations. A dresser from the town arrived by rickshaw bringing a large box containing a bridal wig.

'Someone wake Sachiko and Shuichi up, and, Haruko, you go and have a bath.' Kei was taking Tei-ichi's tea to his study.

'Hallo!' a woman shouted and opened the kitchen door. 'Kané san will bring the others. Are the little tables still in the storehouse?'

'Kiyo,' Shige called. 'Go and ask okkasama for the storehouse key,' and, to the woman, 'You'd better polish the little tables over there before you bring them in. The lacquered bowls have to be taken down, too, but leave the china dishes. I'll come and see to them.' She took out a bundle of rags from the cupboard and handed them to the woman. Some more village wives arrived and they walked towards the storehouse laughing loudly at each other's jokes. On that day, no one was scolded for making merry noises.

Three large baskets full of fish were wheeled in on a cart.

'Good morning. Is it all right to use the pump, Shige san, to clean the fish?'

'Kiyo, put the rest of the cooked rice in the wooden tub and start washing the new rice.' Shige's hips moved this way and that way. 'Eight faces and six bottoms', Haruko thought of the old saying as she passed by the kitchen from her bath. A savoury smell rose from the slightly burnt rice that Kiyo was turning out. Haruko remembered that when she was little, she and the other children used to gather around Shige waiting for her to make rice balls with burnt rice.

'O'Shige san, make me a rice ball.'

'Honestly!' Shige pretended to disapprove, but her eyes were soft. She put her hand in the salt pot, and said, 'Your dannasama will be shocked to see you like this.' She stood for a minute and watched Haruko eat before she went to examine the azuki beans being cooked. Beans were to be mixed with the rice to make the 'red rice' prepared for celebrations. A cook with an assistant arrived from a restaurant in town and started to sharpen his knives.

Ayako and the dresser were waiting for Haruko. A robe and kimonos were draped over stands. The underclothes, obis and many strings were placed neatly in large shallow boxes.

Haruko sat in her cotton kimono. The dresser tied a band around her head to hold her hair out of the way and started to brush her face with thick white liquid. Her throat, neck and hands were also covered in white.

She was pushed and squeezed. First the white underclothes and then the red under-kimono. Then a white kimono. A heavy obi was tied around her middle. The ceremonial robe was of white patterned satin. It had been worn by Ayako and Takeko before her.

'I have dressed many young ladies, but I don't often come across such a beautiful bride.' The dresser stood back and examined her work before she put a bridal hood over the elaborate wig. Kei was called. She sat down quietly just looking at her granddaughter.

Ayako said, 'Haruko san, go and see oji-isama. Say good-bye.' It was good-bye to home. From that day, she no longer belonged to the family she had grown up with. She would be no longer a Miwa.

Normally the bride was taken to the bridegroom's house where the ceremony took place, but no one suggested this as Nozomi's parents lived in a remote mountain area. They could not even attend the wedding and Noriyasu and Takeko were to represent the bridegroom's side.

The dresser held the skirt of the kimono which had swept over the floor and Haruko walked the long corridor to Tei-ichi's study in small steps. She called from outside his room. The dresser opened the sliding door and Haruko knelt down to bow. Her hair ornaments made tinkling noises.

'Oh!' Tei-ichi looked surprised before he admired her. He gazed at her for a while. 'I wish Miwa oji-isama could see you, and your otohsama, of course.' Then he squared his shoulders a little. 'Haruko,' he coughed softly. 'Your husband is a clever man and there is no doubt that he will be successful. He is a graduate of the best university in the country and is very well qualified. That is far more important than family names in this modern age. He is also a fine man. You have nothing to worry about. Now, it is your duty to keep a happy home for him.' Having made his short farewell speech, Tei-ichi let out a little sigh.

'Yes, oji-isama.'

'And . . . You look after yourself. Keep well.'

'Thank you very much, oji-isama, for taking care of me for so long.' Haruko bowed. The mesh of the tatami was blurred. She managed to say, 'Please, oji-isama, you keep yourself well, too,' without breaking down, but she knew that her make-up had to be repaired.

'A lovely day,' Tei-ichi's voice trembled. 'The bridegroom will arrive soon. You'd better go.'

'The bridegroom has come.' Like little waves, the news reached Haruko who was ready and sitting on a stool. The sliding doors between two large rooms had been removed, and when she was taken in there, she saw Nozomi out of the corner of her eye. He was sitting on the other side of the room facing the place where she was to sit. He wore a black kimono and haori, and hakama. Haruko felt Nozomi's eyes on her but she kept hers down. The president of Nozomi's company with his wife had come from Tokyo to act as the go-between couple. Tei-ichi had been reassured of Nozomi's prospects when they accepted the invitation.

A plain wood table was placed in front of the *tokonoma*, the recess for ornaments, and a Shinto priest was sitting by it in his robe and hat which resembled a courtier's costume from the Heian period, a thousand years ago.

The go-between couple gently urged the bridegroom and the bride to move and face the table side by side. The priest stood with his back to the room. In front of a painting of the sun goddess, the legendary ancestor of the emperors, a simple altar with a pair of vases had been set up and the priest chanted the ancient felicitatory address in a continuous monotone. At first Haruko tried to understand its meaning. She wondered if anyone made any sense of the wailing sound. She saw Nozomi's hands placed on his knees. They were fair. His knuckles were smooth.

At last the priest stopped chanting and bowed deeply. He picked up a branch of holy sakaki tree and swished it around over the couple's heads for purification.

After more bowing, the priest went back to his place. Three tiers of the shallow saké cups had been placed on a red lacquered stand. The go-between couple poured a little saké in the top cup. Nozomi and Haruko sipped it three times, and then the same procedure was repeated with the next cup. Every time the cup was handed to her, Haruko had just the taste of saké on her lips. After inhaling the fumes nine times, her head began to feel hot. Then the cup was passed from Nozomi to Tei-ichi, Kei and Ayako, and returned, thus tying the in-law relationship.

Haruko exchanged the cups with Noriyasu and Takeko who were today acting as the bridegroom's relatives.

After the ceremony, Haruko was led out to change into a colourful kimono. When she was taken back to the room again, the dinner was being served. Women from the village were carrying in small lacquered tables one by one to set in front of each guest.

The go-between sang a traditional recitation. He did not have a good voice, but was practised and steady. Haruko sat still. The bride was expected to be like a doll, hardly eating or moving.

Saké was served and the guests started to get up from their places and circulate. Nozomi and Noriyasu were talking to each other, completely relaxed. They even laughed. At one point, Haruko thought that they were looking at her together. She felt her cheeks burn, remembering a picture Kei had given her the night before.

'It's a talisman to protect you against evil,' her grandmother had said and handed her a piece of folded paper. 'Put it in your tissue paper holder.' It was a ukiyoé print by the famous painter, Utamaro. A man and woman held themselves in a position convenient for the great painter to convey the advice that her grandmother thought Haruko would need on her wedding night.

After the wedding, Nozomi and Haruko were to leave for a honeymoon. Two rickshaws arrived to take them to the station and Haruko got in the second one. She was sitting and looking at the back of her new husband when Kei came to her, working her way through the crowd at the gate.

'Haruko, turn your face down. The bride should look modest,' she stood on tiptoe and told her. 'Take care of yourself, and be happy.' Kei was smiling but her voice had an edge. Ayako was standing a little away. Her eyes were moist. Haruko looked for Tei-ichi but she could not see him.

The rickshaw man lifted up the shafts and followed the first rickshaw which had already gone ahead.

'I have to do a little work at my office,' the bridegroom said as soon as the train started to move. 'So we will get off the train at Fukuoka.

I have arranged for my secretary to look after you while I go to the office. He will bring you back to the station and then we will go on.'

Her husband's secretary took Haruko to his own house where his mother gave her tea and they spent a couple of hours in gentle conversation. The secretary then took Haruko back to the station. As she went up to the platform, the train was already there. Sudden panic seized Haruko. She could not remember what her husband looked like, except that he wore glasses. She was not quite sure how tall he was either.

She walked along the train.

But he was there, leaning his head out of the window and waving to her. Obviously he remembered what she looked like.

PART TWO

12

To Manchuria

The sliding doors to the garden were all open. Haruko realised how cold her hands were and how hungry she was. She had been sorting out family possessions since the morning and it was nearly three o'clock. It was empty inside the house. Everything had been taken out to the garden to be packed in crates.

The year was 1941. Haruko was preparing to move to Manchuria, a northern province of China which had been colonised by Japan.

The garden was not large but it had been well tended until two days ago, when a local handyman came and started to pack furniture and various objects. There was a shapely pine tree which the handyman had trimmed now and again. In winter, the same tree was protected by pieces of rope hung from the top and tied to branches so that the weight of snow would not break them. It made the tree look as though it was inside a half-open umbrella. Some azalea bushes and tree peonies had emerged out of straw covers a few weeks before. There was a tiny pond which Nozomi called 'Cats' Pee', making Haruko feel uneasy as she knew that he was laughing at her bourgeois taste.

Small pieces of straw from rope covered the soft moss now. The air felt dusty.

'Where will you have the soba noodles?' the maid Aki asked. The noodle shop boy had just arrived on a bicycle balancing a tower of ten or so trays on his outspread palm and delivered three to the Sanjos. It looked precarious but the noodle shop boys were well trained and seldom caused an accident.

Haruko looked around the empty expanse of tatami floor. 'Bring out . . .' She started to laugh. Of course, the cushions had been packed.

'Never mind, Aki san. We'll sit on the veranda and eat.'

'Takeda-ya san.' She called to the man who was putting his foot on a bundle and tightening thick straw rope around it. 'Come and eat. You must be ready for noodles.'

When Haruko handed him a small tray with a bowl of soba noodles on it, he bowed. 'Thank you. I will eat down here.'

'No, no. Sit on the veranda. Aki san, you come and eat with us, too'.

When he sat down, Takeda-ya wiped his face with a cloth he had twisted and tied around his head. A waft of sweaty odour mingled with the smell of fresh straw. He held the bowl on one hand and, bending his head over it, blew and sucked the noodles quickly and noisily. It was said that a connoisseur of soba noodles should eat without breaking the strands from mouth to stomach.

Having finished eating, he lit his pipe. He lived in a small house nearby. Its front was open to the street and in winter he baked sweet potatoes in a clay oven and sold them. The house had a hardened mud floor and gardening and simple carpentry tools, coils of rope and pieces of wood stood against the walls.

Gently puffing the tobacco, he was surveying the pine tree. He would come with a pair of shears and a ladder. He would cut one branch and snip here and there, come down from the ladder and examine the shape sitting on the veranda as he did now. After a while he might cut another branch. Gardening was a process which took hours of deliberation. If Haruko wanted a camellia in the garden, he would bring the plant, and spend perhaps half an hour considering the best place for it. Towards the end of the day, he would go around over the soft moss picking up leaves and twigs by hand and finished his day by brushing over it.

Today his job was quite different. He continued to puff.

'To us, Manchuria is another world,' he said, almost to himself. 'I thought it was miles and miles of barren land.'

'It is very civilised there now. Life is exactly the same as here or even better.'

Haruko did not know in what way life over the sea would be better but she had heard that the Russians had built a lot of fine houses during their occupation of Manchuria before they were defeated in the Russo-Japanese war in 1905. Until a year ago, she accepted remarks such as, 'Why did the Japanese army have to go as far as Manchuria?' quite naturally. Her knowledge of the northern part of China had come only through newspapers.

When Haruko married and went to live in Kyushu, she had thought that from then on her life would be orderly and predictable. At first it was like playing house. There were only two pots, one for rice and one for soup. A small table was folded away after meals unless she needed it to write a letter.

Haruko smiled, remembering how she had regarded Nozomi as a person of authority.

'Please, may I buy a pot and two tea cups?' she had asked him one night. He looked surprised.

'Of course you may buy whatever you want.'

She bought two tea cups and Nozomi liked his.

'Lovely shape and colour. The tea tastes very good in this.'

But soon after that, Haruko's hand slipped and the cup was broken.

'What happened to my nice tea cup?' he asked that night.

'I am sorry. I broke it.' As she spoke, tears rolled down her cheeks. Nozomi stared at her in incomprehension. Perhaps he never understood what it meant for Haruko to live with a man ten years older than herself who had already achieved so much in life. But he was not a difficult husband. Soon Sachiko, Shuichi and also Hideto found the Sanjos' a pleasant change from home and they spent most of their holidays at Haruko's house in Kyushu until Nozomi was transferred to Tokyo. He was called back to help with the reconstruction of the capital after the Great Earthquake in 1923.

After Haruko's marriage, five years passed before Sachiko married. There had been changes during that time in the Shirai family. Two years after Haruko had left home, Tei-ichi died peacefully in his sleep. Yasuharu had come back from Europe and had been appointed as head of the Ophthalmology Department of the Red Cross Hospital in Tokyo. He had married a senior surgeon's daughter.

The decision-making over the family affairs had shifted from Kitani village to Tokyo, together with the focus of family life. Nozomi and Haruko saw the family often and, eventually, Ayako and Sachiko were spending more time with the Sanjos and at Yasuharu's than at home in Kitani.

A proposal of marriage to Sachiko had come from a student who was the son of a neighbour of the Sanjos'. He lived with his parents in a small rented house. Had Tei-ichi been alive and learned that the young man had fallen in love with Sachiko and taken the initiative to approach the family himself, he would have thought his conduct impudent. He would have disciplined Sachiko even before he had considered the possibility of a match.

Yasuharu had been cautious. As this was the first occasion on which he had to face responsibility as the head of the household, he refused. The young man had not been deterred. He had the advantage of being a graduate of the same university as Yasuharu, although their fields of study were different. He had used the connection to gain Yasuharu's confidence and wrote a long letter. He had also enlisted his friends' help to persuade Yasuharu.

The young man had visited Ayako, which was a little out of the ordinary, and Ayako had hesitated to receive him. But once she had met him, she had been charmed by him. She had said that she would not raise any objection if Yasuharu accepted the proposal. At Ayako's request, Nozomi had invited the student to his club and the two men had talked.

'What did you think of him?' Ayako and Haruko were waiting for him at home and Ayako asked as soon as Nozomi had changed and appeared in the *chanoma*.

'A fine man. He talks well without being chatty. Perhaps it is to be expected from a student of social science.'

'Did you get the impression that he was the passionate sort? Might he cool off?' Ayako was anxious.

'I can't guarantee, okahsan.' Nozomi was amused. 'Hum. At this moment, he might kill me and kill himself if I suggested that.'

'He is a rash, angry kind of man, then?' Haruko had asked.

Nozomi had glanced at Haruko.

'He is, as they say, madly in love with Sachiko san and has all the symptoms of a young man in love. If you ask me, okahsan, you had better rescue him from the fate of the young Werther.'

'Who?' Ayako had asked.

Nozomi had waved his hand and laughed.

In the end Yasuharu had given his consent. Sachiko had married Hitoshi Asada in Tokyo as soon as he completed his doctorate and got a lectureship at his university.

Hitoshi was kind and amusing. He became popular among the family but they were beginning to be aware that economics was a dangerous subject to pursue in the unsettled political climate of Japan in the late 1920s.

Meanwhile, Shuichi had started medical school and come to live with the Sanjos in Tokyo. Nozomi was generous with Shuichi's pocket money and he easily slipped into a fashionable life. He brought home friends who found the Sanjos' comfortable and with them came the atmosphere of cafés, dancing, cinemas, the gay and decadent taste of the time.

'Haruko nesan, I'll teach you how to dance.' Shuichi had grown up to be a tall and good-looking young man. 'Try wearing a European dress.'

'No, really! Niisan would be shocked.'

'He won't mind. Besides, he never comes back early. You can take it off before he comes home.'

That was true. Nozomi was more and more involved in his work and the family hardly saw him.

One of Shuichi's friends was the grandson of a finance minister who, Haruko heard, was an excellent jazz pianist. He brought a gramophone and several friends danced around in a small room on the tatami mats while Namiko, Takeko's daughter, watched them wide-eyed. Shuichi pinned pictures of Mary Pickford and Rudolf Valentino over his desk.

Yet not all was carefree. These acquaintances also brought Haruko into contact with the uneasy atmosphere of the time. Young army officers who advocated imperial power, demanded the reorganisation of the government and shot three government ministers in their homes. One of them was the grandfather of Shuichi's friend. The dissident military group was subsequently suppressed, but the gathering of power around the Emperor gained momentum.

The frenzy of pleasure-seeking in society, on the other hand, seemed to have increased against this background of instability. Only once Nozomi mildly told Shuichi, 'Shu-chan, it's good to enjoy yourself. I wish I'd had time and money to do that when I was young. I might have been able to relax more and do a better job. But just remember: one day you will be entrusted with someone's life.'

*　　　*　　　*

Haruko did not learn to dance but she listened to songs from *The Merry Widow, Rigoletto,* and other operas, and went to see European films with Sachiko. She also saw Anna Pavlova dance the 'Dying Swan'. A famous novelist wrote incongruously that the ballerina was 'a vinegar woman'. Japanese people believed that drinking vinegar would make one supple.

They went to a concert by the violinist Zimbalist. For once Nozomi came as well and listened, sitting between Haruko and her sister in their decorous kimonos. He remarked, 'I like Zimbalist because he did not keep on bowing like a grasshopper. He was quite dignified. If they bow too many times and too deeply, I feel sorry for them.'

'He played beautifully,' Sachiko sighed.

'The Brahms was wonderful, I thought. Well, perhaps because that was the only music I recognised.' He laughed.

'Are you going to treat us tonight?' Haruko asked Nozomi light-heartedly.

'Why should I do such a thing?' He, too, was in a carefree mood. Haruko wanted to say, 'You will be with us tonight instead of being with geishas,' as it was not often that a taxi brought him home before midnight. Most nights he was at exclusive restaurants being entertained by people who were seeking his favour. She did not complain. After all, it was a lifestyle expected of an able and successful man. She knew little about this twilight world of men. Like other wives she knew that high society geishas were not prostitutes, though there was always an edge of ambiguity.

'We haven't got anything prepared at home tonight.'

'Let's go to Alaska, niisan.' Sachiko named an expensive restaurant.

'How did you know about Alaska?'

But he whistled for a taxi and took them there.

On reflection, Haruko had hardly noticed how unproductively she had spent her days. It was a time of her life strewn with glitter. The social climate had been kaleidoscopic, but all the while the world was heading towards chaos.

In September 1931, the Japanese army blew up part of the railway north of Chenyang in Manchuria. Under the pretence that it was a ploy by a Chinese general, the Japanese army swiftly occupied Chenyang, opened the way to invade the whole of Manchuria, and established Manchukuo under the puppet Emperor, Pu Yi. Five years later, near Peking, while training at night, the Japanese army claimed that they had heard gun shots fired by Chinese troops and that they had lost a soldier. This incident would trigger the Sino-Japanese war.

Whenever the family gathered for someone's birthday, to celebrate someone's recovery from illness, or for tasting wild ducks that one of Yasuharu's patients had sent to him, discussions and arguments flourished amongst the men, while the women yawned over repeated 'colonialism', 'military government', 'xenophobia', and retreated among themselves to chat. Since the beginning of the Sino-Japanese war, nationalism had become pervasive. A song sung by Danielle Darrieux in the film *Retour à l'Aube*, which had been heard everywhere, was no longer played on the radio. Luxury goods were gradually squeezed out of the market.

'You know the son of the Saitohs married recently?' Hideto's wife, Kazuko, was saying. She was Haruko's aunt-in-law, but a year younger than her.

'Uh hum.'

'They said on the invitation, "Considering that we are in a national emergency, we think it prudent to make our celebration dinner a small family gathering", or something like that, and the reception was at that big cheap Chinese restaurant, you know, the one like a department store.'

'It was not at the Imperial Hotel?' Takeko pretended to be shocked. 'They must have been relieved not to have to spend a lot of money.' Takeko never missed family gatherings. Recently her visits were more frequent as her son and daughter were living with Haruko and going to school in Tokyo.

'Oh, Takeko san,' Kazuko giggled.

One day Haruko asked Nozomi, 'Are we going in the wrong direction?'

He replied, 'There is a universe. It has no end just as a circle has no beginning and end. I can't tell you more than that because I don't know. And there is the world. And there are families. Each family tries its best to be safe and happy. That is enough, isn't it?'

Typical, Haruko thought, but it struck a chord somehow as they had their own family by then.

After more than ten years of marriage, during which Nozomi and Haruko had given up hope of having their own children and were thinking of adopting Takeko's daughter, Haruko gave birth to a baby girl and a year later they had another daughter.

When the first daughter was born, Nozomi came beaming into the hospital room to visit Haruko and said, 'I have decided to call her Emi. "Blessed with beauty." Isn't it a lovely name? I will go to the register office straight away.' Haruko liked the name but she thought that he could have consulted her before he decided. She pretended to ponder over the name and said, 'You don't have to register today. We can think about it until the naming day.' The naming day was the seventh day after birth, but he did not even hear what she was saying.

'I just went to see her,' he chuckled. 'She saw me and smiled.'

'No, she wouldn't.'

'Why not? She should recognise me. I went to see the doctor, too. He said she was a perfect baby. The nurse said she was very intelligent.'

They must be laughing at him. Haruko smiled helplessly.

'Thank goodness she did not have my thumbnails,' he continued in his jaunty mood.

Nozomi had particularly short thumbnails which made his thumbs look like fat stumps. On one occasion he had shown his thumb to a geisha and said, 'Look, I have only one joint on my thumb.' The geisha made a sympathetic noise over his deformity and after a while cried out, 'Oh, my thumb has only one joint, too.' Haruko thought it was a silly story and that the geisha probably saw straight through him.

After naming the second daughter Mari, once more without asking Haruko's opinion, Nozomi left all the decisions concerning their daughters in the early years of their lives to Haruko. When they were older, Haruko sent them to piano lessons, and also Japanese dancing lessons. It was an expensive business. The teacher was a famous dancer and the assistants were also well known. A Kabuki make-up specialist came and painted faces and a stylist dressed the children in their kimonos. A theatre in the centre of Tokyo was hired. Parents paid for blocks of seats and invited friends and relatives. Sushi was served for lunch and later the guests were given tea and cakes.

Nozomi asked Haruko to let him know when their daughters would appear on stage and came hurrying in just in time. He sat and enjoyed their performances. His satisfaction, though, did not come from their dancing, which even he had to admit did not show any promise. He was pleased that Emi lost her sandal in her twirl and, without getting upset, calmly put it on during the next movement, and that four-year-old Mari did not forget the sequence, simple though it was.

While enjoying her young family, Haruko was becoming increasingly concerned about her brother. In spite of his hearty participation in social activities, Shuichi qualified in medicine and Ayako did not spare her efforts to secure him a good position. He was blessed with the handsome features of the Miwas and the Shirais, and had the advantage of a good upbringing. His professor recommended him to the paediatric team for the newly-born Crown Prince. The appointment was more for the honour than a good salary, but Ayako was overjoyed. She was certain that her father-in-law and her husband would have been delighted. Her responsibility had been fulfilled.

This happiness did not last long. While Ayako had been contemplating his marriage and rejecting a lot of proposals, Shuichi announced his intended bride. She was the daughter of a middle-ranking civil servant and they had met at a dancing hall.

'At a dancing hall!' Ayako was shocked.

'Okahsan, it's just a café. It's called a tea-dance.'

Yaéko was not the kind of girl whom Ayako could have imagined as her daughter-in-law or anybody's wife. The dress she wore to meet her future mother-in-law was low-cut at the neck. Her short hair had been curled and she had worn bright red lipstick.

'Her parents are really nice. They treat me like a prince.' Shuichi was smug.

'You have met her parents already?'

'Why not!'

'You cannot treat marriage so lightly. We have to find out more about her family.'

'What is there to find out, okahsan?'

'Well, there are many things. For instance, there may be someone in the family who has a hereditary illness.'

Shuichi laughed one of his easy laughs. 'I am a doctor. I can assure you the whole family is quite healthy.'

As Shuichi's salary was low, the young couple decided to live with Yaéko's parents until Shuichi was earning more money.

'Living with her parents.' 'Having to earn more money.' Everything was so different from Ayako's idea of her only son's marriage.

Her dream of being able to live with her son was shattered.

'Okahsan, it's just for the first few years,' Shuichi assured her, but she was not convinced that she and Yaéko could be happy together, and Shuichi's three sisters shared her doubts.

A year later, a boy was born, but the happy event was darkened by the discovery that his hearing was impaired.

Ayako whispered to Haruko one day, 'I wonder if there was some ancestor in the Miwa family who did something terrible. There's a curse on the family.'

'No, these things happen in any family, okahsan.' Haruko tried to reassure Ayako.

'But every time things start to go well, something happens to crush it. Who would have thought of having a deaf boy as the heir of the Miwas?' Ayako had wept. 'I thought how pleased oji-isama and otohsama would be when Shuichi san was selected as a court physician. He could have been the Emperor's physician one day.'

'He could still be that.'

Ayako shook her head.

Against everybody's advice, Shuichi had started to work as a general practitioner.

'The salary as the prince's physician is not good at first but that is why they look into the family background carefully. It is stipulated that you will not work as a town doctor at the same time. They will be careful to protect the prince from exposure to contact with normal people. Shuichi san will be dropped from the team soon. If he stayed with me, I would have helped him, or,' then she had stopped.

Haruko guessed what had been in Ayako's mind. Had he married someone whose family could have helped him instead of needing help from him, things would have been different. There had been many proposals that would have offered this security. But Ayako kept this regret to herself and looked at her hands. 'It's sad that Shobei oji isama's grandson has to throw away such an honour for money. He would be distressed if he heard that. And I am afraid Shuichi san is working too hard. He looks tired. He is not too strong, you know. If you have a chance, suggest gently that he ought to relax. I would like to do what I can but Yaéko san is a proud lady, and there is no opportunity for me to talk to Shuichi san alone.'

Not long after that, Nozomi came home and told Haruko, 'Yaéko san came to see me today at my office.'

'Yaéko san?'

Before Haruko asked obvious questions, he said, 'Shu-chan has been taken ill and it seems that he needs to have a good rest. I gave her whatever she wanted to borrow but you'd better go tomorrow to see what is happening.'

For Yaéko to come to borrow money, something serious must have happened. With two small children to look after, Haruko had not been able to visit her brother's family for a while. Haruko and the other members of the family had drifted apart from Shuichi and his wife, partly because he was always working.

When Haruko arrived at Shuichi's house it was quiet and the front door was locked. She stood for a while looking at the dusty leaves of a small fatsia plant. It was the only thing in the short space between a token gate and the front door. Haruko wondered about her brother's thoughts when he came back to the gate every day to a life he had won over the objections and tears of his own family. Did he ever think of the pair of tap shoes he had bought, or the love letters he had received from a film star? How the family had been impressed and talked. His life was full of fun.

After waiting a while, Haruko put down a bag of fruit she had brought for them by the door and opened a cream-coloured crêpe parasol. As she started to walk back to the station, she recognised Yaéko's mother coming from the other direction.

'O'nesama.' A smile spread over her broad face which was drenched with sweat. She had her grandson strapped on her back and shopping bags were dangling from both hands. The little boy's head was rolled backwards and his small face was also shiny with sweat.

'I am sorry, I just went out shopping. Please come back and let me give you a cup of tea.'

Yaéko's mother opened the sliding doors to the garden and gave Haruko a fan. Then she brought a cup of tea and bowed formally. 'Thank you for coming in this weather.'

Haruko learned from Yaéko's mother that Shuichi had not been well for a while but he had decided that the hot weather was to blame. It was true that it had been exceptionally hot.

'But the other day he coughed and found a trace of blood in the phlegm. Shuichi san has a lot of good friends and they told him he had to have a rest. At the moment, he is in hospital and Yaéko is with him.'

Haruko asked how serious his condition was. Yaéko's mother replied that she had been told that he would come home in a day or two.

Before Ayako was told, Yasuharu stepped in. Once he was alerted, everything moved swiftly. Shuichi was moved to a sanatorium in a mountain area away from Tokyo. He stayed there for seven months, during which time Haruko managed to visit him only once. It took six hours to get there by train and bus and Yasuharu gently discouraged 'those with small children' from going to see him.

When she saw Shuichi alive for the last time at the sanatorium, he did not look ill. The mountains Haruko could see from the open window were blue but there was snow on the peaks. They took a short walk following a path in the woods of white birches. The sun was mellow and golden. A woodpecker was tapping a tree trunk and the echoes came back over the valley.

'Nesan, we often walked together from Miwa oji-isama's house, didn't we?' He looked at the mountains through the trees bare of leaves. Haruko was also remembering their childhood walks together.

'In spring, the mountains were covered with cherry blossoms.'

'These mountains will be, too, in spring.'

Like his father, Shuichi died of tuberculosis away from home, without waiting for spring. On that last visit Haruko had worn a pale orange kimono with thin blue stripes. The kimono was lined as it had been autumn. It was kept at the bottom of a drawer. She had never worn it since.

Ayako did not talk about her son for a long time.

It was a year after Shuichi's death that she said to Haruko, 'I sensed that it was coming. All the people around him had done so much for him and one can't say he did not have luck. Only he was not capable of using it.' Her voice had been composed but tears ran down her cheeks.

Not long after Shuichi died, Nozomi told Haruko that his company was expanding its business to Manchuria and that he found the opportunity exciting. He left alone for Chenyang a month later.

Little by little Haruko learned about Manchuria. There were fourteen primary schools for Japanese children, two boys' high schools and three for girls in Chenyang. There were even colleges. They would be able to live in comfort or even in luxury.

Haruko received postcards from Nozomi, written in a formal style: 'I hope everybody is well. It is getting cold. Do not forget to start heating the greenhouse.'

Growing orchids was his only hobby. He had had a greenhouse built and designed a heating system himself. Black iron sheets were arranged over the roof of the house and water trickled down which provided the family with plenty of hot water even in the middle of winter. A pipe led the hot water into the greenhouse and a small gas stove supplemented the heat for the tropical plants.

Now that Haruko was going to join Nozomi in Manchuria, the greenhouse had been dismantled by Takeda-ya, the handyman, and he would take it to Yasuharu's to be reassembled. All the orchids were being kept under cover in Takeda-ya's back yard and would be transported carefully by him on his cart.

He had nearly finished packing and Aki had swept up inside the house. When all the crates were done, he would deliver them himself as Haruko had already instructed. They were to be stored with various relatives.

'Thank you very much, Takeda-ya san. Will you please lock the house after you and give the key back to the owner?'

'Don't worry. Everything will be taken care of.'

'I hope to ask for your help when we come back.'

'I will always be here. Be very careful.'

'I am leaving some clothes and a few things for you in this bundle. Will you take it home?'

'Thank you very much. You have been very kind.'

Haruko was going to Yasuharu's with Aki to stay there for a week before she left for Chenyang. Emi and Mari had been sent ahead to his house. Haruko had to pay visits to say good-bye to relatives and friends. Aki was from Kitani village and was going to work for Yasuharu's household after Haruko had left.

13

The Farewell Party

Haruko went through the big gate of Yasuharu's house followed by Aki. There was not much space between the gate and the entrance but sometimes a black car occupied most of the stone path and a capped chauffeur would be polishing the bonnet with a duster. This performance was for the benefit of distinguished patients whom Yasuharu was receiving at home. By tacit agreement, the family used the back door.

While Yasuharu had been training, Kei used to give her son extra money out of her savings when he returned to Tokyo after his holidays. She had nodded to his thanks and said, 'One day you will live in a house with a big gate, won't you?'

The entrance hall was spacious and his surgery was on the right. Straight ahead a wide staircase of polished wood went up to the guests' rooms. A thick door on the left separated family life from his professional quarters. Beyond this door, there were several rooms, a kitchen, a bathroom, servants' rooms, a narrow steep staircase and more rooms upstairs.

Their *chanoma* was roomy with a large lacquered low table placed in the middle. There were always ten or more beautiful boxes of all shapes and sizes piled high on the sideboard. More boxes were under the table and on the tatami floor. Each contained biscuits, seaweed, tea, rice crackers or *tsukudani* (food boiled down in soy sauce). Most of them were still sealed and wrapped up in gift paper. Patients would bring them as a token of thanks or when they wanted to ask Yasuharu to see them without an appointment. The family called the room 'the general store'. 'I'll take home some tins of biscuits and seaweed,' they would say to Yasuharu's wife, Tatsuko, and she would answer, 'Yes,

yes, take some more. It'll make it easier for us to tidy the room.'

When Haruko arrived for the farewell gathering of the family, Tatsuko was sitting alone in the *chanoma*. She was a large woman. Although Yasuharu was an inch or so taller than her, she looked more imposing than her husband. Haruko and her sisters had whispered 'a flea couple', a common expression for a little man and his big wife.

Tatsuko always wore an expensive kimono and called a taxi even for a distance of five minutes' walk. She loved good food and anyone who visited her around lunch time was treated to dishes supplied from reputed restaurants.

Relatives and friends all benefited from her generosity but had criticised her extravagance behind her back until Kei said, 'Everybody knows Yasuharu san has a lot of wealthy private patients. He is careful with money himself and if his wife was stingy as well, people would say that they were tight-fisted.' She added that a house which had many visitors was a happy and prosperous house and that she had never heard of anyone ruined by mere kimonos and occasional good food.

Haruko sat at the table. Tatsuko looked up at the wall clock and said, 'Emi-chan and Mari-chan went out to the main street with the others. Aren't they lovely! You are lucky to have girls.' She had two sons.

She called for a maid and asked for tea. Her kimono had a pattern of small flowers on reddish brown.

'The colour of your kimono is beautiful. Is it new?'

'This?' Tatsuko drew her chin in and looked down. 'Oh, no. Do you remember that ochre-coloured kimono? I got it redyed, but it came out all right, didn't it?' She stretched her arm out and looked at the sleeve. Then she went on to say that she could not have many new kimonos made as Yasuharu would tell her off. She rolled up her eyes and pursed her lips to imitate her husband's face when he was displeased.

'Do you have to tell him whenever you have a new kimono made?'

'But of course. I can't buy anything without him knowing. But I have an arrangement with Kogiku-ya when I want an expensive kimono.' She mentioned the name of her favourite kimono dealer. 'They send me an invoice with a much lower price and add a little to other orders throughout the year.' Tatsuko touched her neat hairdo. 'One has to use up here, Haruko san.'

She had sent Haruko a roll of brocade as a going away present. It was a generous gift. Haruko wondered if the invoice carried an extra sum to help pay for Tatsuko's other expenses.

Cheerful voices outside the room meant the four generations of women, Kei, Ayako and Sachiko, followed by Emi and Mari, had come back.

'Okahsan! When did you come?' The girls were pleased to see Haruko. They spread out on the tatami toys and books which had been bought for them.

Soon Sachiko's son Sakaé came in with his father, Hitoshi.

'Everything finished all right, nesan? There is always so much to do to shut up a house. You must have worked like a coolie.' Hitoshi sat by Haruko and after formal greetings, spoke comfortingly to her.

'She is all right. She will be able to live like a queen in Manchuria.' Sachiko pouted, 'It's me who forever works like a coolie.'

'I know. I know. You are my queen but you work like a coolie. You are the ideal wife for a man like me.' Hitoshi smiled at Sachiko across the table. Haruko had seen them play at arm-wrestling and, on another occasion, kicking each other's ankles under the table.

'They are married. If Hitoshi san thinks that that's the way to run his home, I suppose it's none of our business.' Ayako had tried to come to terms with this new type of marital relationship.

There were footsteps in the corridor, and Kazuko, Hideto's wife, poked her head in followed by Akira, Takeko's son.

'Hello.' She walked in cheerfully and sat down heavily. 'Shopping is tiring, especially when you don't know what to buy.'

'That must have been difficult.' Hitoshi assumed a sympathetic tone. 'Why go then?'

'Oh, you men! That's a nice tie.' Kazuko looked at Hitoshi. 'Is that Sachiko san's taste? Akira san, you go and ask for a cup of tea for me. You must look after your elders you know, not just the young ones.'

'I am always polite, especially to the old ones,' Akira retorted.

'Well done!' Kei put in, and everybody laughed.

Shuichi's widow Yaéko came in, carrying her small son.

'I am sorry I am late.' She put her hands on the tatami floor in front of her and bowed to her in-laws.

She told Haruko that her mother should have come as well but she had a slight cold and stayed home, although she would be at Tokyo station to stay good-bye when Haruko left.

'Yaéko san, you should not have worried so, but how serious is your mother's cold?'

Yaéko thought that her mother would recover by the next day.

While this conversation was going on, Yaéko's son, Hajimé, was sitting by his mother quietly holding his stuffed toy and looking at everybody with his clear intelligent eyes.

Haruko smiled at him. He was a good boy. He had never been any bother to anyone but everybody wondered how much his calm looks were due to his being deaf.

Yaéko had been defiant and refused to accept proposals of financial assistance suggested by Ayako after Shuichi's death. She was the first among the Miwa and Shirai women to gain a degree from a women's college and also the first to have a job. She left Hajimé in her mother's care every day and worked for a newspaper. In a society where journalists were considered immoral dirt-diggers and gossip-mongers, it was a bold step.

'I saw your sister-in-law the other day having lunch at a sushi bar.' The other women of the family heard their friends talk about Yaéko now and again. 'But I did not say hello to her because she was with someone else.' They all knew the intended implication.

Takeko's daughter, Namiko, and the children wore European clothes, but Yaéko was the only woman who did not wear a kimono. Her white blouse was tired and her black skirt shiny with wear.

'Can't you give her some of your kimonos?' Ayako had asked Haruko once. 'Mine are too sombre-coloured for her age.' To outsiders, the Miwas and the Shirais kept up a common front, but inside the household, Ayako was uncomfortable that her only daughter-in-law looked shabby and stood out among the carefree, gregarious members of the family. Haruko had never dared to suggest that her sister-in-law should wear her kimonos. She remembered that she, too, had thought of getting a job and independence. She admired Yaéko's courage.

By the time Yasuharu came home, the entrance hall was full of footwear.

Everybody made their way to two large rooms which were made into one by opening the partition. Three low tables were set in a line on which three gas burners with thick iron pans had been prepared

129

for cooking sukiyaki. Yasuharu's household was used to catering for such large gatherings of people.

'Okahsan, how are you?' Yasuharu came in to sit next to Kei who had arrived while he was working. 'Did you have a good journey? You look well.'

'I am wonderful as always. Thank you. And you? How is the prince? Has he recovered?' Kei was proud that a brother of the Emperor was one of her son's patients.

'He is fine now. It was nothing serious.'

Another table was set for the young people and the children a little away from the adults. Emi sat Hajimé between herself and Mari on a folded *zabuton*. Altogether there were eight children of the extended family. Hideto's son did a handstand in the narrow space between the wall and the table and Yasuharu's son copied him.

'Obachan!' Tatsuko's niece called. 'It's dangerous.'

'I'll sit with you to protect you.' Namiko, Takeko's seventeen-year-old daughter, came to sit next to Mari.

'Akira san.' Tatsuko spotted Akira sitting several people away and addressed him. 'Come here and supervise the young ones.'

'Me?'

'You're not so much older. Come on.'

For the children, a sukiyaki pan was set on the floor and cooked pieces were put on a dish in the middle of the table. Akira sat by the pan and another maid came to help him.

'Okahsan.' Yasuharu's son called to Tatsuko. 'It's not fair. You have one pan for five people and we are ten.'

'We believe in Spartan upbringing,' Hideto answered before Tatsuko turned to her son. 'Children should not eat too much good food.'

'What's Spartan?'

But Hideto's attention was elsewhere, and the boys started to hit their rice bowls with chopsticks.

'Hey, stop!' Akira told them off.

Large plates piled high with meat, negi, sticks of bean jelly and tofu were carried in and placed on the table. The smell of cooking started to fill the room. The sound of cracking eggs followed. Hot cooked meat and vegetables were picked from the pan and dipped into raw egg to be cooled before they were eaten.

Shige came in with more warmed saké bottles.

'I brought o'Shige san with me because it's a good opportunity for her to see Tokyo. Mata san as well. Last time they were here, they did not have much time to see around. They should see the Imperial Palace this time.' Kei felt the need to tell them about Shige's presence.

'Shige, you look well.' Hideto was pleased to see her.

Haruko was tired after days of packing and preparation. She sat down to enjoy the fast-flowing conversation at the adult table with occasional interruptions from the children. Everybody had something to say.

'It's a pity that Masakazu san and Miki san could not come. He is so busy. They sent regards.' With the family around her, Kei missed those who could not make it. Masakazu had married the daughter of the local headmaster and had two children. The post office where he worked had expanded to cover a wider area and he had been made post master. He also looked after the family land and their tenants. He still rode the same bicycle that Kei had bought for him.

'Otohsan!' One of the boys raised himself on his knees on a *zabuton* and called, 'Can we go home by taxi tonight?'

'Why?'

'Because you always drink too much and sleep on the train. It's embarrassing.'

Everybody laughed.

Tatsuko explained that she had chosen to serve sukiyaki, because the storm the night before made it difficult to get the fish she wanted.

'I thought Chenyang is so far away from the sea and Haruko san may not be able to get good fish. I wanted her to enjoy it before she leaves.'

'There must be river fish.' One of the relatives turned to Haruko.

Takeko wondered if all the rivers in China were muddy.

'Haruko, I told Yohei san to come and meet you at Bofu as your express train does not stop at our station. He'll bring the dried fish Nozomi san loves and some sweet dumplings for the girls in case they are hungry,' Kei said.

'Poor Haruko san,' Kazuko whispered. 'You have to carry fish all the way to Manchuria.'

Haruko leant forward and thanked Kei who was sitting at the top of the table.

'You must be careful with water there,' Kei raised her voice. 'Their water has amoebae in it.'

'Amoebae, okahsan?' Yasuharu turned to her, wide-eyed. 'But the water system there must be more modern than ours.'

'How about giving a lecture tour over there, Hitoshi san?' Hideto poured saké for Hitoshi across the table. Hideto was an army surgeon but the family had never seen him in uniform. That night he was wearing a kimono which had belonged to Tei-ichi.

Yasuharu spoke to Hitoshi about the suppression of books written by Professor Kawai, a professor of economics and a well-known liberalist. Having criticised militarism, Professor Kawai's books had been taken out of circulation by the government.

'The war in China seems to be going extremely well.' One of Kazuko's brothers was heard talking before Hitoshi responded. 'But I have read that the Chinese leader Chiang Kai-shek refused to accept the terms offered by Japan.' He turned to Hideto and asked whether he thought there was a possibility of war between Japan and America. America and Great Britain, he said, were squeezing Japan out of South-East Asia.

'I have no idea.' Hideto shook his head. 'I deal with only physical illness and injuries.' His eyelids were pink. He poured more saké into his cup and Hitoshi's. Hitoshi drained his immediately.

'Don't men love talking about wars,' Kazuko interrupted. 'There would be no war without men.'

'Hitoshi san,' Takeko flapped her hand at her brother-in-law to draw his attention. 'What's all this talk about socialism? If there were no rich people to start business, the working-class people would not have jobs, would they? Why are they making trouble and disturbing the peace? Why are the rights of the proletariat different from anybody else's?'

Haruko saw Yaéko's lips were drawn into a smile.

Hitoshi flashed a charming grin. 'Well, it's just a point of view, nesan.'

Takeko complained to Ayako. 'Okahsan, Noriyasu said he couldn't come to Tokyo this time because he was too busy. He said, "Us working-class people have to unite. We always have to work hard." He keeps on saying that he is a member of the working class. It's annoying.'

'He is just teasing you. You know he is, nesan, because he knows that it annoys you.' Haruko could imagine her brother-in-law talking to Takeko in a serious voice. Takeko should have noticed his eyes twinkling.

'But he is right, Takeko nesan.' Hitoshi laughed. 'I am a member of the working class, too. We are not capitalists. We are honest, hard-working people.'

'In any case, we don't want to hear such dangerous words.' Tatsuko finished the exchange.

'Haruko.' Yasuharu stretched his neck and called: 'Did you notice something inside the gate when you came in?'

Haruko had noticed a piece of stone set on the path which was carved in the shape of a stylised carnation although it was inconspicuous.

'The piece of stone like a flower?'

'Um. I thought you'd notice. The idea is not mine. I saw it a temple. You come through the gate, and you find a flower.'

The next morning, Haruko was woken by her daughters' chattering voices. They had slept in the same room. The two girls were sitting on their futons and playing with stuffed white monkeys that Yaéko had given them the day before.

'Okusama!' Mari imitated the surprised voice of a woman. 'I didn't expect to see you. Where are you going? Shopping?'

'I am going to Mitsukoshi Department Store to buy a present for Mrs Matsumo. Do you know she has to leave a little earlier because she is leaving from Kobe rather than Yokohama? So we are having a lunch party for her today to say good-bye.' Emi finished the long conversation and giggled.

Mari took over in a serious tone.

'Oh, I didn't know. By the way, okusama, have you heard about Mrs Tamaki's daughter's wedding?'

'I hear that she married the son of a noble man.'

'Okusama.' Mari lowered her voice to a whisper. 'You know, her trousseau is magnificent. She will take a hundred obis. I hear that her kimonos have taken two years to prepare.'

Haruko was amazed how well they were imitating some of her friends. They had wrapped up the white monkeys with their own clothes and made them bow and put their heads together as they talked. The monkeys had wise expressions.

Haruko had been given many farewell presents. She had gone to the Mitsukoshi Department Store and chosen lacquered dishes as 'return gifts'. She had selected them carefully so that they were not too expensive nor cheap. After she left for Manchuria, the store would deliver them according to her instructions. It was a convention in the orderly society in which she lived, but, having heard her daughters, she felt as though she was part of a satirical play.

It was comfortable at home and she would miss it, but she was looking forward to a new life. Since she had not had the opportunity to study, she reflected, she could at least find out more about the world for herself. She felt excited.

14

The City of Acacia

The day they arrived in Chenyang was sunny but the wind was cold as they stood at the station after the long train journey to Kyushu from Tokyo, then the overnight ferry to Korea and another long train journey.

'In Tokyo, the cherry blossoms were just about to open,' Haruko said, holding her stole closely around her and giving an anxious glance towards her daughters who were neat in their blue double-breasted coats.

'You arrived at a good time. From now on, everything starts blossoming all at once. Prunus varieties here are much darker pink than Japanese cherry blossom. They open in late April.'

Nozomi helped the children up on to a horse-drawn carriage. It was driven by a white-bearded old Russian with a noble face, a refugee from the revolution.

Before the revolution, he must have been driven in a carriage himself, Haruko thought fleetingly, but his expression was serene. A little bucket hung behind the horse to collect droppings. The streets were paved but muddy, and the carriage had strings of large bells.

'It is beginning to thaw everywhere. You are a bit late for skating this year.'

'Oh! Can we skate?'

'Of course you can next winter. We have to buy you skating boots. During the winter, schoolchildren do nothing but skating for exercise.'

The large house that Nozomi had rented was managed by a Japanese couple. Haruko thought that they might not be married, although the woman was called Mrs Ono. They lived in a small apartment near the kitchen. Whenever she was called, even in the morning, Mrs Ono would come out red in the face and smelling strongly of alcohol.

'Where did you find them?' Haruko asked Nozomi.

'They were in this house when I took it. They worked for a German company which had the house before me and I have not had time to find a new housekeeper.'

The massive, red-brick house was built at the turn of the century for a Russian general and his family. The walls were thick, the doors were tall and heavy, the banisters were chunky, the rooms were large. Everything was the opposite of what they were used to in Tokyo.

Haruko thought that people who lived in such a house ought to drink quantities of vodka over a zakuska table. They should talk in a language with sonorous sounds like the man who had read Pushkin poems in a film she had seen.

'Come and see the bathroom.' Mari came running. 'It is like a swimming pool.'

It was a large room surrounded by white tiles. Complicated and over-sized golden taps, pipes and showers were set along a wall. The bath tub in the middle of the room was also big.

'The one upstairs is even bigger,' Nozomi laughed. 'It's like a bathroom for bears.'

Haruko pictured out of a hazy memory the Russian doctor whom she had met with her father. No wonder I was scared, she thought. He must have been really big.

'I need both hands to turn this tap.' Emi tried and still failed. That first night, Nozomi had to be called to turn the tap on while his wife and two daughters stood and watched, holding towels around themselves.

He put his foot on the rim of the far side of the tub and turned the tap with an exaggerated shout. Hot water gushed out, gurgled and swirled into the tub. Everything steamed up instantly. Mari shrieked with delight. The tub was large enough for the three of them to get in together.

'It is like living in an auditorium,' Haruko remarked, looking up at the ceiling of the living room which was far away.

'There are not many houses to let,' Nozomi said, as though to excuse himself. 'The more suitable houses have been built by people who have decided to settle here and are living in them themselves, or have been allocated to big organisations like banks, universities, the consulate . . .'

'Oh, I love this house. It's such fun.' Mari came in giggling, having looked into a linen cupboard, which was the size of a large room. 'But,' she looked at everybody, 'can I wake you up when I want to go to the toilet?'

'Mm. But you will be all right. The ghosts will get lost, too, in this house.'

'But there might be lots of them,' Emi joined in. 'Big ones.'

As both Mr and Mrs Ono were neither willing nor experienced workers, and Haruko felt uncomfortable about their heavy drinking, they were tactfully dismissed. To replace them, a Chinese cook was employed. He was called a cook but he did almost everything but cooking. Haruko did not need a cook, besides there were few Japanese in Chenyang who were looking for domestic employment. To help the cook, a young girl called Shun-ren was hired. The cook's name was Mah, and the family called him Mah san. Shun-ren, which meant spring lotus, became Ren-chan and was delighted with her new Japanese name. Both of them spoke broken Japanese.

Mah was a tall, well-built man and lived in a small house in the back yard. Mari often visited him. The house was built of bricks and a part of it was earth-floored. The other part was raised quite high and hot water pipes underneath made the room very warm in winter. Mah's bedding was rolled up to a wall and his clothes and few possessions were neatly kept in a corner. He went home to his family every weekend.

Shun-ren slept in a room inside the house. She had an unframed mirror and a box full of cosmetics.

Both Mah and Shun-ren had been introduced to the family by the owner of a shop called Ten-sei-sho. Mah was the owner's cousin. The owner was a fat man with a sleepy expression and seldom appeared in front of customers. His tall nephew managed the shop, made visits for orders and for monthly accounts. Wearing a long Chinese robe, which made him look even taller, the young man was cool and handsome.

'Madam, Ten-sei-sho san here.' Shun-ren flapped around breathless. She had unbound large feet. She wore rouge like a pair of red patches on her thickly-painted white cheeks. On days when Ten-sei-sho was due to come, the rouge was even darker and the smell of hair oil was overpowering.

She would noisily announce his arrival and rush back to him at the back entrance to chatter. The nephew would receive her offer of a chair and listen to her gossip without taking much notice. Sometimes his left cheek twitched slightly in a sarcastic smile.

Ten-sei-sho provided the household with sundries as well as most basic food. While Haruko was making orders, Shun-ren hovered around to exclaim eagerly, 'Madam, we want oil', 'Soap', 'Scrubbing brush not good', 'Sugar too little', and once in a while was told to be quiet and get on with her work.

Haruko admitted that he was good-looking. He had a haughty expression which made him look intellectual, but that impression lasted only until he turned his head sideways, pinched his nose and with a loud noise cleared his nose to the ground. His breath also smelt strongly of garlic and Haruko felt obliged to open a window after he left.

Mah did not approve of Haruko or her daughters picking up Chinese words from local people, although they hardly had contact with them anyway.

'Manchuria Chinese not good,' he told them. 'Pekingese Chinese, good.'

'I try to learn Chinese but he corrects my pronunciation so much that it gets nowhere,' Haruko complained, but, in spite of mild difficulties, Mah and Shun-ren became part of the household. She trusted them and went out without the bother of locking everything away as a lot of her friends said they had to.

Haruko and her daughters spent two summer holidays at a hotel at Golden Hill in Port Arthur. Nozomi joined them whenever he could. The hotel had green hills behind and from the verandah, they could see the sea. Waiters in white jackets brought tea in the afternoon. They each had a lily-of-the-valley-shaped lamp on a little desk, and at night a billowing white mosquito net was spread like a canopy over their beds.

They made frequent day-trips to the nearby town of Dalian. Dalian was romantically called the City of Acacia, although Nozomi said the trees in the boulevards were really Robinia Pseudoacacia. The season was late for Haruko and her daughters to enjoy the white flowers, but the light green leaves gave the streets a cool shade. The sun in Dalian was brighter than in their northern city and there was the clean, fresh atmosphere of a harbour town.

'I love Dalian because there is a lot of air and I can breathe as much as I like,' Mari said, and Nozomi reflected to Haruko, 'Children are so uninhibited in expressing themselves.'

The shops in Dalian sold chic imported goods from Europe brought through China. Haruko bought the children's shoes and dress material, French cosmetics, perfume and always three purple glass jars of Coty face cream.

'You will give me the jar when you finish with the cream, won't you?' Mari asked. The jars had glass lids and Mari's was soon broken. Emi handled hers more carefully, keeping trinkets inside. Mari lost her 'jewellery' easily but did not seem to care much.

The first summer in Port Arthur, Haruko bought a crocodile handbag which was in fashion. She took a long time to choose and eventually decided on a plain one without adornment. She looked at the other bags of beige-coloured knobbled skin from the crocodile back.

'Those are too showy, and a little vulgar.' Haruko ruminated upon her decision.

'I am glad you chose this one,' Emi whispered into her ear. 'The larger and more expensive ones are grotesque and hideous, okahsan.'

'I need a pencil case,' Mari said. 'May I have one?'

'Of course.'

Her celluloid case had split but she had stuck it together with a piece of adhesive tape and waited till she came to Dalian. They could get these things easily in Chenyang but they appreciated different markings and patterns. The pencils they bought in Dalian were stamped with gold 'English' letters.

After shopping, the three of them carried several boxes each and took a horse-drawn carriage to a restaurant at a seaside hotel. Emi had fair skin but dark hair. Mari was dark and her hair had a brown tinge. She had long limbs and Haruko suddenly saw the tall and agile Shobei out of memories from long ago as Mari climbed up into the carriage after her.

Later, when Nozomi was shown the handbag, he laughed. 'I am glad I don't have to come any closer to the back of a crocodile. If this one was less expensive, so much the better.'

The second summer the waiters whom they had known had been replaced by waitresses and there were fewer of them. The young men had gone to war.

In 1941, nine months after Haruko arrived in Manchuria, the Japanese attacked the American naval base on Hawaii. To the Japanese, 'Pearl Harbor', the virtual elimination of the American navy, was a magnificent victory. To the Americans, the death of two thousand three hundred men killed at dawn as they slept was an atrocity which would finally bring them into the Second World War.

An incident happened when Nozomi took the family for dinner at a restaurant in Port Arthur on that second holiday. The sea was dark, only dotted with the shimmering lights of fishing boats far away. Emi and Mari looked out, pushing their foreheads against the cold window glass, but the dining room was lit up by glittering chandeliers and the white tablecloths were luminous.

'Those confounded fools talk about winning the war against the United States and United Kingdom.' A loud voice came from the next table where the dinner was well advanced. The person speaking was a famous industrialist and the founder of a consortium in Japan, Nozomi observed. He was expanding business in Manchuria as well. Ripples of attention spread out to the tables around him, and gradually the jangling of knives and forks subsided. Astonished or curious faces surreptitiously turned to the table from which more strong words were coming. 'Ridiculous! Fight against them with what?'

'Otohsama, please.' A slender young lady in a cream-coloured dress was putting her hand over his arm. He patted her hand and continued. 'The Greater East Asia Co-Prosperity Sphere! If you ask me, it's the Greater East Asia Co-Poverty Sphere.' The other four men around the same table laughed noisily in an effort to smother the embarrassing argument. The industrialist raised his voice.

'America is far more advanced in science and technology. Who can deny that? We don't have natural resources. They have them in abundance. They have a larger army, fleet ... I know what you innocent lot are thinking. How about Pearl Harbor? How about the sinking of the two British ships, the *Prince of Wales* and the *Repulse*? Manila. Singapore. Rangoon. Mandalay. We are fighting splendidly and winning, you are thinking. Of course you'll win, attacking someone who is asleep.'

'The enemy don't have the samurai spirit of our soldiers, sir,' a man said.

'Come, come. You need areoplanes and submarines and modern tactics to fight in the twentieth century.'

He held up his hand and silenced one of the men who was about to protest.

'We have gone as far as we can. We have been running wild for six months since Pearl Harbor while the Allies were recovering. Now is the time to lay down our arms and think about how to compromise and make peace. Trouble is, no one dares to speak up.'

Haruko could see the daughter, the only woman of the group, between two backs in dark suits. Frills of gossamer encircled her slender neck. She now said to her father, 'Let's go,' and pushed her chair back to stand up. The diners at other tables had resumed their conversations and the industrialist left the room surrounded by his four co-diners and his daughter.

'He said we would lose,' Mari whispered. 'Is he a spy?'

'Mari-chan, he had a little too much wine and was saying things he did not mean to say,' Nozomi said, leaning towards her. But he was shaken by the speech of the industrialist. Since Pearl Harbor, the Japanese army had rampaged southwards. He had heard talk of the miraculous recovery of the American navy. It was obvious to any expatriate that supply lines and communications with Japan could easily be severed.

'I wonder if that man will be safe,' Emi muttered later that night. Haruko was surprised at the mixed fear and concern in her tone.

'What do you mean by "safe", Emi-chan?'

'Okahsan, do you think he will be shot dead?'

'Shot! Why?'

'People who talk about losing the war are traitors and if the police know about them, they are taken to prison and shot.'

'Emi-chan, he won't be shot. He is a famous man and I saw an article about him in the newspapers the other day. Remember, he had a lot of wine today, and nobody would report him.'

'I hope not,' Emi said. 'I don't want his lovely daughter to lose her father.'

At the end of each school year, Nozomi invited his daughters' teachers to a restaurant to thank them, just as years ago Shobei had asked his grandchildren's teachers for a dinner party at his home. When Nozomi learned that both Emi's teacher and Mari's teacher were thinking of going to Port Arthur during the summer, he invited them to the hotel at Golden Hill.

Emi and Mari's teachers were both cultured and well-mannered men. The education of Japanese children was subsidised by the Japanese-owned Southern Manchurian Railway Company. Teachers who were sent to Manchuria were carefully chosen among the graduates from teaching colleges.

When the teachers arrived at the hotel, a boisterous music teacher came with them. He wore a pair of gold-rimmed spectacles and a colourful striped jacket. He did not hesitate to open the cover of the grand piano and he played with panache. He was vivacious and enjoying the plentiful house wine. Haruko felt a little ill at ease but Nozomi looked relaxed. There were few other children at the hotel and the girls were delighted by the lively visitor. The next day Haruko went out to watch the others enjoying tennis, ping pong, swimming and cycling, but the music teacher did not appear.

Nozomi showed off by jumping over a mound on a bicycle.

'Goodness, Sanjo san!'

'Otohsan!'

'I am an expert cyclist, as I was going to work at a noodle shop as a delivery boy.' He circled around pulling up the front wheel. Emi and Mari looked at each other.

'Otohsan, what a story!' Haruko never got used to Nozomi's claims to unlikely professions.

'Where is Ryo sensei?' the girls wondered sometimes. The music teacher regularly appeared at meal times but disappeared again the next day.

On the third day after the teachers arrived, Nozomi and Haruko were having coffee in the airy and light lounge. The ceiling fan was sending a gentle breeze and plants around the room sparkled from their morning wash.

Haruko was wearing a kimono of dark blue silk gauze and a white obi which had dragonflies on faint green leaves painted in watercolour. She wore a jade ornament on her obi. The effect was cool and sophisticated. She felt people's eyes on her and noticed that the industrialist whom they had seen at the restaurant in Dalian was sitting at the far side of the lounge with his wife and daughter. The wife was looking at her. Haruko was relaxed.

The two teachers joined Nozomi and Haruko. As soon as they had said, 'Good morning,' one of them began, 'We have to talk to you. We found out where Ryo san has been every day.'

Haruko noticed his grave tone.

'He was visiting Mizuki san's chalet every day.' Mizuki was the industrialist's name.

'But why?' Why should Ryo sensei want to visit the Mizukis and why should the two teachers look so serious, Haruko wondered.

'You know Mizuki san has a daughter.'

'Yes, she is there. She is very pretty.' Haruko lowered her voice although they were far away on the other side of the spacious room.

'That's the trouble. Ryo san fell in love with her. He has asked her to marry him.'

Haruko opened her eyes wide. 'Asked her to marry him? When? He hardly knows her.'

Mari's teacher continued. 'Falling in love with her is only part of the problem. He called on them and introduced himself as your nephew.'

'My nephew?' Nozomi started to laugh. 'Well, well.'

'Oh, dear.' Haruko was trapped in a whirl of embarrassment. She had thought that Mrs Mizuki was looking at her appraisingly! She must have been wondering who were these impertinent people with an ill-mannered relative.

Haruko found her handkerchief in her sleeve and held it in her hand.

'Oh, well.' Nozomi called a waiter and asked him to order a taxi in ten minutes.

'You know about these things better than I,' he said to Haruko, 'Talk it over with sensei and sort it out. I will see you perhaps next Friday if I can get away.'

'The best thing is, Mrs Sanjo,' Emi's teacher said, 'that we leave here today and persuade Ryo san to come with us. We are really sorry. We were having a lovely time.'

'I thought the teachers were going to stay for a week,' Emi said to Haruko later. 'Why did they go today?'

'They remembered something they had to do.'

'Why did they suddenly remember something to do in the middle of a holiday? Didn't they get ready before they came?' Mari asked.

'Mari-chan, don't be so insistent. It's a bad habit.'

Haruko knew that neither of them was satisfied by her explanation and that they were busily working out what had happened.

'Okahsan, may I leave the rest of the ice cream?' Mari brought Haruko's attention back.

'Yes, you may. Wipe your mouth with the napkin. Shall we go?'

The next week, they took a train back to Chenyang. In the evening, the blood-red sun gradually became larger as it moved down towards the horizon and flooded their carriage with a flaming glow. Eventually it sank far away beyond the miles and miles of golden kaolian fields.

Years later, when Haruko thought back on this holiday, she was incredulous that the incident with the music teacher had upset her more than the news of war.

15

Gathering Clouds

The gentle pattern of life had to be broken as war began to encroach upon their lives. The hotel where they had stayed was requisitioned by the army. They missed the detached villa belonging to the hotel in which they had spent two summers. They could no longer buy luxurious things and freely eat cakes and ice cream. Nozomi brought back two pairs of shoes from Japan for his children. They were made of shark skin. He also brought back spoons made of bamboo and ceramic cooking pots to show Haruko.

'A lot of things are either in short supply or not obtainable at all. The few things one can buy are mostly substitutes.'

The streets in Chenyang, like those everywhere else, were full of slogans. They proclaimed from the walls:

LUXURY MEANS LOSING TO THE ENEMY.
WE WANT NOTHING TILL WE WIN.

At the corners of the busy streets, women stood wearing sashes on which was written, 'Patriotic Women's Association of Great Japan'. They handed out leaflets which said, 'We are at war. Cut your wide sleeves off immediately.' Haruko walked past, growing pensive. What were they suggesting should be done with the pieces of material? On the other hand, she could not wear a kimono for the air-raid training practice with the neighbourhood group.

Instead of cutting the material off the sleeves of her kimonos, she went to Kikuya, the biggest material shop in the town. Its window no longer exhibited streams of colourful material. Now mannequins stood in 'National Emergency Clothes'. One was dressed in a rough shirt and a wrap-around skirt in sombre khaki. Another mannequin was in *mompe* (wide trousers) and the same rough shirt. Haruko started to select less drab material to make a 'Patriotic Women's Uniform'. She was not going to make trousers and skirts out of her favourite kimonos as many of her friends had done. Emergency clothes were based on the design of peasants' working clothes. Haruko thought they looked ugly in town. She wondered what Kei and Ayako were making of the situation. At seventy-nine, Kei was still in good health.

Good kimonos and obis were chosen to last for many years and were looked after with care. Some were bought as white material, then dyed and patterned to individual taste. Each kimono held many happy memories. When the colours and patterns were no longer suitable, they were still used and loved as cushions, futon covers, little bags and underclothes. The material could be bleached and dyed again. Haruko thought it sacrilege to turn kimonos into ugly working clothes.

'Mrs Sanjo.' The owner's wife came out, having been informed by one of the employees that Haruko was there. 'Please come in for tea.' She had been a good customer.

Haruko was taken into the private rooms at the back of the shop. There was a small but elaborate garden with a little pond. A shapely tree was leaning over the water. A stone lantern was placed by a miniature hill. The shopkeeper's family were living graciously and quietly behind the buzz of the street and their trade.

A law had been issued to prohibit the production of luxury items, which included good quality kimonos. The wife brought out a few obi and kimono materials.

'We cannot sell them openly in the shop any more and will not get new supplies for some time,' she said. 'These are the last special ones we have. I thought with two daughters, you might like to have a look.'

With Nozomi's financial status, there should be no worry about getting the substantial trousseau that Haruko wanted for her daughters. But the war might create difficulties.

Haruko looked at the kimonos which were loosely stitched together into shape. The patterns had been dyed, embroidered and painted. There was one with a design of white peonies with gold centres on a salmon pink background and another with red camellias on gold and pale blue background. Having chosen two more kimonos, suitable obis and ample lengths of dark blue velvet for evening dresses, Haruko left the shop.

Haruko had no intention of marrying her daughters young before they completed their education. Both were bright girls. They could take a profession if they chose. Marriage preparations had seemed far away in the future until Kikuya's wife had reminded her.

Her hopes for her daughters were confused. She wanted them to fulfil her own ambition of becoming well educated and independent. Yet she wanted them each to be married, beautifully dressed as the daughter of a successful man. Each should be married with a suitable trousseau to a man whom Nozomi and Haruko found for them, or at least approved of.

Whatever future they chose, she would like her daughters to appreciate the beauty of kimonos and understand the enjoyment of wearing them. However, she had a foreboding that their future lay in a different kind of world.

Since she felt powerless, Haruko tried to stop herself worrying about the gloomy news of the war, but when she thought about her daughters, she found it hard not to feel depressed.

The situation in Japan had become worse, Nozomi told Haruko when he came back from a business trip in the summer of 1944. It would be his last trip for a while as crossing the channel between Korea and Japan became increasingly dangerous with air-raids and possible attacks by submarines. The passenger ferries no longer operated regularly. Many families who had sent their children to Japan to be educated were bringing them back.

Although Nozomi did not tell Haruko in detail, Japan was faring badly in the South Pacific. Imperial Headquarters announced 'a tactical withdrawal' from Guadalcanal, but most people were beginning to realise that this meant nothing less than retreat. The entire garrison of Attu Island had perished 'for the sake of upholding the honour of the Emperor'. Takeko's oldest son, Akira, who was a naval purser told Nozomi.

'Ojisan, we haven't a single aircraft carrier left now. It is an open secret among us.'

'You think there'll be a final battle on the mainland?'

'Yes. The navy doesn't want it, but the army is insistent. In any case, I can't think the war will last long.'

The outcome of the war grew increasingly bleak, but at the same time Japan was holding out with surprising tenacity.

'My teacher said, "When you have a sword fight, you have to draw the sword to you first and then strike away." That is what we are doing now,' Emi said, 'Otohsan, is that true?'

'What?' Nozomi looked up from the newspaper which had diminished to a few pages.

'In kendo, yes, that's what one does.'

'Is that what we are going to do really?'

'Mm.'

Listening to European music was considered unpatriotic. The radios played a lot of minor-key music using Japanese traditional instruments. There were frequent extra news bulletins cutting in on other programmes. These always started with stirring patriotic music and the announcer's excited voice: 'An announcement from Imperial Headquarters. Early this morning, the Japanese Imperial Navy was engaged in a sea battle with the navy of the United States and . . .' A glance at the map told the listeners that the battles were fought closer and closer to the Japanese mainland. The losses suffered by the enemy became less and less compared with the losses on the Japanese side. The garrisons were annihilated one after another. Guam, Saipan, Marianas . . . and bombs began to fall on Tokyo.

Chaos invaded life in many other ways. Nozomi was worried about the way the children were educated. There must have been other parents who shared his view, but they were helpless. Nozomi had to sit back and watch as his children's creativity was nipped in the bud by zealous teachers. Everything they wrote or painted had to be related to the war, gallant soldiers and the wicked enemy.

As a summer holiday project, Emi had studied clouds. She had painted every day in water-colour, cirrocumulus, cumulonimbus, sunset, sunrise and many more clouds and skies. Under them she wrote as much information as she could find about the clouds and weather. It was a beautiful collection of paintings as well as an interesting study.

'It is well done!' One night Nozomi commented on the work. 'She must have taken after you. She paints beautifully,' he said to Haruko.

'Me?'

'You used to do water-colours, didn't you?'

'Oh, a long time ago.'

The project was presented to Emi's teacher. It was returned with one comment: 'The study of clouds does not help our country defeat the enemy.'

'The teacher did not like it,' Emi said. 'I have never had such a bad mark in any subject.'

It was not just the education of the future generation that was under threat, Nozomi said to Haruko, but the whole nation was being brainwashed and persuaded to believe in a myth. Haruko, who had been brought up in a prosperous upper-class country family, had not experienced the life of the average person, but Nozomi, as a peasant's son, had been one of the ordinary millions at the turn of the century. He had never worn shoes as a child. In winter, he had had home-made straw footwear. His meals had been rice, millet, wheat and hardly anything else. While most of the nation had lived like him, and without any industry to speak of, the country had spent nearly half of its national budget on military expenses. Within ten years, it had created a navy which was one of the five strongest in the world.

That had been the Japanese navy which defeated the Russians, the mightiest nation in the world, Nozomi reflected. The previous generation had not relied on miracles to win. Under the present government, people were forced to believe that the Emperor was God. It was said that the country of God would be always protected at times of national crisis. In the thirteenth century, the Mongols had invaded Japan. During the night there was a typhoon and the entire Mongolian fleet had either sunk or dispersed. In the middle of the twentieth century, the military government revived the incident in peoples' minds and claimed that the typhoon was divine intervention.

'In the thirteenth century, meteorology did not exist. In any case, the Mongols did not know that in Japan we have typhoons almost every year in September.' Nozomi pushed a cup towards Haruko for more tea.

She poured tea for him and protested, 'But it is important that they did come in September.'

'That was their stupidity and bad luck. There is nothing divine about autumn typhoons in Japan.'

'Don't talk like that in front of Emi and Mari.'

'No.' Nozomi drank tea. 'But I don't like the children to be taught nonsense all the time.'

*　　　*　　　*

Soon Nozomi and Haruko did not have to worry about how their children were taught. The classrooms were turned into factories and there were no lessons. In the morning, children of the neighbourhood gathered together at street corners to go to school to work. Confucius said that after seven years of age, boys and girls should not be together, so the boys and girls gathered at different corners.

The walk to school was part of a military-style training. Like all the others, Emi and Mari wore trousers gathered at the ankle and took a padded anti-air-raid hood. Instead of books and pens, they carried a regulation bundle of hard biscuits and water and a minimum emergency kit in their khaki canvas shoulder bags.

'Attention!' the senior girl shouted in a high-pitched voice as loud as she could. 'March!'

At school, she would be reprimanded if she did not scream.

'Give a command from your belly,' the instructor shouted. 'Walk like soldiers. Is it a funeral march?' he yelled. The drill was torture. 'You, in the second line. What is your name?'

Once he grabbed Emi by the shoulder and dragged her out of the march.

Mari had told Haruko that Emi had been humiliated in front of the whole school, yet neither Emi herself nor Mari could understand what she had done wrong.

'O'nesan is too ashamed to tell you, okahsan,' Mari said.

'What do you think was wrong with her walk?'

'I don't know. We were practising for our sports day march. O'nesan's class was coming to the rostrum where the big people are supposed to stand and receive our salute or something. A senior girl yelled "March in step", and they started marching.'

'Didn't she do that?'

'Of course she did.'

When Haruko told this to Nozomi, he folded his arms and did not say anything. Both of them had seen Emi walking with other children. Both of them realised that Emi stood out as a pretty girl. Nozomi shook his head involuntarily.

'Did she not tell you about this?'

'No. Nothing.'

'And you didn't ask her about it?'

'No.'

'If this kind of thing happens again, I'll talk to the headmaster.'

Now, without the instructor's eyes on them, all the girls looked a little more relaxed. Having said good-bye to her daughters at the gate, Haruko stood and watched the two retreating lines of shapeless grey. When a dozen or so young girls gathered together, there should be an irresistible gaiety, Haruko thought. If Haruko and her two sisters had been together in public when they were that age, her grandfather would have cast a glance of restraint towards them now and again. Almost anything had been funny to them and a dam of mirth could have burst with the slightest provocation. There was none of this youthful energy among this group. They looked as though they were being led to a sad fate. They were afraid. Emi must be terrified in case the instructor should single her out again.

Walking back to the front door, Haruko thought of Mari as well. She had been made to stand at the back of her class room holding up her lunch box in both hands. It was a shocking experience for her.

Haruko always put a sour pickled plum with the cooked rice in the lunch box. It was to prevent the rice going bad in the sealed container.

'I left the plum as I did not want to eat it. There were a few grains of rice stuck to it,' Mari explained. That day the teacher inspected everybody's lunch box and anyone who had left even one grain of rice was punished. He had said in a harsh voice, 'We are given precious rice which our hard-working farmers have grown with their sweat and blood. To waste it is traitorous conduct. Why did you leave rice?'

'I didn't know what to say.' Mari appealed to Haruko. 'So I answered, "The plum was sour, and I left the rice with it." He said, "Don't make excuses. Have you forgotten that we are fighting a war?"'

'I won't put plum pickles in your lunch box any more.' What else could Haruko say?

'Did you, by the way, give me only cooked string beans and rice for my lunch?'

'No, Mari-chan. There were pieces of chicken, carrots and mushroom as well.'

'I thought it was funny. I forgot to tell you. The other day, there were holes in my rice. I think you must have put in a boiled egg cut into half and buried in the bed of rice. Okahsan, someone is pinching my lunch.'

'We'd better tell your teacher.'

'Oh, no, please, okahsan. I don't know what he will say. He might say my lunch is too luxurious and we are not considering the soldiers fighting without food, or something.'

'He is mad,' Emi said about Mari's teacher. 'I don't think the other teachers support him, but he is the deputy head, and they cannot say much. Anyway, we have hardly any teachers left.'

That was so. All the male teachers up to the age of forty had been drafted.

'Okahsan, you know Miss Suzuki?'

'Oh, yes, the very beautiful teacher.'

'We know she was crying because Mari's teacher had said something about her hair style.'

'Her hair style?'

'My friend Setsuko heard him telling off Miss Suzuki because her hair style was not suitable for the war effort. Her hair was curled like a European film star.'

At school every morning, the children lined up in the playground for roll call. The flag was raised and the Imperial Declaration of War was read aloud by the headmaster. A copy of the Declaration was mounted on silk, rolled and kept under a piece of purple cloth with white lining. The headmaster bowed deeply before he took off the cover, reverently handling the scroll with white gloved hands. Having been taught the meaning of the contents, the pupils knew what was being read, but the imperial language was peculiar and most words were of the kind only used by the Emperor himself.

The Emperor called himself by a word derived from one used by an ancient Chinese emperor in the third century B.C. It sounded similar to a word for dogs standing on their hind legs to beg. All the children sensed the funny side but even the wildest boy did not dare make jokes about it.

After the ceremony, the children were marched off to their class rooms to the sound of patriotic music. Emi spent her days on an assembly line, sitting at her desk sewing buttons on military clothes. Mari was counting and putting hard biscuits into bags to be sent to the front. They were taken outside occasionally for military drill.

Housewives had to attend anti-air-raid training. Sergeant Tanaka, the head of the neighbourhood group, would go round with a megaphone, 'Air-raid alarm! Air-raid alarm! There is a formation of bombers heading towards Chenyang.'

All the housewives were supposed to rush out with buckets and mops.

'Your man said just now that enemy planes were coming. Why are you going out?' Nozomi was amused when he happened to be at home. 'You should stay home under cover if there is an air-raid.'

'We have to put out fires, attend to the wounded . . .'

'You will be injured yourself even before the fire starts. And these houses won't catch fire easily as they are made of brick.'

'Oh, do be quiet! I must go!'

She put on Emi's old gym shoes and ran out.

Sergeant Tanaka was anxious to be recognised as a good drill master in the hope of being commended by the government. Now and again, officers came round to carry out inspections.

Haruko knew that Sergeant Tanaka bore a grudge against her and two other women in the group, Mrs Suzuki and Mrs Matsuda. The three of them were educated and middle class and were not in awe of his authority. He sensed a suppressed attitude of derision.

Mrs Suzuki's husband was the president of a bank. She was a tall and graceful lady of about fifty whom Haruko had hardly seen before. She lived opposite the Sanjos in a house which was quiet behind a large iron gate and many mature trees.

There had been a Japanese maid who picked up newspapers from the letter box and opened the gate every morning. Employing a maid from Japan rather than hiring a local girl meant a step up the social ladder. But after the registration of Japanese household members, all the unmarried girls had to work in factories. Perhaps the Suzukis had sent her back to Japan. The plump young girl with quick steps no longer came out to the paved path, and Haruko missed the accustomed scene from the window while she was combing her hair. Now it was Mr Suzuki who opened the gate and walked out as he went to work.

For the first air-raid training session, Mrs Suzuki came out wearing an old checked coat and a pair of baggy knickerbockers. They were obviously her husband's and very likely made in England for playing golf. Nozomi had a similar pair kept somewhere at the bottom of a trunk left in Japan.

There was a chilly wind. Although Mrs Suzuki looked comical, the woollen jacket and tweed knickerbockers were more sensible than the cotton 'national uniform for women'. She greeted everyone and stood next to Haruko. She smiled self-consciously.

'I know I look like an English beggar.'

Sergeant Tanaka cast a glance at her and it was obvious that he did not approve of the outfit.

Haruko remembered what Nozomi had told her once: 'In London, beggars draw pictures of rural scenes and churches with chalk on the pavement and write "Thank you" above them. Then they quietly sit and wait. Unlike our chaps, they don't noisily demand pity and money. I suppose in the country of gentlemen, even beggars behave politely.'

'Attention!' Sergeant Tanaka shouted.

About thirty women of various ages straightened up, each with a bucket dangling from one hand and holding a mop in the other.

'We are not here to play a game,' Sergeant Tanaka began his lecture. 'Our sacred country is fighting a war to set the world right. Although you are not soldiers' – he made it sound as though anybody who was not a soldier was a second-rate citizen – 'the Emperor with his generosity deigns to call us all his children. We must live up to his graciousness. Now.' He raised his voice even higher and surveyed the lined-up women from one side to the other, 'I see some of you wearing the leisure clothes of the enemy. You are, all of you, requested to wear the national uniform for women as the government has told you. One of the important things for soldiers is to look neat.' Haruko thought: You just said we are not soldiers. Sergeant Tanaka continued. 'You have to wear the khaki national uniform.'

Haruko was wearing a rough shirt and *mompe*, loose trousers, made of black wool. Red yarn was woven into the cloth. Mrs Matsuda wore an old jumper of her husband's.

'Sorry, I did not know we had to wear a uniform. I did not know we had a uniform, come to think of it,' Mrs Matsuda said boldly. She was right. On the circular about the training, there was no mention of having to wear a khaki national uniform for women. It was not a uniform in the strict sense.

The sergeant's face became red.

'We are at war, Mrs Matsuda.' He breathed hard. 'Are you going to say when the enemy is in front of you, "Oh, sorry, I did not know we were fighting"?' He imitated Mrs Matsuda's cultured accent and manner. Ripples of suppressed laughter spread among the women clad in flimsy khaki clothes and he was a little mollified.

Haruko had found out that the sergeant was a foreman in an aluminium production company. The president of the company had been a contemporary of Nozomi's at university and a good friend of his. She had an urge to say, 'I'll tell Wakabayashi san on you, treating us like stupid children!', although she knew that it was a large company and the president would not recognise him.

There were water butts provided in front of Haruko's house and it was the Sanjos' duty to keep them full of water at all times. The women lined up and the first person scooped up water in a bucket and handed it to the next. At the end of the line, whatever was left in the bucket was thrown at the high wall of the Akashis. The Akashis had been settled in Manchuria for a long time and their house looked safe behind its high walls.

'Come on, come on, quickly,' the sergeant urged, his whistle and a stop-watch hanging from his neck. As they tried to pass buckets quickly, most of the water was spilled and everybody was thoroughly soaked.

'Number three, don't pass the bucket so high.' That was Haruko. She was aware of the mistake of wearing Emi's gym shoes. As the surface of the road got wet, the rubber soles became slippery and she had difficulty keeping her balance.

'Number four, you are too slow.' That was Mrs Suzuki.

Just before the training began, Mrs Matsuda took a scarf out from her pocket and tied up her hair. It came untied and fell to the ground. It had a pretty flower pattern. As it lay in a pool of water, Mrs Suzuki bent down and picked it up before it was trodden on. It was a natural reaction and the chain of activity was temporarily broken. The sergeant looked at her but did not say anything.

The Matsudas had six children and they were named A, Ayako; B, Binko; C, Chuichi; D, Doji; E, Eiko; and F, Fumiko. There were six hooks on the wall by the back door in their house, and above them was written the letters A to F to indicate where each child should hang his or her coat.

Dr Matsuda would not entrust his children to the local expatriate schools and the older children, A to D, had been sent back to Tokyo to specially chosen schools. Only E and F were with the parents. The children called their parents 'Papa' and 'Mama', which was considered unpatriotic, but having confidence in their father's opinion, the two girls in Emi and Mari's classes were defiant when challenged.

'Papa said Italians call their parents Papa and Mama, too, and the Italians are our allies. In any case, what we call our parents in our own home is our own business.'

Hearing this, Emi was shocked and frightened by the daring of the statement but at the same time she was impressed.

Nozomi mused one day to Haruko, 'The Matsudas must have been quite confident that they would have many children.'

'Why?'

'Because it is only worthwhile naming children alphabetically when there are many of them. For one or two, the effort would not be noticed. Don't you agree? Anyway, Binko is a bit hard, poor kid.' He chuckled.

To socialise with Mrs Matsuda, you had to be well educated or the wife of a well-educated man. If, like Dr Matsuda, you were a graduate of a renowned high school and an élite university, then Mrs Matsuda would bestow not only her friendship but also her respect. Haruko scored highly. This was the path taken by her husband, as well as by her father.

'I worked hard to pass the entrance examination so that you could be Mrs Matsuda's friend,' Nozomi said in a specially grave voice as was his habit when he thought his joke was good.

Haruko did not know what university Mr Suzuki had graduated from but, seeing Mrs Matsuda talking to Mrs Suzuki, she surmised that it must be a prestigious one as well.

When training was finished one day, and they were walking back towards their homes, Mrs Suzuki said to Haruko. 'I have not done any exercise since I left school and I ache all over after training.'

After the first session, Haruko had bought a cheap uniform and kept it for the training sessions. Mrs Suzuki did the same. Mrs Matsuda did not wear a jumper, but wore a rough shirt which was of a khaki-like colour. She did not think that it made sense to buy a useless garment.

When Mrs Suzuki became more friendly with Haruko, she learned that the Suzukis' only son and their son-in-law were both naval officers somewhere in the Pacific.

'My husband ridicules me, but I pray to everything. I pray to the ancestors' spirits. I pray to God, gods, any god, and I pray to Christ. I feel someone should help them. I know I have given them to the Emperor, but I am sure they are more useful alive than dead, don't you agree?'

Another day, she said, 'My son was not strong as a child, and we had a lot of worries about him.'

She did not say anything further, but yet another day she said,

'The worst time is when I wake up during the night, and then I am afraid that somewhere in the sea, one of them might be dying and calling me.' She had tears in her eyes.

16

Bamboo Spears

Early in 1945 Hideto, who was the surgeon-general, visited Manchuria as part of an inspection tour. When Nozomi and Haruko went to the station to meet him, the platform where the first-class carriage was to stop was full of army officers glittering with gold epaulets, stripes and decorations. They seemed rigid with hierarchy and formality.

'I don't think he will come first class,' Haruko said. Meeting Hideto at the station reminded her of the days after her marriage when she lived in Kyushu. Sachiko was a regular visitor, as was Hideto during his university holidays, and Shuichi often came from school as well. Nozomi used to give his young uncle-in-law pocket money and send them all to Beppu, a nearby hot spring resort, joining them over the weekend. Until a few years ago, they saw Hideto at family gatherings fairly regularly, but for Haruko he was always 'Hiden sama', a companion for fun despite the passage of time.

'Of course he will come first class,' Nozomi said, and did not move.

When the train glided into the station and gently came to a halt, a whole group of officers lined up on both sides of a door which was opened from inside by a khaki-clad figure. The air was electrified with the attention of saluting officers. Some seconds later, a smiling figure emerged from the train and came down the steps.

'That's Hiden sama,' Haruko was amazed. He looked even more handsome than usual and at ease.

She knew, of course, that Hideto had attained the highest rank in the army as a medical officer and was one of the youngest to achieve this rank, but she had never seen him in full uniform and amongst other officers.

'Welcome, your excellency,' the officer nearest the door said.

'Your excellency!' Haruko opened her eyes wide and nearly laughed.

'This is quite a welcome. Thank you very much.' The atmosphere surrounding him relaxed. After a few exchanges, he walked to Nozomi and Haruko.

'Very nice to see you,' he said to Nozomi, and looked at Haruko. 'You look well.'

'I am impressed,' Haruko said.

'The army likes the theatrical.' He smiled. 'I have told them that I don't need any hotel arrangements. I will come to you later.'

He came in the evening. Having had a bath and changed to a *yukata*, a cotton kimono, which had been prepared for him, he asked over a cup of saké, 'Have you had any news from Japan recently?'

No, they had not received any news from Japan for several months except something bordering on rumour. Civilian communication was difficult even within the Japanese mainland. With so many air-raids it was understandable. Besides, people did not have the time, place or inclination to write letters when taking refuge in dug-out air-raid shelters or while living in someone else's house if their own had burnt down. Paper and ink were scarce, too.

'A large part of Tokyo has been destroyed by B-29 bombers. From my station you can see nothing except charred tree trunks here and there and black stone walls. My house has also gone.'

'That was a lovely house,' Haruko said minutes later.

'It wasn't bad.'

'Where is Kazuko san?' She asked about his wife.

'She escaped from the inferno before the house burnt down. She is with okahsan in Kitani.'

'Oh, with Kei obahsama. Is she well? And okahsan?'

'They are all very well in Kitani. Yasuharu niisan's house was also bombed, and nesan has also gone to Kitani. The Shirais' house is full of evacuees from Tokyo. Yasuharu niisan is sleeping at the hospital where he works.'

Among the bright sons of the Shirais, Haruko's grandfather, Tei-ichi, had thought that Masakazu had been a sad exception and a failure. But after the others had flown away, kind, cheerful and hard-working Masakazu had become the mainstay of the family. When Tei-ichi had died, it was to this son that he had entrusted the household. Now it was to him that everybody turned for shelter. He and his wife welcomed family members as though it was a matter of course.

His successful brothers had married smart young ladies from Tokyo and in the past they had criticised Masakazu for keeping the old house. 'Why don't you knock it down and have a smaller but modern house built?' Kazuko had said. To Haruko, she had once complained, 'I know I have to visit my mother-in-law now and again, but I can't possibly go in winter. That house is too draughty. I wish Masakazu san would do something. It's so unhygienic and surely very uneconomical.'

They had thought that the kitchen was primitive. There were too many rooms. Some rooms were too big and dark. How could they use a bath built outside the house? How could they wash their faces outside by the well? Why did he not have modern houses built in the big yard or sell a part of it? Who would want to keep a moat and old stone walls? Masakazu san, as always, lacked enterprise.

Masakazu used to explain gently, 'Yes, I agree, but okahsan will be upset if we knock down the house. Besides, we don't mind. We like the old house. We are happy frogs in a well. We do not know how wonderful the outside world is.'

Haruko, too, was reminded how inconvenient life had been in Kitani, but those of the family who had been brought up in the house were grateful that Masakazu kept the house as it always had been with all its memories.

Now Yasuharu and Hideto's wives did not have relatives to turn to in the country. Everybody must be glad that the large house had enough rooms to accommodate all the people from Tokyo comfortably. There was a garden for growing vegetables to supply the large household. All the fruit trees were thriving. They could gather fuel from the woods as well. None of those things could be bought now even if one had money.

'Matabei is working at the station,' Hideto said. He was beyond conscription age but nobody was allowed to keep servants.

'You have never seen your okahsan working, have you?'

'No, what does she do?'

'She works in the garden, cleans, washes . . . She seems well for it. Okahasan, too, looks ten years younger as she herself claims and she is full of energy. I was scolded by her. She said I should be doing something more to win the war quickly and what is the use of hanging around with a lot of medals if I am so incompetent. Shige came to my defence saying there had to be a lot of obstinate people preventing my good intentions. Things never change in Kitani.'

Hideto scratched his head and they all laughed but Haruko knew how proud Kei was of her youngest son.

'Did obahsama see you in your uniform?'

'Yes. When I went to the Sasebo naval base to review their hospital arrangements, I took the opportunity to make a little detour and saw her.'

'She must have been proud.' Haruko remembered her own surprise when she saw Hideto at the station.

'I was immediately taken to the ancestors' graves to thank them. It was a sunny spring afternoon and I am sure all the ancestor sama must have been aroused from their nice nap with a shock.' Emi and Mari giggled. According to army regulation, Hideto's hair was cropped short and there was the arc of a scar above his left ear from his childhood.

'You must have so many scars, Hide ojichan,' Emi remarked. She had been well versed in the legendary adventures of Uncle Hideto.

'I was always naughty,' he chuckled, 'but I was more afraid of okahsan than otohsan. Her principle is that it is stupid and irresponsible to get hurt. That is quite true, of course. It was always Shige who sorted me out. You remember, Haruko, when I stepped on some nails climbing up a forbidden tree in the shrine to steal hawk's eggs? What a thing to do! Okahsan insisted that I should go to school. If I did what I should not have done, at least take the consequences, she said. Otohsan would have only locked me up in the storehouse until I was allowed to apologise. I could not put my foot on the ground, so the only thing I could do was to crawl. As I started to school with great difficulty, Mata came and carried me on his back. Shige must have told him. No one is as naughty as I was and no one is brought up like that these days.'

Hideto's only son was a student but the students had lost their prerogative of being exempt from conscription.

'He is somewhere not far away from Tokyo digging trenches. There are not enough weapons for them, and the army must have realised that shipping them away to some Pacific island means simply losing them. Kazuko apparently sent him away with sane advice. "Forget about being brave or trying to distinguish yourself. Just come back alive."' Hideto laughed in his easy-going way, 'There's the family of "His Excellency" for you.'

'I agree with Kazuko san,' Haruko was grave. She thought of the Kamikaze units of sixteen- or seventeen-year-old boys. They were given aeroplanes made of glued veneer, she had been told, with just enough petrol to reach enemy ships. They would attack the target; they themselves became the bomb. Veneer aeroplanes were one thing, but sending the boys out for a mission without any possibility of coming back alive was not human. 'For the sake of the Emperor,' sounded incongruous for such sacrifice. 'I am unpatriotic and a coward.' Haruko was ashamed, yet she could not deny that she was glad Emi and Mari were girls.

She felt a pang as she thought of the boys who were so carefree and happy at her farewell party five years ago: Shinichi, Hideto's son, yelling as he fell back from doing a handstand; Sakaé, Sachiko's son, frowning as he was making a paper hat for Yaéko's little Hajimé; Kohji, Yasuharu's younger son, big for his fifteen years with his floppy fringe; Goro, Kazuko's nephew, trying saké and screwing up his face.

'Hide ojichan, can we win the war?' Mari asked.

'Mari-chan, I don't know. I am asked to look after the wounded and the sick. I came here to see how adequate the hospital facilities are in case the war spreads in Manchuria. I don't know what the real army people are doing or thinking.'

'What happens if we lose? My teacher said that the Americans would kill us all or make us slaves.'

'Win or lose, war is cruel and miserable. More so if the country is defeated, of course. If Japan loses, I think the Imperial Army and Navy will be wiped out. We have to take the consequences of our actions as Kei obahsama told me a long time ago,' Hideto said. 'But for civilians, there are politicians whose job it is to protect the country and its people and sort things out. It will never come to killing everybody whichever side wins, or certainly it will not come to making people slaves.'

'I am not too afraid of being killed,' Emi said quietly. 'What I am most afraid of is being left alone accidentally if all my family were killed.'

'Oi! Cheer up!' Hideto said, 'Good times will come. You young people are the ones who will make the world better after we messed it up. Oh, I nearly forgot.' He got up and brought out from his suitcase a bundle wrapped up in old newspaper. It had three little coats made out of old silk kimono material.

'I remember this kimono. It was Kei obahsama's,' Haruko said, looking at hers, and then, 'and that was okahsan's!' pointing at her daughters.'

They sent Nozomi an antique Chinese bowl. Haruko could see Kei and Ayako unstitching the old kimonos and making the garments sitting on cushions facing each other.

'Aya san, will you thread the needle?' Haruko could hear Kei's voice. She was eighty. But Ayako was no longer young, either. She was over sixty. Now she would need a pair of glasses and the sunlight to see the small hole of a needle. Holding the present and trying not to cry, she said, 'We should be celebrating Kei obahsama's eightieth birthday this year.'

'She insists she is only seventy, so we'll celebrate it in ten years' time.' Hideto grinned.

After the girls had gone to bed, he said, 'Poor girls. We have taken the war too far. It's like a few firemen trying to cope with a big fire. They are jumping around all over the place but cannot contain all the sparks. They started this war based on a total miscalculation of the enemy power. The navy objected to the war, though, having had the chance to study the outside world. They are better educated than the army.'

'Hiden sama,' Haruko said, 'I read in the newspaper that the national policy is not to surrender, and the whole nation will die a death of honour. Surely it is not realistic, is it?'

'It sounds hysterical.'

'By the way, Hiden sama, what happened to Teiko san? Someone told me that he had heard from someone else who had heard a vague story that she had gone mad and died.'

'Oh, it's a tragedy. So far, our family has miraculously escaped death in action. We have, how many? Two of Yasuharu niisan's sons, one of Masakazu niisan's, one of mine, one of Takeko's. Five young men of our family have been called up. Oh, there is Namiko's husband as well. That makes six of them. They are, thank God, all still alive, Teiko is the only victim of the war.' Hideto winced, and was silent for a while. Eventually, he said, 'You know they were married.' 'They' meant Yasuharu's eldest son, Ryoichi, and Teiko. They had been engaged, Ryoichi was a medical student still under training. 'As he was drafted, they decided to get married in a hurry. He had permission to stay home for three days.'

Marriage was encouraged, following the national policy of Bear Children for the Future of the Country. The actual slogan was more crude. It said, 'Bear and Increase'. French power had been weakened, the people were told, because French women avoided having children to keep their looks.

'It was just the two of them at the wedding,' Hideto explained. 'They went to the Yasukuni shrine together and bowed. That was all. I hear Ryoichi was wearing an officer's uniform but Teiko had baggy work clothes on. Her mother had made her wear a beautiful kimono with work clothes over it so that no one could accuse her of being a traitor idling away in a luxurious kimono! Her mother could not bear her daughter to get married in that women's national uniform. At home they exchanged the wedding saké cup with several relations present.

'Ryoichi was held up in Hiroshima for nearly a month after the wedding, waiting for transport. He asked for permission to call his wife. She had to buy a train ticket on the black market and took nearly two days to get there. When she arrived at the barracks, two guards met her. You know what Teiko looked like.'

Haruko remembered Teiko well. She had large eyes with folded lids and wavy hair with a brown tinge which was not common among Japanese, either. She was tall and cut a striking figure.

'She is, was, a beautiful girl.'

'Yes, quite exotic. There is a film star who looks almost exactly like her. You know the one I mean.'

Even in shabby clothes, she could not have escaped drawing attention. Would she have put on a little make-up perhaps? Then she would have looked really attractive and impressive.

'She arrived at the barracks and two guards stopped her at the gate,' Hideto repeated. 'It appears that she was taken to a room and kept there while other guards one after another came to look at her. Eventually she was taken somewhere else under the pretext of a body search and was stripped. Several soldiers assaulted her one after another . . .'

'Oh, no!'

'By the time Ryoichi was informed about her arrival, she could not speak or recognise anybody. She was just staring in the air. She never recovered. Her father went to take her home and she died a week later.'

After a while, Haruko asked, 'Was there something done about those guards?'

'No. I was away going round the South Pacific field hospitals at the time. The soldiers were taken to the front very soon afterwards.'

'Surely one could find out their names and . . .'

'War is making everybody insane. Nothing is normal. I have been thinking about it a lot. You have no idea what is happening, especially abroad. Yet, they are the Emperor's honourable soldiers. The army will do their best to hush up such scandals. How and when I can fight against such power and win, I can't even begin to think. By the way,' he said, as though to shake off the gloomy atmosphere, 'did you hear your okahsan was honoured by an audience with the Empress?'

'Oh, really?'

'Yes, she is the president of the Red Cross in our area. She is still quite something when she is dressed up. Some people might fall off the bridge yet.'

The next morning, a young officer came with an orderly who brushed Hideto's uniform, polished his boots and laid out clean underclothes and an ironed shirt.

Hideto finished his cup of tea and stood up. He hung his sword from his belt with a chain and secured it. Although some modern adaptation had been made to its hilt and sheath, it was the same seventeenth-century antique sword that had been given to him by his father when he was a boy.

The night before, Emi and Mari wanted to see the famous sword. Nozomi and Haruko had not seen it, either. Hideto took it out of its leather sheath and held it with both hands in front of him. The waveform of the edge threw out a bluish light.

'It's beautiful. It's like moonlight,' Emi said, without taking her eyes off the sword.

'It isn't a bit sinister.' Mari also looked at it intently.

'You are very perceptive. You are right. The swordsmith was an artist. His swords are famous for their quality of clearing your mind when you look at them. His swords were made to kill evil in the mind.'

By the time he left, Emi and Mari had gone to school.

'Say good-bye to Emi-chan and Mari-chan for me. They are such lovely girls. Very intelligent, too. Let's hope that the war will end and they can grow up in a peaceful world. This situation cannot go on. Perhaps peace will come soon.' His sunburnt face wore the same lively expression of the boy whom the Miwa children followed around in Kitani village.

'Peace.' Haruko was awed by the word which she had just heard. She had thought that it was taboo.

'It was marvellous to have seen you. Look after yourselves. Good-bye.' He climbed into a car with an insignia on the sides and a stiff-backed young officer at the wheel. He waved cheerfully and was gone.

The radio noisily broadcast a new song, 'The Americans and English, brute and savage . . .'

Haruko got up and turned off the radio. At the beginning of the war, although the underlying messages were equally militant and patriotic, the words in songs were decent. Falling cherry blossoms, silver wings of fighter planes in the blue sky over the Pacific Ocean, palm trees and the Southern Cross . . . some songs were made up of classical words and their lyricism was touching.

A modern composer had succeeded in putting a poem written by a soldier around the eighth century to a dignified tune. The feeling of devotion to the Emperor was beautiful in its simplicity. As the war progressed and the situation deteriorated daily, despair spread to every corner of life. As though people had no time to be pleasant, the songs, too, became nakedly ugly and hateful.

A newspaper had showed the prime minister, a general, inspecting people's rubbish bins. He told the gathered journalists, 'There are still lots of useful things among the nation's rubbish. We have not reached the end of our supplies. We can win the war.'

'What "rubbish"! What an undignified thing to do! The prime minister should be doing more important things than poking around in the rubbish bins,' Haruko complained to Nozomi. Her dislike of him was increased a few days later when she saw a photograph of him in a pair of patched boots.

'Of all the people in Japan, he should be the one who can afford a good pair of boots. It is nothing but affectation.' But he had resigned, and a new Cabinet came and went. It was as though no one wanted to take responsibility.

Neither Nozomi nor Haruko said it aloud, but they knew the war would be lost. They heard that, in Japan, everybody left was trained to fight with spears made of bamboo. In the sixteenth century, farmers who could not afford to have weapons used sharpened bamboo poles to defend themselves. What and how were they expected to defend or attack with bamboo spears in the twentieth century?

17

The Summer of 1945

Although Haruko had taken part in many air-raid practices, or perhaps because of this, when the real siren sounded, it was a surprise.

No neighbours rushed out into the street with buckets. The Sanjos had had a shelter dug in the garden and covered it with a sheet of corrugated iron as had been ordered, but there was nothing they could do about the knee-deep stagnant water which had seeped in and stayed. Haruko remained inside the house and thought of going into the cupboard under the staircase.

It was a spring afternoon and the sky was powder blue. Through the window, high above, she could see a formation of silver wings trailing white lines of vapour. The bombers looked as though they were hardly moving. It was her first confrontation with the enemy and she was frightened.

The Americans were going to drop bombs on them and kill them. The Americans, the British, they were all enemies. Yet who were 'they' really? They were rich and beautiful like the lady in the pendant of the dead Russian officer she had seen as a child. They lived in magnificent castles and large houses. They were friendly like the landlady in whose house Yasuharu, Nozomi and Sachiko's husband had stayed as young men. 'My children,' she had written to them at Christmas. Also, Professor Arensburg and his wife had been kind to Nozomi and often invited them to his house for dinner.

Her uncles, husband, brother-in-law, they had all had a good time once with the enemy. Haruko still had a pair of opera glasses and faded photographs of a young Nozomi in skating boots, 'At Saint Moritz 1922' written casually on the back. And lots of picture postcards: 'I am sitting at Café de la Paix having an aperitif in the evening sunshine'; 'Dear Haruko, I am having tea at the Hotel Ritz. There are a lot of ladies in pretty dresses. I wondered what you would look like dressed as they are.' That was as near a love letter as she had ever received in her life. Hotel Ritz. What an evocative name. Chandeliers and pink ribbons.

These images were so different from the propaganda posters of large-nosed, red-faced and big-booted men with savage smiles and hands spread out to grab and squeeze one.

She sighed and called Shun-ren. At least her gripping fear had subsided. Both squatted under the staircase but Mah refused to come. He stood in the garden and watched the aeroplanes, shading his eyes with his hand.

Haruko felt irrationally that he had secret information about the target of the enemy. He could be a spy. Soon distant but unmistakable booms were heard and windows rattled. Plates and dishes in the cupboards made clattering noises. It lasted a few minutes.

'It finish.' Mah came in. Haruko was worried about Nozomi at his office and Emi and Mari at school.

'Only station,' Mah said confidently. Another siren told them that the air-raid was over. Soon an errand boy came from the office to tell Haruko that Nozomi was safe. Emi and Mari walked in twenty minutes later.

The station was undamaged but nearby buildings had been hit. Tattered clothing from the cupboards of the bombed houses had been blown up by the blast and caught in the trees, like Christmas trees painted by children, Nozomi said when he came home. No Chinese casualties. Only a few Japanese were hurt.

A week later, Mah wanted a few days off to visit his relatives. There was a wedding and also someone was ill.

Two days later, Shun-ren disappeared during the night. Her room was empty. The house was quiet without Shun-ren's singing and chatter. At the breakfast table, the strong perfume of hair oil had been difficult to bear but Emi and Mari almost missed it.

'Okahsan, you haven't told her off for something, have you?'

'No, of course not. I don't think I have ever told her off severely. She has simply gone during the night. I wonder if someone came to fetch her. She could not have carried all her belongings herself.'

'I think she took her things bit by bit,' Mari said. She had been specially friendly with Shun-ren. 'I noticed that she had hardly any clothes in her room last week.'

'They must be frightened of air-raids,' Emi said. 'I would go home, too, if I were her.'

Haruko wondered if they had wanted to distance themselves from their Japanese employers. She felt as though she and her family had been left on a ship abandoned by its crew.

To her surprise, Haruko found that she missed the air-raid practices. It was the only time in her life, she realised, that she had been thrown into a situation in which she had to mix with people who were virtually strangers. Imperceptibly, over the last year and a half, her social life had come to a halt. Before she could begin to dwell on these thoughts, she could hear Kei's voice saying, 'This is no time for self-indulgence. If you have a hard journey ahead of you, don't sit beside the road.'

Rice, sugar, salt and other necessary items had been rationed and were in short supply, but Ten-sei-sho could bring Haruko anything she asked for at a black market price. Abruptly he stopped turning up. Haruko knew where the shop was but, without Mah, she did not feel like going into a Chinese shop on her own.

The White Russians disappeared as well. A shop where Haruko had bought music cases, hats and trinkets for the children had fewer and fewer goods, and finally closed down. Other White Russians had built a settlement called Romanov Village. They put up wooden huts and grew food. They had often come up to town to sell buckets and buckets of fresh vegetables. Haruko heard that the entire village had been deserted overnight.

From April, Emi had started at a girls' high school. It was the last school that the Southern Manchurian Railway Company had built and it was luxuriously equipped. A small Japanese tea-house had been built inside to teach the girls manners and the tea ceremony. The row of cubicles for practising music and the airy, well-furnished chemistry and physics rooms delighted Emi. The teachers were more liberal than at the primary school. That summer, there was no school holiday. The war had to go on. Mari groaned but Emi was pleased. There was nowhere to go and nothing to do without school.

'Okahsan, why are you wearing all your rings?' Emi asked.

Haruko spread out her fingers and looked at them. 'I am saying good-bye to my rings. I have to donate all my jewellery.'

'What are they going to do with it?'

'They will sell them to raise funds.'

'Who buys them?'

'I have no idea.'

'If you don't know what is going to happen to them, do you have to part with those? How do they know that you have them?'

'They went to Nakatani, our jewellers, and looked at the records. These two, I bought from the Nakatanis. I had them alter the design of this one. This one, well, they don't know about it.'

The one that was not included in Nakatani's records was a ruby ring. Ayako had bought it for Haruko when she married.

'I haven't had as many kimonos made for you as I wanted. Nozomi san says that he does not want a lot of things, but a ring won't take a lot of space, will it?' Ayako had smiled and put it on Haruko's finger.

'Haruko san, I have read somewhere that wearing ruby makes you happy. I hope you will be happy.'

The stone was deep red. The shimmer of the colour would make one's heart dance, Haruko thought.

That night, there was chocolate after dinner.

'Wow!' Mari said.

'It's lucky that there are four of us. It would be difficult to divide it exactly into three or five pieces.' Nozomi joined in the spirit of the occasion. 'How did you get it? Is it from the army?'

Like most large-scale operations, Nozomi's work was connected with the army and the Sanjos often benefited from unobtainable goods.

'Oh, no. It is a most legitimate present from the government to me.'

Haruko had been given a coupon to get a large bar of chocolate for giving up her jewellery.

'It is the most expensive chocolate you will ever get,' she said. 'Let's enjoy it.'

In August, the atomic bombs fell on Hiroshima and Nagasaki. They heard the news over the radio. Only Nozomi understood the full implications of the horror.

In April, the Russians had refused to renew the Russo-Japanese Neutral Treaty. On the eighth of August, between the two atomic bombs, they declared war against Japan, a nation on the brink of defeat. They started to invade Manchuria, and met little resistance from the Japanese army.

Nozomi thought of sending his wife and daughters further south, but Haruko was adamant. She insisted that the family should stay together and share their fate and Nozomi was not confident that his family could find greater security elsewhere. No matter how far they went, it would still be inside Manchuria, and eventually they would all be under Russian occupation. It was a matter of time. For more than a year it had been practically impossible for civilians to travel because the army had monopolised the railway.

'We'll all die together,' Haruko said.

'That's not the kind of thing which you should mention casually.'

Nozomi restrained her, but when Haruko persisted in asking, 'What can we do, if the Russians come with guns and surround the city?' he did not have an answer.

'I'd rather die than be taken captive, and Emi and Mari, too,' Haruko muttered. 'I won't let them become prisoners of the Russians.'

'Don't be dramatic.'

August the fifteenth 1945 was a strange day from morning onwards. News spread. There would be an important broadcast by the Emperor at noon. Ordinary people would hear the Emperor's voice for the first time.

It was a hot day. Already in the morning, the asphalt was getting soft. At midday, the streets were empty. Nozomi came home.

'Are you going to listen to the broadcast?' Mrs Matsuda called. 'I wonder if we could join you? Our radio is not working.'

'Of course. Come in.'

Haruko made tea and they all sat down.

'Are your children still in Tokyo?' Haruko asked.

'They have been evacuated with their schools. Our older daughters have graduated and both of them are working as nurses.'

Nozomi and Dr Matsuda were quiet and the two women carried on their conversation in low voices as though they were at a funeral.

There was no sound from the usually noisy radio. No military marches. No special news. At twelve, after an announcer's introduction, the broadcast began. The transmission was poor. The voice of the Emperor sounded as though it was constantly drowned by rolling waves. Haruko just about grasped what he was saying. In an almost choking voice, or was it interference, he announced that he would surrender as he could not bear his nation to suffer any longer.

Nozomi sat with his arms folded when the broadcast was over. As though there was nothing else to add, the radio became silent except for static noises.

'It was a foregone conclusion,' Dr Matsuda said.

Haruko felt as though a heavy burden had fallen from her shoulders. No more fear of air-raids. No more siege by the Russians. Her husband and the children would come home safely every day. All the relations who had been safe so far were going to be all right. Mrs Suzuki did not have to wake up in the middle of the night afraid about her son's and son-in-law's fate. The war was over. They had survived. They had come through it relatively lightly.

A part of Chenyang was surrounded by walls. This was the old city where no Japanese lived and seldom visited. Low houses lined streets which were either muddy or dusty. Carts, carriages and rickshaws churned up animal droppings and debris. Blocked-up gutters and a labyrinth of alleys made up the rest. Once Haruko had been taken there with her daughters by one of Nozomi's employees. She remembered an incident in which a fat man in a black shiny damask robe had had an epileptic fit in a dismal department store which smelled strongly of garlic. He had been carried away sitting in a carved chair. He was wearing a black pill-box hat with a small red button on top and was dribbling copiously.

The Russians had built a railway station away from the walled city. The three broad roads that fanned out from the station were named after the three historical capitals of Japan. Streets which crossed them had the names of fauna representing the twelve months and other favourite plants of Japan. Japanese children went to Japanese schools. People shopped mostly at stores owned by the Japanese. There was not much to remind them that they were in somebody else's country until the Emperor declared the surrender.

Nozomi went back to his office after the broadcast but came home much earlier than usual. Haruko noticed from her upstairs window that the Suzukis' big iron gate had been closed early in the afternoon.

'You are early today. How are things in town?' Haruko asked, although the centre of the town was in walking distance.

'It's quiet now, but unsettling,' Nozomi said. 'We'd better stay home for a few days and see what happens.'

'Mr Suzuki must have come home early today, too. Their gate is already closed. What will happen?'

'The bank must be in serious trouble.'

Manchukoku, which had been set up by the Japanese government with a puppet Emperor, was no more, Nozomi explained to Haruko.

'All those bank notes printed with the Manchurian Emperor's face are worthless as of today.'

'You mean all the money we have is worthless now?'

'That's right. But I was warned by our bank manager a few months ago. I have taken most of our money out.'

'Oh!' Why was I not told, Haruko thought, but aloud she asked, 'Is that what everybody else has done as well?'

'No, I don't think so.'

Not everybody anyway, he said. The banks certainly would avoid people flooding in to take money out and cause panic. It was only as a favour to a special friend that he had been given hints of the oncoming trouble. It was the most confidential information, although it might not be difficult to surmise if one had foresight.

The Chinese people would not suffer. They had learned from history. Few trusted banks. They trusted their walls and under-floor niches.

'But then you mean my little savings are gone?'

'If you had savings.'

'I did have some.'

Nozomi laughed. 'It's punishment for having kept a secret hoard from your husband.'

No banks, then. But neither had a clear idea until the next day what it would mean to have no police or army.

18

The Chinese and the Russians

The sun set over the silent city. When night fell, there was whispering and furtive movements among Chinese people in the alleys and back streets. The Japanese realised abruptly that they had been oppressive invaders. Now they were left defenceless in a hostile and foreign land, with no protective power behind them. Darkness enhanced their uneasiness.

It was not as unfamiliar a situation for the Chinese people as it was for the Japanese. When Haruko had read Pearl Buck's *The Good Earth*, sitting on a sunny verandah in Japan, she had never associated the story with her own experience. The history of the Chinese was a repetition of power struggles and, won or lost, life had been hard for ordinary people. The interim vacuum between rulers was an opportunity for swift gain.

Tension was mounting all through the next day. As night came again, a distant murmur became louder as though the waves lapping at a beach were increasing in volume. The Chinese people had started to come out from their homes. At every corner, the number increased. They pushed and shoved and began to run as a mass. It was not with liberated feelings that they moved. It was not an exultation that carried them. Some were uncertain, some were afraid, and some were agitated, but for most of them, the definite aim was not clear.

They started to growl and roar like an animal whose force became a tidal wave.

'A riot!'

Japanese men in blocks of flats got together and began to bang pots and pans to chase away the crowd. This had some effect at first, but it was impossible to defend themselves against the whole city. More and more Chinese people flooded out of the walled city to join the riot.

Nozomi and Haruko woke their daughters up.

'Get into here quick.' Nozomi pushed his wife and two daughters through a door by the staircase into a small flat. He dragged a large box in front of the door and piled up empty crates on top. The door was in shadow and well concealed.

The flat had two small rooms, a bathroom and a kitchenette. The windows were facing the back and were barred. Since the Onos had left, no one had used the flat and there was a faint musty smell.

As Haruko stood and looked around the empty rooms, repeated banging started to shake the air.

'Is otohsan going to be all right?' Mari asked, clutching her stuffed toy.

'I am sure he is all right,' Haruko answered automatically.

The banging continued and they heard the smashing and splintering of wood. The front doors must have been broken down. Haruko imagined a mob swarming at the entrance flourishing a big hatchet. Now that the heavy double doors were smashed down, they must be pouring in. What would happen to Nozomi? She should have dragged him in as well, but there had been no time to think.

'Come here,' she told her daughters, and raised a hatch door inside a cupboard. Standing on a box, she climbed up into the loft and urged the girls to follow her. They sat on a beam in the darkness. The shattering of china dropped on the stone floor. A lot of shouts. Something heavy being dragged over the floor.

Haruko noticed that Emi and Mari were not as frightened as she was. It was an unexpected new experience for them and they were even enjoying themselves a little. They were secure so long as they were with their parents.

It was dusty and hot.

No one had a watch. Even if one did, it was too dark to read the time. The commotion seemed to continue for a long time. Gradually the house became quiet.

They stayed on in the loft.

'Where are you? You can come out now.' At the sound of Nozomi's voice, Mari scrambled down and ran to him.

'Otohsan! I was worried about you. Weren't you hurt?'

'I am all right.'

Outside the apartment, the air was fresh and the early morning sun cast long shadows on bare floors.

'Where were you?'

'I was watching from a corner.'

'They might have killed you,' Haruko said hotly. 'Why didn't you come in with us?' Now that she saw him safe, she became angry.

'They wouldn't kill me. What's the use of killing me? They were too busy. They are not thugs. They are ordinary people. They are perhaps honest people. They are just seizing an opportunity.'

Nozomi put his hands on his daughters' shoulders, but Haruko saw that he was a little breathless and that short sentences were jerked out of him.

'But they hate us now. They are getting revenge on us.'

'As far as I am concerned, they have had enough revenge.' Nozomi managed to smile.

Haruko looked at the scene for the first time. Most of the doors had been wrenched off their hinges and taken away. They left ugly scars on the door frames. The furniture had gone. Some floorboards had been ripped up and exposed the concrete base underneath.

'Oh!' Emi exclaimed. 'They have taken the piano!'

The devastation of the house was complete. They had carried off tables, chairs, sideboard, ornaments, paintings . . . The deserted room looked bigger than they remembered. The bare floor was criss-crossed with scars where heavy pieces of furniture had been dragged across it. From the dining room, a large ebony table had gone. It was carved and heavy.

'How did they carry it?'

'They were like ants around sticky sweets.'

'They took that carpet as well!' Haruko sounded awed.

'Yes, it took more than ten men to drag it out. A lot of scuffles among themselves. A man was struggling to carry out our armchair, and another man was trying to snatch it, while someone else was rolling out the round table.'

'You stood and watched it all?'

'What else could I have done? I thought of telling them to take their time and treat the furniture carefully. It's all theirs anyway, but everybody was too excited to listen. Someone threw that heavy ash-tray at me but luckily it missed me.'

'Thank God! That would have killed you.'

Haruko went to the kitchen. Her favourite bowl was smashed and the pieces were scattered on the floor. They had left chaos as they tried to take as many small objects as possible from the cupboards.

'We'll live in this apartment for a while,' Nozomi said, when they gathered to have dry biscuits and tinned soup from the air-raid emergency stock.

'By the way, among the mob, I saw Ten-sei-sho,' Nozomi said, and waited for Haruko's reaction.

'No! Not that shopkeeper, surely.'

'Oh, yes. That sleepy-looking fat chap. Always so courteous but inert. He was very agile. He had brought several young men and ordered them around as though he was the boss of a removal company. Together they took quite a lot of stuff. That cynical young chap Ten-sei-sho's nephew who used to come to get orders, was there too. He carried off our celadon vase. The carpet was taken by Ten-sei-sho, I think.'

A large thick carpet with a blue pattern. How pleased and proud she had been when it had been delivered.

'We weren't allowed to have tea on it,' Mari said wistfully.

'Ten-sei-sho will be grateful for that, Mari-chan.' Emi's remark made Haruko think of the age difference between her two daughters.

'Didn't they notice you?' Haruko asked Nozomi.

'It wasn't quite light yet, and I pretended to be busy taking things as well.'

Mari laughed hilariously.

'Mari-chan, it's not funny,' Haruko said, a little crossly. They had just lost most of their possessions. She had planned to ship everything to Japan one day when they had a house built. Some could have been passed on to their daughters.

'Haruko, we were lucky. They were too busy downstairs and did not go upstairs. We have clothes to put on, and bedding to sleep in. And we are safe. Let's not worry about a few sticks of furniture.'

'You two, come and help me.'

Nozomi found a hammer and while Emi and Mari held the broken front doors, he nailed various pieces of board over them.

'Will there be more mobs?'

'I hope they are looking for a better bargain elsewhere now, but wood is precious for them and we still have floorboards.' For many years, no one had planted trees in China. 'That's why the hills and countryside are so bare,' he explained to his daughters. 'They never have enough fuel at any time.'

Later that day, Nozomi put a couple of shelves on the door of the apartment and placed a few empty cardboard boxes on them. In the dim corner, the door became even less conspicuous.

'You are clever.' Mari looked up at him.

All the windows of the house were double. In summer, the inside glass panels were replaced by screens, but without Mah only a few of the windows had been attended to that year. The apartment was no exception and the glass was dirty, but the girls were happy.

'It's like a holiday,' Mari said. 'How long are we going to stay here?'

'Um.'

The Suzukis' gate was three-quarters open, and the path was strewn with colours. A woman's silk under-kimono was on the border as though someone had thrown herself down. Nozomi and Haruko wanted to call on them to see how they were but did not dare step out of the house.

In the afternoon, the Suzukis had closed the gate and cleared most of the debris. The iron bars of the gate had been bent.

The Sanjos took their belongings, little by little, into the apartment from the messy kitchen and bedrooms. Emi and Mari brought lots of books and settled down to read.

'The Suzukis are all right. They were hiding in the loft. The Matsudas are also safe. The mob did not go in their house,' Nozomi came in and told them. 'Mrs Matsuda was laughing that the mob knew they were not rich.'

With many children, the Matsudas' lifestyle had not been luxurious.

Haruko wondered if the whole ransacking operation was under Ten-sei-sho's directions. He must have good knowledge of the circumstances of each family in the area. And he was Mah's relation. Would Mah have told him about the Sanjos' possessions, and would Ten-sei-sho have decided that it was not worth spending time upstairs?

'You did not see Mah in the mob, did you?'

'No, he was not among the lot who came here.'

*   *   *

179

Two days later, the Russians marched in. The Russian soldiers had cropped hair, and were uncouth and disorderly.

Rumour had it that the Russians would send out a company made up of convicts ahead of the real army. The riots by the Chinese people were quickly suppressed, but the Russians were an unknown threat to the Japanese and more menacing than the Chinese.

The Japanese and Chinese alike were disturbed by random shots and sharp cries night and day. Armoured vehicles sped by, one after another, in no particular direction. Posters in Japanese were pasted on walls and electricity poles: 'If one Russian is killed, we will kill a hundred Japanese. General Constantine Kevich.'

One night, there was a thunderstorm. The Sanjos were woken up by the roaring and flashes of lightning but also by Russians running about outside shouting and shooting their guns up towards the sky.

'Don't they have thunder in Russia, otohsan? They sound scared,' Emi said from her bed.

'Aren't they stupid, shooting up at the thunder,' Mari added.

The Russian soldiers demanded watches from passers-by at gunpoint. Most of them had collected several watches and strapped them all the way up their thick hairy arms. Some had as many as a dozen.

'I was told that if they sell a watch in Siberia, they can live for five years without working.' Mrs Matsuda passed on the information.

'In that case, they will spend their entire lives in luxury.'

By this time, the four girls had made a hole in the wall separating the gardens of the two families and the adults started to use it, too.

Haruko could not imagine an economy where one watch would be enough to live on for five years.

'Your "great future" has not reached Russia yet,' Haruko teased Nozomi.

'That's not what I meant.' But he did not elaborate. 'I am an engineer,' he had often said, 'I'm not good at arguing and I don't have to be.'

On his way back to Japan from Europe years ago, he had chosen to return via the newly formed Soviet Union. He was interested in how the Soviet Union was developing its electricity industry and in its plans for mechanisation. He had also wanted to see Dresden, and to travel in Austria and Poland.

'Everything was behind and primitive, but even someone like me who is completely ignorant of politics and economics, can sense that there is energy and lively hope. There is a feeling that something immense has started and that the Soviet Union is moving towards a great future,' he remembered telling Haruko. He had also thought to himself with a wry smile that the excessively feminine hotel room in which he had stayed in Vienna might have had an effect. The room had pale wallpaper with pretty flowers also in pale colours, decorative gilded mirrors, tulip-shaped lamps, delicate chandeliers, laces, frills and a little silver dish of chocolate. He had imagined that he had smelt of sweet perfume all day. He had thought of changing his hotel but did not get round to it. After a week of feeling a total misfit, the odd hospitality of a hotel in Moscow had been refreshing. He would have liked to have stayed there longer to understand more about the new country emerging out of feudalism.

Haruko had listened to his description of Paris and Dresden and other European cities with interest and pleasure, but she had not shown any sympathy with his comments on Moscow.

'But you are not going to become a communist, are you?' she had said, half anxiously and half joking, and that was that.

Nozomi was surprised that Haruko remembered the conversation.

'I am not strong-minded and knowledgeable enough to qualify as a communist. Not then and not now, either,' he muttered.

'Otohsan, where did you put your dirty underclothes?' Haruko asked.

'I am wearing them. I put them on inside out.'

'Otohsan!'

'We wore the same thing for weeks as a student. We all had fleas. We used to have flea-catching competitions.'

'Otohsan, stop!' Emi shivered. 'I feel itchy all over. Do you think we have fleas?'

'So give me your clothes.'

Everything took time but they had all day to do housework. Nozomi made a clothes horse with pieces of old pipe and rope.

'What a funny thing,' Mari giggled. 'When you hang the clothes up, it looks like a giant squatting and begging.' Everybody laughed.

A simple meal took a long time to cook over an electric ring but they had to be grateful that the electricity supply was unaffected, although there were occasional power-cuts.

'Ah, that's the first thing the Russians made sure of, I imagine,' Nozomi said.

'Okahsan, Eiko-chan's otohsan had her hair shaved so that the Russian soldiers would think she is a boy. Do you think I have to, too?' Emi had just crawled back through the hole from next door. It was something which had never occurred to Haruko and it jolted her. Emi was eleven and still looked like a little girl. There was nothing womanly about her.

'I don't think so, but be careful. Don't go outside.'

It was a new worry.

'I don't think it is necessary, do you?' Haruko put the question to Nozomi.

He, too, looked surprised. 'Emi? Oh, I don't think so.'

'Fumi-chan's got soot on her face. Her father said she had to look as ugly as possible.'

'I don't know about soot, but it may be better not to let her wear a pretty dress or anything like that.'

'She doesn't have pretty dresses, anyway.'

For the past two years, the young girls had not had any occasion to wear dresses, and Emi's old dresses had been outgrown.

'What a time we are living in,' Nozomi said.

Their hiding place was violated one day. Haruko and Mari were at the Matsudas' and Emi was alone. She saw a shadow flit across the windows. The windows were kept unwashed so that from the outside the house looked deserted. A Russian soldier had sauntered into what he had obviously thought was an empty house.

As the days passed, the family had relaxed and the door with the shelves was open and Emi did not have time to shut it. Seeing someone, the soldier seemed more surprised than Emi. He quickly hid his bulk in a doorway and aimed his pistol at her.

Emi stood there with her arms dangling. The only thing she could see was a round shiny muzzle. Everything else was in shadow. Keeping the pistol aimed at her, the soldier cautiously came into the apartment. His big boots trod on the tatami floor. As Emi watched him, Haruko, alarmed by another neighbour, came running in with Mari after her. The soldier sharply turned to them, then he imitated a watch ticking, 'Chi, chi, chi,' and pointed at his wrist.

Haruko stuck both her wrists in front of him and shook her head. Emi and Mari copied her. He looked around a little more, poked in their small bathroom and left.

The cicadas were singing noisily, and it was such a hot day.

19

A Journey to Chenyang

'Okahsan, there's someone wandering in front of our house. She keeps on coming back to look at our front door. She is like a beggar,' Emi said, coming downstairs. A month after the riot, the family began to walk around in the rest of the house more freely.

'Is she Japanese?'

'I don't know.'

Haruko went upstairs and peeped out of a window. She drew a sharp breath and hurried downstairs. The front doors were boarded up. Haruko hurried from the back door round the side of the house to the gate.

'Obasan!' the woman screamed, and with arms outstretched staggered towards Haruko. 'Obasan, I thought you had all gone!' Tears started to run down her dirty cheeks and she crouched down on the ground.

'Come in, come in. We are all here.'

Haruko had to half drag her into the house. She smelt of unwashed hair, soiled nappies, rotten vegetables, and as soon as she came into the house through the back door, she collapsed on the floor and broke into uncontrollable sobbing.

'Emi-chan, Mari-chan, it's Toshié san,' Haruko said to her daughters who stood gaping. Toshié was wearing a tattered 'national uniform', and her feet were wrapped in rags.

'Oh!' Recognition dawned on Emi's face. 'What happened? Where are . . .'

Haruko quickly looked up, stared hard at her and shook her head. Emi held her hands over her mouth.

'You two can go and put a kettle on the spirit stove for tea, and let's find her something to eat.'

Toshié was Nozomi's niece. She had married and lived in a town about six hours' train journey away. She had a daughter of three years old and a son who was just a few months old. Haruko did not want to ask what had happened to Toshié's children yet. The fact that they were not with her and her distress told her of their fate.

Haruko had never been close to Nozomi's relations except to one of his younger brothers who had lived at their house as a student, but Nozomi had always been generous to his family. Toshié was his sister's daughter. Since she had married and come to live in Manchuria, liberal amounts of money had been sent to her for the births and illnesses of the children, and every New Year.

Having eaten and washed and changed into Haruko's clothes, she sat and put her hands in front of her on the tatami floor. She bowed.

'I am sorry to be in such a dishevelled state. I didn't know what to do if you weren't here,' but the end of the sentence was swallowed in fresh sobbing and she crumpled down on her face.

The news that the Russians were invading Manchuria across the river Amur (the Black Dragon river) sent the Japanese community where Toshié lived into confusion. The Russian advance was swift. Japan was on the brink of defeat and there was no army left to defend Manchuria. Communication with people in the cities further north was broken off within a day of the invasion.

Although this action on the part of the Soviet Union had been anticipated by the higher authorities in Japan, they no longer had the power to resist or to protect the Japanese citizens who were living in Manchuria. The only measure taken by the authorities was to hide the vulnerability of the Japanese expatriates and let events take their course. The expatriates had long been abandoned and they were unaware of this.

Toshié lived in one of a group of houses provided by the Manchurian Railway Company, for which her husband worked. Her house was in a large compound, with rows of bungalows neatly lined up. Several blocks away, there were bigger and better houses which belonged to the people of higher rank, and, further up, a few even bigger houses surrounded by large gardens for executives.

The people who lived around Toshié conformed more or less to the same style of life with identical houses and almost the same salary, yet differences emerged after a while. Toshié's family was better off than most others because she had extra financial help from Nozomi. She and her children often made trips to Chenyang. Their meals were a little better than the other families and they could treat themselves to lunch and tea at restaurants more often than the others. Toshié could shop at department stores now and again without money worries.

She was a good-natured and cheerful woman and, in spite of the fact that she boasted about 'my uncle in Chenyang' a little too much so that her envious neighbours sometimes gossiped about her behind her back, she was popular among the other wives.

The company took good care of its employees and their families even after most husbands had been conscripted and taken away. Toshié's husband was one of them. When it was known that the Russians would arrive any day, panic set in. The company gathered the residents together and informed them that it would provide them with a train going to Chenyang within a few hours. This meant that they should leave immediately. In Chenyang, further plans would be decided. The residents scrambled home and tried to prepare for the exodus.

After the announcement Toshié was more relaxed than the others. Once in Chenyang, she and her children would be safe.

'We advise you to leave just as you are and go to the station as soon as possible,' said the man in charge. His surname was Hayashi and he had been a section head in the finance department. He was known as a capable and conscientious man. There had always been gossip about why he was a bachelor, but nobody had really found out much about him. 'The train will leave when you are ready. Don't miss it. I am afraid this will be the only train,' he told the crowd.

At home, Toshié put down her baby on the tatami floor, and gathered a few children's clothes and nappies into a small bundle. She also took biscuits, arrowroot for emergencies and a small bottle of water, and pushed them among the clothes. She had to throw away half the arrowroot from the bag she had kept it in, and in spite of the circumstances, she felt guilty. In her kitchen, the clay charcoal stove was cold. She turned off the gas cock at the mains. The rubbish outside had to be left as it was. She locked the back door and kitchen windows.

Coming back, she looked around her small house of three rooms.

The sliding doors were all open. It was a humble but cosy home where the first four years of her uneventful married life had been spent. A basket of toys, futons in the cupboards, clothes in the chest of drawers, she had to leave them all now. She walked to the chest of drawers and from a case took out a pearl ring that Haruko had given her. She put it on. This, and the clothes she was wearing, were her only possessions now.

'Toshié san, are you ready? Hurry up,' her neighbour and a specially close friend Kimiko called.

'Coming, coming,' Toshié shouted, thinking that perhaps she should take some photographs. Most of the children's photographs were not in albums but still in a box. These were the things she could never replace.

'We'll miss the train. What are you doing?' Now Kimiko's voice was high-pitched. Toshié gave up. No time to get the box out from under various other things and find an envelope or something to put the photographs in.

'Coming, coming,' Toshié repeated and strapped her baby on her back. She put on her shoes at the entrance and her daughter's.

Kimiko had started to walk. She had tied a small child on her back and carried a baby in front. Her four-year-old son was walking by her.

Toshié locked the front door and put a long string attached to the key around her neck.

'What are you locking your door for?' Kimiko stopped irritably and said, 'Come on! Hurry!'

Under ordinary circumstances, Kimiko was a cheerful woman and gentle with her children, but now she yanked her son by the hand. He looked surprised and began to whimper.

'Stop it,' she scolded the boy. 'I am going to leave you here all alone, if you don't stop crying. Do you understand? All alone!'

Toshié meant to let her daughter walk but realised that it would take too long. She carried her. Soon, sweat started to run down her face. Her daughter in her arms traced the running sweat with her finger. Toshié's back was drenched from the effort and by the warmth of the baby.

Kimiko's son was being pulled and pushed, half running. Tears were rolling down his cheeks but he was trying not to make a noise. Toshié put her daughter down and said, 'Tett-chan, hold Mii-chan's hand. You are a big boy. You take care of Mii-chan, won't you?'

They had to slow down but Tetsuo cheered up a little and walked with Toshié's daughter.

'We must hurry,' Kimiko said again, turning round and waiting, but they were not the only ones heading to the station and everyone else had their own burden. A boy of about fourteen was carrying a young girl on his back. They were a family who lived in one of the bigger houses. Their father had gone to Dalian for a business trip about a month ago and had not been able to get a train to come back. His wife was walking by their sick daughter. Everybody knew about the girl, who had been bedridden with tuberculosis. Her complexion was translucent. Her cheeks were soft pink and she had shiny black hair. She rested the side of her face on her brother's back and with her large eyes was quietly taking in the confusion around her.

Not a hundred metres away from home, people had already started to abandon their possessions they had thought precious enough to carry with them. A little case, a bag, a bundle of paper were left on the side of a street. Toshié noticed a pair of smart women's shoes neatly placed together.

A dog was following a family wagging his tail, and two children were crying and tried to chase him back home.

'Let him come,' a kindly middle-aged man said. 'He'll be better off around the station. We might even find him a place on the train. Cheer up, boys.'

When there was not enough food around, few people kept pets. The dog must be specially loved by the family, Toshié thought.

'I want a drink,' Toshié's daughter said.

'Be good and wait till we get to the station.'

'Is otohsan there?'

'No, otohsan is not there but we will take a train to Nozomi ojichan and Haruko obachan. You remember Emi-chan and Mari-chan, don't you?'

'Are we going there, too?' Tetsuo looked up at Kimiko.

'No.'

The sun was strong. At first Toshié was thankful that it was not in the middle of winter, when the temperature was minus thirty or even forty degrees, but soon realised that walking in temperatures of thirty degrees above freezing point was also torture.

The station was in a turmoil. People were overflowing from the station building to the square in front. The Manchurians had rolled up mattresses. Old women with pointed feet, deformed and dwarfed from binding, tottered along precariously with their families and their bundled possessions. They had grey hair tied in a small bun at the nape of their necks and most of them had withered yellow faces from opium smoking. In the heat everybody looked wilted and some squatted on the ground with hands dangling in front. Young people and children, too, sat exhausted.

As Toshié's group started to arrive, Hayashi was waiting. He told them to skirt the station building and walk along the railway further down.

The executives' families had been alerted to the evacuation before the others and carts had been provided for them. They were already sitting and waiting on their suitcases in the shade of a goods train. Together with the others, Toshié and Kimiko sat down on the pebbles a little apart from their bosses' families. Their babies were exhausted in the heat and were sleeping drenched in sweat. Toshié gave water to her daughter and Tetsuo and drank some herself. When she passed the bottle to Kimiko, it was nearly empty. Once she had found out what was going to happen, she would go and fill the bottle from a tap further away.

As soon as they were cooled a little in the shade, they began to be restless and anxious to know what was happening.

Hayashi was talking to the executives' group and then came to the others.

'I am sorry but you have to wait. As far as I know, the train should have been prepared by now. I hope it will arrive soon.'

'Where is it arriving, Hayashi san?' someone asked.

'Somewhere near here,' he said. 'We are avoiding the platform to prevent confusion.'

One hour passed, and the children dozed. Babies cried and were fed. Toshié got more water from a tap and gave the children biscuits. Sensing the unusual atmosphere, most children stayed with their parents without admonition. Toshié piled up some stones for Michiko and Tetsuo and they played together with a few more children. Nearby, the dog which had followed his family sat quietly panting.

The wet clothes which stuck to her gradually dried out. Toshié dreamed of the big bath and shining shower at Haruko's house. The Sanjos used imported towels. They were large and thick, unlike the little piece of cotton that most people used both as a face cloth and for drying.

The pebbles were too uncomfortable to put down the babies and Toshié and Kimiko rested them supported by their bent legs. A few others copied them and the atmosphere relaxed a little. There was nothing they could do except wait. Once they were on the train and had escaped from the city, they would be safe.

Toshié began to think of things she had left. It had not seemed to matter when she left home a few hours ago, but now she regretted that she had to lose the kimonos which she had brought with her as a bride and had had no chance to wear. She thought of a handbag that she bought when Nozomi gave her New Year's money, and with a jolt, of a gold watch belonging to her husband. She had saved up the money and they chose it together.

'This is the most expensive thing I have ever owned,' her husband said, and kept on looking at his wrist like a child with a new toy at the restaurant they went to afterwards.

She closed her eyes.

There were about two hundred people, mostly women and children, at the station. Towards evening, everybody became restless. They were getting hungry and impatient.

'Since we have had to wait here so long, we needn't have been rushed like that,' a woman began to complain. 'I wish I'd brought a few more things.'

'Are we going or not? The Russians will catch us up.'

After a while, Hayashi came back and said, 'Anyone who can help carrying food, come with me, please. The more people, the better.' Young boys and girls, women without small children, including executives and their families, got up and followed him. Soon an assortment of incongruous items, large bags of biscuits, tins of fish, meat, fruits, vegetables, bags of sweets, rice, saké, rice cakes, seaweed, sugar, tea, powdered milk, spirit stoves, torches, candles, matches, cigarettes, blankets, were brought back and welcomed with involuntary exclamations of pleasure.

'Hayashi san found out about an army depot and we went there,' one of the neighbours explained. The depot was guarded by a few soldiers who were ready to abandon the place. 'We'll go back and stock ourselves up,' they said. 'These things might be useful in Chenyang.'

Everybody was busy. Together they lit the stoves, cooked rice, toasted rice cakes and made tea. They were cheerful and became friendly once again. It would be about six hours' train journey to Chenyang, and from there they would be able to go back to Japan. What would happen after that did not worry anyone. They would be home.

The tea, made with powdered milk and sugar, was delicious and Toshié was relaxed in the knowledge that her children were fed and happy, at least till the next morning. Everything would be all right after the next day.

The men smoked and gradually the excited chatter subsided. Mothers managed to rinse out soiled nappies and hang them over the hedge. They were still waiting but the mood was less desperate.

Finally, around midnight, they were told that the train was ready. Someone whispered that the problem had been finding a driver who was willing to make the journey to Chenyang. Under Hayashi's instructions, silent and in an orderly fashion, they climbed on board and the train finally started to move.

Toshié had no sentimental feeling about parting. Her mind was full of relief that she had escaped and of the pleasure of going back to Japan after four years. With the war going on, she had not been able to visit her parents since she married. She had no news of her husband, but tonight, she thought, she had to be grateful that she and her children were fed and safe. She would think of her husband and start making inquiries when she got to Chenyang.

The children and babies were settled. Toshié and her friends talked a little but eventually one after another they were quiet. The lights were off in the carriages and it was dark outside. Toshié was too agitated to fall asleep at first, but soon, lulled by the rhythmic motion of the train, she, too, slipped into unconsciousness. She had been through more than enough for one day.

She was not sure where she was, but she heard beans jumping on a hot pan.

'Okahsan, why are you roasting salty beans there?' she was going to ask. Roasted beans were a treat that she and her brothers and sisters had as a child. There were no cakes and sweets on ordinary days. In her dream her mother was sitting by a thundering waterfall. Toshié was still half awake when she remembered that she was on the train. She was about to be dragged back to sleep again when someone shouted, 'Bandits!'

Everybody stirred and looked around drowsily. The word 'bandits' did not sink in with them. It sounded like a film about a nineteenth-century story.

'Get down on the floor.' They heard Hayashi's voice.

A child started to cry which set off a few others. The train roared on. Before she crouched down, Toshié saw through the window the flicker of fire. It was still dark outside.

The train slowed down and stopped. Shouts, galloping horses and firing guns were audible now that the train was quiet. Everybody in Toshié's carriage remained on the floor and did not move.

Someone came in with a hand lamp. Deprived of the protective darkness, they all felt vulnerable.

Hayashi's voice said, 'If you have any money or anything precious, put it on the seats, and leave the carriage as quietly as possible. You'll be all right. Don't panic. Just leave the train quietly and stay out-side.'

Hayashi was being pushed from behind by a bandit in filthy rags with a gun. Several equally dirty and smelly men weaved through the people on the floor to the next carriage. Toshié and her friends scrambled up and one by one climbed down from the train. Once on the ground, Toshié thought of running away. No doubt the idea must have occurred to the others as well, but it was too dark, and they had nowhere to go. They remained huddled on the embankment.

The executive families who had occupied a separate carriage also came down and joined the others. Now, like everybody else, they were empty-handed. The lights went up and down the carriages as the bandits gathered their booty. Two horse-drawn carts appeared from the darkness. The bandits set to work piling up their plunder, including the food supplies from the army depot, on the carts.

It was cool. Toshié's little daughter was awake but the baby was asleep on her back. A streak of light appeared in the eastern sky and the stars began to fade. Dawn would bring another unknown day. Had they not been attacked, by this time they should have been almost at their destination, Chenyang.

After the bandits had gone, they sat on, numbed by the experience. Hayashi had climbed back on to the train. He came down and said to the dismayed people, 'I am sorry, the driver has gone. We bribed him so that he would not stop the train but he was too scared. The only way I can think of to get to Chenyang is to walk.'

'Hayashi kun,' one of the executives called to him, 'how far do you think it is to Chenyang?'

'My guess is about one hundred and fifty kilometres.'

'Humm.'

'I suggest,' Hayashi said, 'that those who do not want to walk can remain in the train. The Russians will come soon, I think, but if they see that you do not have any intention of resisting, they will not harm you. Of course, there may be more bandits. Someone has to find food and drink. Nobody knows how long you have to be here. But there will be problems and risks for the walkers, too.'

'That is so.'

Most of the executive families and women with small children decided to stay.

'I will go and do my best to get help to rescue you. Keep your spirits up.' Hayashi stood among the people who were going to stay. 'I am sure you have heard about mirages. This is the kind of place that they appear.'

Toshié had made up her mind. She wanted to reach Chenyang as soon as possible. A hundred and fifty kilometre march with the children and without food and drink sounded crazy, but it would be better than sitting day after day starved and waiting for Russians who might come and might kill them all in the end.

The mother with the sick daughter tried to persuade her son to go.

'If you get to Dalian, you can find otohsan and tell him what happened to us. Otohsan will rescue us.'

'How do you know I can reach Dalian?' the son was saying. 'If I get lost or taken by the bandits, we will be all separated. Besides, in case we have to walk after all, Momoko nesan will need me.'

'He is right, okahsan. Don't let him go.' The girl was holding her brother's hand. 'We don't want to be separated now.'

Kimiko decided to stay.

'When you reach Chenyang, send a rescue team for us.' Tears streamed down her cheeks. With one hand she held Tetsuo, who was watching wide-eyed, tightly, and with the other she held Toshié's hand. 'I won't say good-bye. I'll see you soon.'

Hayashi looked around. 'Those who want to walk, come this way, please. I want to know how many we are.'

There were about thirty people but no one else had small children. He looked at Toshié.

'Are you sure you want to come?'

She looked up at him and nodded.

'Good luck.'

'Be careful.'

'We'll see each other soon,' everybody cried.

After two hours, the walking group could still see the train standing far away over the flat barren land, but the people who were standing and looking after them were no longer recognisable.

'So long as we walk along the railway, we won't get lost. We should reach Chenyang, whether we want to or not,' Hayashi, who had tied a piece of cotton cloth over his head, said cheerfully.

Toshié trudged on. Some who had hurried at first were found sitting exhausted. She was not going to give up. The baby who was crying weakly on her back stopped crying. She felt him heavier than usual. It was hot again.

'Don't think about the heat, or the weight of the children. Just one step ahead and I'll be that much nearer to Chenyang. Soon, I will sit and feed him. When I find a cool little wood, we will sit down,' she kept on saying to herself, but there were no woods. Not even a tree as far as she could see.

The group gradually spread out. Hayashi often stopped and waited for everybody to catch up, but soon some were hopelessly behind. There was nothing more he could do except tell them to go back to the train.

'If I find a village, I will try to ask for help. There must be a village somewhere.' Toshié thought that he was saying it to encourage them.

'Think of sucking lemons,' he suggested. 'You'll feel your mouth water a little.'

They never found cool little woods where damp ground gave them soft beds to lie down, but there was a mound and about twenty people who had made it so far sat down in a little shade.

Toshié put down her baby. He was limp as she lowered him to the ground and remained motionless. Toshié did not understand. She held him and sat there. She heard her daughter whimper, 'Okahsan, I want a drink.'

'Yes, I will get you a drink,' she said mechanically, and stared at the parched land spread in front of her.

'What can I do with him?' she vaguely wondered. 'I don't want to leave him.'

'We want to walk as much as we can before nightfall,' Hayashi said. 'Let's go. There must be a stream.'

Toshié sat there holding her baby.

'Let's go,' Hayashi repeated.

'I don't want to leave my baby.' Tears started. They tasted salty.

Hayashi looked surprised and then understood. He said gently, 'We'll bury him here by this mound. You can come back one day. Look, this mound is very old. It will be here for a long time.'

As Toshié stood and watched, silently crying, a few of the men made a shallow dent in the ground with their hands and put scanty soil over the baby.

'Let's go,' they urged her. She put her daughter on her back and dumbly followed the others.

In the evening, in the last rays of sunshine, they saw mud huts huddled over the horizon encircled by mud walls. Wisps of smoke were rising and kaolian fields surrounded the hamlet. A line of willow trees meant a stream. It looked a picture of peaceful life.

'We'll beg them to help us!' Everybody started to walk more briskly. But before they were near enough, they could see a group of people running towards them holding sticks and shouting.

'Stop!' Hayashi stared. 'You stay here. I'll go and talk to them.'

'I'll come with you,' a couple of men volunteered.

For the group which stood and watched, it became clear that the Manchurians did not have any intention of giving them hospitality or listening to their pleas. They could see their wide-open mouths and raised sticks. The men ran back and everybody started to run. Toshié followed them. She had been a good runner, but with a three-year-old girl on her back, she was not fast enough. She heard running steps and shouts close behind. She felt something hot on her shoulder. Her head was hit repeatedly. She stumbled and rolled on the ground. She was stamped on and kicked. She stayed still.

Some flies buzzed. A long time passed. It became cool and dark. A big moon rose. It was quiet, not even insects singing. She slowly raised her head. There was a burning sensation on her shoulder and her head ached. As she stood up, stiff and staggering because of the weight on her back, she saw several people still lying down ahead of her. She went and touched the nearest person. Her former neighbour did not move. She was half naked and her blood was black in the moonlight.

Toshié staggered on until she came to a muddy stream not far from the hamlet. Dogs were barking. There was a row of willow trees. She sat and put down her daughter gently on the ground. She knew that Michiko was dead on her back. She had been shielded by her daughter and Michiko had been beaten to death.

'I am sorry. Okahsan was wrong to carry you on her back,' she stroked Michiko's injured head. 'It must have hurt.'

She felt her tears running down and remembered the touch of a little finger tracing trickles of sweat on her face on the way to the station. She was so alive only yesterday. She held her daughter tightly and sobbed.

'I will join you very soon,' she whispered again and again.

When the sun rose, she stood up and began to walk. She could not decide how to kill herself but if she went on, she would eventually die of starvation or of exhaustion, or she would meet more Manchurians and they would kill her, she thought.

It was on the second or the third evening that she came to the ruin of a small mud hut. It had been painted white, but had half fallen down. There were a few trees around it and pieces of rags clung to sticks stuck in the ground. It seemed like an old shrine or a grave.

'I will lie down there,' she thought. 'That is a nice place to die.'

As she was going in, she nearly screamed. A man was coming out.

'It's me,' a voice said. It was Hayashi who had seen her approaching.

Nozomi had come in and listened to Toshié. He folded his arms and did not say a word. Haruko, too, was quiet.

'Ojisan, obasan, should I have stayed in the train as the war ended soon after that?' Toshié asked half to herself.

'No, there would not have been any chance for little children to survive,' Haruko said.

'The Russians have not brought your people to Chenyang. I have not heard about any one from your group,' Nozomi assured her. He had been asked to join a committee organising a centre for Japanese refugees, and was busy negotiating with the Russians.

'I wish I were dead. I want to kill myself,' Toshié wailed.

'Toshié.' Emi and Mari looked scared by the severity of their father's voice. 'Aren't you forgetting an important thing? Wherever he is, your husband must be worried about you. He must be trying hard to survive so that he can come back to you.'

Toshié recovered her composure.

Haruko looked at Nozomi and asked, 'Otohsan, what did you do with your belt?'

All of them including Tochié looked at him. Nozomi himself looked, too, and said, 'I was talking to one of the Russian officers today, and he admired it so much that I gave it to him.'

'And he gave you the string?'

'I seem to have lost weight. I couldn't keep my trousers up so I asked for the replacement. He was going to give me his dirty old belt but I told him I didn't want it.'

'Otohsan!' Haruko laughed a little helplessly and even Toshié's face had a ghost of a smile.

'Aren't you afraid of the Russians?' Mari asked.

'No. They are friendly and guileless chaps.'

'The way they sneaked in from the back door so that they could join in getting the spoils of war seems artful enough to me,' Haruko said.

'Don't you think that doing things in a way that even we can see through is artless?'

'Otohsan likes the Russians.'

'I try not to have enemies.'

'Come and eat, Toshié san,' Haruko called, and as Toshié sat at the table, she handed her chopsticks. Toshié looked at them as though they were unfamiliar objects and exclaimed, 'Oh!'

Haruko turned to her inquiringly.

'Obasan, I still have my pearl ring on my finger.'

20

Survival

'Toshié san, these days, otohsan does all our shopping,' Haruko told Toshié over the meal. 'I haven't been out at all. He brings back fresh vegetables and meat. Apparently there are men on the road selling these things.'

People cannot hide and do nothing for ever. Even after a few days, they need to have food, earn a living somehow, and have contact with the outside world.

'Are things more expensive than before?' Toshié asked.

'I don't know how much they cost before,' Nozomi said, and Haruko laughed.

'There are Japanese people selling their possessions.'

Along the former busiest street all the shops were boarded up but in front of them on the pavement, people put down mats and spread out many different things to sell.

That night, Toshié and the two girls slept in the same room with Emi in the middle. Haruko heard suppressed sobbing during the night. She got up quietly and sat by Toshié. She gently stroked her head. Toshié took Haruko's hand and wept for a while.

'Obasan, what is in there?' Toshié asked, pointing at a garage in the front garden. Towards the end of the war, under the assumption that Nozomi's work had a military purpose, incongruous materials had been offered to him by the army. He did not scrutinise where and how they had been obtained, but just paid and stored them in his empty garage where a Russian general had kept his car or a carriage half a century ago.

There were rolls of wire, insulating tape, boxes of nails, tools, all of which were nothing to do with his work.

'Why do you waste money on something you do not need?' Haruko had complained about Nozomi's careless way of spending a lot of money.

Characteristically, Nozomi had not given any answer.

Haruko went with Toshié to the garage and showed her inside. 'Either the mob was not aware of them, or they did not realise their value. Now, I suppose, we will sell them all.'

It must be worth quite a lot of money, she thought, and had to admit that Nozomi's purchases had been a good investment.

'Isn't that the same fuse wire that we buy in short lengths wound round a piece of cardboard?' Toshié asked.

'It looks like it, but I must ask otohsan.'

'Obasan, if it is, instead of selling it as big rolls like this, why don't we make little coils and sell them in the street?'

'Sell them in the street?'

'Not you, obasan.' Toshié smiled. 'I will take them and sell them.'

Nozomi did not oppose the idea.

'Otohsan, after all we might make a profit out of them.'

'I don't know about profit, but those things are always in demand.'

'How much shall we sell, ojisan?'

As though the question triggered his memory, Nozomi said, 'I met Suzuki kun today.' Suzuki was his manager. 'He told me that his wife has died.'

She had never been strong. During the riot, she had suffered from pneumonia, and he had not been able to get a doctor, or any sort of medicine.

Suzuki would be the right person to find out the price and what best to do with the stored materials, Nozomi said. In any case, he had been thinking of offering him support. Later, Nozomi said to Haruko that it would be good for Toshié to occupy herself and at the same time help them, but if they asked Suzuki for advice, he would have to bring his fourteen-month-old son now that no one else could look after him. He thought that Haruko should warn Toshié. Toshié accepted the situation bravely.

'Obasan, I decided to live. And I cannot spend all my life avoiding little children.'

Suzuki brought the little boy.

'What a beautiful boy!' Although it was not the first time that the Sanjos had seen him, everybody admired him. He had pink cheeks and large liquid eyes. Toshié held him and he was quiet in her lap. Emi and Mari were delighted and made a lot of fuss, to which he responded sweetly.

In the evening, Suzuki looked at his little son, and said, 'Shall we go home now? Say bye-bye and thank you.'

The little boy stood facing the door. With his little bottom towards everybody, he bowed deeply. They all laughed.

'He is beautiful. So quiet and good,' the four women chattered after they left.

'I thought he was rather hot,' Toshié said. She was reminded of the girl on her brother's back going to the station. She had the same translucent skin and pink cheeks.

'I hope he is all right.' She could not help uttering her thoughts aloud, 'He looks too beautiful,' but everybody took it as a general remark.

'Suzuki san seems to be coping all right. The little boy was very clean,' Haruko said.

Suzuki had promised to return but he did not come for a few days. When he came, he was alone. His little son had died that night from miliary tuberculosis.

'He must have been suffering from it for a long time. He might have died hardly knowing how it is to be well. I was too occupied with my wife's health and I have never had him checked since he was born. I had no experience with children and thought he was a quiet boy. Most of the time he just sat and watched me.'

With those eyes . . . Haruko sat, incapable of knowing how to take the news. His memory was too poignant.

There were not many doctors or facilities. War had killed, and was still killing, directly or indirectly, so many people.

'He said good-bye to us, facing the wrong way,' Emi sobbed. Suzuki bowed his head and covered his eyes with one hand. His shoulders shook.

School started and Emi and Mari went back, not to the same school but to newly organised classes. There were no lessons which required facilities, but English was added as a new subject.

A lot of girls of Emi's age had had their hair clipped and it grew back in spikes. They wore scarves over their heads and to snatch off someone else's scarf was a popular practical joke.

Haruko and Toshié sat at home and rolled fuse wire into coils. Suzuki helped to bring out the heavy rolls and cut them. He also negotiated selling tools and thick wire. When they made twenty coils of wire, Toshié wanted to take them to the street and try to sell them. She should not take too many.

'I'll pretend that there are not many more.'

'Have you done anything like this before, Toshié san?'

'Not really, obasan, but my mother often had to sell vegetables, straw boots and rope, things like that. My grandfather used to make baskets in winter, and sometimes I went with my grandmother to sell them.'

'I see.'

Toshié's grandparents were Haruko's parents-in-law. As their son, had Nozomi been to market carrying baskets his father had made in winter, sitting on the hardened earth floor?

Nozomi's mother had told Haruko, in a dialect which she found difficult to understand, that Nozomi had a good knowledge of cows, and since he was about five years old, people had asked his opinion when they wanted to sell or buy a cow.

'You don't know how peasants live,' Nozomi had laughed indulgently.

'His stuck-up wife.' Her sisters-in-law had been unfriendly.

'Be careful. The peasants are perverse,' her grandmother Kei had said.

Toshié put the coils in an old canvas bag and was going out.

'Don't you need a stand?'

'No, obasan, I'll try leaving them in a bag. People will be curious and gather around it. That way I'll get more customers.'

Toshié came home triumphantly after about two hours. 'I sold them all. I was asked if there were more. I said I didn't know and told them to come back and see me tomorrow. I won't take too many at a time and won't take fuse wire every day. But I will take other things like the insulating tape.'

They found a dozen shiny square tins about thirty centimetres high. The records of Nozomi's purchases had been lost since his office had been taken over by the Chinese, but Suzuki remembered that there had been many tins of nails.

'They don't sound like nails.' Nozomi lifted one of the tins. He prised it open. They all looked inside the round hole. The tin was full of pine-needle-shaped chocolates in many colours. They looked at each other like a bunch of children who had come across hidden treasure. It was Haruko who picked one out and put it on her tongue.

'Oi, wait! It might be poisoned.' Nozomi looked at his wife.

'No, they are chocolates all right,' she responded matter-of-factly.

Haruko and Toshié were busy again, dividing the chocolate into bags. That afternoon, Toshié brought back dumplings filled with juicy meat.

'I hope you don't mind that I spent the takings without asking you first, obasan, but they looked delicious. You know, there are Japanese people steaming these in the street and selling them.'

For the first time in weeks, Haruko went out shopping. As Toshié had described, the main street was lined with vendors and most of them were Japanese. Not many were selling their possessions any more. They were venturing into producing things, mostly food, to sell.

The couple who were selling the dumplings were a former bank manager and his wife whom Haruko knew well. The husband was calling, 'Steamed dumplings, steamed dumplings,' and his wife was squatting and fanning charcoal. A small push cart was parked by them. The dumplings were almost identical in shape, and were selling well.

She wondered if she should avoid the couple in case they were embarrassed at being recognised but decided that many of their acquaintances would pass, and this was no ordinary time.

'Otani san, you seem to be very busy.' Haruko approached them.

'Ah, Mrs Sanjo.' He looked delighted to see her.

'I had your dumplings yesterday. They were delicious. How do you know such a recipe?'

'Aha!' Otani smiled, as he wrapped up five dumplings for a customer and received money. 'Mrs Sanjo, my parents and my brother, before he was drafted, ran a Chinese restaurant. I used to help them and learnt a few things.'

'Oh, no wonder.'

Another customer came, and he was busy wrapping more dumplings.

By him, his wife shyly nodded.

'She didn't like it.' He turned to his wife and said to Haruko, 'But we've got to live.'

Holding a warm parcel, Haruko walked on. There was someone selling kimonos. A Chinese man picked one out and held it up. It had a stream of cherry blossoms diagonally from one shoulder on the palest blue background. The man's gnarled fingers handled the delicate material, turned it around and then abruptly dropped it on the mat. The kimono was left in a heap as though a woman had discarded it. It looked licentious.

'We are people of a ruined country.' She felt depressed.

'Okahsan, Etsuko-chan is selling cigarettes. Can I sell cigarettes, too?' Mari asked.

'No, you cannot.'

'Why, okahsan? I'll bring back money for you.'

'Otohsan gives us money. You do not have to earn money. Besides, you have school.'

'After school. Toshié san is selling things, too.'

'Toshié san is grown up.'

'But Etsuko-chan is doing it. She is the same age as me.'

'Mari-chan, okahsan said you cannot. You have a lot of school work to do.'

'Otohsan.' Mari was waiting for Nozomi at the back door one day and said in a small voice, 'Otohsan, do you think you can give me a little money? When I grow up, I will give it back to you.'

'Why do you want money all of a sudden?'

'Otohsan, please, will you?'

'Tell me what it is for.'

Mari fidgeted. 'Will you promise not to tell okahsan?'

'It depends. You tell me what it is first.'

Mari blushed a little and stood looking at her feet.

'All right, I won't tell okahsan, so tell me what it is.'

Mari had begged Etsuko to let her have her cigarette tray. It had looked such fun to sell things. Everybody was selling things. As the parents of a lot of her schoolfriends were in financial difficulties, some of the children were helping their fathers or mothers in the street.

Etsuko had acquiesced and gone away to look at other displays.

Mari had found that selling cigarettes was not such fun as it seemed. The tray was heavy and soon her neck hurt. The Russians were large and scary. She did not want to approach them and offer a packet as Etsuko did. How did she know they wanted cigarettes? She felt shy about thrusting the tray towards them. The Chinese and Japanese were rude or indifferent.

Just as she was going to give the tray back to Etsuko, a Chinese boy ran up to her, snatched a couple of packets from the tray and ran away.

Etsuko's father had been taken from the street by the Russians in the first days of the occupation and had not been heard of since. His family believed that, together with others like him, he had been taken to Siberia for forced labour. Her mother was cooking and washing at the Russian officers' club and her two brothers were cleaning.

'You see, if she loses two packets, she has no profit. Actually she lost money today, and . . .' Mari started to cry.

'I see. Come along then. We'll go and pay Etsuko-chan now. Tell okahsan that we'll go out together.'

Mari wiped her tears and smiled.

She took Nozomi's hand and they walked out together.

'So, it was not much fun, was it?' Nozomi asked.

Mari shook her head. 'No, it was awful. I thought I'd try and then I wanted to help you, too.'

'You don't have to sell cigarettes to help me,' Nozomi said, and added rather thoughtfully, 'Well, not yet anyway.'

'Otohsan, how can you communicate with the Russians?' Emi asked.

'A lot of them speak French and German. Some of them know a little English, too.'

'And do you speak all those languages?'

'I can't say I speak any of them fluently and I am rusty since I haven't spoken them for so long, but, yes, I manage to make myself understood and understand what they want if it is not too complicated. We exchange jokes and laugh together. Language is an important bridge among people.'

'Aren't you afraid of them?' Mari looked at him.

'No, the officers are, on the whole, well educated and decent.'

'Do they still want things like a leather belt?' Haruko joined in.

'They gave me bread and a jar of caviar to thank me, didn't they?'

'But, otohsan, their bread was black,' Emi said. The word the Japanese used for bread was 'pan' which had come either from the French 'pain' or Portuguese 'pão'. 'Pan' was white. Black bread was a symbol of poverty.

'We'll invite some of the Russian officers for dinner,' Nozomi said, and Haruko was astonished.

'No, otohsan, don't be ridiculous. We can't have them here.'

'You know, they asked me if I wanted to go to Russia. They'd give me national guest status as an engineer.'

'What does that mean, national guest status?' Emi asked.

'I don't know precisely, but they will give me a place to live, a decent salary, a dacha perhaps, and a holiday on the Black Sea.'

'Can we go to school?'

'Of course you can. You can go to Moscow University when you grow up. It has splendid buildings.'

'Don't be absurd, otohsan.' Haruko was horrified and hastily cut in. 'You don't know what would happen to us. They might take you to Siberia. We don't know what they are thinking about. We can't trust them. Besides, they say you can't eat if you don't work. I don't want to be a lavatory cleaner.'

21

Going Home

Nozomi went out every day until the evening working for the refugee committee. At night he often sat at a small dining table with his daughters and seemed to Haruko to be composing letters in a foreign language.

'What are you writing, otohsan?'

'Mm?'

Emi, who had started to learn English, leaned over. 'Oh, I can read this bit. "It is" in English.'

'That's the trouble. It is hard going beyond "it is".' Nozomi scratched his head. 'I have never learnt practical English.'

'What did you learn?'

'Our readers were Goldsmith's *The Vicar of Wakefield*, Macaulay's *History of England*, and, oh, yes, Gibbon's *Decline and Fall of the Roman Empire*, books like that. "In the second century of the Christian era the empire of Rome comprehended the fairest part of the earth,"' he recited, although nobody else understood. 'Funny one does not forget things that one learnt while young. The teachers made us memorise passages. Not a bad way to learn a foreign language, but we thought that the modern English man wrote and spoke like that. I bet the teacher himself did not know that what he was teaching was archaic and we were trying to speak like nineteenth-century gentlemen. They looked at me curiously when I talked to people in London.'

They all laughed but Haruko still did not find out why he was trying to write letters in English.

Toshié said one day, 'Obasan, do you know ojisan is very popular?'

'Popular among whom?'

'You should come, and see ojisan working at the refugee centre. Even in the streets, women clamour around him.'

'Really, Toshié san, why?'

'Because he is the only one who will help. He is wonderful. He does not hesitate to go to the Russian army headquarters and meet the commander-in-chief. He negotiates to retrieve blankets, clothes and all kinds of things that the Russians had confiscated from the Japanese army stores. The refugee centre has stoves installed for winter now and he managed to get sufficient amounts of coal as well. He listens, not just to refugees, but to those women whose husbands have not come back yet and are left with children without any income.'

The refugee centre had been set up in a former school building and it had also become the information centre. Toshié went there every day to see if she could get news about her husband and also about her friends who had stayed on the train. The railway had been used daily by the Russians for transportation of recruits and supplies, but so far nothing had been heard about the train left on the track. Nobody seemed to know about it.

'Hayashi san is helping ojisan, now. He said that ojisan insists on seeing the top people at the Russian army headquarters and waits till they give up refusing him. Ojisan argues so forcefully that they listen. Even Hayashi san, who is pretty courageous himself, is impressed.'

It was not a description of Nozomi that Haruko recognised, even after twenty-five years of marriage.

He had never gone out willingly among people, particularly among people of high rank. It seemed to Haruko that he had felt an aversion to meeting people with names and distinctions. She frowned, trying to elicit from memory evidence of this hitherto hidden side of his personality.

Haruko's grandfather, Tei-ichi, had been a close friend of many powerful politicians. Even Shobei Miwa had not been forgotten among a certain circle of people. Ayako had said now and again, 'The new Minister of Industry and Commerce used to come to see your Shirai oji-isama for advice and help. You must make sure that Nozomi san goes to see him. He will be very useful,' or 'Tell Nozomi san to see Goto san. Your Miwa oji-isama helped him when he was a student. He is now a famous industrialist, but still keeps in touch with us. He never forgets to send "incense money" for the anniversary of oji-isama's death. He will be very happy to see and help Nozomi san.'

When Haruko passed on the message and urged him to go and get acquainted with these famous people, Nozomi had been noncommittal. If she persisted, his answer would be, 'I am an engineer and I am quite happy as I am. I am not interested in politics.'

'It has nothing to do with politics,' Haruko used to protest hotly. 'Why don't you just go and see him? I am sure you will benefit. In any case, no harm will be done by meeting him. That's how people get on in life.'

He would not answer her. When it came to an argument, he would be silent. So there had never been a quarrel between them but it was impossible to persuade him to do something he was not interested in.

'Why don't you want to see him? Is there any particular reason?' she had once pestered him, when the person in question had been a well-known social figure.

'We have nothing in common. He does not have anything to offer me, nor I him.'

'How do you know? He would open up good connections for you.'

'I am an engineer and not a society figure. I don't need connections.'

'You can be an engineer and still enjoy a social life. You are the most bigoted person I have ever met.' Haruko had thrown the remark at him in frustration.

Nozomi had refused to respond. Haruko had decided that, after all these years, he still suffered from the shyness of a poor peasant boy. 'That's it,' she had thought, 'he is not confident enough socially. I must do something about it. I must break the ice for him.'

'If you don't need connections, they will help Emi and Mari,' Haruko had ventured. She had been confident that this would move him.

'Emi and Mari?' He had looked unexpectedly amused. 'I thought you were a disciple of that famous lady. What is her name? The proponent of the feminist movement. I think they are too intelligent to depend on such connections to find husbands, if that is what you mean. They are my daughters and I will make sure that counts.'

Haruko had pondered: Those people have titles and financial empires that Nozomi would never even dream of achieving. Emi and Mari's pictures could be in society magazines as beautiful and intelligent young ladies through those people, and a lot of good families with young men would notice them. It is a shame that he can never get away from his poor family background. He does not understand. He cannot be comfortable in such a circle of people.

Nozomi might be obstinate in some ways but he was not a domineering husband. He had not interfered with what Haruko did or wanted to do. He had never complained about her decisions.

When the house they lived in was no longer suitable, it was Haruko who would decide to move. On one occasion Nozomi had come home to a new place from his work, having asked the nearby noodle shop if they knew people who had moved in on that day.

'Otohsan! I have told you about it many times. I gave you the address once more this morning. I explained to you exactly where it is.'

'I remembered the name of the station. It was quite ingenious of me to have asked at the noodle shop, I think,' he had chuckled. When people were busy moving or spring-cleaning, it was common to have bowls of noodles delivered instead of cooking.

'Even so.'

Not many people had owned a house, but Haruko had thought that it was a good time to buy. People rarely bought old houses. The normal procedure was to buy a piece of land and have a house built. Ayako, who had been visiting them, had come to Haruko's aid.

'Nozomi san, space on this earth is limited. With population growth, land prices will always go up. You never lose by owning a piece of land.'

Nozomi had smiled. 'Yes, okahsan, you are right. We'll think about it.' He was always polite and obliging to his mother-in-law. Ayako had still been young and a journalist who had come to interview Nozomi had mistaken her for his wife. The age difference between Ayako and Nozomi was less than that between Nozomi and Haruko. The article had mentioned that a remarkable engineer, Nozomi Sanjo, was a gentleman and very polite to his wife.

Backed by Ayako, Haruko had started enquiries about land for sale. When she had thought she had found a suitable place, Nozomi had said, 'Rather out-of-the-way, isn't it?'

'I know. But they say there will be a new line for the trains soon and that's why it is a good buy now. The price will soon shoot up.'

'Is that what the developer said?'

'Isn't it obvious if a new line for trains is being planned?'

'Mm.'

'What do you think?'

'It is too far from my office. It means wasting at least three hours a day. That would mean within a year I'll lose . . .'

'Otohsan, it's meant to be an investment. You can sell it when the price goes up.'

'Why do we have to go through such a tiresome process? Buying, selling, buying. Why don't we find a good place and live there?'

After several similar conversations, Haruko had begun to be irritated. To her, he was simply indecisive, and also indifferent.

'Is there any law that engineers cannot engage in things other than engineering?' she had said one night. She immediately felt that she had gone too far, but then thought that, as always, Nozomi would ignore her stinging remark. To Haruko's surprise and apprehension, he had responded. He had lowered the newspaper which he had held in front of him and looked at her.

'As a matter of fact, there is a rule. I shouldn't waste my time finding out whether the land is a former graveyard, or recently reclaimed land so that it is too soft to build a decent house on. That after all the promised rail line is not going to happen, and all the other flaws in our future asset. I have to be in my office or on site doing my work. I am willing to go along and buy a park or have a castle built just as you like, but I am not chasing after those developers who think of nothing but cheating people.'

'Why didn't you tell me before? Then I didn't have to waste my time.' Haruko was not expecting a reply.

'If I told you in the beginning, you would think that I was making an excuse to avoid buying the land, and accuse me of not being ambitious enough or deliberately avoiding an affluent style of life.'

'Oh!'

'But I must admit land prices are much higher than I expected. You have found that out for me.'

At that time Nozomi had been earning a good salary as the head of the engineering department of a well-established company which was still expanding. Yet, Haruko reflected, their income had never been sufficient. This was because Nozomi's relatives had constantly demanded money: 'The family grave ought to be reconstructed', 'So and so is getting married', 'So and so is ill'.

'They think we have a money-growing tree,' she had complained to Ayako, and had been obliged to look for land in an area where the price was relatively modest.

When Nozomi's older brother had asked for money for the third time to buy more 'very productive land for an amazing price', Haruko had objected for the first time. She was aware that her in-laws were better off by then.

Nozomi had replied, 'I know we have done a lot, and I understand what you feel, but I always remember when I was living at my teacher's house, my family could not afford my board and lodging, and every month, niisan brought a bag of rice as a part of my keep. I cannot forget him walking home in the snow. He did not even have a coat.'

Haruko had acquiesced, but had suggested, 'In that case, why don't you give him the money but ask him to put the land in Emi's and Mari's name? Niisan can use the land as he likes.'

Nozomi had agreed that that was a good idea.

'I'll tell niisan.'

Haruko reflected and still could not see any evidence of a tough negotiator or a good organiser, or, above everything else, of his willingness to meet authoritative figures at the top.

'Otohsan has changed.' She shook her head.

'Haruko, we haven't got my old dictionaries here, have we?'

They must have been packed with the other things they had left in Japan, or they might have been thrown away when she had cleared the house in Tokyo before she came to Manchuria. Nozomi wanted dictionaries to write to the newly established offices of the British Consulate, the American Consulate and the International Red Cross.

As Nozomi walked in the busy street, still trying to compose English sentences in his head, he saw a young engineer he knew well standing behind a small stand.

'Hirai kun, how are you? I am very pleased to see you. Obviously you came back all right. Is your family well?' Delighted to see a young colleague, he was unusually chatty.

'Sanjo san! I am pleased to see you, too.' Hirai's face lit up. 'I was lucky. As I suffered from pleurisy as a student, I was branded Grade C and not called till late on. I had not reached anywhere far by the time the war ended.'

Nozomi had always regarded the young man as exceptionally brilliant. He looked at his display of crockery, clothes, some books. He spotted an English–Japanese and a Japanese–English dictionary.

'Just the things I want.' He picked them up. 'I am trying to write to whatever organisation I can think of for help, and I really need them.'

'No response from our own government?'

'No. They must be in chaos. Anyway, there is no way of getting in touch with them directly. How much are these?'

'Oh, please, take them.'

'No, I can't do that.'

'Yes. I wouldn't get much, anyway. Please. I hope they will help you to get what we need.'

'You are not a good businessman, are you?' Nozomi laughed, and added in a comradely way, 'My wife would say all engineers are no good at business. I might add all good engineers.'

Hirai smiled and said, 'Well, as part of the bargain, then, I will come and ask for your help when we get back to Japan.' He had always looked up to Sanjo san.

Nozomi's eyes wandered to the far end of the street. He gazed at nothing in particular for a moment. He looked forlorn. He turned back.

'You are young and capable. You don't need my help. Besides, I won't be in a position to help you when I go back to Japan.' Then he smiled, 'Thank you for these. Look after yourself. Winter is coming.'

He put the dictionaries under his arm and walked away into the crowd.

In spite of inadequate facilities and food, the harsh winter had left very few casualties among over a thousand refugees. Outside the temperature was so low that, when you breathed in, the hair froze stiff inside your nostrils, but the refugee centre was kept sufficiently warm. There was enough bedding and clothes, especially for the children and babies. The place was kept clean due to Hayashi's hard work.

Nozomi had organised doctors and nurses and established two clinics. He had appealed for medicine from the International Red Cross through the British Consulate and succeeded to a certain extent.

*　　*　　*

When the ice began to melt, and the wind became less harsh, the people realised that their town had turned far more dreary than they remembered. The trees, which had lined the streets, had been felled. The Monument to the Loyal Dead had been vandalised and the almond trees around it had been savagely mutilated. But spring had come.

Haruko was surprised and pleased to see a Chinese vegetable vendor selling a basket of daffodils. The vendor wrapped bunches in a piece of yellowed newspaper and impassively handed them to her.

Then the Mongolian wind swept over the area. Every spring, after the thaw, the sky would become yellow. The wind brought tiny particles of sand all the way from the Gobi Desert. Mouths were gritty, and faces, especially eyebrows, became yellow as though dusted with soybean flour. Furniture was covered with dust. It was a common practice to seal windows with narrow tape but still tiny particles of grit somehow seeped into the house.

When the wind was gone, the evacuation started. It was done in an orderly fashion. The refugees and the women with children went first. By the time the summer was over, the entire Japanese population had gone and the Chinese had recovered their city for themselves after so many years.

The least destitute families left the city last, and Haruko's family was among them.

Early in the morning, the Sanjos got on a horse-drawn cart. They were taken to a small station, beyond the main station. When they arrived, their fellow travellers had begun to assemble. Most of them were former owners of big shops, large factories and companies. They were not the intellectuals of the city but the people with financial means. All their rucksacks were new. They wore tidy new clothes prepared for the journey and the children were well fed.

'Sanjo san.' A man who had been the deputy mayor came looking for Nozomi. The two men walked away from the gathered crowd. Three more men joined them. All five men stood talking for a while. Then Nozomi broke away from them and called out, 'Will one person from each family come here, please.'

News had spread that the richest group among the evacuees would be travelling that day and the obvious danger was that bandits were waiting for them.

'The only way we can get through is to keep on bribing the drivers. There are two of them and we can trust them. But it would help if we contribute whatever we can. By the way, we need not alarm your families.'

The money was collected in Nozomi's hat. Hayashi, who had stayed on to finalise the evacuation, volunteered to keep an eye on the drivers.

The train came to the platform, and everybody started to move. It was the first time that Haruko had put a rucksack on her back. She had packed carefully. The things inside were her last possessions from Manchuria. They had been told that nothing precious should be taken. There would be a customs check.

The rucksack was heavier than she had imagined. In fact, when she was packing, she had not remembered that she would have to carry it herself. Emi and Mari hoisted Haruko's rucksack on her back. She staggered. Finally, Nozomi lifted his on to a bench and put his arms through. A couple of the men helped him to stand up.

They had to climb up the stairs to the bridge over the railway. Haruko had to bend forwards and hold on to the hand-rail otherwise she would have been dragged backwards. She went unsteadily one step after another. She was not thinking of Nozomi or Emi or Mari or anybody else.

A locomotive with several open goods wagons was waiting at the platform. Some men climbed up on the train and others handed rucksacks up to them from the platform.

'Where is Sanjo san?' Somebody looked around. 'He was on the other side of the bridge.'

Haruko thought that it was just like him. Whenever they went away as part of a sightseeing group, he would be the last one to come back to the bus. 'Is everyone here?' And it had always been, 'What happened to Sanjo san?'

'What can he be doing?' Haruko asked in annoyance, as Nozomi appeared at the top of the stairs. He was coming down slowly. He was holding a walking stick horizontally and a small child with a tear-stained face was hanging on to the other end. Between them, a tiny rucksack was dangling from the stick. Nozomi was imitating the sound of the train. His face was shiny with sweat.

'Oh, isn't that Masao?' a man called Onari said.

The Onaris had seven children. As 'Onari' meant big harvest or large amount of produce, they were often the target of good-natured jokes.

'We forgot him. He was left on the other side!' Onari said to his wife.

'Oh, my goodness, I completely forgot about him.' Mrs Onari stood in the middle of her flock and held her hands over her mouth.

Each child had his or her own rucksack according to their size. Masao, hardly out of the toddler stage, was the second youngest of the family.

'Thank you, thank you, Sanjo san.' Onari ran to them, 'I am sorry we lost count.'

Everybody laughed, relieved. The Onari children all looked alike and had to be counted at every move.

It was just like Nozomi, Haruko thought, half exasperated, half admiring, to find a helpless and miserable child, humour him and bring him along while he himself had to struggle with a bundle that he could hardly cope with.

The train finally started and journeyed through the crimson sunset into the starry night. The bandits did not appear. All the people slept curled up around their rucksacks.

Early in the morning, Mari woke up and saw Nozomi standing up.

'Oh, how lovely!' She woke Emi. 'Emi-chan, wake up. The sky is magnificent!' The dawn was beginning to throw gold and rose shafts into the sky.

'Your face is black,' Emi laughed.

'Yours, too.' Mari rubbed her soot-smudged nose, making it worse.

Haruko woke up and handed them a small damp towel. The others were still asleep.

On the horizon to the west, where the sky was still grey, stood massive bottle-shaped chimneys. No smoke was coming out of any of them. They were silently standing there waiting for action.

'Look,' Nozomi said. 'That's where otohsan's work was. It was going to be one of the biggest power stations in the orient.'

'Did you build the power station?'

'I did the planning.'

The four of them stood and watched. Nozomi put his arms around his two daughters who were on either side of him.

'I thought I would send you to any school and any university you wanted at home or abroad. I was going to make sure you were well provided for. When you wanted to get married, I was going to do a lot for you as my daughters. But,' his eyes stayed on the retreating scenery, 'from now on, you both have to stand on your own feet.'

It came as a realisation to Haruko, who had been preoccupied with the immediate problems of the evacuation, that she and Nozomi were leaving what they had been building up for their future. It was the end of a chapter of their history.

PART THREE

22

The Ruined City

The train deposited its passengers at a port. The drivers with thin waists slunk away in the midday sun, with extra money in their pockets as had been promised. Wind-blown and sun-tanned, the evacuees were herded to the customs point, where Chinese soldiers did a spot-check, and then into a former army barracks. It was a building with a stretch of bare boards and a tin roof without any furniture. They immediately opened the small square windows but the heat was stifling.

After the customs point they had left Chinese territory and come under the protection of the Allied Forces.

There were a few officials sent from Japan. Clad in the khaki fatigues of the former Imperial Army, they instructed the new arrivals to go to another building for meals at the sound of a gong. They were cool in response to the relief of the people who had come through a perilous journey and found themselves under the care of their fellow countrymen.

'What is it like in Japan? Life in general, I mean,' someone asked. 'Pretty bad.'

They all wanted to know what that remark implied, but the official's preoccupied manner told them that he was not going to spend time elaborating. In any case, they would find out themselves within a few days. Another Japanese man slowly moved among the unsettled crowd, writing down their family names and counting them.

There was a hut with temporary latrines, sinks and shower cubicles. Having had a wash, they queued up for a meal. They were handed aluminium plates, spoons and cups. Each was stamped with the words 'USA Armed Forces'. A Chinese man in a white apron and cap scooped rice on to the plates and then poured stew over it. They were to take the food to an adjacent tent where there were tables and metal chairs.

Nobody spoke. No one was sure whether to be pleased to be given a meal or whether they should feel resentment at being treated like prisoners. Even the children were quietly spooning the food into their mouths.

For small children and babies, powdered milk was supplied. The mothers felt grateful to the Americans. They were conquerors, but they were benign, unlike the Chinese. Their material generosity impressed the refugees.

After the meal, bars of milky chocolate were distributed among the women and children. To their surprise, the men were each given a packet of cigarettes. The white packet had a round red design in the middle and was sealed with a blue tape to distinguish it from other cigarettes on the market.

Most of the men were impressed.

'If we won the war, things would not have been like this.'

'After all, it's a big and rich country.'

'That's what they want to hear.' One man was cynical but the remark did not break the general harmonious atmosphere. They all sat around and enjoyed smoking.

'Thank goodness, the bandits did not attack us.'

'Sanjo san, you stayed up all night, didn't you?'

'Hayashi kun had a tough time,' Nozomi said. 'I was just awake thinking of one thing or another.'

Mari stood with some other children and looked inside a tent. The flaps were held open and thick cables snaked all over the floor. There were lots of radios and telephones. A nisei (American-born Japanese) soldier with an oriental face came out and said in English with an American accent, 'Chewing gum?'

The children stared at him. He offered them a packet but they ran away.

After three days of waiting, they picked up their rucksacks again and walked up the gangway into an American Liberty Boat. Built to transport tanks, heavy vehicles and armoury, it had a large open hold into which hundreds of evacuees were packed. The boundaries between each family were made out of their own rucksacks. Army blankets were spread out on the iron floor to sit on. Among wailing babies and screaming, running children, they began crossing the sea back to a southern port of their home country.

Time became meaningless for the evacuees who were cooped up in the bottom of the boat lit by shadowless fluorescent light high above. The incessant drone of the engine was the only reminder that they were on a journey.

Haruko noticed that no one was seized with joy on arriving home. No one even expressed relief after the perilous journey. The refugees looked numb as though they had no expectations and had come to accept that tomorrow was unknown.

On the second day, a young man came walking between the ruck-sack walls.

'Are you by any chance Miwa san from Kitani?'

'Kitani?' Haruko sat up. 'Yes, I am from Kitani.'

'Are you Miwa san? Miss Haruko?'

'I used to be.'

'I was told by Mata san to watch out for you.'

He was employed for miscellaneous services on board, he explained, and was the son of a villager from Kitani.

The young man lowered himself to a squatting position and whispered, 'I can arrange for you to have a hot bath and a cup of tea if you all follow me.'

As they climbed up a narrow and steep iron ladder, he turned round and said, 'My name is Tei-suke. Right after I was born, I nearly died of some infection and Dr Shirai saved my life by taking me to his own home to look after me. That is why I am named Tei-suke, having been given a part of Dr Shirai's name. My parents told me never to sleep with my feet towards Dr Shirai's house.

'Matabei san told my parents that you must be coming back one day and my parents contacted me. I have been looking for you for four months.'

The bathroom was small but white-tiled and they were supplied with fragrant soap. Emi and Mari were delighted and sniffed the soap, wrinkling their noses.

'Okahsan, you used to smell like this,' Emi said. 'When you bought perfume at Dalian.'

'Yes, I had beautiful bottles of perfume.'

'Okahsan, look!' As they rubbed, dirt rolled off their skin and the two girls giggled.

'Don't rub too hard. You'll abrase your skin.'

When Nozomi finished his bath, they were taken to a corner of a dining room and given tea and cake.

'Otohsan.' Haruko touched his chin with a little towel she carried around. 'You cut yourself.'

'Okahsan's face is so shiny,' Mari said.

'One day, shall we all go to a hot spring?' Nozomi put his elbows on the table and clasped his hands together looking around at his family.

When they arrived at Sasebo port after three days, the front of the boat was opened like a gigantic mouth. The sunshine streamed into the semi-darkness in the bottom of the boat. The green mountains appeared in front of them beyond the calm sea.

After scrubby plains and craggy hills, the luxuriant mountains were a welcoming sight for the home-coming travellers.

It was a Chinese poet who wrote in the eighth century:

> The country was defeated,
> Yet its mountains and rivers are unchanged . . .

As Haruko indulged herself in such sentiments, the boat jolted and a piercing 'Help! Someone, quick!' was heard. A commotion followed. People rushed to the opening. A mother had been standing at the edge of the opening holding a child. The sudden movement of the boat had made her lose her balance and both she and the child had tumbled down into the water. They were not recovered from the sea alive.

When the evacuees landed, all their possessions and they themselves were sprayed with DDT powder, which they had never heard of but took to be an advanced way of treating vermin and a panacea for hygiene. With this baptism, they were admitted into a modern and civilised society as its members.

Then they were interviewed by government officials. None of them had documents of any kind. There had been a rumour that any written paper would draw suspicion. Why this should be, and where the information had come from, no one knew, but the evacuees had been nervously trying to avoid any obstacles to their passage home. So many hazardous incidents had happened to them since the end of the war, for which no legitimate explanations could be given.

After the interviews, documentation was completed, and a ration book was handed to each person with a train ticket to their home town or destination. The procedure took a long time. Finally they were free to go and boarded the train which had been specially arranged for evacuees.

The packed train stopped at each main station, and some people got off. Families, having come down from the train, gathered themselves on the platform away from the jostling crowd. They looked relieved and happy. Men by themselves casually walked away carrying their rucksacks. But the people who were still on the train hardly had time to say good-bye to their friends.

At every stop, the platform was full of people. There were shouts and scuffles as men surged to climb into the train. They pushed and shoved. Although each carriage had a clear sign stating 'For Evacuees' on its side, men clambered in regardless. Some banged menacingly on windows demanding to be let in. Somewhere glass was shattered and women cried out. Children screamed and the angry voices of men were heard.

'Evacuees only,' the station speaker was repeatedly announcing to no avail. The intruders were all men with rucksacks. Their faces were gaunt and their expressions were harsh. Each man was intent on his own purpose and defended a small space he secured with hostility.

When the train stopped at the main station nearest Kitani, a middle-aged man was seen fighting his way amid the confusion along the train, trying to see inside at the same time. Haruko saw him.

'Mata san!' she shouted, and knocked at the window.

Nozomi pushed open the window a little. Matabei saw her.

'Haruko ojosama!' his face crumpled. He came up and held on to the window frame. 'Oh, welcome home. You are safe. Dannasama and little ojosama, too! You must have had a hard time.' Tears started to roll down his wrinkled cheeks. He breathlessly told them that everybody, especially Ayako, had wanted to come but he had stopped them.

'The station is not a place for ladies these days. Besides, there is no transport to come here now. But you will come back and see the family as soon as the situation gets better, won't you, ojosama? They want so much to see you.'

'Of course I will.'

Sniffing, Matabei lifted a bundle and Nozomi pushed the window up a little further.

'Sushi for your journey. Okkasama and Ayako okusama cooked them last night. There are some bean cakes for little ojosama, and some rice for you when you get to Tokyo. It is very difficult to get rice these days. I put some miso in, too.'

'Thank you Mata san. How did you come carrying such a heavy thing?'

'I walked.'

'It must have taken hours.'

'I am glad to see all of you. Tei-suke sent us a telegram.' Hearing the whistle his speech became rapid. 'Please take care of yourselves. There are a lot of pickpockets about. You guard your purse carefully, Haruko ojosama, and don't let anyone know that you have money.'

'No, Mata san.'

'Don't let little ojosama go out at night. And don't go out yourself. People are very wicked these days.'

As the train started to move, he walked alongside it, bumping against people. Tears were still streaming down his face and he did not bother to wipe them away. From a distance, Haruko noticed that his back was stooped.

Haruko held the bundle on her lap. The four corners of a piece of striped cotton cloth were gathered and tied together. She clasped the knotted top tightly.

'Okahsan, he called you Haruko ojosama,' Emi said.

Haruko just nodded. If she opened her mouth, she would have started to weep. Nozomi, who was gazing at the passing scenery, took out a soiled handkerchief from his pocket and carefully polished his spectacles.

It had occurred to Haruko to stop at Kitani before she went back to Tokyo. A week or two staying with Kei, Ayako and Masakazu's family would be a tonic before starting a new life. But in Tokyo, there were problems of housing, schooling, transport, and in every facet of life, as a wide area had been burnt down or demolished. The metropolitan authority severely restricted the entry of people to Tokyo as residents. If the Sanjos did not exercise their privilege as refugees to go to Tokyo immediately, they would forfeit their residency. For Nozomi to stand any chance of finding work, they had to live in Tokyo.

At Tokyo station, Nozomi told Haruko and the girls to wait. He would look for one of his younger brothers, Genzo, who had become a police chief of a district in Tokyo. He also hoped to find Takeko's son, Akira. Both he and his sister, Namiko, had been treated like the Sanjos' own son and daughter while they had gone to school from their house.

Nozomi and his brother looked alike, except Genzo was a little taller. They came walking towards Haruko with Takeko's son behind.

'Thank you for coming to meet us,' Haruko bowed to them.

'Obasan!' Akira smiled, showing healthy white teeth. 'We have been very worried about you.' He turned to his young cousins. 'How was the trip?'

'Why hasn't Nami-chan come?' asked Emi who adored her older cousin. 'Where is she?'

Akira ignored the question. 'If I met you two in the street, I wouldn't recognise you. You have really grown up.'

'I would recognise you,' Mari said. 'You are always so dark.'

'Mari-chan!' Emi reproved her.

Akira laughed.

A car was waiting for them outside the station.

'Ojisan, obasan, I am so glad to see you. Now I have to go back to work. I'll call on you soon.' Akira left them.

They arrived at the official house of the police chief. It had been hastily built with poor materials and stood in the middle of a burnt-out area. Flimsy doors slid open to an entrance. The driver helped to carry their rucksacks into a small room on the right.

Genzo's wife, Yoshi, came out and unsmilingly bowed.

Haruko remembered when Yoshi had first been brought to Tokyo accompanied by her mother and one of Nozomi's older brothers who was a Buddhist priest.

The years had not changed her demeanour.

Genzo's first wife was a pretty girl. She used to come to Haruko's house almost every day. At that time Haruko's younger brother Shuichi and Nozomi's younger brother Seiji were staying at the Sanjos' together with Akira and Namiko and the atmosphere of the house was always lively.

Haruko had to remind Genzo's young wife who would be still sitting and chatting in the evening, 'You had better go home. Genzo san will be back soon.' Often Haruko wrapped up a couple of fish or whatever she had and told her, 'Take this and then you don't have to spend too long shopping. Hurry up. You just have time to cook rice and make miso soup for your supper. Have you got some vegetables?'

'I'll see you tomorrow.'

'Tomorrow I have to go to Mitsukoshi department store to look for kimono material for my mother, and a neckpiece for my grandmother at Eri-han shop. Do you want to come with me?'

'Oh, yes, please. I'll come early.'

'Make sure you lock your house well. You are out every day.'

Although Haruko's house had been a refuge, life with Genzo must have been boring for her.

'He says novels are immoral and reading them is a waste of time,' she complained. 'We have nothing to talk about and we just sit without saying anything to each other. He doesn't laugh at all.'

She went away to visit her parents after six months of marriage and never came back. According to country custom, the marriage had not been registered until the first child was born. There was an apology from the go-between to Genzo's oldest brother, and she had disappeared from Haruko's circle.

About a year later, Haruko had a telephone call from Nozomi. Not many private houses had a telephone installed. A glass-fronted telephone room at the end of the corridor was a symbol of prestige.

Nozomi's voice sounded metallic.

'Haruko? I just received a telegram from niisan of the Jodo Temple that he is arriving at Tokyo station this afternoon with a bride for Genzo.'

'A what? A bride?'

'Hello, hello,' Nozomi called. Haruko sensed that he was busy. 'Can you hear me?'

'Yes, yes. Have you been told about it before?'

'No, no, I didn't know anything about it. So will you please go to the station and meet them? They are arriving at three thirty. Three thirty. Then they want to get married tonight.'

Haruko was flabbergasted. 'What do you mean, get married tonight?'

There were muffled noises.

'Hello.'

Nozomi was obviously talking to someone else. 'Yes, go ahead,' he said to someone, and then, 'Sorry. There will only be a few people. I'll come home as soon as I can. Order something appropriate for dinner.' He rang off.

Haruko looked at the clock and called a maid. 'Will you go to the fishmonger's and ask him if he could put together ten red sea bream for tonight. I know it's short notice but I'm sure he will manage. Ask him to grill them and bring them at eight o'clock. It's for Genzo san's wedding.'

The maid opened her eyes in surprise.

'I know,' Haruko felt that she had to make an excuse. 'The priest is busy. He wants to go home as soon as he can.'

'By the way,' she called out to the maid as she headed off, 'tell the fishmonger that the fish is for a family gathering. You do not have to mention the wedding.' She was ashamed that a close relative was getting married in such a casual way. She was also annoyed: whoever are the parents of the girl, what a way to get a daughter married. Something which would have been unthinkable among the Miwas and the Shirais. At least they could have written to ask beforehand.

She sat in front of her dressing table, creamed and powdered her face carefully, then took out a new kimono from its wrapping. It had white irregular stripes on a black background.

She bought a platform ticket at the station and waited for the train. It duly arrived and people, some carrying lidded baskets tied up with string, some with suitcases, started to walk towards the gate.

Haruko noticed the priest in a black robe waving his arm. The wide sleeve flapped. As she approached, she saw behind him a woman in a large shimada bridal coiffure and a kimono with long dangling sleeves. A middle-aged woman in a black haori coat was with her.

'Ah, Haruko san,' the priest said, and wiped his face with a towel. 'Thank goodness. I was worried about what I should do if you were not here.' He turned round and said nonchalantly in a loud voice, 'I thought of bringing her up to meet Genzo but instead of wasting time and money, we decided to go ahead and get them married.'

Haruko was about to ask, 'You mean Genzo san did not know about his own marriage till today?' but was taken aback by the look of the bride. Her kimono had too many strong colours and a rustic impression was inescapable. She had a bulbous nose and thick curled-up lips.

It was difficult to see her sentiments under the thickly painted face. She was not young, either. Perhaps after the first wife, the relatives might have been careful to choose someone who was not fun-loving and pretty. Rough red hands stuck out from her sleeves which were made shorter than they should be. Haruko had forgotten to greet the bride's mother whose face was tanned and wrinkled.

Haruko was conscious that she was too smart and fashionable among them. The three following her were like a group of travelling performers. It was a totally incongruous group who walked the platform together after a porter. The priest was unaffected. As he walked clicking his wooden *geta* footwear, he continued to chat loudly to Haruko, 'It is already autumn here, isn't it?'

Haruko thought, 'It must have been an ordeal for the girl to be dressed like that and travel for thirty hours.' Aloud she said, 'The bride could have changed at home before the wedding.'

'Oh, they insisted that she had to look her best when she arrived in Tokyo.'

'To impress whom?' Haruko wondered. Perhaps they expected Genzo to meet them. She hoped that Nozomi had managed to get in touch with him.

Haruko paid the porter and called a taxi. The trousseau was not much but still there was a basket and a suitcase to cope with. As she sat in a taxi with them, Haruko began to feel sorry for Genzo.

Her maid looked surprised when she opened the door.

The four young people, Shuichi, Akira and Namiko and Nozomi's youngest brother, also a student, came home almost at the same time. She called them aside and whispered, 'There will be no other guests but you. Put on something smart and sit down when I ask you.'

The priest performed the ceremony and they all sat down to a celebration dinner. The good tableware which was kept wrapped up except at New Year was brought out from a cupboard.

The bride and the bridegroom left for his small house, and the bride's mother went with them.

'Where did they find such an ugly woman?' Nozomi said that night, taking off his trousers.

'She might be a very good-natured woman.' Haruko felt that she should defend the bride, but the dour, uncommunicative expression had not seemed promising.

*   *   *

Whenever Nozomi came back to Tokyo from Chenyang for business, he stayed with Genzo and Yoshi. It would have been more convenient for him to have stayed in a hotel near the city centre but it was his way of helping them by paying them an amount almost equal to the hotel expenses. At least Genzo had expressed his appreciation and welcomed niisan.

At Nozomi's instruction, a few pieces of furniture and antique china which Haruko had wanted to keep when she left Tokyo for Chenyang had been entrusted to Genzo and Yoshi. She had also left a few sets of good bedding, which Nozomi had used when he stayed with them.

Nozomi and his family were put in a small room about four metres by three. A glass-fronted bookcase and a tall chest of drawers, both of which belonged to Nozomi, were standing along one wall. Haruko opened the drawers and found that most of the contents had gone. She had packed them with antique pieces of china and silverware. In the cupboard they found their bedding. The blankets had the names of Genzo's son and daughter written on them. Obviously they had been taken with them when the children had been evacuated with their school during the air-raids.

In the evening, when Genzo came home, he called them for a meal. Emi and Mari were looking forward to talking to their cousins. Eita was a year older than Emi and his sister Teruko was a year younger than Mari.

They were shy with a boy of their age, and perhaps Eita also felt shy of them, but Teruko did not show any friendliness. Her manners were abrupt and she seemed purposefully busy going between the kitchen and the small *chanoma*.

They sat around a low small table, almost touching each other. Teruko looked very much like her mother. All through the meal, no one spoke.

Nozomi liked meat. He would eat fish and enjoy it when grilled or fried, but not boiled. Now he quietly ate a small portion of boiled fish given to him on a mean little plate. No cup of tea was offered.

After the meal, Haruko helped with the washing up. She was amazed that her antique plates, the eighteenth-century Kutani set, were in the cupboard. Out of the original set of five, there were only four and one was badly chipped.

'We thought you were all dead,' Genzo said the next day. 'It was a surprise when Toshié told us about you.'

'Is Toshié san all right? Did her husband come home?' Haruko asked.

'He has. I was told that he escaped from a train heading towards Siberia and had an awful time getting back.'

'Where are they now?'

'In Tokyo somewhere. He might be doing something not entirely legal.'

Haruko remembered that Genzo was a policeman. Toshié would not be likely to come near Genzo's house if her husband was involved in something illegal.

There was a bathroom but no hot water seemed available. After eating, Haruko's family walked twenty minutes in the dark streets to the nearest public bath. Many public bath houses had been burnt down and the shortage of fuel made it difficult for them to operate. On the way back, Mari said. 'I am hungry.'

'Let's go to the market and eat something decent,' Nozomi said, and walked into a maze of assembled shacks and covered stalls. A delicious smell of grilled chicken wafted towards them. 'Mmmmn!' Mari sniffed the air, 'Oh, I have a stomach ache.'

Nozomi parted the short curtains which served as doors of one of the stalls. Inside, in a narrow room, high stools were placed in front of a counter. It was empty. Outside, at the back, a woman was fanning a charcoal burner on which skewered chicken pieces were being barbecued.

'What a little restaurant,' Emi whispered to Nozomi.

'It's a *yakitoriya*. It's a place where men drop in to drink saké and have a snack.'

Nozomi ordered a small bottle of saké and grilled chicken pieces.

'Can you give us four saké cups?'

'Four? Oh, for the little girls, as well?'

'Yes, we want to celebrate because we are safely back home.'

'Oh, where from?'

The *yakitoriya* gave Emi and Mari extra pieces of chicken.

'Pretty girls, aren't you? Glad you came home safe. War is a terrible thing. We had a small but good restaurant but it has been burnt to ashes. We lost everything.'

'Will you and your wife join us?' Nozomi poured saké into six tiny saké cups.

'Kanpai!' the man said. His wife came in and joined them. 'Good luck for all of us.'

'Even the man who did not know us was pleased for us and wished us good luck,' Emi said to Haruko. That was exactly what Haruko was thinking.

'Oh, wasn't it delicious! I don't think I have ever had such a delicious thing in my whole life,' Mari said, walking with Nozomi a few steps ahead.

'In your whole young life?' Nozomi looked at Mari. 'What about the restaurants we took you to in Dalian?'

'I was not so hungry at that time. I wish I did not leave half that banana split last time. I could eat two of them now.'

Inflation, devaluation of the currency, and the freezing of savings made everybody's life hard, especially people whose property had burnt down. Haruko's uncles, Yasuharu and Hideto, and their families had left Toyko. Their life was not easy.

The Americans released surplus food and distributed it but this was fruit juice or brown sugar instead of the staple diet of rice. Other food could not be obtained without bartering with farmers.

Genzo's family was better off. Under the pretext of presents, eggs, vegetables, fruit, rice, miso, sugar, cake were brought in to them by merchants. Sometimes a rigid enforcement of regulations brought many confiscated items from black markets and they were distributed among policemen. Yoshi took everything they were given into their bedroom. When and how they would be eaten, Haruko did not know, but in return, she was not going to share the rice and miso that Matabei had brought to the train.

In the morning, a police car came to take Genzo to work. Their two children left for school. Not having found a school for Emi and Mari, Nozomi and Haruko deliberately stayed in bed till everybody had gone in order to avoid adding confusion to their busy routine.

Nobody was around when the four got up. On the table four cold grey dumplings had been left. Yoshi had kneaded dough the night before. When she had kneaded it sufficiently, she had pinched a small portion and put it aside for the next day's yeast supply. The yeast must have been used like that for months. It had nearly lost its function as a leavening agent and produced a hard sour roll. There was no oven and the dough was steamed, which made it soggy.

Nozomi picked it up and made a comical face but tore off a little and chewed it. Eventually he swallowed the mouthful. No one else could finish their dumpling.

Changed into a suit, Nozomi had to go out to look for a job for the first time in his life. Jobs had always waited for him or come to him.

There was an acute shortage of homes. Even a year after the surrender, a lot of families lived in shacks of assembled corrugated iron sheets and odd boards. Some lived in air-raid shelters in the garden. A room in a house would be snatched up for high rent. Schools which had escaped air-raids were over-crowded and were reluctant to accept new pupils.

But by the end of the week, Nozomi had become a consultant of a company through a university friend. He was not excited about the prospect, but at least there would be a little income.

Meanwhile Genzo had a small house he owned vacated for them, and through the influence of a son of Ayako's friend, one of the ministers in the government, the two girls were admitted to a school.

23

The Ming Dish

The house that Genzo owned was in an area which was beginning to be incorporated into Greater Tokyo. It squatted at the end of a muddy lane. The wooden panels of the outer walls were blackened with age and the whole structure, which had been built some thirty years before, looked as though it was ready to crumble under the weight of the roof.

Haruko could not imagine what circumstance had made Genzo purchase the undistinguished house, or any house at all. But it could be said that he had had more foresight than his brother, or he might have just been lucky.

We were unlucky, she thought. Had we stayed in Japan, we might have had a decent house. I did try to buy a piece of land. I was right in thinking of acquiring property. He should have listened to me. Haruko was discontented as she approached Genzo's house in a small van on the back of which their few possessions swayed as it bumped along pockmarked roads.

Although she had toyed with the idea that she could have been better off had she owned a piece of land, the chances were that she would have lost it as an absentee landlord. Her two uncles whose families had been evacuated from Tokyo and had not come back immediately after the war had forfeited their right to their property. They should have come back and put together corrugated iron sheets and pieces of board as a hut on the land if building a house had been a difficulty. But neither had shown such initiative, and neither had bothered to start a legal battle when the authorities had relentlessly launched the replanning of streets. After a short period, there had been nothing left to indicate where their houses used to stand.

'The genteel class is the loser now.' She felt that the world she had known had slipped away for good and been replaced by pragmatic and tough people, but rather than grieving for the good old days, she felt resentment against the weakness of the ones she had loved and respected. Most of her relations were highly qualified and clever people, but their inability to cope with the untoward had been exposed by recent circumstances.

She did not feel any grudge against the Americans or the British. As far as she was concerned, these nations were chess pieces moved by the forces of history. The war, like many big or small crises in life, was an inevitability and people should show their worth at moments of difficulty.

'It was an expensive lesson,' she pondered, 'I had to throw away practically everything to learn it.' Perhaps the realisation came too late for her, but Emi and Mari had to be brought up to be strong and confident, ready to get through any unexpected event.

The house was small and square, divided more or less equally into an entrance and three rooms. They were connected with each other by *fusuma*, paper sliding doors. The kitchen was built out at the back. Its floor was uneven, because some joists had rotted away. Nozomi described it as 'a dwarf's golf course'. Depending on where one trod, the floor made a surprisingly loud noise and a piece of board jumped up. There was no running water, and by the zinc-lined sink was a large crock with a wooden lid. One rusty gas ring, a clay hearth, a small stand and a shelf completed the kitchen. A narrow window was black with soot and so pressed down by the weight from above that not only did it remain closed but it was bulging out at the bottom. The sliding back door needed strength and coaxing to open. 'No need for locks,' Nozomi said.

A wooden bath tub with a fuel hole underneath was set in a shack outside and by it there was a hand-operated pump.

In one of the rooms, a heavy gas stove had been left.

The houses of middle-class families often had a room called the reception room or the European room. It was usually built by the entrance and had floorboards instead of tatami, windows instead of openings to the garden, and had a coffee table and sofas.

The house in which the Sanjos lived in Tokyo before they moved to Manchuria had had such a room and Nozomi used to spend most of his weekends in their European room meeting people who had come to get a contract or to ask a favour. The more important the person, the more visitors, and Nozomi had had many people coming to see him. The stove had taken up a corner of the room with its three large panels and filigree ornamentation. In the room with its heavy draperies and soft furnishing, the red glow and blue flames had added to an affluent image on cold days.

Now, on the yellowed tatami floor, the same stove stood as an incongruous cold mass of metal and an ugly nuisance.

If Haruko's mood was gloomy, though, the rest of the family did not share it. The two girls particularly were in high spirits.

'Oh, look. We can sleep on our own futon tonight and don't have to be squashed together.'

'Can we have this room to ourselves?'

Haruko unpacked and cooked the rice Matabei had brought to the station. It was shining white and each grain was fluffy.

'I have never had such tasty rice,' Mari said.

'You seem to be having a lot of first-time experiences,' Nozomi teased her, but he, too, asked for more helpings than usual.

'Otohsan, you used to stay with them when you came back to Tokyo. Do they always eat things like that? Isn't she a terrible cook!' Haruko ventured.

'I stayed with them but I never had meals with them. But I suppose they used to eat better things before the war.'

Haruko wanted to say, 'She does not have any affection or consideration for people eating what she has cooked. She has never even tried to make people enjoy food, or enjoy anything at all,' but restrained herself. After all, Yoshi was one of Nozomi's relations.

'That bread! You know that woman hid nice food from us and deliberately gave us the rubbish.'

'Mari-chan!' Haruko upbraided her. 'What a way to talk! You cannot call your aunt "that woman".'

'She is no aunt of mine.'

'Mari-chan!' In spite of herself, Haruko was appalled.

'I admit that Genzo ojisan is my uncle because he is otohsan's brother, but she is just his wife. If he divorced her, she would be nobody to me.'

Nozomi shook his head and smiled wryly. Seeing that he was not getting angry, Mari put on a cheeky grin.

'Mari-chan!'

Nozomi put up his hand to Haruko.

'All right. Let's not be unpleasant to each other tonight. Do you know the story of "Gonta and the thieves"?'

'No, only Ali Baba.'

'Once upon a time . . .'

'Oh, no.'

'Listen. Once upon a time there was a notorious band of thieves. They lived in the mountains and now and again descended on rich people in villages and towns. They killed entire households and took their treasures. One day, when they were about to leave a house, they heard a sneeze.'

'Poor Gonta.'

'Yes, that was Gonta. He pleaded for his life and told them that he was an only son and his mother was depending on him. The thieves felt sorry for once, because some of them thought of their own mothers. But they had been discussing where to hide the treasure. So they told Gonta if he could keep the secret, they would let him go. But if he betrayed them, etcetera.

'Gonta, of course, did not tell anyone where the treasure was hidden, but after a while the secret began to worry him and then it became a hard knot in his stomach. He lost weight, and got ill.

'When a famous priest heard this, he told Gonta to go to the mountains where there was no one else and find a tree and shout his secret aloud to the tree. He did as he was told and the knot disappeared and he was cured, but when you go to the tree on a windy day, the tree still shouts Gonta's secret even today.'

Nozomi looked at his family. 'So you may say what you have kept to yourself just tonight, then we'll forget about it.'

'It will be embarrassing if this wall starts shouting what we are saying tonight,' Haruko said, and Emi and Mari laughed.

'Ah, it was a good meal. Okahsan, don't forget to make tea.' Nozomi finally put down his chopsticks.

'It was funny to leave the table after a meal without having tea, wasn't it?' Emi remarked. 'That's what I wanted to say all the time.'

Haruko stepped into the kitchen to put a kettle on the gas. Nozomi used to come home late almost every night. Some nights geisha girls had accompanied him home and they had had another party. Nozomi had become so used to good food from expensive restaurants that

Haruko had been obliged to make an effort to cook something special for him when he had been at home. She used to take trouble getting particularly fresh fish or meat of quality. He had never complained but left dishes untouched if they had not interested him.

As she put tea cups on a tray, she wondered if he was resigned to his present life and regarded luxury as belonging to bygone days. Would he have the ambition and mental stamina to stand up again, or would he be quite happy to stagger along from day to day without any hope of getting back to a decent life?

Emi and Mari did not find it too difficult to catch up at school in general but English lessons distressed Emi.

'She says that all the other girls are so advanced that she does not understand what they are doing. All she knows is the alphabet and a few basic words. Do something for her, otohsan.'

At first Nozomi did not pay much attention to Haruko's plea. He said to Emi, 'If you have a dictionary and patience, you can read any foreign books.'

'I don't understand.' She was in tears.

'Let me see. You don't have to cry. It's only a language. Even the most uneducated beggar can speak English in London.'

Nozomi picked up the reader. No new textbooks had been published and he noticed that the contents were old-fashioned. He read, 'He who would enjoy the spring . . .'

'You see, otohsan, I know "he". It is a personal pronoun, singular, the third person. Then I looked at "who". It said, "an interrogative pronoun". So, he who? but I left it and looked at the next word, "the past tense of will". I looked up "will". It is an auxiliary verb and seems to suggest future.'

Nozomi burst out laughing. 'Oh, I am sorry. But what a sentence!'

'Didn't you learn English at school?' Mari asked Haruko.

'Yes, but our English is to repeat like a song, "Cat is *neko* and C-A-T". "Dog is *inu* and D-O-G".'

Mari giggled and Emi joined her, wiping her tears.

'Is that all?'

'We learnt a bit more but I can't remember it now.'

Fortunately their next-door neighbour, Tsuchiya, was a small-scale timber merchant. With the demand for construction materials rising, he was doing good business. Although the noise of the incessant electric saw in his yard was disturbing, Haruko could get sufficient wood for her cooking and for heating bath water. The neighbour knew that her family was connected with a policeman and was as pleasant as could be. The traders never knew when a police connection would be useful.

It was not so easy to find a route to food sources. Most families had established their special supplier by then which they would not disclose as it was illegal to sell and buy rice directly. The fact that no one could survive without acquiring extra food in addition to legally provided items was a matter left uninvestigated.

The newspapers had published an article not long before about a judge who, in protest at the unreasonable enforcement of the law, had refused to eat anything but legally distributed food and died of malnutrition.

Every family had plenty of brown sugar released from American army surplus. Some clever people had cashed in on it and started to sell a simple ladle with a stick for 'calmelo' making. This caught the imagination of the people and it became a pastime of almost every household.

One put some sugar in the ladle over heat and, as it melted, stirred it with the stick dipped in bicarbonate of soda. The sugar puffed up, but, for one reason or another, sometimes it did not work and that uncertainty increased the fun. At the Sanjos', Nozomi was the most skilled. He sat cross-legged in front of a charcoal burner and produced perfect round calmelo one after another, although he did not eat it himself.

Ground maize was distributed next. Mixed with dough, it made yellow and gritty bread which was most unpalatable. It crumbled as one picked it up.

Haruko went to a black market and, among other things, bought milk, sugar and tea to please the family but she had to acquire more essential food somehow.

Nozomi said one day that he had met Wakabayashi, who had been the president of the aluminium-producing company in Chenyang. His wife had come from a peripheral prefecture of Tokyo, and her cousin might be able to introduce Haruko to a farmer.

A few days later when the girls were on half-term, Haruko got up at four o'clock in the morning. Moving around her kitchen, she carefully avoided the hazardous spots in the floor which she had become familiar with by then. She cooked rice and prepared miso soup. Then she woke Emi and Mari.

When they were about to leave the house with rucksacks, Nozomi came out to the entrance.

'Take care of yourselves.'

'Otohsan, I left a note but there is miso soup that you can heat up and the fried fish from last night. We'll be home as soon as we can. I've told Tsuchiva san that nobody will be home today. Will you lock up the front and leave from the verandah? The back door won't shut from outside.'

It was still dark and the sky was full of stars. They had to walk nearly half an hour to reach the nearest station and then had to change trains three times. As they were travelling against the main stream of commuters the trains were not too crowded but they were few and far between. The last line they took was an ancient local railway which looked as though it was at the end of its useful life. The train made husky whistling sounds and swayed dangerously over a bridge. The seats were bare boards. Most of the passengers had rucksacks.

The cousin of Wakabayashi's wife was a pleasant woman and, having giving them a cup of Japanese tea, accepted a piece of brocade Haruko had brought as a present. Then she took them to a nearby farmhouse.

'They are back from Chenyang like my cousin and don't know anyone. Would you be so kind as to help them?' The cousin talked to someone whom Haruko could not see as only a part of the paper sliding door was open. After a few more exchanges which did not reach Haruko's ear, a woman poked out her red face and looked at Haruko.

'She says she may sell you some rice.' The cousin bowed to Haruko. 'I'll leave you to talk to her.'

'Thank you so much.' Haruko bowed as well, and then turned to the woman inside the house. She felt awkward: How do I start such a negotiation? Should I treat her as a friend or a vendor or like a farmer in Kitani village? 'I brought kimono and obi material for you,' she began.

'Let's see.'

Haruko put down her rucksack and took out a kimono. When she had bought it at Kikuya in Chenyang, she had had Emi in mind. Emi would look graceful in the delicate salmon pink. The painted pattern of the newly opened soft peonies would bring out her seemingly quiet but bright personality.

The woman's rough hands spread it out with accustomed nonchalance. In the dark old farmhouse, it released an air of rich abandon. Haruko could discern greed in the woman's eyes.

Haruko bought rice, Chinese leaves, aubergines, carrots, giant radishes and filled the three rucksacks. They dropped in at the house of the Wakabayashis' cousin to thank her again, and walked back to the station.

'I am sorry we had to give away your kimono,' Haruko said to Emi.

'It's all right, okahsan. I have never worn it so I did not feel it was mine, but it was a beautiful kimono.'

'One day, we'll buy you another one like that,' she wanted to say, but swallowed her words. When could she do such a thing? Rather, she should be pleased that for a few weeks they would have enough food for proper meals.

There were no benches at the station. They sat on the concrete floor, ate rice balls and pickles that Haruko had packed in the morning and drank cold tea from Mari's water bottle. Nobody took any notice of them. It was a common sight.

The rucksack was heavy and they took nearly an hour to walk home from the station. As they turned into the lane leading to the house, they saw that the house was in darkness.

Haruko exclaimed, 'What has happened to otohsan?'

Surely he should have been home hours before.

The front door was still locked. Having dropped her rucksack, Haruko ran round to the back.

'Otohsan!'

'Oh!' Nozomi came out to the verandah.

'Why were you sitting in the dark?' Haruko's heart was pounding.

'The moon is so bright tonight. I must have nodded off.'

Why was I so frightened? she wondered later.

When Haruko had pressed him for more money and accused him of not doing anything a few days before, he had muttered, 'The training I had seems no use at all for earning a living now. The only place fit for me is an uninhabited island or better still somewhere one doesn't have to eat.'

*   *   *

Haruko sat on the tatami floor and placed a large flat box in front of her. It must have been Shobei who had had the box made. The writing in brush and ink on the lid was his. It said 'Large Ming Dish: Possession of the Miwas'. The box was made of *kiri* (paulownia) wood which was light and damp-proof.

The dish was wrapped up in three layers of silk and cotton material and packed with silk floss. Haruko sat straight. This was a habit of training by Shobei in childhood and later by Ayako: when you handle antique pieces of china, they had told Haruko, you have to sit properly. Your upper arms ought to be kept at your sides close to the body. But relax, they both had said. Try to look at the object and enjoy it. Turn it around. So long as you hold it gently, you will never harm it.

Haruko untied the cloth. The dish was blue-grey. It was one of the treasures that Shobei had given to Ayako personally after she had gone back to live with her own parents. He had had his servant carry the box. He had said to Ayako, 'It is one of the most precious antique pieces I have and I thought I would make sure that it goes to you.'

It had seemed to Ayako that after she had left with the children, even though it had been at his suggestion, his daughter-in-law and grandchildren's future had become Shobei's prime concern. He had been well and repeated that he would live till Shuichi graduated from university, but perhaps he had had a premonition.

When Shuichi started university and came to live with the Sanjos, Nozomi had told Ayako that he had been supporting his own brothers and why not Haruko's? By that time Ayako's financial status had not been comfortable.

For Shuichi's graduation, Ayako had come up to Tokyo and formally thanked Nozomi and Haruko. She had brought an obi for Haruko, and the dish for Nozomi.

'Okahsan, this is an honour to handle such a precious dish. I accept your goodwill but let me say I will keep it till Shu-chan has established his own home,' Nozomi had said. 'This should belong to him if not to a museum.'

'Thank you, Nozomi san, whatever you say, it is yours. I cannot thank you enough for having Shuichi for all these years and for caring for him, and you deserve this from the Miwas.'

The obi, Ayako had said, had been woven as one of a pair for a trousseau of a princess and through Mikuniya, Kei's and Ayako's long-standing kimono dealer in Kyoto, she had managed to buy it for a reasonable price. Golden threads were woven into the back and gave it a subdued glow, over which there was a design of scattered fans each with intricate patterns.

'You can wear this for any occasion, for anyone to see.' In front of her daughter, she had not hidden her pleasure and pride in giving her a special present.

When Haruko had left for Chenyang, she had considered leaving the dish in Yasuharu's safekeeping but in the end had left it with other possessions at Genzo and Yoshi's home. The obi had been brought back in her rucksack in the hope that the customs officers would not know its value and confiscate it, although when she reflected on this back in Japan, it seemed unlikely that they would be interested in a Japanese obi.

Perhaps because the dish was large and also did not look pretty, Yoshi had left it in the box.

The night before, after her daughters had gone to bed, Haruko had said to Nozomi, 'Otohsan, let's sell the Ming dish.'

Nozomi put down his newspaper.

'Now that Shu-chan is dead, we do not have to keep it. Okahsan will not mind if it is for Emi's and Mari's education.'

'We'll wait for a while before we do such a thing.'

'What for? It'll never be of any use to us,' Haruko said bitterly. If her brother Shuichi were alive . . . It had been years since he died, but the sense of loss was still acute.

Haruko often thought of her sister-in-law and her nephew. They lived as sitting tenants with Yaéko's widowed mother in an even smaller and shabbier house than Haruko's present place, and rented out one of the two rooms to a government official whose family still remained in the country.

'The neighbours talk about us, and my mother is worried,' Yaéko had said once to Haruko, 'But I told them, "Don't be silly. What can I do in such a small place?"' Her skin had become mottled, but her eyes were large as they had always been, and she had long curled eyelashes. Her lips were still full and sensuous.

Haruko felt a family obligation to go and see them now and again. Yaéko's mother would call the boy from outside and tell him, 'Say how are you to obasama.' The boy watched his grandmother's lips and responded in a nasal airy voice. 'Obasama brought for you sweet potatoes. You love them, don't you? I will cook them for you later. Say thank you to obasama.' Yaéko's mother always distressed Haruko. She would continue talking to Haruko, 'He cannot hear of course, o'nesama, but he is very good at maths and can write beautifully.' She smiled at her grandson. 'Bring for obasama your school exercise books.' Haruko was obliged to look at them, nodded and smiled at the boy.

'He is getting more and more like Shuichi san,' Yaéko's mother said, perhaps to reassure Haruko that she had not forgotten where the boy belonged.

It was a long time ago that Haruko had helped Shuichi with his school work. He had been good-looking even as a little boy. She tried to see her brother's image in her nephew, but it was sad to remember her brother in a cramped room crowded with odd furniture and dirty old tatami. Still holding the exercise book, Haruko reflected how circumstances were different between the father and the son. No doubt the war had contributed to the further fall of the Miwas, but the decline had set in long before that when Shobei died and Shuichi had gone down with it.

She sighed and put the dish carefully on the table. She got up. She was going to make sushi tonight and arrange them on the dish. It would be her way of saying farewell to the precious antique piece that her ancestors had passed from one generation to another. Now it would be going from the family for ever. But, after all, what else was left with the family except its name? What was the good of worrying about one last piece of the prosperous past, of the Miwas as well as her own?

24

Struggle

One night Nozomi was late coming home. He was usually home by seven o'clock and it was getting towards eight. While the public in general was struggling on the brink of starvation, there was an undercurrent of unrest, and when a family member did not adhere to routine, the others felt more than ordinarily anxious.

At night, the centre of the city was bright and lively. Tall lanky American soldiers strode around with short Japanese girls on their arms. The girls looked shorter and dumpier in excessively high-heeled shoes. With thick make-up and brightly coloured clothes, they looked cut off from other Japanese, as though they were people from a strange land. Petty crime was abundant. Streetwise orphans roamed around, stealing to survive.

Around the train stations, temporary buildings had mushroomed, and during the day, a black market did brisk business. In the evening, humble drinking and eating places flourished. A few blocks away, the streets were unlit and vacant land stretched between clusters of houses which had escaped destruction. After dark, leaving the train, people walked quickly, conscious of following steps and any shadow in front.

'He might have met an old friend or someone he knew.' Haruko decided not to worry too much. 'Let's eat.'

The table was cleared after the meal so that Emi and Mari could do their homework. Haruko opened a newspaper. The newspaper was yesterday's. Before the war, the Sanjos used to subscribe to three major papers as well as evening papers as a matter of course. One paper was considered good for political articles, another was read for social events and the third was well known for sports. Now she did not have even one delivered. When Haruko told Nozomi that she was not going to have the paper every day as the settlement of the monthly account was a burden, he did not object. He bought a paper himself every day.

Haruko had not looked at the papers for some time. She had to spend so much of her time keeping the family fed. Shopping took up a good deal of the day. Nothing could be bought in a straightforward way. Flour had to be bought with coupons after waiting in a long queue and some of it had to be taken to a baker in order to get bread. There was a queue there as well because the baker did not bake bread every day as fuel was in short supply. After all this waiting, all that was available was spindle-shaped bread called 'koppe-pan'.

'Why is it called koppe-pan?' Mari asked.

'It sounds like German. Is it from Kuppe, hilltop, perhaps? I wonder who named it,' Nozomi answered.

Unless Haruko had bought it from the black market, there was no butter and the bread was not popular in the family. In order to pay a little less for eggs, she would walk fifteen minutes in the other direction from the market to a house where a family kept hens, though they might or might not have eggs to sell on the day. Someone else might have bought them up already or it might have been the hens' day off.

She had thought she would keep hens herself. She had paid money for six chicks and also given a piece of cotton cloth, because nothing could be acquired without an additional gift. The chicks had been kept in a wooden box outside the verandah. Woken by a commotion at night, Haruko had gone to the glass door to look outside. At first, she had thought that a pack of wolves had come. In fact it was several dogs surrounding the chicks' box. The big ones had been large, like German shepherd dogs. In the bright moonlight, their fur had bristled and shone silver. Nozomi had come out and banged the glass panel. They had retreated unhurriedly in an orderly way through a garden gate into an adjacent vacant plot. They had obviously managed to open the gate themselves.

'They looked like wild animals in the mountains.' Haruko was still standing on the verandah.

'It would not take long for them to go back to their natural habits I expect,' Nozomi said from the bed. She had known that it was not just robbers and unknown villains who lurked in the dark. There were bands of semi-wild animals as well in the capital city. Since that night there had been an additional job for her before she went to bed. Her potential egg suppliers had to be taken into the shed every night and various heavy objects had to be piled up in front of its rotten rickety door.

For the family to have a bath, she had to push the pump up and down for more than one hour to fill the bath tub. She did not change the water in the tub every day. To heat the water she squatted in front of the fuel hole and fed in wood chips that she had carried from the yard next door.

The worst thing was worry about money. With the war widow of a doctor, she started to make paper bags. They were supplied with newspaper cut to size. They sat and pasted newspaper all morning. The work was simple and boring and the pay was insignificant. At lunch time, they counted and tied the finished bags into several bundles and Haruko made tea.

'We might have just earned a cup of tea,' Haruko laughed.

'Oh, I am not so sure,' her friend sighed, and then giggled. 'Yesterday on my way home from your house, I thought I had worked so hard that I would buy a piece of cake or something at the black market to console myself. But perhaps that might have wiped out all the money I earned for a week. Eventually I gave the cake to my children. One piece of cake among the three!'

'I often think I could do something better.' Haruko added hot water to the teapot and poured more tea into their cups. The cups were good Imari pottery. She reminded herself that she had to buy cheap cups as soon as she could, as they were too precious for daily use, and then continued, 'But I don't know where to start. Whenever I hear something, there is always a hitch. I am useless. I even thought of working at one of those drinking places.'

'I know.' Her friend nodded. 'I thought of that, too. Anyway I think I am too old for that.'

Both knew that they would never work at drinking places anyway. They would not have the courage to start.

'Our education was wrong,' Haruko said. 'We are from a class who were brought up with stupid sayings like "The samurai glories in honourable poverty".'

'Yes, that's right. The trouble is poverty is poverty. There is no difference between honourable poverty and simple poverty. If anything, poverty with old fetters is worse.'

'I can sew but these days my hands are so rough that I can't handle silk material.' She spread her hands on her lap under the table. How she had slighted Yoshi when she had first met her at Tokyo station years ago. One of the reasons was that her hands had been coarse and red. She thought, I was wrong to have judged her from her hands. Perhaps it was my fault that we were never close. Now her own hands were not only red and coarse, but they were cracked and covered with corns. When she combed and put up her hair, sometimes a few strands went into a crack and made her draw breath. The maids she used to have had never been asked to work as hard as she did now.

'My only hope is,' her friend was saying, 'for my son to grow up. But then with the new family law, the oldest son does not have any obligation to look after his parents or his family any more.'

Haruko looked up at the clock. 'Let's have lunch,' she said brightly and resolutely. 'I can make fried rice. I have eggs and even a tiny bit of bacon.'

'Oh, no, I am going. I can't eat your food. You must keep it for supper or for tomorrow.'

'Tomorrow is another day. Let's not worry about a tiny scrap of bacon and a morsel of rice. We both need to eat.'

After her friend had gone, having thanked her for lunch, Haruko decided to work in the garden. The aubergines and tomato plants had flowers. Bending down to pull up weeds, she reflected that even though they had lost the war, she had not expected that her life would change so much.

At the beginning of the war, the prime minister, General Hideki Tojo, had written in the children's newspaper on New Year's Day: 'Boys and girls, I am happy to see you enjoying a victorious New Year.' He had gone on to say that the Japanese Empire had drawn a sword of righteousness against America and the United Kingdom. 'Ours is the sword of God which will bring victory. As we advance, the enemy is defeated and scattered. The enemy can never touch the land of God. I congratulate you for having been born in such a glorious country which is unequalled in the world.'

Since then one flowery word after another had deceived the nation and intoxicated them, and the facts had been carefully hidden. Now the newspapers and magazines were full of disclosures and reproaches for the events of the war. Haruko read that the Midway sea battle in June 1942 had been a complete disaster for Japan and that the military high command had never analysed the error in strategy after the battle. They had only been too anxious to conceal the defeat from the nation so that morale would not be affected. The pilots and sailors had been confined to an island in the Inland Sea and were forbidden all contact with their families. Radio and newspapers had given a cursory report: 'The result was a shining achievement with very little loss on our side.'

For thirty-eight months after that, Japan had dragged on the fighting. In the middle of 1943, when the situation had grown worse, the prime minister, General Tojo, had said: 'Victory or defeat is decided by spiritual strength. Defeat is only possible when we believe we are defeated.'

The war had killed, on the Japanese side alone, over three million people. That did not include Toshié's small children and Nozomi's manager's little son. Had they stopped the war after Midway, it might not have destroyed the peace of so many families, including Haruko's, since there had been no death in the family up to that stage of the war.

The military high command were now in prison as war criminals.

She thought of the lady she had seen in a queue in front of a bakery. Her manners and the style of kimono she wore reminded Haruko of her mother. She was graceful, but she was standing as though she was cold in the spring sunshine. She quietly left with a few pieces of koppe-pan in her macramé bag.

'That's General Akagi's wife,' the baker's wife whispered as she left. 'He'll be hung soon.'

'Poor lady.'

What else could one say?

'Yes, but then they are responsible for so many lives. They are getting what they deserve. The wives, too, they had a good life during the war.'

How quickly people changed their allegiance.

On the day Japan surrendered, thousands of people had swarmed in front of the Imperial Palace. They had knelt down and cried. Some had killed themselves then and there.

'One hundred and eighty degrees turn.'

'Upside down.'

'About face.'

These were the expressions used to describe the social climate. The hitherto abhorred words like democracy and freedom were now adored and former enemies became model nations.

No one would make heroes of those who had killed themselves in order 'to uphold our honour' or 'to apologise to the Emperor for the humiliation he had to suffer', on the day of the Emperor's broadcast. Wartime had been a moment of madness in history, and people who had been too emotionally involved had been dismissed as hysterical. Now everyone wanted to wipe the memory from their consciences.

Society applauded the new words, 'freedom', 'individualism' and 'democracy'. The Emperor, who had been a living God, declared himself a human being. He was called the human Emperor and went out to talk to people who had never seen him before. During the war, anybody spreading rumours about him would have ended up being interrogated by the military police and imprisoned for disloyalty.

Someone had said that the Emperor must use a toilet. A neighbour had informed on him to the secret police and he had been arrested. Haruko could laugh now and was amazed at the stupidity of the authorities, but at that time she had felt only terror. She had changed, too, without realising.

It had not been appropriate to talk about one particular god who was supposed to be an ancestor of the Emperor. He was a brother of the sun goddess and notorious for his pranks, according to one of the oldest Japanese books. Eventually the brother's behaviour got on the nerves of the sun goddess and she hid herself in a cave. Recently Haruko heard a discussion over the radio that the legendary incident of the hiding of the sun goddess might have been a reference to a solar eclipse. How quickly the country had changed. How fragile it had been and how adaptive people were.

Their new masters were the Americans. They had ordered the abolition of the former school curriculum of history, geography and moral studies. The Japanese welcomed the changes. The Americans had reorganised the school system. They had introduced land reform. They had worked out a new constitution. No one rebelled.

Democracy permeated into the Kabuki theatre as well. The traditional theatre had performed plays on feudal themes for centuries. One of the most popular plays was about a war between two domains. The victorious side demanded that the son of the defeated lord was killed and that his head be presented. The son's nurse killed her own child and sent his head to the enemy. When the play was performed for the first time after the war, and the box which was supposed to contain the head appeared on the stage, the police rushed up and ordered the curtains to be dropped immediately.

That was the first incident of censorship of Kabuki. Stories of vendetta, death, brutality, harakiri were prohibited. For a while, it had been impossible to carry on the Kabuki theatre.

It was an American scholar of Japanese art who had offered himself as an inspector of art and had saved Kabuki plays. The Japanese were helpless in this situation. Some had supported the idea of total abolition of the theatre.

The front door was opened and broke the quiet of the night. Haruko was brought back from her thoughts.

'Otohsan!' The three of them stood up.

'What happened to you?' Following Nozomi back to the *chanoma*, Haruko looked at the clock on the wall. 'It's nearly eleven o'clock.'

In the light she could see that his face was a little flushed.

She quickly gave him a kimono to change into before he sat down. He had brought four suits back from Chenyang out of the many he used to have. She wanted them to last as long as possible. She was afraid that it would be a long time before he could have new suits made.

She brushed the mud caked on the bottom of his trousers and carefully hung them. She took out everything from his pockets and put the contents on a tray.

'Have you eaten?'

'Yes.'

'Will you have tea?'

'Um. I'd like a cup of tea.'

He went back to the *chanoma*, tying an obi around his middle. Sitting down at his usual place he said, 'I went to a restaurant with Wakabayashi.'

'Oh, I see.'

Haruko talked from the kitchen as she made tea.

'Did you and Wakabayashi san have something nice to talk about?'

Nozomi had said a week ago that he had been asked to do the planning for an independent power plant to be installed at a famous shrine.

'Wakabayashi is enthusiastic to start a new company. We might work together,' he had said.

'So you two had a drink in anticipation of success?' Haruko's voice was cheerful.

'Kajiwara was there as well.'

'Kajiwara san?' Haruko frowned a little. Like Wakabayashi, he was one of Nozomi's contemporaries at university. He had never seemed to be able to settle into a job but always had a scheme which, according to him, would turn him and anybody involved into millionaires. He would go around among his friends offering them partnerships in land development. Once he had tried to persuade Nozomi to buy an island. Another time, a share in a copper mine. Other friends of Nozomi's became established as scholars, engineers, businessmen and treated Kajiwara not unkindly but as a joke or an amiable crook.

He was a handsome man but, with years, he had come to look like a faded flower.

'He is married, isn't he?' Haruko had asked Nozomi when Kajiwara had visited Chenyang and stayed with the Sanjos. He seemed to be constantly moving around.

'I have never asked.'

After a while he had added, 'He always had one woman or another following him.'

The purpose of his visit to Chenyang had been to persuade Nozomi to join his silver-mining company.

'It's ridiculous. If silver is lying around everywhere for an amateur to find, the world would be full of millionaires,' Haruko had whispered to Nozomi in private. 'But he hasn't said gold yet. He must have some sense left.'

Haruko had found out that Nozomi had given him money.

'Why do you have to throw away money?' she grumbled. 'If you have so much, you could have given it to me.' But it had not mattered much at that time. As always Nozomi had been silent.

As far as Haruko was concerned, Kajiwara was not the kind of man to have around.

'Why did you have to involve him?'

'Wakabayashi met him and brought him. Kajiwara's nephew knows a nisei who could introduce us to someone to provide American Occupation Army funds.'

'You haven't believed such a story, have you? Why does this nisei think that the American Army would give you funds? You and Waka-bayashi san are not going to trust Kajiwara san, are you?'

'We just listened.'

Haruko was full of misgivings. At least Nozomi was not alone. Wakabayashi seemed less gullible.

'Be careful, otohsan. Don't you remember that Kajiwara san sold you a piece of so-called precious stone for making a seal? He said it was bloodstone, or something. You bought it for a lot of money. I told you not to trust him. The seal carver said it was too soft to work with. And what happened to the money you have given him for the silver mine? You were cheated right and left. You can't be swindled by a man like that now.' Anxiety made her go on.

'I won't be cheated by him. We just met and talked,' Nozomi was defensive.

'That is what I am worried about. Just met and talked. It was always like that. I warn you, otohsan, if you are cheated by him again, and throw us into trouble, I'll leave.' Days of frustration exploded. Her voice sounded harsh even to herself. Her own words surprised her.

The room was silent. Emi and Mari stared at her. Mari was about to cry. Nozomi laughed feebly.

'You don't need to get excited for nothing. Wakabayashi is a good fellow and intelligent, if I am not.' Then he said to his daughters, 'Okahsan has to be Gonta, too, now and again, and get rid of the knot in her stomach. It's late. Let's go to bed. We all have work to do tomorrow.'

Nozomi had been offered the kind of work that he was good at. He handled similar projects such as planning an independent electric power plant for the Kabuki theatre and auditoriums and a few small scale hydro-electric power plants covering specific areas around Tokyo after the Great Earthquake. It was this combination of being able to provide for special electrical requirements and the civil engineering needed for a difficult site that were Nozomi's expert contribution to the project and had made his name. But Haruko could see that he needed capital. He needed to find money before the likes of Kajiwara gathered around him.

Several years before, she had talked about the swindler with her brother-in-law, Noriyasu.

'Niisan, do you remember Kajiwara san from your university days?'

'Oh, yes. The one who looks like a woman.'

She had blinked. She would not have gone so far in describing him.

Her brother-in-law had added, 'The kind of looks that Takeko falls for.'

In spite of herself, Haruko had smiled. She had thought: After all, niisan is sharp. She had remembered the incident many years ago when she had been intent on saving Noriyasu from Takeko's stupidity and had burnt the Count's photograph.

'Why ask about Kajiwara? You are too intelligent to fall for him. He is a crook. He came to me once to borrow money. He brought a wad of paper and said it was a bundle of share certificates. I chased him out, because, number one, I didn't have money. Number two, more importantly, although the bundle of paper was sealed, I could tell that only the top paper was a certificate.'

'What was the rest?'

'Just pieces of white paper cut in the same size.'

'Did you cut the seal and see?'

'I suspected that it would be the kind of cheap thing he would do and when I looked closely, I could tell from the edge that the rest were slightly different.'

'Niisan, he brought the same bundle to Nozomi, and Nozomi paid him.'

The bundle of paper had been kept in the safe with the seal still unbroken.

'Sanjo has always been like that.' He laughed. 'He trusts anyone. No, that's not correct. When we were students, a lot of friends used to go to him with all kinds of promises, and he would give them his last penny. When he saw Kajiwara, he must have thought that here he was with money and Kajiwara didn't have any. A cheat or not let's help him. I can tell you, Sanjo will never be a good businessman, ha, ha.'

'Niisan, you are irresponsible,' Haruko laughed, too. 'If you knew his weaknesses so well, why did you bring us together?'

'But he is the best friend I've ever had. Now he is a successful, kind, and good husband, unlike me, although I am more handsome. He is well off, in spite of his lack of business acumen. What more do you want? Treat him well and keep him happy.'

Haruko wished heartily that she could talk to Noriyasu, especially about Kajiwara, and Nozomi's vulnerability. As the years had gone by, her brother-in-law had become more and more sarcastic, but she had always liked him. He had died just before the war had started. Kei and Ayako had been convinced that he had died from excessive drinking. Takeko had long dismissed him as debauched. Haruko knew that he was a romantic. Takeko had never understood him. He had always been lonely.

When he had died, the Sanjos had been in Chenyang. Haruko had not been able to go because both Emi and Mari were seriously ill with scarlet fever. When Nozomi had come back, he had been even quieter than usual. He had only said, 'He died alone.'

'Why don't you go and talk to your niisan,' Haruko said to Nozomi the next day, meaning his brother. 'You have done so much for him. I think he could afford to help you now. And, remember, there is some land you bought for him which was put in Emi and Mari's names . . .'

Haruko had heard that Nozomi's oldest brother was well-off like other farmers. He had expanded his land with Nozomi's help and, while their parents had been alive, had had a new house built as well.

His younger brother also might help. He had bought land in the mountains and now there was a constant stream of buyers of timber who paid any price he demanded. He invested the money from the profit at high interest and was getting richer.

'You paid for all his education, don't forget.'

Nozomi looked out the window.

'Otohsan, are you listening? Why don't you go to niisan's and ask? He did not hesitate whenever he needed money.'

'I'll think about it.'

'Why do you have to think about it? It is time that they should help you after all these years. If we had not spent money on them, we would have been better off. It's stupid to be used by them. If they have a little decency, they should know they have to help you.'

It was not with great enthusiasm that Nozomi went to see his brother.

'It's a good time to visit your parents' grave.' Haruko had to persuade him. 'And really, you don't have to ask for help if you don't want to. Just sort out what belongs to us.'

But she had a premonition that nothing would come of the visit.

When he came home, she knew that no negotiation had taken place the moment she saw him. He brought back rice, rice cakes and azuki beans. A young man followed him into the house.

'This is Toku's son,' Nozomi said, and the young man bowed a little. Toku was one of Nozomi's many sisters. When they all sat around the table, Nozomi said, 'His name is Kensaku. He wants to go to college in Tokyo.'

There were only two rooms to sleep in. Kensaku's futon had to be spread in the small entrance room. After he was settled in bed, Haruko whispered. 'So what happened to the land?'

'Mm?'

'What did niisan say?'

'He says that there is no such land belonging to our daughters.'

'Why?'

'He says he does not remember such a request.'

'Otohsan!' As Kensaku was sleeping on the other side of paper screens, she could not raise her voice. 'How could they say that? Didn't you tell him that's what you wanted when you sent the money? Didn't you ask for documentation?'

'No, I just wrote to niisan.'

Haruko was infuriated. She had to be silent for a while, then said as quietly as possible, 'But they did buy the land, didn't they? They can find out which part of the land was bought at that time. Surely he would remember that you paid for it.'

Something about Nozomi made her stop. Whatever his thoughts were, he was not thinking of the land. His eyes were focused far away.

The hope for the settlement of land had come to nothing. Instead, Haruko had acquired another mouth to feed. She felt she could not be bothered to get angry.

25

Kei, Her Sons and Daughter

A year had gone by since Haruko had come back to Japan and she had not seen Kei or Ayako. It had been a difficult year for Haruko. She could not see the prospect of their life getting better soon, but in her letters Ayako had expressed her wish to see her daughter and grandchildren who had survived so much danger. Haruko had been pondering a trip to Kitani.

Although it was no longer necessary to have a certificate to buy a train ticket, it was still difficult to acquire one. It meant a long queue. Before getting on the train, there was another queue behind a barrier. When the gate was opened, it was a single-minded dash down the platform to the train to secure a seat, all the while being jostled in a stream of people carrying luggage.

Nozomi said, 'If there are three of you, queuing will not be too bad, and you can let the girls do the running.'

'But how are you going to cope with shopping, cooking and preparing the bath?'

'Don't worry. Kensaku will help.'

After an overnight journey, Haruko and her daughters arrived at the main railway station near Kitani. Matabei was waiting on the platform by the stairs. His chin was jutted out in the effort to lift his eye level as high as possible. When he saw the three of them, he beamed. As he bowed, his knees were bent.

'It is very nice to see you. I am glad you look well.' He tried to take Haruko's rucksack from her back and stretched out the other hand to Emi and Mari.

'No, no, no, Mata san, we can carry them.'

'You should not carry such a thing,' he admonished Haruko. 'It does not suit you. They say men and women are equal these days, but men are still stronger than ladies.'

Haruko could not tell whether he was serious or joking. Emi and Mari kept their rucksacks on their backs and they walked over the bridge.

A station employee who was collecting the tickets at the gate smiled at Matabei. 'Arrived safely, have they?' To Haruko and her daughters he said, 'Good afternoon. I hope you will have a good holiday.'

The bus had started to run a couple of months ago, they were told. Matabei took a piece of cotton cloth hanging from his trousers and wiped his tanned and wrinkled face. The autumn midday sun was stronger than in Tokyo. His raised arm was sinewy and reminded Haruko of a bronze statue.

'Which route does the bus take? Does it pass through Takao?'

At the name of the Miwas' village, Matabei stiffened a little. 'Haruko ojosama, don't go there. It'll only make you sad.'

'Isn't Rinji ojisama well?'

'He is well,' he answered bluntly, and turned to look the other way.

Haruko had not seen her uncle since the day she married and left home. Kei and Ayako had not been enthusiastic about inviting Rinji for Takeko and Haruko's weddings, but Tei-ichi had been adamant that the Miwa side should be represented. He told them, 'We should always present ourselves to the people as a decent family.'

Kei and Ayako had kept the custom that Tei-ichi had insisted on, even after his death, and Matabei was still sent to the Miwas twice a year taking seasonal presents and greetings, but he had never been reconciled to the fact that Rinji had usurped what had been due to Shuichi.

'Oh, Haruko ojosama, Shuichi dansama's son Hajimé dansama is a lovely boy.' Matabei's thoughts seemed to have gone back to Shuichi, and then to his son. Haruko had heard that Hajimé had visited his paternal grandmother for the first time during the recent school holiday.

There were some more people gathered around the bus stop, and Matabei exchanged greetings. After they climbed up on the bus and sat down, Haruko continued the conversation.

'Did okahsan like Hajimé-chan?'

'Like him? Haruko ojosama, both of them were crying when he went home. I expect we will see him again soon.'

'That is a good news. I am very glad.'

'I am very fond of him,' Matabei said. 'Anybody would be. Even the village kids like him. They ask me when he is coming back. There were one or two who came every day to play with him. Okkasama says it's because Ayako okusama gave them treats.'

Kei would say that. Haruko laughed.

The bus bumped along the dirt road raising a cloud of dust. Hard benches were arranged along the windows leaving a space in the middle. Most of the seats were taken. The driver called Matabei without taking his eyes off the road.

'Mata san, did you tell Dr Yasuharu about Eisaku's son?'

'The next time Yasu dansama comes, I'll tell him. I won't forget.'

'Eisaku's son is very keen to become an eye doctor.'

'I know.'

'Mata san.' One of the women raised her voice above the din. 'I haven't seen okkasama for a long time. Is she well?'

'Very well. This is Haruko ojosama and her daughters. They came back from Manchuria and now live in Tokyo.' Matabei talked back loudly.

'Ah!' The woman bowed from her seat. 'I wondered.'

'This is Matsu's sister, Haruko ojosama. Her son is now working at the post office.'

'Thanks to Masakazu dansama.'

'How is Matsu san?' Haruko remembered Matsukichi who had been a big boy and a bully.

'Thank you. He is still working at the town office. Dr Shirai wrote a letter of recommendation for him, if you remember. Now he has three children. The youngest is exactly like Matsu at that age.'

'He must be a strong boy, then.' Haruko smiled.

'He is one of the children who came to play with Hajimé dansama,' Matabei put in.

No one was embarrassed remembering Kei's remark except Emi and Mari.

'Matsu was awful.' His sister shook her head. 'Every day he was made to stand at the corner of the classroom, and I used to be ashamed of him. His sons are not so bad.'

'Matsu was rough but Haruko ojosama was not going to give in easily. She hitched her kimono skirt up,' Matabei gestured to pull a skirt up, 'and fought back with a bamboo stick. She was a fast runner, too. She was also very clever in argument. Tei-ichi dansama pretended not to know, but he used to say, "Pity, she could have been a prime minister, if she were a boy".' Matabei spoke for the benefit of Emi and Mari.

'Mata san!'

'You two young ojosama, believe me, it is true.'

'I could have been a lawyer, a general, a fireman. Only I was the wrong sex. The world could have been very different, if I were a man.' Haruko was light-hearted.

'A fireman? I did not know that.'

'Yes, Kei obahsama thought I should be a fireman as I was often caught climbing up trees.'

'Now I remember. You were like a squirrel, very good at climbing up trees.'

Emi and Mari were happy listening.

'Sachiko ojosama was another tomboy. She was always following you.'

'Sachiko ojosama's son must have grown up now,' another passenger with a large basket in front of her said. 'I have not seen them for a while.'

Haruko and Sachiko were still called ojosama as though they had never married. Takeko alone had acquired the title okusama as she lived nearby.

They had passed Takao village and Haruko could see the black roof tiles of the Miwas' surrounded by dark green cypress trees. The house where Rinji used to live was not far. She had been younger than Mari when she was sent there and made to work hard in the house. Now it was a part of an endearing memory. Sachiko had come to take her back home and both of them had run this same road as though they had been escaping from a fearful fate. But it was a complicated story to tell her daughters on the noisy bus journey.

Nearer Kitani village, Haruko said to them, 'Okahsan walked this road to school with Sachiko obachan carrying books wrapped up in a *furoshiki*.'

'Didn't Takeko obachan go with you?'

'She was always late. She did not like the kimono that she was told to wear or she was not feeling well. She often hadn't done her home-work and made lots of excuses.'

'Takeko okusama has gone to Keisen hot spring resort with friends. She said she had planned it for some time before she knew you would be back, but she will be home in a couple of days.'

'The sky is clear and the horses are well fed.' The traditional description of autumn was true around Kitani village. Nothing had changed. The war bypassed this place, Haruko thought.

'Give okkasama and the family my regards.' The driver stopped in front of the Shirais' house and helped to take the luggage down. 'Have a good time.'

'Can you post this? I forgot about it.' Matabei climbed back into the bus and handed the driver a letter taken from his hip pocket. The driver put it on the dashboard. He blared the horn and the bus moved off.

The gate of the Shirais was standing solidly on the other side of the moat. Its tiled roof was over twenty metres wide and five metres deep. The thick oak doors were usually barred by a square heavy pole from inside. The family and visitors normally used the small side door. The moss-clad stone walls of the moat curved up from the water just as they always had. Vivid green weeds were swaying below the clear water.

Haruko stopped before she crossed the bridge. Matabei stood by her with her rucksack in hand.

'It's been a long time,' Haruko said.

'Twenty-one years,' Matabei said.

'Is that right?'

'Yes. And it's been twenty-six years since you left this gate as a bride.'

He walked over the bridge ahead of them and pushed the small side gate. He let Haruko and her daughters in.

'Oh!' Emi and Mari were both surprised to see the spacious court-yard. At the far end mats were spread out and halved heads of Chinese leaves were being sunned ready to be pickled. Chickens were scuttling away. The persimmon trees had lots of fruits. The burrs on the Japan-ese chestnuts were still green among the large leaves. It was a secluded kingdom.

Ayako hurried out on the stone path alerted by the bus driver's horn. Masakazu's wife, Miki, followed her.

'Haruko san, it's been such a long time. We were so worried about you, but I am glad you came back to Japan safe and well.' Miki came near and bowed.

'Thank you.' Haruko bowed as well. 'It is lovely to be back here.'

'You must be hungry. There are some somen noodles waiting for you. Otohsan will be home early today.' Miki went back into the house.

'Haruko, I am so glad to see you,' Ayako said. 'But you look thin. You must make an effort to eat fresh fruit and vegetables.'

Haruko laughed to herself as she followed her mother who was now walking ahead with her granddaughters on either side. Ayako was talking to them, turning to one and then to the other. Tears ran down Haruko's cheeks and she wiped her face with the back of her hand.

Kei was sitting like a doll in a small back room. It had its own verandah open to a garden. There was a little stone lantern and a hollowed-out rock filled with water. She had a handful of hair tied in a neat bun. Her skin had not lost its glow and there was a waft of eau-de-Cologne as she stirred.

'Haruko san.' Kei smiled. 'It's been such a long time.' She nodded. 'And, I have forgotten the names of these beautiful young girls.' She laughed, covering her mouth with her small bony hand.

'They are Emi and Mari.'

'Oh, yes, of course. Silly of me. My brains are like a bamboo basket these days. I am so glad that you came home safe and well. When you passed here on your way back to Tokyo, we all wanted to come and see you. Last time I saw you, you were only babies. Haruko san, you have done very well to bring up such lovely girls. How is Nozomi san? Is he well?'

Kei happily chatted on. Although she was well looked after, she did not often have visitors to talk to.

The room was next to the back staircase which had many drawers set under it. Kei asked Haruko to open one of them and take out a lacquered box. Kei opened the lid with both hands and put it aside. Inside were dry rice flour cakes moulded into pink and white chrysanthemum shapes. A chrysanthemum with sixteen petals was the crest of the imperial family.

'Emi san and Mari san. Such smart names, aren't they? These cakes are from the Emperor,' Kei explained. 'Hideto ojisan used to be given these whenever he went to the palace to pay his respects to the Emperor. Hideto ojisan used to send them to me. These,' she took out pieces still wrapped up in paper stamped with the crest, 'were given to me when Hideto san took me to the palace to be received in an audience by the Emperor.'

Nobody in the family had been allowed to forget the event. Kei had ordered new underclothes and a new kimono, and she had practised steps for weeks. Ayako had been worried that she might fall ill from excitement.

'I have never eaten any of them myself. I keep them for the family,' she said.

She took out pieces of paper from a small chest of drawers kept beside her and carefully wrapped each of them. The pieces of paper were ironed out old letters and wrapping paper. Kei wasted nothing.

'You can eat it when you have tea.'

'But, obahsama, you will not be able to get any more,' Mari said.

'It is all right. You are very special.' Kei put the lid back and handed the box to Haruko to be returned to the drawer.

'So, they are saying now that the Emperor is a human being as though he was ever something else. Silly of them. Of course he has always been a human being and everybody knew it,' Kei continued. 'They are making a lot of fuss because the country has lost the war. You need two to quarrel. Nobody can dispute that. And both sides have to be equally blamed for quarrels. I don't understand those flighty people who were upset and telling us that everything on our side has been wrong. The victorious side always over-rides the defeated side, that is natural, but I do not agree that winning means being on the side of justice.'

'But, obahsama,' Mari ventured, 'the military government was really wrong. We were oppressed by special police and military police. We did not have freedom of speech . . .'

'That is what they teach you at school now, is it?' Kei responded with a little sarcastic smile. 'A war was going on, young lady. It was our duty to serve the country. I did my best to win the war and I am not ashamed of it. I shall never apologise for the part I played in the war. I have always said what I wanted to say. Nobody has ever restricted my speech.'

Ayako smiled indulgently and met Haruko's eyes.

'Emi san and Mari san,' Kei carried on, 'the world is confused. Men are lost, bewildered and useless. The war seems to have taken the stuffing out of them. They are all too miserable. It's up to us women now to stand up and do things.'

Miki had come in and waited for this moment to ask, 'Okahsama, shall I bring tea here?'

'Ho, ho, ho.' Kei laughed, making tinkling noises. 'Miki san and Aya san know when I am on my hobby horse. No, thank you, you all go and have tea in the *chanoma*. I will join you later for supper when Masakazu san comes home.'

Later, Haruko realised that Kei's comments to Emi and Mari stemmed from the disappointment and frustration she felt for her two sons. The war had, after all, left a scar on this seemingly peaceful household.

When the war ended, Yasuharu went back to Kitani where his wife had moved after being evacuated. He declared then that he would retire and spend the rest of his life painting, making pottery and contemplating haiku poems.

'I'll live away from onerous human society. From now on birds and flowers are my companions,' he smiled affectedly.

Kei was surprised and felt betrayed. She had expected him to be full of enthusiasm to resume research in his own field of medicine which he had been forced to abandon.

A long time ago – 'It was such a fine summer's day,' Kei often reminisced – Yasuharu had left for Germany. That was the first time Kei went to Tokyo and was taken to see the palace. She bowed deeply like the other tourists in the direction of the Emperor's residence across the Double Bridge and old pine trees. But in her mind, she was different from ordinary sightseers. She took a personal message to the Emperor that her son was going to Europe to study. 'When he comes back, he will serve your country by saving a lot of people from misery. I will do my best to help him.' She closed her eyes and promised.

Haruko, standing by, had to urge her grandmother to get up and go, as Kei had been so long kneeling with her hands clasped.

With other members of the family, Haruko accompanied Kei to Yokohama to see the great ocean liner sail away.

'Obahchan, it will take a month to get to Marseille,' Shuichi told her, as he had studied a map the night before. 'It will go through the Indian Ocean and Suez Canal. You could have a camel ride. Then you go to Naples. I wish I could go, too.'

'If you work hard, you can, too.' The grandmother's trite remark did not dampen the enthusiasm of the boy, but the world Shuichi grew up into was quite different . . .

There were thousands of colourful streamers swaying down from the deck high above. With the gong of departure, Auld Lang Syne struck up, and the tangible connection between Yasuharu and his family was snapped. He stood a little away from the other passengers and waved his panama hat. Soon the ship sounded a melancholy siren. It changed direction and moved away leaving a white wake.

After Yasuharu came home and married, he invited Kei to live with him in Tokyo. He was Kei's eldest son and he did not forget his duty. Kei stayed back not because she was reluctant to leave the house she had lived in most of her life but because she thought that she should look after Yasuharu's assets.

Tei-ichi had left the house and surrounding land to Masakazu but Yasuharu had also inherited some property. Kei decided to take care of it so that Yasuharu would be free of financial concern when he wanted to pursue his research on curing trachoma. Kei had never forgotten the excitement she had felt when Yasuharu had told her his ambition. Kei's ambition was that he would be the best eye doctor in Japan, if not in the world, and eradicate the misery of gummed eyes for all children.

The war had destroyed the happiness of Yasuharu's oldest son and his daughter-in-law. He had also lost his second son on Guadalcanal Island. His house had been burnt down together with most of his collection of paintings and antiques. Kei sympathised with him, but she could not accept that tragedy should make him a broken reed.

'Born a samurai, die a samurai,' Kei said.

'Obahsama!' The family giggled.

'Die a man, then.' She was not daunted.

As for Hideto, having been a medical officer, he was not tried as a war criminal, but he had come back and said, 'I have seen too much suffering, too many deaths. The only wish I have is to become a Buddhist priest.'

He had abandoned the idea of going back to Tokyo to live and wanted to settle down in a village in the mountains somewhere. In spite of his wife's protest, he insisted on trying to find an isolated temple where he could spend days meditating. He soon found out though that it was not practical for him to be anything else than a doctor. Without assets, he had to make a living. He had refused to take up a position at a university hospital with a teaching post attached. He had chosen instead a small village without a doctor, not far away from Kitani, and settled there with Kazuko. Their son who had been conscripted at a late stage in the war and had never seen a battle, had come home and resumed his studies at a university in Tokyo. Hideto had to support him as well.

Hideto had been popular as a boy not only because he had been athletic but also because he had been kind and considerate. He had always been easily moved to tears.

As the war progressed, with one inspection tour after another, it had become difficult for Hideto to walk between rows of wounded soldiers, to see one with his back split open, another with his shoulder blown away, another having lost his eyesight. What had they done to deserve such sufferings? Of what use could his medical education and training be in that inferno? When there had been a shortage of morphine, he had shouted at soldiers writhing in agony, 'Bear it like an honourable soldier of the Emperor!' At night alone in his tent, he had wept about his own cruelty and deceitfulness. The war will end. It must end. I will go home and spend the rest of my life praying for them, he had kept on telling himself, trying not to go mad.

Kei knew about her son. Yet, 'I understand how you feel, but you are only forty-nine, not fifty. Why do you have to scuttle into a hole and be miserable? It wasn't your fault that there was a war. There's enough time to start a new life. Get on again in the world. Have another house built and be cheerful. You are wasting your ability and education. Repay your soldiers by being useful again.'

Hideto was still handsome but Kei felt that his laughter had lost the ringing tone that once enlivened the people around him.

'You sound like an autumn wind,' she told him. 'A young man like you should be full of spirits.'

Forty years before, she would have dragged him to the well and poured a bucketful of cold water over him.

*   *   *

Masakazu was the only one among her sons who seemed steady. He had managed the main post office and the telephone and telegram office without staff, and at home had supported the whole extended family throughout and after the war.

'Haruko, did we tell you that this house and the gate have been classified as national treasures?' he asked when they sat down for the evening meal.

'The house and the gate are national treasures?' Haruko involuntarily looked around. The pillars were twice as thick as the ones used in modern houses. They had a dull sheen from years of polishing. Each sliding door was wide and the frames were solid.

She cast her mind back to familiar scenes. Inside the gate, the front garden was now used as a farm yard where fruit was dried under the sun and rice was winnowed. At the end of the long and straight stone path from the gate stood the house with its wide entrance to a hall with a polished wooden floor. A brush and ink painted screen was still standing in the same place. The wooden shutters were always open during the day, even in the middle of winter, but only special guests or the men of the family on some occasions used the front entrance.

A corridor ran to the left of the house to the walled formal garden with ornamental rocks. It did not have much colour except in the autumn when guests stopped and exclaimed at the sight of the maple trees in the evening sun. There was a stone bridge over the pond. Haruko used to walk over it with the other children to pray at the small family shrine built by a little waterfall. The two large reception rooms facing the garden could be made into one and the marriage ceremonies and the parties for both Takeko and Haruko had been held there. At the end of the corridor was the room which Tei-ichi had used as his study.

On the right-hand side of the entrance, another long corridor led to many rooms. Small gardens, in between the rooms, provided light and air. The store with its thick mud walls was in the innermost part of the house.

Kei said, 'It is all here because Masakazu san worked hard to keep it this way. Everybody else said that he should get rid of it and build a modern house and gate, bury the moat and sell the land. It would have been much easier.'

'I knew okahsan thought it should all be kept, and you were right.'

'Whatever you thought, it is yours. You could have done with it as you liked. No, no, it was your prudence which has made our house a national treasure.'

Kei was pleased and proud.

The bath was as it always had been, built away from the house, but a long covered passage had been added connecting the house to the bath, and a proper bath house had been built instead of several posts and a corrugated iron roof.

'It is too cold for okahsan to walk to the bath in winter,' Masakazu replied to Haruko's remark. 'She walks rather slowly these days. I thought of adding a bathroom to the house but a lot of houses get burnt down by embers, you know.'

He walked with Haruko to the back of the house.

'These peach, Japanese chestnut, and persimmon trees were planted the year you married. Those over there are Takeko's. Peach and Japanese chestnut take three years and persimmon eight to bear fruit. So they have been producing fruit for a long time. Everybody was delighted when they arrived here from the air-raids and found delicious fruit.'

'You must have had a hard time looking after so many people.'

'We survived.'

'I am glad Nobuhiko san came home safe.' Haruko mentioned Masakazu's son.

'Um. He was lucky. His destroyer was sunk, and he was in the sea for over ten hours before he was rescued. That was a miracle. But Reiko's young man died near Okinawa, right at the end of the war.' There was an inconsolable sadness in Masakazu's simple statement about his daughter's lost happiness.

'Oh, I did not know that.'

'He was a nice chap. He was working in local government. Reiko says she will never marry. I don't mind, of course, she can always live with us. She is my daughter. But I wonder if she won't be lonely when we are gone. What will she do when she gets old? Where will she live? A woman cannot live and manage this house alone. The agricultural reform has taken the mountains from us and there is hardly any income from the land. Will Reiko be able to live with Nobuhiko's family? When I wake up in the middle of the night, I start thinking about this and that and cannot go back to sleep.'

You did not look changed, Haruko thought, but you are not the same carefree Masakazu ojisan any more. The war has not spared you from worry.

'We used to run in the rain and snow to the bath,' Haruko told her daughters as they walked down the passage. She opened a glass door. 'This is new. We only had a roof.'

'You had a bath in the open? Nothing to hide you?'

'No. But it was normal. Nobody came near while we were having a bath, unless we called. When oji-isama had a bath, he sometimes shouted and Mata san came to blow the fire underneath to make the water hotter, or took cold water, because oji-isama was always the first one to have a bath. And obahsama went in with her kimono hitched up and the sleeves tied to wash oji-isama's back.'

'Gosh! How feudal!'

Kei's answer for such a remark would have been, 'Why, that is only proper. He is a man.'

'If there was one piece of cake, half of it would be given to Shu ojichan and the rest was divided into three for us.'

'Unbelievable! Didn't you say anything?'

'What was the use? Obahsama would say, "What are you talking about! He is a boy." Anyway, we did not think there was anything wrong with it. But,' Haruko added, 'obahsama seems to be changing.'

The tub was a large iron pot. The bath water was heated from underneath and in order to avoid the contact with the scorching bottom of the pot directly above the fire, there was a round piece of wood floating on the surface.

'It is called a Goémon bath. You have to step right in the middle of the board and balance as you sink, otherwise you will overturn the board,' Haruko explained and showed them how to get in. A legendary robber at the end of the sixteenth century called Goémon had been persecuted in such a pot of boiling water.

'Without a board?'

'Without a board. He said as the water got hotter and hotter, "Ah, a nice bath, a nice bath." He was such a stubborn man. "Even when all the sands of the beach have gone, robbers will still be thriving in the world," he said before he died.'

'Okahsan, the side of the bath is hot, too.'

'You have to sit quietly in the middle.'

Haruko and Sachiko had always had a bath together and she could almost hear their shrill cries as one of them misstepped on the board and upset it.

There was a persimmon tree outside the bath hut. They used to pluck orange-coloured fruit in the autumn and eat them in the bath. They were cold and sweet.

That night, Emi was delighted when Reiko invited her to sleep in her room. Mari was asked by Kei and happily went to share a room with her great-grandmother. They found that they liked each other. Haruko took her futon into Ayako's room and they lay side by side.

After she said a prayer and turned the light off, Ayako asked, 'Did you know that Hajimé-chan came to stay?'

'Yes, Yaéko san told me.'

There was a silence and then Ayako said, 'God is merciful. God is kind. Hajimé-chan is a lovely boy. He has beautiful eyes. They are Shu-chan's eyes.'

'Yes, and also your eyes.'

'What a kind thing to say, Haruko san . . . He slept where you are now. We prayed together and before I turned the light off, he touched me so gently. That was his good night. I realised that once in the darkness, there was no way for me to communicate with him. I felt sad.'

'I know.'

'He is very sensitive. He understood that I was sad. He said he would give me a wonderful present the next day. His voice is much more controlled now. He has a very good teacher.'

'So what did he give you?'

'He taught me the Morse Code. That was his present.'

'Oh.'

'I pressed his hand in the darkness. At first I could do only simple words. He was very patient when I could not remember, or made mistakes. I quite forgot that he was only nine years old. I got better and better. That reminds me. I have homework to do before Hajimé-chan comes back.' Ayako's voice was clear and youthful.

'Haruko san, both Yasuharu san and Hideto san tell me that he might be able to see a specialist. They think that a lot of research has been done for problems like Hajimé-chan's in America. They seem to think that he could be at least partially cured. I am praying that he will be cured for his sake. But as far as I am concerned, he is wonderful as he is. He is very intelligent. He is kind. He is really like Shintaro san, I mean your otohsan. I am looking forward to seeing him grow up.'

Then she turned and added, 'A lot has to be said for Yaéko san, too.'

Among the Shirai family, the men who had been intelligent and capable had given up on the future. Kei and Ayako were unbroken.

Haruko pictured in her mind two green shoots of wheat coming straight up from winter soil to the sunshine. The wind would be cold still but they would grow. It was a pleasing image.

I wonder if I can be equal to them, Haruko thought, but what lulled her to sleep that night was the warmth between Ayako and Hajimé.

26

The Sisters

The next day, Haruko and Ayako were peeling astringent persimmons on a sunny verandah. Astringent persimmons were not fit for eating directly from the tree, but dried in the sun they were fleshy and sweet. Emi and Mari were stringing the peeled fruit. After hanging in the sun, they would be stored for winter.

'When I was a child, there were not many kinds of cakes and sweets except the bean cakes that obahsama bought. These dried persimmons were the main treat during the winter months,' Haruko explained to her daughters.

It was hot in the sun and soon beads of sweat appeared on Ayako's forehead.

'We somehow believed that beads of sweat on someone's face meant that person was beautiful. Sachiko obachan and I dabbed our face with water trying to leave beads on our faces but never succeeded.' Haruko chuckled.

'What a funny idea. Look, you have sweat beads, too, around your mouth.' Mari scrutinised Haruko's face.

'Pity, that would have made me so happy. I'd have been careful not to disturb them and shown off to Sachiko obachan.'

As though on cue, there were quick sliding footsteps over the tatami floor and Sachiko arrived without warning. She lived in Kyoto now, several hours' train journey away. It was the first time Haruko had seen her for several years.

'Obachan!' Emi and Mari stood up. Sachiko went straight to her nieces, gathered them in her arms and held them tight. 'Oh, oh, so good to see you. Glad you came back safely.' Tears rolled down her cheeks. Sachiko had always been easily moved to tears but on this occasion, Haruko was also close to tears herself seeing her sister weep with joy for them.

'It must have been scary and awful. Brave girls. So good to have you back,' she put her wet cheeks against her nieces'. They were almost as tall as Sachiko. She talked to Haruko between the girls' heads with her eyes full of fresh tears. She did not bother to wipe them away.

'I thought for a long while that you were all dead.' She finally let Emi and Mari go and sat down between Ayako and Haruko. 'I wondered how one would erect graves without any remains.' Now she laughed merrily, dabbing her eyes with a handkerchief she had taken out of her sleeve.

Ayako looked at Sachiko reproachfully but was resigned and smiled.

Sachiko had put on weight, which suited her. Her hair was professionally put up and she wore a new kimono. To anyone's eyes, she was the well-looked-after wife of a successful man.

Haruko had been surprised to see how Sachiko's husband had gained popularity as an emergent economist when she came back to Japan. His articles were in newspapers and magazines and he was often talking or being interviewed on the radio. His name was on school textbooks as one of the editors. It was from one of those media sources that she had learnt of his imprisonment during the last part of the war.

Recently Haruko had seen him often. Whenever he came up to Tokyo, he stayed with the Sanjos for one or two nights at a time. Nozomi and Haruko knew that it was inconvenient for him to come to their small house away from the centre and their relationship with him had become closer. Prison life had turned his hair completely white. It had taken some time for him to recover from a chronic stomach problem and he had not yet started to put on any weight, but his sincerity and infectious bright smile had not left him.

'Nesan, now we can talk about it, but what a time we have gone through.' That night, Haruko and Sachiko put their futons in Ayako's room and the three women lay down with Haruko in the middle. Haruko remembered that Ayako had always been well mannered, even in her sleep. In summer, under a thin cover, her prone figure had hardly moved till morning.

Haruko turned and looked at her mother's profile on the pillow.

Her eyes were closed and she was breathing regularly. She seemed asleep.

'I can't sleep while the light is on,' Haruko whispered to Sachiko.

Sachiko raised herself on her elbow to see Ayako and remarked, 'But she always slept anywhere any time. She is naturally sanguine. I think she is one of God's favourites.'

'God has not been unkind to you, either, has he?' Haruko considered her sister. Sachiko was not depressive by nature, and people would feel happy being with her and help her. There had always been other people who would carry her worries for her. I used to be her minder-in-chief, Haruko thought.

'Nesan, you say so because you don't know anything about what happened to us. Did you receive my letters during the year before the war ended?'

'No, I didn't hear from anyone in our family and I am gradually catching up on the news. But so far, everybody has been busy and I have not seen much of our family.'

'The letters must have been vigorously censored. Particularly mine.'

The special branch of the police had visited Hitoshi at home and at the university where he had been teaching, again and again. They had asked the same questions until Hitoshi grew weary and became sarcastic. They had wanted to know what he thought of the Emperor, the Soviet Union, Stalin, Yesenin, Gorky . . . They had rummaged through Hitoshi's desks and bookcases.

Hitoshi had never slipped. He had not shown his impatience. They had not been able to break him. They had resented him as he had not been afraid of them. In the end they had accused him of naming his son, Sakaé, after Sakaé Ohsugi, who was an anarchist. His name was associated with the assassination plot of the Emperor.

'Surely, it's too ridiculous.' Haruko was incredulous.

'But, nesan, they had decided to take Hitoshi. The reason did not matter. That was the "evidence" which they used to prosecute most people they called "communist sympathisers" or "a person who would endanger the country". Hitoshi has never been interested in anarchy nor advocated communism for Japan.'

'I know.'

One night Hitoshi and Sachiko heard a whistle and realised that their house had been surrounded. There had been about twenty police. Some had climbed up on the roof. It had been a starry night and the roofs had been glistening with frost. They had seen black shadows flitting across the garden from the bedroom window. The shrill sound of the door bell had made Sachiko jump.

Hitoshi had gone downstairs in his pyjamas and opened the front door. He had asked them to wait at the entrance while he changed. They would not. They had followed him in their muddy shoes on the tatami floor and upstairs. Hitoshi had winked at Sachiko and had told her to put something warm on, go into their son's room and stay there. He would not have been able to say, 'I will be back. Don't worry.' Four of them had gone with Hitoshi. The rest had gone to take away the owner of their house to interrogate him.

'When the owner was released and came back, he was scared and cross. He told me that he did not want to let his house to "reds", and that he did not want to have anything to do with traitors. So Sakaé and I had to find a place to live.'

'You should have come home with Sakaé-chan,' Ayako said matter-of-factly, without stirring.

Haruko and Sachiko were quiet for a moment.

'I wanted to, so much, but that would have meant that the special branch might have come here, okahsan. I could not involve you. Unlike Takeko nesan and Haruko nesan, I chose my husband myself. No one told me to marry him. If something happened to our marriage, I had to take the consequences myself and be responsible.'

That was not at all like the sister Haruko had known. She was impressed by the strength of the bond between Sachiko and Hitoshi.

'I wish you had come home all the same,' Ayako repeated. 'What could they have done here? Ask obahsama about Marxism and Tolstoy or whoever it is that otohsan used to tell me about . . . and what kind of answer would they get?'

The three laughed, but Haruko understood. The investigation might have involved Hideto and Masakazu and their positions might have been threatened or at least they might have been put under observation.

'Even Hiden sama did not know till much later. He was not in Japan, anyway. As it happened, communication was very poor and newspapers would not write about the unmentionables.'

Sachiko had gone to live with Hitoshi's parents as he had instructed when the interrogation had become serious. She had not received any letters from Hitoshi. The only piece of information which had been given to Sachiko at the Home Office was that Hitoshi had been taken to the prison in Abashiri, a town in the north-east of the northern island of Hokkaido. The town faced the Sea of Okhotsk where an icy wind blew straight from Siberia.

She and her son had had their fair share of air-raid experiences.

'We had to run with Hitoshi's parents. Sakaé carried Hitoshi's mother on his back if the air-raid was at night and he was with us. We were surrounded by burning houses once and Sakaé poured water from butts over us and literally dragged Hitoshi's mother and me out through the fire.

'Sakaé was sent from school to work at a munitions factory but it was bombed one night. After that, he was clearing the ruins of the air-raids. It was just as dangerous as working in the factory. He was glad to go because the students were given some food every day for the work. It was awful stuff but they were so hungry. Once, when they were working, there was an air-raid and Sakaé stole two pieces of koppe bread before he ran away. He brought them home and Hitoshi's parents and I divided one of them into three and ate it, sprinkling a tiny bit of sugar on it. We thought it was delicious.'

'We still eat something like that at home.' Haruko sighed.

'Well, yes, sometimes army officers came to train the students how to use guns in preparation for the landing of the enemy. Sakaé told me that the guns were the same type of guns used for the Russo-Japanese war over forty years ago.'

'I can imagine.'

'When the war was ended, I was simply happy. The worries over the Emperor or sovereignty or honour had not entered my head. It took me a while to get used to the idea that I could walk outside without incendiary bombs falling from the sky. At first it was odd to see that the sky was just blue and quiet. Then I realised that I could say "good-bye" and "see you" to anyone without qualms.

'When I really understood that we were safe, I wept. I danced in the garden when no one was looking. Then I read in the paper that all the political prisoners had been released. I took some food and water and went to Ueno station every day for a week. I sat by the gate on folded newspapers and waited and waited until he finally appeared, unshaven and in old army fatigue clothes carrying a small rucksack . . .

'I was all right until . . . I saw him put down his hands on the tatami floor in front of his parents and bow to say he was sorry to have caused them trouble and . . . I knew he would never have put down those hands on the prison floor to bow and apologise. He has horrible scars on his back and across the back of his hands.'

In the quiet of the room, a cricket was chirping. Was it the first cricket in the autumn that Haruko had heard or had she not noticed it the night before?

'He is a favourite of the mass media now.' Ayako's voice lightened the atmosphere. 'You will be all right now.'

'The war ended just in time,' Sachiko continued. 'In a year, Sakaé would have gone to war even if he entered a university. Oh, I hate war. I hope we will never have war again.'

Nobody moved for a while. Haruko thought that Sachiko had gone to sleep and turned the light off.

'Nesan.' Sachiko turned her head on the pillow and whispered. 'Do you know what happened to Nami-chan?'

Takeko's daughter, Namiko, had spent nearly ten years at Haruko's house as a school girl and later as a student at a women's college. She had become a sophisticated beauty from a little girl with puppy fat under Haruko's influence. Haruko had been Namiko's confidante.

Someone had brought a proposal from a family which was said to be descended from a vassal of a feudal lord. Both Haruko and Sachiko had thought it was hilarious.

'What is the matter with Takeko nesan?' They had made fun of her. 'Goodness, it was over a hundred years ago that his ancestor with a topknot walked or maybe rode a horse by the palanquin of his lord and went up and down the Tokaido road. What has it got to do with the young man? Besides, the family is impoverished now.'

'She has always been like that, Haruko nesan. She likes feudal lords and descendants of a nobleman. Give her an illegitimate grandson of an aristocrat, and she is overjoyed.' They giggled at their older sister's expense.

But Takeko's mind had been set on the son of the family. He had had his own merit. He was a bright student of medicine.

Nozomi had restrained the conspiratorial tendency of his wife and sister-in-law against their older sister.

'You two behave yourselves. Since nesan wants us to, let's invite the young man and let Nami-chan meet him.'

He had arranged a meeting at a club which he had belonged to.

When Haruko had arrived with Namiko, Nozomi was already waiting for them, and soon they were joined by the young man.

His suit had been tired. He had walked, dragging his shapeless shoes. His appearance had been out of place in the exquisite decor of the club, but Haruko had been prepared to excuse him. After all, he was still training. He had a round face and sleepy eyes.

Haruko had bought a new kimono for Namiko for the occasion and she had looked radiant. Many people had turned to look at her, but Haruko had not been able to see that the young man's face had registered any excitement on meeting a lovely young lady.

Namiko had completely written him off. She had not even offered an opinion.

'He will be well qualified. He is intelligent. We intelligent and upright men don't wag our tails as soon as we see a beautiful young lady. We keep our feelings deep inside.' Nozomi had done his best to defend him in a taxi on their way home, and Namiko had burst out laughing.

'Ojisan, you surprise me!'

Nozomi scratched the back of his ear.

Haruko had thought that Nozomi might have been right. She had put a gardenia on Namiko's hair before they had left home. The young man had certainly noticed the white flower and its fragrance.

His name had never come up between Haruko and Namiko after that. That was how Namiko's marriage proposal had stood when Haruko had left for Manchuria.

Haruko did not know how Takeko had persuaded Namiko to accept the young man. It seemed that Takeko's concern over her daughter's marriage had increased after her own husband died. Haruko had also understood that a smart and beautiful young girl who was well brought up and had a talent for painting, and who could read a little English and French, would not have the ability to cope with life outside her family.

The marriage had been quickly arranged. Takeko had worried about gathering opposition, but the haste was mainly because the young man had been drafted. No one in the family had been invited for the wedding. There had been no time for preparations. A photograph sent to Haruko later showed a man in uniform and Namiko in the same kimono that Haruko had bought for her for the occasion of their first meeting. Namiko was wearing a diamond clip of a butterfly design in her hair which Nozomi had given her when she graduated from college. 'My most beautiful and precious treasure' – Namiko used to express the pleasure of having it.

Three days after the wedding, Namiko's new husband had gone to the South Pacific and she never saw him again.

'She lived with her in-laws. Four women,' Sachiko said. 'Two unmarried sisters and one who had come back with a child as her husband had gone to war, and her mother-in-law.'

There had been very little food to share. After Namiko died, they had found no clothes to speak of left in her closet. They had been exchanged for food. Her dressing table had been used by her sisters-in-law. Her hair clip had been sold. The day before she died, she had received the news that her husband was safe and coming home. Kiyoshi, her little boy, was over two years old.

'Tell me, Sachiko san, everybody is secretive when the conversation is about Nami-chan. I meant to ask you. I understand both Kiyoshi-chan and Nami-chan died at the same time?'

A short while ago, Hitoshi had published a collection of his articles on the change in Japanese society since the war. The book had been dedicated to 'Namiko and her son Kiyoshi, for whom the dawn came too late.'

'She killed Kiyoshi-chan and committed suicide, Nesan.'

'Why?'

The two sisters put their heads together.

Had Namiko lived a little longer, as Hitoshi had written, she could have seen that family law had changed. A woman could initiate divorce, a woman could own property, a woman could share an inheritance. A woman could work without bringing social degradation to her family.

One of Namiko's sisters-in-law had found the crouched body of Namiko with the little boy's limp body stretched out on her lap. Namiko's arm hung loosely with her slit wrist held into a wide-necked pot filled with water. There had not been a will.

'You know,' Sachiko whispered, 'when nesan was called, Nami-chan was still alive. She had lost a lot of blood and she was almost unconscious but there was a chance that she could have been saved. Kiyoshi-chan was dead. She had suffocated him. How could she have done that?'

Haruko had no answer to that. She thought of an anecdote in *The Story of the Heike Clan* written in the twelfth century. The Heike Clan had been defeated and well-dressed young courtiers and colourful ladies spilled out to the sea in many open boats. They could run away no further. A lady-in-waiting held the six-year-old Emperor and told him, 'There is a beautiful city under the waves,' and jumped into the water holding him . . .

Perhaps Namiko had held the little boy and whispered to him, 'Okahsan will take you to a beautiful place where we can be happy. We will go together.' Haruko was sure that little Kiyoshi must have been asleep.

In the silence, a wall clock in the *chanoma* struck three.

27

Ayako and Her Daughters

Haruko asked Sachiko if she would like to come with her to visit their uncle Rinji.

'Are you walking?' Sachiko took a long and sturdy U-shaped pin from her hair and scratched her scalp with it, trying not to disturb her hairdo.

'We can wait for the bus but it's not far. We used to walk.' And then Haruko added, 'We ran together, too.'

Sachiko considered. 'It is still hot. You go on your own. I'll visit him next time.'

Although Haruko had asked, she was glad that Sachiko had declined to accompany her. It would be easier to carry out what she had in mind on her own. Before she left the house, there was another person whom Haruko had to tell of the visit. When she went round to the back of the house, she found Matabei chopping wood. He stopped and wiped his forehead with the back of his hand.

'Hard work, Mata san.'

'It's easy to prepare a bath now that we have running water.'

Haruko told him where she was going.

'Mata san, don't worry. I'll be all right. I won't feel depressed. I just want to see how ojisan is and also how the house is.'

'There won't be a house much longer if it's left like that. It is only walls and a roof over them as it is. One big storm, and it will be gone.'

He saw that Haruko was not persuaded and conceded.

'You have to go round the house through the back to the dansama's old study. There are a lot of stinging nettles by the back door. Go carefully.'

She opened a parasol that Ayako told her to take. The white material and the frills on the edge had yellowed. It had a long handle with an elaborate tassel hanging from the end. A small label attached to it had the name of a defunct import and export goods shop in Yokohama. She wondered who could have bought it. Kei must know. She had seen a lady in an impressionist painting holding a similar parasol. It was one of the relics from the period when her father, Shintaro, had been a young student. Society ladies had worn European-style evening dresses then and had attended parties at a building called Rokumei-kan designed by an English man. It was a time when material culture had flooded into Japan from Europe and members of the upper class had vied with each other in imitating European fashions and lifestyles.

Then nationalism had swept Japan and everything European and American had been rejected.

Now, everything American was valued. American goods were considered superior. The American armed forces took over a large department store in the middle of Tokyo and made it off-limits for Japanese. The windows and doors were shaded and nobody knew what was happening inside. It was a forbidden treasure house for passers-by.

Young women bought second-hand clothes disposed of by the families of the American armed forces. Old cardigans, jumpers, skirts were not cheap, but they were American, something that was not ordinarily available. There were women who darned ladders in nylon stockings using tiny hooks, and sold them to young women. Nylon stockings were highly coveted.

On both sides of the road along which Haruko was walking, the rice plants were bending heavily. It was nearly harvest time. The rice plants undulated in the wind, creating shiny white waves. Haruko thought that Japan was like a rice plant. It rustled and swayed this way and that as the wind blew.

As she came near the Miwas' village, she regretted that she had not brought a present for her uncle, but then she would not know what to give an old man who was living alone.

Under the guise of investments to various ventures, a considerable amount of money had gone to Tetsu's family in order to pay the gambling debts of her nephew. It had been public knowledge. Everyone knew except for Rinji himself, who had been left with a lot of sham certificates. On the advice of his relatives, in order to save himself from becoming the laughing stock of the village, Rinji had divorced Tetsu.

She understood why Matabei had not wanted her to go, when she came to the gate. She had not been there since Shobei's wife, her Miwa grandmother, died. It had been before she married. The thick oak doors were closed, but as she pushed one, it shuddered and moved easily. A piece of board holding the bottom of the door had rotted away. The locking bar had gone.

When Shobei had been alive, the gate used to be opened by a maid in the morning. She would bring out a bucket of water at the same time and wipe the doors and pillars. After rain, she would carefully wash away mud splashed on them.

The path leading to the front door was curved and used to be lined with well-manicured bushes and trees. Now they were overgrown and the stepping stones were hidden under rich leaf mould. Large trees stretched their branches from both sides and made a tunnel.

It had been a house full of people. Three generations of the family had made it their home and there had always been guests, especially at election time. The path had been a thoroughfare of visitors.

She walked along the house to the back. Just as Matabei had said, around the kitchen door where broken gutters poured water into an open drain, the damp ground was covered in nettles. Mushrooms of many sizes were flourishing on a rotten wall. She walked further along the house picking her way carefully. The pond in which Shobei used to keep koi fish was stagnant and the edges had caved in. A stone lantern had lost the ball which used to sit on top and it stood comically under a pine tree as though taking its hat off and laughing.

From the garden side, she saw that all the wooden shutters of the main house were closed but the sliding doors of the study were open and she could see Rinji cleaning a copper hibachi, an elaborate charcoal burner. Haruko was relieved, as she had been afraid that he might be sitting in the ruin of the house vacantly staring in front of him. The room was tidy. He was sitting straight, wearing an apron made out of striped cotton material.

'Ojisan,' Haruko called gently, trying not to surprise him. Rinji turned his face to her and stared.

'Yes?'

'Rinji ojisan, I am Haruko.'

It took a few seconds until recognition dawned on him. He was obviously more shocked than pleased at first and sat gaping at her.

'I am sorry I have not warned you. May I come in?'

He recovered himself. 'Yes, yes, come in, come in.'

He took off his glasses and put them on again.

'You have grown into a fine woman.' He peered at her over the horn-rimmed round spectacles, drawing his chin deep into his chest, and then took off his spectacles as Haruko sat down.

'You have not changed much, ojisan.' It was true. He was in his mid-seventies, but he had a lot of black hair. He looked robust.

The rooms were exactly as they had been when Shobei was alive. Shobei's wife used to live in this annex but she had not changed it, either. On the ornamental shelves, there were the same vase and carvings. A scroll hung in the recess, and an elaborate iron incense burner was standing on an ebony base. But she could not see the box Shobei had been so anxious that she should hand to Tei-ichi.

'Sit down, sit down. You want a cup of tea?' Before Haruko answered, he stood up and disappeared behind *shoji*, sliding doors. He seemed to have a simple kitchen built somewhere nearby. Haruko thought for the first time that his movements had grace and he was a well-mannered man. It was a pleasing discovery. After all, he had been well brought up as a son of a wealthy landowner. She felt sorry that his life had been poorly directed. Shobei's excessive concern had backfired.

Rinji came back with a solid tray made of mulberry wood, which Haruko recognised. It was well polished and showed up the beautifully complicated pattern of the grain. He pushed away the hibachi he had been cleaning and placed a large and deep tea cup in front of Haruko. The tea was not too hot and easy to drink. The cup contained enough tea to satisfy her thirst. Haruko did not realise how thirsty she had been. When she finished drinking the tea, Rinji put the cup back on the tray and unhurriedly left the room again. When he reappeared, he had two small blue and white cups on the tray. They were on carved wooden saucers. He also had two lacquered plates with a large cooked chestnut on each.

As though he was performing a tea ceremony, and with perfect ease, he placed a cup and a plate in front of Haruko.

'I cooked and stored the chestnuts last year.'

She ate it with a small lacquered fork. It was sweet and delicious.

The tea was refined green tea called Gyokuro which meant 'dew drop'.

She could not suppress her curiosity. 'Where did you get Gyokuro, ojisan? These days it is almost impossible to get it, isn't it? I haven't had such good tea since I came back to Japan.'

He sipped his tea and smiled. 'That is what is good about an old house. It has been sealed and stored for a long time. I am sure nobody remembered that we had tins of it. I will give you some to take back to . . '

'Nozomi.'

'Of course.'

'What made you think of giving me a large cup of tea first to prepare me for the Gyokuro, ojisan?'

He lowered his hands to his lap in which he held his cup. 'Oh, you would not appreciate a small amount of good hot tea with something sweet if you were thirsty. That's common sense.'

He was companionable and generous, which Haruko had not expected.

'When your ojiisama died, I thought I had to be responsible and manage the family finance well. That scared me. I was worried about what would become of the Miwa household. I might have behaved a little hastily, a little disorderly. I was young and uncouth.' He smiled his old timid smile.

It was outside the room in which they were sitting that he had collided with Haruko and nearly knocked her off her feet trying to reach the box full of the Miwa family's important documents. Greed must have been his prime motivation, but it was a long time ago and Shuichi, the person who had been the centre of the following dispute, was dead.

'The world has changed since. Money is like sand in one's hands. Once it has started to run, it is gone so quickly.'

'Never mind, ojisan.'

Haruko wanted to reminisce. She thought of the way that Shobei had taken care of his koi fish but, looking at the pond, decided it would not be a good subject. She would have liked to talk about Rinji's mother, her grandmother, but this seemed too sad.

Rinji muttered, 'If you stayed with us, everything might have been all right.'

'No, ojisan, as you said, the world has changed. It would not have worked out.'

He became animated. 'Haruko, I have not forgotten you. I have kept something for you. I have disposed of a lot of our things but there are still valuable works of art that I can pass on to you. Do you remember the screens? The ones with pine trees and a crane?'

Yes, she remembered. A pair of screens by a painter of the Kano school. They were precious and brought out only for special occasions. When Shuichi was little he used to be scared of the yellow eyes of the cranes. They looked alive.

'I have more things. Do you want to see them? I have given a lot of things to Takeko. She visits me now and again, but I have kept the most precious things for you.'

Haruko's mind wavered for a moment. As though to shake off temptation, she started to address Rinji.

'Ojisan, I came today to see how you are, of course, but there is something I wanted to ask you.'

A veil of the old cautiousness shadowed his eyes. Haruko became a little tense.

'Ojisan,' she began again. 'Before oji-sama died, what he was most worried about was Shu-chan's future and the continuation of the Miwa family. He might not have told you' – she was sure he had done – 'but oji-isama asked me to give the box he always kept by him to Shirai oji-isama and okahsan should something happen to him. Since you went away with the box, I could not keep my promise to oji-isama. I did not understand how important the box was.' She stopped. Her uncle was rubbing his hands and looking at them.

'Unfortunately,' she continued, 'Shu-chan is dead but he has a son called Hajimé. He is a lovely boy and the only Miwa who is left to us. I would like to fulfil what I have promised oji-isama and otohsan by helping him.'

She pressed on. 'Ojisan, those screens and Kutani bowls and Ming plates and whatever else there is, and if I may suggest, this house and land when you do not need them, will you please pass them all on to Hajimé-chan? Those things belong to him. Then oji-isama would be able to rest in peace.'

To Haruko's surprise, Rinji had tears in his eyes.

'Haruko, I have often thought of otohsan. I am sorry. I have been hoping that you would come one day and I could talk these things over with you. It is true, I really wanted you to come. I have asked Takeko to tell you so. I have been thinking that I was going to give you whatever I have. After all, I was going to adopt you as my child. But if you wish, and I am sure you are right, let Shuichi's son inherit everything which is left.'

Haruko gently let a sigh of relief escape from her.

'Ojisan, thank you. I am so relieved. Hajimé-chan has been on my conscience for a long time.'

'I'll do whatever you wish.'

After a while, at Haruko's suggestion, Rinji wrote down what they had discussed.

'We'll take this to a solicitor in town and make the matter legal. Is that all right?'

'A solicitor?' He was alarmed. 'We do not need a solicitor. They charge a lot of money and it's a waste. There is no need. I shall not change my mind. I am happy about our decision.'

'It would not cost much, ojisan.' Haruko shook her head gently and smiled. 'And we do not have to carry around a lot of documents in a cumbersome box which could be stolen.'

'Just as you say, then. More tea?'

A little later Haruko asked, 'Can I go through the house, ojisan?'

'I haven't opened those blinds for more than ten years. I didn't need those rooms.'

The rooms were dark, and the air was musty. The tatamis had rotted and the stuffing was bulging out.

'Careful.' Rinji held Haruko's arm. His grip was strong.

Some of the floorboards were about to collapse.

'We'd better see if we can do something now that we know what will happen to the house. I haven't done anything to these rooms, you see. It worried me whenever I wondered what would happen to it, but why should I bother if no one was going to have it.'

Haruko thought that she would ask Masakazu to discuss with Rinji what to do about repairs.

'It was so good of you to come. When are you coming back?' Rinji walked to the gate with her.

'I'll try to come back to see you, soon. Next time, I will bring my daughters and if possible, Hajimé-chan as well. You look after yourself.'

He nodded. Haruko turned to look back after a while. He raised his hand.

Haruko suddenly felt tired.

What have I done? Had I accepted the screens and those precious antiques, I would have been relieved of money worries for quite a while. The thought upset her. Hajimé-chan could have the house and that bit of land. She felt a tinge of regret and wondered if she had been stupid. Perhaps she could have accepted just the screens or one or two things.

But, no, she could not have betrayed the trust her father and grand-father had placed in her.

When Nozomi had been doing well in his business, Haruko had been confident that, when the time came, she would be able to provide for Hajimé. Since her circumstances had changed, she had been waiting for a chance to meet Rinji. She had been prepared to argue with him. She had thought that she might have to bring out the old story and point out how wrong he had been. But there had been no need for even remotely ugly scenes. He had been repentant. She was pleased to find her uncle gentle and kind, and congratulated herself on what she had achieved. She was beginning to feel excited, thinking of how happy Ayako would be when she heard the news.

Lively voices were heard as Haruko arrived back at the Shirais'. She washed her face and feet by the well and dried them carefully with a small towel she carried with her before she went inside.

As she walked into the *chanoma*, five women turned and looked up at her. Kei was there and Masakazu's wife was pouring tea. Takeko, who had come back from a trip with her friends, was cutting a cake she had brought as a present.

'Haru-chan!' Takeko put the knife down. It had been thirty years since Takeko had called her 'Haru-chan'. Since they had grown up, Takeko had always called her 'Haruko san'.

Haruko's relationship with her older sister had not been as close as her relationship with Sachiko. Takeko had always behaved as though she was grown up and different from her tomboy sisters.

The night before, when Sachiko had told Haruko that it might have been possible to save Namiko, Haruko had been angry with her sister. She knew that, had Namiko been saved, she would have been tor-mented by remorse all her life for having killed her son. No doubt it would have been merciful to let her die. But it seemed to Haruko that there had been a cold calculation on Takeko's part. The worries over the tarnished family name, rumours, scandals must have been the predominant problems that had been in Takeko's mind when she had been confronted with her suffering daughter.

These thoughts had not made Haruko feel warm towards her sister.

In spite of all this, when she met her sister after such a long time, and seeing her obvious pleasure, Haruko was overwhelmed by feelings of affection. She forgot all the disturbing feelings that she had harboured and found she had totally forgiven her.

'How have you been, Takeko nesan?'

'I am all right, but you had a terrible time. I am so glad you are safe. Haven't Emi-chan and Mari-chan grown up! I did not recognise them. You have to worry about getting them married soon.'

'Nesan, not so soon. They are much too young. Besides, they will find their own husbands. Times have changed.'

'Stay here tonight,' Ayako persuaded Takeko after dinner.

When four futons were laid down, there was no room in between and they even overlapped a little.

'When was the last time that we slept together in one room?' Sachiko was in high spirits.

'Have we ever done it?' Haruko could not remember. 'Takeko nesan always slept with obahsama. We slept with Shu-chan until he went to High School. You and Shu-chan always smelt of urine when you were little.'

'No, we didn't.'

'We went to the latrine together,' Haruko remembered.

'You were awful, Takeko nesan. I pleaded and pleaded with you to wait for me but you always ran away screaming. I felt so scared that I thought I'd die. I couldn't come out until I finished using the latrine, could I?' Sachiko said.

'You came out once without finishing if I remember correctly.'

'Very likely.'

'Oh, dear.' Ayako wrinkled her nose.

They all laughed.

'The guests' toilet in this house is still scary.'

It was built into the garden. One opened a sliding door, put on wooden footwear, passed a small patio paved with pebbles and planted with bamboo. Then there were two more doors.

'Hem!' Masakazu cleared his throat passing outside the room. 'Aren't you a little too noisy? What time do you think it is?' Everybody knew that he was imitating Tei-ichi. 'Ayako, why can't you keep them quiet!'

They were more merry after that.

'Takeko nesan, why didn't you accept the marriage proposal?' Sachiko turned to look at Takeko.

'Has someone proposed to you?' It was the first time that Haruko had heard about it.

'A judge whom Hitoshi knows well. He was looking for a second wife and another friend asked Hitoshi if nesan was suitable.'

'Takeko nesan, why don't you marry him? He sounds good. You don't have to worry about having to depend on Akira san. We'll put a trousseau together for you.' Haruko was half joking but half serious.

'Oh, shut up. How can I get married now? It's embarrassing!'

'Why are you so coy about it? You know what marriage means.'

They all laughed again.

'Haruko san, I saw an American military policeman directing traffic at Ginza. Don't they move their bottoms around.' Takeko stood up and, making a whistling noise, waved her arms and swayed her hips.

'Honestly, how old do you think you are?' Ayako opened her eyes wide and indicated how shocked she was.

'Why do those Europeans have such long and slender legs?' Takeko ignored Ayako's remark and, lying down, stretched her leg up in the air.

'Oh, Takeko nesan.' But Sachiko, too, stuck up her unscarred leg.

'Aren't your legs thick, Takeko nesan.'

'My masseuse said "Your body and legs look as though they belong to different people".'

'No.' Haruko and Sachiko giggled and Ayako joined them.

'It's because of the way we kneel. We have sat on our legs for generations.' Takeko examined her leg.

'Haruko san, you must get chairs for your house and don't let your girls sit as we did.'

'Aren't we Japanese long in the torso! Look at Yasu ojisama. There is not much difference in height between him sitting and standing.' Sachiko put her leg down and covered it.

'We have flat large faces. That's why we look silly when we wear western dresses.'

'But Kei obahsama has long legs and a small face.'

'Haruko san, you have long legs. Mari-chan inherited them.'

289

'I should wear a dress, then.'

'Okahsan, you put your leg up.'

To her daughters' amazement, Ayako put her leg up and said, 'There! Are my legs good enough to wear a western dress?'

28

A God to Rescue You

A milky glow shone through the frosted glass of the front door. Back to the small old house. Back to the struggle to survive. But for a moment, Haruko felt relief. It was their home.

'Otohsan! Tadaima!' We are back. Mari put down her heavy ruck-sack and kicked her shoes off. Emi followed. Haruko gathered the scattered shoes of her daughters and paired them up neatly. She went in.

'What time is it? You arrived earlier than I thought. I was coming to the station to meet you,' Nozomi looked up at the flushed faces of his family. There was one tea cup and an open newspaper on the table.

'Where is Kensaku san?'

'I arranged for him to start at a night school. We found a good lodging near his school.'

Haruko was pleased.

'Have you eaten? I made miso soup and cooked rice in case you were hungry.'

As Haruko was going to the kitchen, she glanced at the clock. The pendulum was hanging motionless. Nozomi must have forgotten the weekly winding.

'Otohsan, what time is it?'

'Mm? I haven't got my watch with me.' That was unusual, Haruko thought. 'I'll put the radio on.'

Kensaku, his school, his lodging, all those expenses must have something to do with his missing watch, which was his last expensive possession from a vanished time. Haruko sighed. She herself had forsaken assets that had been within her reach. After all, we are, as they say, two badgers in the same hole.

'Otohsan,' Mari was chatting. 'Kei obahsama said that you went to that house to meet okahsan and you liked her so much that you asked oji-isama straight away to let you marry her. She said okahsan was very very beautiful.'

'That's nice of obahsama to tell you that.'

'Otohsan, have you seen Takeko obachan's legs?'

'Good heavens, no!'

'Reiko san and I peeped through the gap of *fusuma* because they were making such a lot of noise. Sachiko obachan and Takeko obachan were stretching their legs up and giggling.'

'That must have been a splendid sight. You all seem to have had a good time.'

Haruko decided that she was not going to interrogate Nozomi about the watch.

'We brought back rice, azuko beans and what else, Emi-chan? There are a lot of things.' She started to bring heated miso soup and rice back into the *chanoma*.

'Mata san gave me a pair of gardening gloves and told me how to grow tomatoes. Okahsan, we must go and see Hajimé-chan soon. Obahsama sent oji-isama's drawing set for him and Mata san asked me to take him dried fruits.'

Haruko would tell Nozomi what she had done for Hajimé and she was sure he would be pleased. It's not just Nozomi who is stupid, she thought. As far as helping others, we are both the same. Both of us forget our own situation, and behave as though we are generous benefactors. Or are we? No, no, that is not true. We simply try to do the right thing.

Haruko was on her way home from meeting a woman who sewed dolls' clothes. They were for special dolls modelled after famous Kabuki actors and had to be clothed exactly as if they were in the traditional plays and dances. The material used for the dolls was dyed with the miniature patterns of the real costumes. The accessories used in Kabuki plays were not make-believe jewels and stage props; real gold, silver and precious stones were abundantly sewn in resplendent hair ornaments, fans, costumes, furniture, and each had its own value. An army of specially assigned men looked after them, checking, cleaning and storing. The dolls had tiny but elaborate copies of all these accessories. To clothe the dolls and set them in certain postures from scenes in the plays required an understanding of Kabuki plays.

An acquaintance had introduced Haruko to an agent who handled the trade, and Haruko was fairly confident in herself: she knew enough about Kabuki plays; she knew she was dexterous. With the better weather, her hands were no longer too rough. She remembered the days when Takeko and Haruko had sat with Kei, learning to sew.

'You are sloppy,' Kei would mildly rebuke Takeko. 'The corners have to be sharp, not round and bulgy as though you had left a nut inside. Let's see, these two pieces of material, the top and the lining, have to fit together exactly, as though they are one piece. You are not supposed to be making a bag.' She would laugh and Takeko had sulked. Then Kei would pick up Haruko's work. 'Look at Haruko's. Her corners are so neat. The whole thing is crisp. Here is a punctilious young lady.' Kei had a tendency to describe personality based on unconnected daily behaviour or achievements.

It was obvious that making those dolls' kimonos was not just a matter of sewing under-sized kimonos, but it did not take long for Haruko to acquire the knack. She tried her hand and the woman was impressed and pleased. She had passed the initial test with flying colours. But in order to make a serious income, she was told that she had to attend a course lasting several weeks and get a certificate.

Haruko had to consider the merits of spending several weeks to get the certificate. The first problem was that she could not afford the substantial fees, the expenses for material to practise and the train fares, although the agent explained that the fees could be deducted every month from her wages after she started to work.

'That's exploitation,' Mari would have said. Her perception of society and her language had recently become more and more left-wing. Haruko wondered if their reduced circumstances had influenced her daughter's way of thinking. According to Mari, her uncle Dr Hitoshi Asada was a reactionary.

The student movement was at its height. The Metropolitan Police Headquarters had suppressed demonstrations and mass meetings and Mari had been highly agitated when she had read in the newspaper that General MacArthur had purged all the Central Committee members of the Japanese Communist Party and stopped the publication of the Communist Party newspaper *The Red Flag* for a month.

'Do you think she is getting too radical?' Haruko had asked Nozomi once.

'She will settle down like most intelligent young people. They won't go on running around helping bus drivers' strikes when they are thirty.'

'Thirty!'

'Well, we just have to leave her alone at the moment but keep an eye on her.'

Yes, there was that problem. Haruko did not want to be out every day learning how to sew dolls' kimonos while her daughters came home from school to an empty house. There had been student arrests. Emi was working hard for the entrance examination for a highly competitive university. She needed to be looked after as well.

And ultimately, she was not sure if she would like to be a professional kimono-maker of Kabuki dolls and spend the rest of her life surrounded by tiny scraps of material. There were not many types of work that she could choose from. She had no formal experience of any sort, no certificates, only pride and confidence that she was as clever or cleverer than average, and she wondered if there might not be something else more worthwhile to do.

There was a song that she used to sing with Hiden sama and her sisters:

Over the mountains lives Happiness, they say,
I climb the mountains and search for it in vain.
'Go further,' they say, 'It lives over the farther mountains.'

When she had been happily chanting, she had not thought of its meaning . . .

'Obasan!' Haruko's contemplation was interrupted. Somebody called but she did not stop walking. There must be many obasans in the market. 'Obasan!' the same voice called again, and Haruko heard running steps behind her. She turned. Toshié caught up with her, panting.

'Obasan, it's been such a long time. I am sorry I haven't come to see you. What are you doing here?'

It was not necessary to explain what she had been doing and thinking. She was so pleased to see Toshié and wanted to find out everything that had happened since she last saw her in Chenyang.

'Obasan, are you very busy?'

'I am on my way home now. I am not very busy.' Emi and Mari would not be home for another couple of hours. 'Shall we sit somewhere?' Haruko looked around. A banana seller was shouting. Next to him was a stand with only an incongruous collection of items. If one asked, though, the man behind the stand would scrutinise the customer and might produce sugar, a tin of American instant coffee, a tin of Lipton tea, American cigarettes; all were goods illegally acquired from American soldiers. Haruko remembered she had just passed a coffee shop and quickly calculated how much money she had in her purse. Could she afford two cups of coffee and perhaps some cake? Would there be enough money left to buy food for their supper? They might have to do with something basic tonight, but never mind. She would treat Toshié.

Toshié seemed to have interpreted Haruko's hesitation as a worry about time.

'Obasan, can you come to my place? I won't keep you long, I promise. Once you know, you can come back again another time.'

'Do you live near here?'

Toshié put her hand on Haruko's back and gently pushed her. 'Come on.' The gesture suggested more confidence and maturity than Haruko remembered.

They came to a small restaurant which was closed. Toshié opened the door and Haruko saw three tables and a counter. A man was preparing fish but it was not Toshié's husband.

'This is Sugimoto san. He is a professional chef and I am learning from him how to cook. This is my aunt, Sugimoto san, the one who lived in Manchuria. Come through, obasan.' Toshié pushed up a part of the counter and took her into a little back room with just enough space for one person to lie down.

'Are you hungry, obasan?'

Haruko had not had lunch but it was taboo to confess. 'I am all right.'

Toshié looked at her, nodded, and called out, 'Sugimoto san, could you cook some chicken for us? I haven't had lunch yet, either.

'Don't worry, obasan. This is my own restaurant. Sugimoto san was in the army, and came back recently. He knows my brother well,' she added, to reassure Haruko. 'He is married and his wife is working at another restaurant near here. We are good friends.'

Haruko looked around. A small cardboard box, a futon which was rolled up and pushed in a corner, an old radio. A naked electric bulb was hanging from a black cord stretched from the front through a hole above the flimsy door. The walls were wooden boards with newspapers pasted up to prevent draughts.

'It's such a small and shabby place but it's all mine and mine alone, obasan.'

'That's wonderful. Is the restaurant going well?'

'People always have to eat, don't they? Whatever else is going on. I am doing fine. I still have debts but I have paid back quite a lot.'

'And . . .'

'Yes, he has come back.'

The delicious smell of barbecued chicken wafted in as they sat with cups of tea.

'Sugimoto san is really good. We don't do elaborate dishes but he makes use of things you don't think of, like the skin of chicken, and makes delicious savoury dishes to go with saké. We are popular.'

'So where is your husband?'

'To be honest, I don't know. I haven't seen him for over a year.'

After he had come back from China, Toshié said, he had not been able to find a job for a long time. 'He is not like ojisan. He has no special skills and qualifications.'

'Well, ojisan is in the same boat with all his qualifications and skills.'

At first Toshié and her husband had rented a room and then, when they could not afford it, had lived in a hut built with half-burnt timber, sheets of corrugated iron, and scraps, on a burnt-out piece of land for which they had paid a small fee. They had made an enclosure over a pit, and moved it around as a lavatory. She had felt as though they were living like animals but she had been willing to work hard with him to re-establish themselves.

Since her husband had received a draft call and left home until he had appeared at the door-step of Toshié's brother's house without warning, Toshié had received only two letters from him and none of hers had reached him. She had had no idea that his regiment had been fighting deep in mainland China. After two years of separation, Toshié had noticed that he had changed. Gone was the sincere and affectionate family man. He had never been a light-hearted man but he had become gloomy and morose. He had hardly spoken to her. Sometimes she had been scared of him, particularly at night when she had been lying down listening to the iron sheets rattling in the wind and thinking of her children. She had sensed that he was awake.

Month after month he could not find work and they both had become desperate. Toshié had rummaged through other people's rubbish. She had stolen bread from the shopping basket of a woman walking in front of her. He had tried manual labour but he had found that he was not robust enough. All the time he had ignored her. She had tried to talk to him. He would not touch her and would not let her touch him.

She had thought of finding work herself, but from the beginning she had been in rags and, by then, no one would have come near her.

'You knew where we were,' Haruko reminded her.

'I went to your house once. But I decided that I could not be a burden. When you were more than comfortably off, I enjoyed being helped by you, but times have changed.'

There had not been any way to lock up the hut in which they lived. He had been out every day till night. One of them had to stay behind to guard their few miserable but essential possessions such as bedding, a couple of pots and bowls, a handful of wood, charcoal.

One night he had come home heavily drunk and tossed some money at her. From then on he had brought money back but he had never been sober. He had become voluble and violent. He had tormented her every night that she had failed to bring back the children. She had accepted his accusations and never excused herself or protested. Then he had started to censure her for her relationship with Hayashi.

'Without him, I would not have made the journey. I trusted him and liked him, but there was nothing between us. I was traumatised after losing the children. I was not in a state to have a relationship with anybody. Will you believe me?

'I might have been stupid and it might have been my fault that our children had died. I am sorry that I was too scared and confused and relied on the protection of another man but why should this make my husband behave like a lunatic? He would sleep till midday and then go out without speaking. Sometimes he abused me like a mad man. We never made love.

'One night he did not come home. I was afraid when he was home but being alone in that place was eerie. It rained hard during the night but there was sunshine in the morning. A policeman came and told me that my husband had been arrested. I learned for the first time, although I had suspected, that he and his friends were in illegal trade, selling large quantities of stolen sugar mixed with white sand, flour with chalk, methyl alcohol with low-class spirits, and many other things.

'I did not go and see him in prison. I was afraid of his reaction when he saw me. I just left. I started to work in a restaurant, washing and cleaning. One day I picked up a magazine that a customer had left.

'There was an article about atrocities committed by Japanese soldiers in China. They raped women, killed babies, burned old people alive, did unimaginable brutal deeds. I know he was in the area which was mentioned in the article.

'He is not really a cruel man. But he is not a strong man. In the frenzy of war, he must have been scared and lost himself. He must have been driven by fear, desperation. When he came home and realised that his children were killed, he was tormented by the memory of his own atrocities. He could not wipe out his suspicion that other men might have raped his wife, having committed such crimes himself. He is filled with remorse and cannot cope with himself. Other men survived, but not him.

'If our children were alive, I might have tried to stay with him. He is their father. But the best thing for him to do now is to forget about the war completely and start afresh.

'I went to see Hayashi san because I needed to talk to someone who would understand. He had been a teacher before he worked for the Southern Manchurian Railway and now he has gone back to teaching. He is also going to night school.

'He helped me to borrow money and I also borrowed from my brothers to open this eating place. We are building this place up together. It was Hayashi san who brought Sugimoto san to work here. Only last week we put a new sink in.

'Hayashi san asked me to marry him. I said, "But you don't want a wife who runs a cheap eating and drinking place," and he replied, "Do I look like a man who would be ashamed of someone who is working hard and honestly?"

'I do want to be with him, too, but right now, I am still a little tormented by the memory of my children. At first, whenever I thought of them, and it was often, I was in pain. Then gradually they became sweet memories. I have one photograph of Michiko as a baby, which I had sent to my parents. There is not a single memento of my little son. He might never have existed ... Anyway, I began to be able to think of them without tears. I long to hold them, and talk to them, but I do not feel desolate. I love them and I feel they are with me all the time. I am almost happy thinking that I had them. I know they never leave me. They belong to me.

'Hayashi san and I often meet. We talk, we go to cinemas, we enjoy each other's company. I think I am beginning to be ready for a new life. We will see.

'Obasan, please come again. Sorry I kept you so long. I hope you won't be late for Emi-chan and Mari-chan coming back from school. Please bring ojisan, and Emi-chan and Mari-chan. Obasan, please take this for your supper. No, no, please. I will come and say thank you properly to both of you one day. Hayashi san often talks about ojisan. He'd like to see him, too. Look after yourself, obasan, and see all of you soon.'

Haruko smiled to herself wryly and thought that she had sunk low as she felt optimistic about life in general, having eaten delicious food to her heart's content. She was ashamed that her view of life had been so influenced by such a basic need as hunger.

She decided that she was not going to be 'exploited' by taking the course. Making newspaper bags meant appallingly low wages – here was even worse exploitation – but, however small, an income was helpful. She could not do without it for six weeks while she attended the course. She almost giggled to herself remembering that, as of the next week, she would be promoted to the status of area manager. The august title would mean doing paperwork, counting money and distributing it among her 'sub-employees', less pasting the bags herself and a tiny increase in her wages. Who knows, at this rate, one day she might become an executive of the paper bag production company. She smiled at her own joke.

'There is a god who will desert you,' Kei had told her last time she saw her. 'But remember, there is also a god who will come to your rescue.'

Haruko hurried on.

And indeed there was a god who had descended to help her. A local doctor, whose wife had befriended Haruko, asked her if she could help sort out health insurance claims. She was asked to go to his house for two or three days at the end of every month and prepare claim forms for him. It was complicated work and would require an ability for calculation, she was told. She bought an old abacus at a junk shop and started her new job in high spirits. Soon, three more doctors enlisted her help.

She was surprised at her own enthusiasm and enjoyment. Once she had wanted to be a doctor. Hiden sama had said that she would be capable. Her art teacher had told her that she should go to art school and become a painter. She used to think that a lot of work had been beneath her. She wondered if she had finally come to terms with her circumstances and understood who she really was. She was not sad. She felt relieved.

'I am glad they don't ask me to attend courses or show them a certificate,' Haruko said to Nozomi.

'Your top mark at the Prefectural School for Girls and the Award for Abacus are the perfect testimonials, I should have thought,' Nozomi teased her. It was not often that he was in a cheerful mood these days. 'Have you shown them to Dr Miyagi?'

'Don't be silly.' She was surprised that Nozomi had known about her Award for Abacus and, furthermore, remembered it. 'Who told you about my Award for Abacus?'

'It was your Shirai oji-isama. He told me that you would have made a brilliant vassal who would have made some lord's domain prosper.'

29

For Better Times to Come

'It was so sudden.' Sachiko's eyes were red.

It was sudden in a way.

A few days before, Nozomi had collapsed. The ambulance had taken a long time to come. The kindly doctor Miyagi had patiently waited with Haruko but eventually he had to go.

After the initial rush of activity, when Haruko had sat down alone by Nozomi who seemed asleep, she felt that she had been expecting this kind of catastrophe for a long time.

He had been well when Emi had graduated from university the year before. He had been delighted and proud that Emi had the top grade. After her first degree, she had won a scholarship to go to a university in the United States. The Japanese currency, yen, had not yet acquired international recognition and private travelling outside the country was almost impossible. One needed strong financial backing and a guarantee from abroad.

On the day Emi had flown to New York, a group of her school friends came to Haneda airport for a send-off. They had given her a large bouquet and surrounded her. Waves of laughter had swayed the group with Emi in the middle, her face hidden behind the flowers. Takeko and Sachiko had stood together watching and smiling. Haruko had been anxious in case there was something she had forgotten.

The time had come for Emi to leave. At the last minute, Emi's eyes had swept over the crowd searching for someone. Obviously failing to find the person, she had gone with a wave of her hand.

'Well.' There had been an inaudible sigh from everyone. In random order, they had started to walk towards the exit. The young girls had gone ahead still entangled with each other chatting and giggling. The

Sanjos' relatives, in a loose group, followed them. Only then had Haruko realised that Emi must have been looking for Nozomi at the last minute. He had been standing alone away from everyone by a pillar. That had been the first time Haruko had noticed that there was something wrong with Nozomi. His suit hung loose and his shoulders had sagged. He had looked tired.

'Mari-chan, bring otohsan,' Haruko had told her daughter and watched her run to him. He had remained standing abstractedly until Mari had come up to him. His illness must have already started to eat into him.

It had been Mari's turn to graduate a month before. She had gone to a party after the ceremony with friends but when she came home, she took her certificate out from its protective cardboard cylinder and unrolled it. She gave it to Nozomi and Haruko and formally said, 'Otosan, okahsan, thank you very much.'

'It was one of the best days of my life. Thank you.' Nozomi had looked at the certificate carefully, and had smiled at Mari. Haruko had thought that they would all go out for dinner to celebrate the next day but Nozomi had been unwilling. Instead, Haruko had made sushi. He had obviously been making an effort, but he did not have any appetite.

The hospital to which Haruko had accompanied him was indifferent and Nozomi had been left on his mobile bed in the corridor for a long time. Finally they were called into a consulting room. The young doctor's manners showed that Nozomi was a nuisance, one of the poor and ignorant, brought in at the last minute. He looked at Haruko haughtily and perfunctorily asked the name and the details of the patient. He ignored Haruko's anxious and inquiring look.

'We cannot do much for him. Do you want us to keep him or take him home?'

Haruko was speechless and looked at Nozomi in case he had heard. The doctor tapped at the table with his pen and then he abruptly called a nurse to tell her to take the patient to a bed. The nurse was equally brusque and banged the wheeled bed against a corner on the way to a large ward, chatting and laughing with a colleague who came out from a room and joined the journey.

As Haruko sat by Nozomi and watched his ashen face, anger began to seethe in her. Nobody should treat him like this, or anyone else for that matter. Born a doctor's daughter, brought up as a doctor's granddaughter, she had grown up with doctors who took a different attitude to their patients. It was her first experience of being treated as though she might not be able to pay medical expenses easily.

She stood up and went out of the ward to search for a telephone. Half an hour later, Nozomi had been transferred to a private room and was being attended to by a senior doctor, flanked by two young ones. One of them was the insolent young man who had been so dismissive. He looked embarrassed.

Haruko had enlisted Hideto's help. She had been convinced that he could find someone who had been an army surgeon.

'How is Dr Shirai?' The senior doctor asked after Hideto when his examination had finished. 'Dr Shirai and I have gone through a lot of hardships, but we also had a good time together. He was a wonderful teacher for me.' Then in a different, quiet tone, he told Haruko, 'We will do our best to make him comfortable.'

'I haven't said anything wrong, have I?' the young doctor said to Haruko in a low voice as he followed the others out. This was a real measly character not fit to be a doctor in the tradition that Tei-ichi had upheld, Haruko thought, a modern young professional who should not be left to take responsibility for patients. It was not worth treating him magnanimously.

She dismissively replied, 'I do not know what you are talking about.'

Hanging bottles, tubes, an electrocardiograph, a tray of injections had been brought in in procession and made Nozomi look like part of a machine. A nurse came every ten minutes and checked the instruments. The young doctor, now polite and earnest, came in and out.

Mari arrived. Both of them sat looking at Nozomi without a word.

'Shall we let o'nesan know?' Mari whispered after a while. Haruko had already made up her mind. She shook her head. If Emi was called back, there was no way that she could go back and continue her studies. Nozomi would not regain consciousness, Haruko was sure. There was no point calling her back.

Nozomi died the next day. Emi would not have arrived in time, Haruko thought, and felt relieved. When all the gadgets had been cleared away, he lay peacefully.

He must have been feeling ill for some time, Haruko thought. A few times when he had looked really ill, Haruko had urged him to go to a doctor.

'When one is ill, the best cure is to rest. I know what is wrong. It is just indigestion and a cold together. I don't want a fuss.' He had smiled ruefully, and Haruko had not pressed him. Their living expenses were managed to the limit. There had always lurked the fear of an additional bill. She had pretended not to notice the obvious.

He used to say that he upheld the principle of non-aggression. It had sounded feeble, but it must have required courage to watch his own life slipping away without resisting. He had tried not to give his family a financial burden right up to the last minute.

The senior doctor came and said gently, 'I am sorry.'

Haruko bowed and thanked him, and asked, 'Doctor, please tell me honestly. Had he started treatment earlier, I mean several months ago, would he have lived?'

The doctor shook his head.

'No, I am afraid not. Had he started treatment earlier, he might have lived two or three months longer, perhaps six months, but not longer than that. It meant that he would have gone through painful and unnecessary treatment. It was best for him as well as for everybody else around him that he has gone like this. You should not have any regrets.'

Takeko's son, Akira, arranged the funeral and Hajimé, in his high school uniform, assiduously helped him. Akira had hired a large room in the temple and Hayashi and Toshié brought Sugimoto, and took charge of the vegetarian lunch according to the Buddhist custom.

Yasuharu could not come but Ayako came with Takeko and Miki and brought from him a white envelope with black edging, a customary envelope for the offering for the departed. It had 'Incense Money' written on it, and contained more than the normal amount of money. Kei sent her mourning kimono for which Haruko was grateful. She had been about to borrow an old one from Sachiko as she knew that she had had a new black kimono made recently. Hideto had been to see the doctor at the hospital and thanked him from the family.

Many people attended the funeral. There was an atmosphere of intimacy in the gathering, which enveloped Haruko and Mari warmly. Hitoshi arrived just in time for the sutra reading, having cancelled his lecture tour. Kensaku came and sat with his head bowed. Nozomi's university friend, who had employed him, was there as well. Apart from 'Incense Money', after the funeral, he had given Haruko an envelope with money inside.

'This is his salary for the last two months since he became ill and was absent from the office.' Seeing Haruko's hesitation, he added, 'Please take it. I am sorry it is not much for a man of his ability, but I am honoured to pay the last salary Sanjo kun earned on earth.'

Nozomi had gone out from home every day till the day he had collapsed. Although Haruko had tried to deny that it was Nozomi, a sad image was etched in her mind. One evening she had been hurrying home from her work later than usual. She had taken a path through a gap in the hedge across a park to save time. As she had walked on, she had noticed a man sitting on a bench on the other side of the park. The setting sun had cut a black silhouette and the lonely figure had been motionless till she had left the park. It was when Nozomi arrived home after her, that the realisation began to torment her.

The space for the grave was expensive to buy. Haruko had asked Nozomi's brother, the Buddhist priest, if Nozomi could be buried in his ancestral grave. It had been built by him a long time ago at the request of his family. There had been no reply. She did not hesitate any longer. She went ahead and arranged for his grave to be built in a temple precinct near Yokohama on top of a hill. The grave overlooked the sea. Like many people who had been brought up in the mountains, Nozomi had adored the sea.

The old and gentle priest promised, 'I am an old man, but my son is going to succeed to this temple and will look after the grave.'

There was no gravestone for him yet but a clean piece of narrow board was standing with Nozomi's posthumous Buddhist name written in brush and ink. The sea was sparkling with thousands of waves and an ocean liner was sailing out to the horizon.

She knelt down, feeling the gentle sunshine on her back.

'Otohsan, I chose this place for you so that you could look at the sea. I remember you told me that after a long voyage from Yokohama, when your ship called at Naples, you were homesick and you sat on a hill looking at the sea for a long time. Then you found a grave which had a Japanese name engraved on it. I can't recall what the surname was but the first name was Kappei. On the grave his friends' dedication said that he was a painter and that he had always hoped that one day he would be successful and go home. You told me that story and you had tears in your eyes. By the way, otohsan, over there, on the other side of the sea, there's America where Emi is and Mari will be soon. You can watch them, can't you, otohsan?' The breeze was not enough to dry her cheeks.

Underneath the graveyard, in the little woods, someone whistled for a dog. Haruko recalled that Nozomi had begun to put on weight in his forties but he had looked well with it. He had looked lively and active. Haruko and Sachiko had often gone to see him at his office, having been in Ginza for shopping, and he would take them for lunch in a small but smart restaurant in the back streets. He would stand at the kerb and whistle for a taxi.

'Niisan's whistle sounds clean and clear,' Sachiko had remarked.

'This is how I used to tell the cows to come home,' he had laughed.

'Otohsan, you said once that you did not want a funeral. You wanted the three of us to take your ashes and scatter them in the sea. Well, Sachiko san insisted on paying for the funeral and after that we had a gathering among the people who are close to us. I am glad we did that. You had not told me but during the time when the special branch of the police were tormenting Hitoshi san, you went to see Sachiko san. You had come back for business from Manchuria and you gave Sachiko san a lot of money wrapped up in a piece of cloth. You said to her to use it when the situation became difficult. Sachiko san told me this after the funeral. She said people had been trying to avoid them at that time and the money had helped her so much.'

Haruko was sitting at the table and counting money.

'Otohsan, this is all we got out of a lot of trouble,' she talked to Nozomi silently as was her habit these days when she was alone. Haruko had been persuaded by an agent to take out a life insurance policy on Nozomi.

'I am not sure if I can keep up the premiums,' she remembered telling the agent.

'That's perfectly all right, Mrs Sanjo. You pay me when you can.'

But he did not make it as easy as he had promised when the money was not there to pay.

'It is not that I owe you the money, is it?' Haruko raised her voice once or twice and when the man finally left with an unsettled air, she stayed sitting in desolation. She envied Ayako or Sachiko who would never have to involve themselves in cheap arguments and could remain graceful.

She wished she had never thought of insuring Nozomi's life when she was paid. According to them, because of the arrears, the sum she finally received was so little that it made Nozomi's life look as though it had been valueless.

'Otohsan, I will spend all this money that the insurance company sent to me to buy Mari-chan a pearl necklace. Let's think that you left the money to give Mari-chan a last present.'

Haruko would go to one of the best jewellers in Ginza. She changed to what she called her uniform. Every time she needed to dress up, she had to put on the same kimono.

It was quiet and cool inside the main branch of Mikimoto's. Haruko felt that she no longer belonged to the class of people who were the casual customers of such a shop. She was a little awed and felt herself shabby, but the employees of Mikimoto's were well trained and did not indulge themselves in petty arrogance. The girl who was attending her was just as polite and patient as the one with an American couple who were choosing long strips of enormous pearls, and as the one with a smartly dressed man at the counter on the other side. He was a well-built man in his fifties and had pleasant manners. He was cheerfully choosing earrings, brooches, tie pins without much scrutiny. Quickly, velvet-covered boxes were piled on the counter by him.

Haruko's shopping was modest. The year before, when Emi had graduated from university, Haruko had come here with Nozomi and they had bought a necklace for her. That was one of the rare shopping trips they had made together and also one of the last. Now Haruko was going to buy a similar present for Mari who had done equally well at university, and was to follow her sister to study in America. Nozomi had chosen a choker of white pearls for Emi. Haruko wondered if a longer necklace with graduated pearls might suit Mari who was taller. Perhaps pink pearls would be good for Mari's dark skin. Haruko was taking time to decide.

She had the feeling that the man who had bought so many gifts was glancing at her now and again.

He left the shop at the same time as Haruko and held the door for her. When they were on the pavement he said, 'Excuse me, you are Haruko san.'

Surprised, Haruko looked at him for a few seconds and then smiled. 'You are Kenji san.'

'It's been a long time since we were in the medicine trade together.' Kenji laughed.

He inquired after her evening plans, and invited her to a quiet restaurant not far away.

'How did you recognise me? You cannot possibly say "You have not changed",' Haruko asked.

'I have seen you before, twice as a matter of fact. Once, a long time ago, I was on the same train with you but I recognised you only when I was leaving, and recently I saw you out of my train window again. You were with your very good-looking daughters at the station and Mata san was meeting you. I could not do anything because my train was just about to move out.'

'It sounds like a popular melodrama of the Meiji period.' Haruko was relaxed in spite of the fact that she hardly knew him.

The Little Cuckoo, ha ha. I have often seen your photograph at the Shirais', as well. By the way, how did you recognise me? I was afraid you might not remember me at all.'

'I saw your name and your photograph in the newspaper. You were appointed to be the first Japanese judge for the International Supreme Court of Justice and you are going to Geneva for five years.'

'Ah.'

'Are you not married?' Haruko asked, when they had ordered. He did not have the atmosphere of a family man.

'She ran away.'

'Oh!'

'It's a long time ago. Since then I thought of getting married again once or twice but somehow I have been too busy to sort out that side of my life.'

Haruko felt friendly enough towards him to ask, 'Why did she run away?'

'Hardships, well, from her point of view. I tried to help my parents with my small salary. I thought my salary was wonderful, but she didn't. Her father was a successful lawyer and tried to persuade me to have financial help, which I refused.' He laughed. 'As headstrong and stupidly proud as ever.'

'It's hereditary in Kitani village.'

'I went back home recently to say good-bye. I always call on the

Shirais when I am in Kitani. Your mother told me that Sanjo san died.'

Haruko told him about Nozomi's illness, and about her daughters.

'What amazing children you have! So you are going to be alone?'

'Oh, Kenji san, you yourself said that the world is getting smaller. I have a dream that one day I will go to Europe. I would like to go to Naples, sit on the hill overlooking the blue Mediterranean, and think about how Nozomi would have felt.'

She continued, 'And I am preparing myself for a day when I will perhaps have great grandchildren with blue eyes and golden curly hair.' She smiled. 'It seems that the world is getting smaller in that sense, too,' and she changed the subject. 'After five years, will you come back to Japan?'

'Who knows. Perhaps I shall retire and run a medicine shop.' They both laughed hilariously and the people at the next table turned to look at them.

'I laughed so much tonight. I don't think I have laughed like this for years.'

'Neither have I.'

'Japan is beginning to emerge out of the ruins. I am sorry Sanjo san died without seeing better times.'

'Kenji san, Nozomi and I missed the boat. It does not matter for us. But I hope Emi and Mari and young people like Hajimé will be able to live in a better world.'

He fumbled in his bag and brought out two boxes of earrings. 'They are not good enough. I only bought them to take with me as impersonal presents. But will you please give these to your daughters with my sincerest congratulations and good luck. They are not only intelligent but beautiful girls. You have done very well. I am only sorry that these haven't been bought specially for them.' Then he chuckled like a boy. 'I still have the dictionary and the grammar book. I said to you I'd come back and thank you one day, remember? It needed a lot of courage to say that to you that night. I must have been bare-foot and smelly.'

'You might have been.'

They both laughed again.

They came out into a crowded and brightly lit street and started to walk together. He looked around, 'It's good-bye to Ginza for a while.'

'Thank you very much for tonight.' Haruko bowed at the corner of Yurakucho. 'Look after yourself.'

'You look after yourself, too. I enjoyed myself so much tonight. It will be a good memory of Japan.'

Mari had not come home yet. There was a blue air-mail envelope dropped behind the door. Haruko made tea, sat in the *chanoma* and opened the letter.

Okahsan, Mari-chan,

I hope both of you are well. I am sorry I have not written to you for some time. I am beginning to settle down to do my work. It has taken longer than I expected to get used to the way of life in this country.

I had never thought of myself as materialistic, but when I arrived, I kept being amazed at such stupid things like shoe shops displaying 'American' shoes and if I wanted to buy a pair of them, I could do so within the budget of my student grant. In Japan, a pair of shoes costs a month's salary of ordinary people, doesn't it? I was impressed that the students' hall where I live is equipped with large refrigerators, the sort that I have seen only in Hollywood films. We post-graduate students are given self-catering apartments to share and four of us go shopping to a super-market once a week. We buy a lot of frozen foods and store them in our deep freeze. We buy a big tub of ice cream and keep it at home! But I think I have already written to you about such things.

People are really kind. Lots of people living nearby are involved in activities with the church and we foreign students are invited to participate. The people are interested in us, and before I realised what was happening, I ended up spending the first few months being taken out in their huge cars to all sorts of parties and meetings almost every night and I had no time left to do my work or write a serious letter to you. I shan't make that mistake again.

Their knowledge of countries outside America is quite limited and they are anxious to invite us to ask questions like, 'Do Japanese men still wear a topknot?' or, 'Are your feet bound?' (unfortunately, the Chinese student had small feet) or, 'Can a man have more than one wife?' or, 'You have mixed baths, don't you?' (I am not sure what they mean.) They do not mean to offend but sometimes it is difficult to treat their questions seriously.

We are asked to wear the national costume for those meetings and they are surprised when I tell them that I have never worn my 'national costume' since I grew up before I came to the United States.

The other day, I was invited by a family for dinner with a few other foreign students. The house was pretty, like a house in an American film. There were ten of us around a large table and we had a large roast. (I have never seen such a large dripping piece of meat brought to the table. I am sure it would be a whole year's ration for us.) They asked me what I am doing and when I told them I am studying thermodynamics, the husband whistled, rolled his eyes up and down and asked, 'What is it? A car part?'

Thermodynamics cannot be a topic of conversation but a Philipino student who is studying T. S. Eliot wasn't making himself popular either nor a Taiwanese historian. The host and the hostess do not understand how we, without speaking English fluently, would be able to cope with English Literature or English history. Mari-chan's nineteenth-century Labour Movement certainly would not have gone down well.

I asked in my faltering English what they do for a living, and discovered that they run a launderette. No wonder they were not interested in *The Waste Land* or colonialism or oriental despotism. Certainly not in thermodynamics.

The worst time I have had so far is when they invited several Asian students and asked us to talk about ourselves. We lined up in our national costume on the platform. (I always feel silly in my colourful flowery kimono, although I am grateful that you took the trouble to have it made for me.) Anyway, on the platform, a Korean girl said that Japan had occupied her country and deprived the people of their own language and treated them as second-class citizens. A

Philipino boy said that his grandparents, his father, two brothers, five uncles and aunts and so many cousins had been tortured and murdered by Japanese soldiers. A Chinese student spoke of Japanese soldiers who had committed unmentionable atrocities, and had broken down sobbing.

Please, someone tell me what I could say after that!

Okahsan, our great writer, Soseki, wrote that when he went to London at the turn of the century, he found everybody in beautiful clothes, the like of which he would wear only when he presented himself to the Emperor. He always felt like a small, mean, dirty mongrel. Have you read it?

One often feels like that and shares his sense of servile misery, but I am aware that the world is developing, not in technology and economy alone, but trying to reach out towards a better understanding of each other. We are getting less and less preoccupied with boundaries separating people. Otohsan once said that he loved the sea because in front of its vastness, he would feel humble and become a plain human being. I am sorry this letter is beginning to sound like a speech, perhaps because I am forced to make speeches too often. I had better stop both speech-making and this letter now as I am going to Boston to attend a conference tomorrow. It sounds grand but I will be one of the many who just sit and listen. Still, I have to prepare myself in order to be able to listen and hopefully understand.

I am looking forward so much to seeing Mari-chan. Please give my love to the Shirai family when you see them. I will write again soon. Please look after yourselves.

The tea was cold. Haruko put the kettle on. While she stood in front of it and waited for it to boil, she muttered to herself, 'I can't get old idly. The world is changing and there will be so many exciting things to do.'

When Nozomi died, everybody thought she would pack up and go back to Kitani.

'I'm looking forward to having an expert to sort out my patients' health insurance,' Hideto smiled at her, but Haruko knew that he was serious.

Haruko understood that the idea of family as the central support to anyone who was connected with it was disappearing. Shobei Miwa, Haruko's paternal grandfather, died with his mind not entirely at rest, but still believing that the Miwas would retain their old status. Tei-ichi Shirai, her maternal grandfather, had been confident till his last day that his family would remain secure within the big gate in the care of Masakazu. Masakazu did not betray his father's trust. He had supported everybody who turned to him during difficult times. Now he continued to look after his mother and sister and maintain the expensive structure of the house. The old servants, Shige, Matabei, Kiyo and her family would always be taken care of.

Before agricultural reform, when Masakazu had owned inherited tenant farm land and a few more assets, it might have been reasonable to think of the house in Kitani as everybody's home. But as Haruko had said many times to herself and to others, 'Times have changed.' The family unit was getting smaller now. The new family law meant that the care of parents was not the legal obligation of the children.

If Haruko went back to live in Kitani, it would be as another dependant for Masakazu who was nearing his retirement from the post office. Masakazu's only son who survived the war was working for an export and import company which was expanding. He was living away from home in Osaka. Haruko did not think that the Shirais' house could continue as it had done in the next generation. Haruko no longer had a place there.

Kitani was her dear home. It had always been and would be but only in her mind.

'No, I will not be the last of the old family watching the sunset,' she said softly.

She remembered a spring day a long time ago, when she had accompanied Kei to the Shirai family temple. Kei visited the temple twice a year to pay the family dues.

Kei, Haruko and the priest sat on the verandah and appreciated a cherry tree in full bloom in the garden.

'Glorious,' Kei narrowed her eyes.

'You came on the right day. The blossom will be gone tomorrow.

When the time comes, the flowers never linger.' The priest smiled at Kei, holding his tea cup in both hands.

Kei nodded. After a while she looked at him.

'Isn't it marvellous, Osho sama, when the flowers go, the young leaves are just ready to unfurl.'

'Indeed, indeed,' the priest sipped his tea.

The steam was rising from the kettle. Haruko thought of spring mist over the distant hills in Kitani.

GLOSSARY

butsuma	A room where there is a specially designed cabinet which houses Buddhist name tablets of the deceased family members.
chanoma	A dining room cum family living room.
chinu	Black porgy.
endings of titles	(These are used independently in address as 'Mr' etc.) -sama (polite, as in Ojisama) -san (normal usage, as in Okahsan) -chan (Mari-chan, Obachan, etc. used mainly by and for children.)
furoshiki	A square piece of cloth. It can be large and cotton to wrap a large object or small and elaborate to carry small items.
geta	Footwear made of wood.
hakama	Wide trousers worn over kimono. Used by men, or by girl students in the early part of the century.
haori	Open fronted top to be worn over a kimono.
hibachi	An elaborate charcoal burner. It could be of china, bronze or wood.
katsuo	Bonito.
kisu	Sillaginoid.
kotatsu	A source of heat placed inside a wood frame which is covered to keep oneself, specially one's feet warm; often recessed in the floor of the chanoma where the family sit together.
okusama	Madame.
osho sama	Priest.
sensei	Teacher, but also used as a term of respect to address doctors and other people.
shinshi	Very slender bamboo sticks with needles on both ends. They are used to stretch washed kimono material.
sukiyaki	A dish cooked on the table. Thin slices of good quality beef and various vegetables are cooked with soy sauce and sugar.

shoji	Sliding doors usually separating the room from a verandah. The doors are made of thin wood frames with paper.	

titles

	Male	*Female*
Grandparents	Oji-isama	Obahsama
Parents	Otohsan	Okahsan
Uncle, Aunt	Ojisan	Obasan
The next generation	(o) niisan *or* niisan	(o) nesan
husband or master	dannasama *or* dansama	
wife or married woman	okusama	
Prefix [o']	Mainly put in front of a woman's name and shows endearment.	

tokonoma	A recess in a room where ornaments and flowers are placed and a scroll is hung.
yakitoriya	A small eating place mostly with a counter and chairs. The customers drink saké and eat some food, which often includes grilled chicken pieces.
yukata	A cotton kimono worn as casual wear in summer.
zabuton	A cushion used on a tatami floor.
zori	Open footwear for more formal occasions than those at which geta are worn.

AUTHOR'S NOTE

Fish of the Seto Inland Sea is a story based on my mother's life. To write it was the fulfilment of a promise I made to my family.

My mother came to England to live with us after she was widowed. She was a lively and intelligent woman and travelled with us all over the world. In her eighties, she needed increasing care. My husband and the children were kind and gentle to her and she lived with us at home till the end. They fondly remember her as a woman who loved them and was proud of them.

My family wanted me to write about my mother and her life in Japan, which is also my background. For a while after my mother's death, I had not been able to face the task as I felt that I knew too little about her earlier life and I was reluctant to probe into the emotions of someone who had been close to me.

Then one day, Sophie, my younger daughter, suggested that I thought of the story in the form of a novel. I started the same day.

The models which came to my mind were the books by two great writers in Japanese literature, Soseki and Tanizaki, although I would not consider myself as standing near those masters.

Soseki based one of his books on a period of his own domestic life and Tanizaki created a novel around his wife and her daughter with her former husband, and her three sisters. The book of Soseki's is often described as 'a biographical novel'. Tanizaki's is treated simply as a novel, but those who are familiar with the background know how much he drew out of the characters and experiences of those women to write it. They had to be novels otherwise how could they have told people's thoughts and emotions and let the characters laugh and cry?

When I was in Japan recently, I visited the area where my mother was brought up. I tried to make some sense out of many place names that I had heard from her but so much had changed and it was not possible during that brief period to establish any meaningful connection to the past. Even in what had seemed tangible, I could not know how much was my imagination.

It was while I stood on the shore of the Seto Inland Sea with warm water lapping around my ankles and heard the murmur of the waves that I realised I do not need to apologise for creating the places and people which fill the book. The story is true of the lives of Japanese men and women who lived during the period I wrote about.